What Reviewers Say about the Author's Books

"Fast-paced action scenes, intriguing character revelations, and a refreshing approach to the romance thriller genre all make for an enjoyable reading experience in the Big Easy....an engrossing reading experience, a noticeably more literate effort than the first in the Casey Clan series. It is always satisfying to see an author grow as Vali has displayed in this novel. The structural details in the plot, the adept handling of action and suspense, and the more delineated major characters produce a coherent and stylish technique. *The Devil Unleashed* is definitely a novel not to be missed." – *Midwest Book Review*

"*The Devil Inside* by Ali Vali is an unusual, unpredictable, and thought-provoking love story that will have the reader questioning the definition of right and wrong long after she finishes the book....unlike most romance novels. Nothing about the story and its characters is conventional." – *Just About Write*

"*The Devil Inside* is that rarity: a fascinating crime novel which includes a tender love story and leaves the reader with a cliffhanger ending. Look for this excellent read at your favorite gay and lesbian bookstore." – *MegaScene*

"Vali's fluid writing style quickly puts the reader at ease, which makes the story and its characters equally easy to get to know and care about. When you find yourself talking out loud to the characters in a book, you know the work is polished and professional, as well as entertaining." – *Family & Friends Magazine*

"Not only is *The Devil Inside* a ripping mystery, it's also an intimate character study, especially in terms of Cain Casey. As ruthless as she is, Cain is also fiercely loyal and will go to great lengths to protect what she holds dear. The overall plot moves along at just the right pace; nothing feels rushed and nothing lags." – *L-word.com Literature*

"It's no surprise that passion is indeed possible a second time around..." – *Q Syndicate*

By the Author

The Devil Inside

The Devil Unleashed

Carly's Sound

Visit us at www.boldstrokesbooks.com

Second Season

by

Ali Vali

2007

SECOND SEASON

ISBN: 10-digit 1-933110-83-X
13-digit 978-1-933110-83-7

This Trade Paperback Original Is Published By
Bold Strokes Books, Inc.,
New York, USA

First Edition: July, 2007.

Credits
Editors: Shelley Thrasher and Stacia Seaman
Production Design: Stacia Seaman
Cover Design By Sheri (GRAPHICARTIST2020@HOTMAIL.COM)

Author's Note

A hurricane is defined as a tropical storm with winds of 74 mph or more. Such a simple string of mundane words doesn't come close to describing what happened to New Orleans and the Gulf Coast in 2005. On August 29, my partner and I watched the city we love fill with water as Hurricane Katrina came ashore, followed by Hurricane Rita a short twenty-six days later.

We survived, but we were left forever changed as we mourned for all those who did not, and for all those left with nothing. In the two years since then we have celebrated as some of the places and people we took for granted came back to the Big Easy to rebuild and recapture the essence, the rich culture and history that is New Orleans. Recovery is slow, but we are moving forward with the dogged determination that won't let us rest until we are done.

C and I want to thank all of you who came to our aid in the days following Katrina. We are truly blessed to be a part of such an extended loving family.

My profound thanks to my editor Shelley Thrasher for her guidance—as always, you were a great teacher and an even better friend. Thank you to Jennifer Knight and Stacia Seaman for your insight, expertise, and invaluable help. Without the three of you, *Second Season* would not have been possible. Thank you to Sheri for another awesome cover. Thank you to Connie, Jenny, and Beth for your willingness to be my beta readers and cheerleaders to "get it done already." And a big thank you to Emma for your boss list of slang.

No book, as you can see from that list, is written alone. It takes a team, and I'm extremely fortunate to be part of great one at Bold Strokes Books. Thank you, Radclyffe, for gifting us with this extraordinary company, and for your continued support, encouragement, and guidance.

Thanks also to my partner. We weathered the storm and found that the most valuable and precious thing we have is each other.

Dedication

For C
My safe harbor

And to the over 1,900 souls who died
in hurricanes Katrina and Rita
You are lost but never forgotten

Chapter One

"Ugh." Tully Gaston Badeaux studied herself in the large mirror in the master bathroom, wondering where her trim waistline had gone. "Wherever the hell it is, it's there sunning itself with the hair that used to be dark."

"Did you say something? You're mumbling again. Are you practicing another closing argument?"

Tully could barely hear Jessica Badeaux's questions through the closed door, since her lover was getting dressed in the adjoining walk-in closet.

"No." Tully sucked in her stomach, raised her arms, and flexed her biceps. She was beginning to be depressed. "Forty sucked when it finally rolled around, and adding another couple of years didn't help."

"Now I *know* you said something. I can hear you talking." Jessica opened the bathroom door to finish her makeup and hair before she pulled on silk underwear and a white blouse, figuring her partner was done since she rarely if ever bothered with makeup.

In fact, it bothered Jessica how Tully had given in to her graying hair and expanding waistline. She liked that her own hair was still as dark as when they met, her weight hadn't fluctuated much even after each pregnancy, and her face still didn't show signs of her forty years. It didn't matter that some of those secrets were between her and her hairdresser and dermatologist.

Tully's gray eyes were slightly bloodshot, but Jessica noticed they still softened when she smiled and said, "Can I tell you, you're the best-looking girl who's wandered in here all morning?"

Tully pressed up against her and tried to kiss her, but Jessica moved away and put her hands up. "I've got rounds this morning."

"I didn't realize a good-morning kiss chewed up so much of your valuable time." Tully's tone, no longer teasing, now held an icy edge usually reserved for her adversaries.

Before this rebuff escalated into another argument, Tully walked away. She wasn't in the mood for another of Jessica's lame excuses.

Tully didn't have to be in court that day and she hadn't scheduled any clients, so she chose a casual blue seersucker suit. She was dressed and down the hall before Jessica finished in the bathroom.

The room at the other end of the hallway was closed, but Tully could easily hear the stereo blaring from the other side. She had to knock for three minutes before the teenaged inhabitant decided to grace her with an audience. After a few screaming matches, she and Jessica had learned it was a small price to pay to knock and wait instead of just walking in.

"What?"

"And good morning to you, sunshine," Tully went on as if the kid was happy to see her. "Are you almost ready?"

"Why?"

"I thought you might like a ride to school, and I have time this morning."

"Why?"

"Why what?" She detested these conversations, but figured eventually the pod people who'd stolen the cute little girl who once enjoyed bedtime stories would bring her back and retrieve the surly replacement model that had shown up the year before.

"Why would you want to?"

"Why wouldn't I?"

Bailey Badeaux continued to chew her gum, adding a few pops. "We'll see," she answered before closing the door.

Aware that the immediate increase in the stereo volume masked the sound, Tully banged her head softly against the wall a few times. Talking to Bailey often left her in that mood.

The last hope of restoring her faith in the reasons she'd decided to settle down and have a family rested behind the door in the middle of the hall. It opened before she could knock, and Ralph Badeaux looked up at her and smiled.

"Morning, Ralph. You ready, buddy?"

His smile widened, his face displaying the dimples that appeared when he was happy. Seeing them reminded her again of the wonders of genetics and the sense of immortality that ensued if you decided to venture into the uncertain world of parenting. The other blessing in her life was that her two brothers looked so much like her.

As Tully gazed at Ralph, she thought about how both of her children, with their height, dark hair and skin, and light gray eyes, resembled her Cajun family. They also shared her intellect, though only Ralph showed an inkling of her drive. He was also the only one who enjoyed going back to her hometown to spend time with her parents.

She'd been born in Montegut, Louisiana, to Gaston and Alma Badeaux, who both had spent a lifetime working so that Tully's mental gifts wouldn't go to waste. They had also expected their only daughter to pull her share of the workload on Gaston's fishing boat, and she had, working there every summer until after she completed medical school. Then, having decided that she wanted to become a trial lawyer specializing in medical lawsuits, she completed a law degree. Mastering both disciplines had helped make her a successful civil attorney.

However, it was aboard her father's trawler the *Alma Mae* that Tully had learned the value of a day's work and the devastation when people, through no fault of their own, were injured and couldn't put in that day's work to feed their families. Being able to convey the impact of such tragedies to a jury while wearing a suit that cost more than most of them made in two months made her even more successful. "A hometown girl who'd hit the big time" was the way her father liked to put it whenever he had the opportunity.

"Are you taking us today?" Ralph adjusted the book bag on his back and walked quickly after her.

"Sure, unless, like your sister, you'd rather wait for your mother."

"No, we hardly ever get to see you in the morning, so that'd be cool."

He picked up his pace, and Tully could read his mind: he knew that if they were out of the kitchen before Jessica made it downstairs, he'd get to have Pop-Tarts for breakfast instead of whatever nutritious meal she wanted them to have.

"Chocolate or blueberry?" asked Tully, holding up two boxes.

"One of each."

As the silver packages of sugar-coated breakfast treats slid across the counter Bailey entered the room and headed for the refrigerator. Tully could read her mind also: she wasn't about to pass up the opportunity to start her day with a Coke instead of orange juice and scrambled eggs.

"Chocolate or blueberry?" Tully asked again.

"Strawberry," Bailey answered just to be contrary, but chuckled anyway when Tully handed over a package from another box she'd taken out of the pantry. "Let's go, shrimp, before we get busted for something," Bailey told Ralph.

❖

On any normal day Tully would've been listening to her secretary on the speakerphone, but now the phone in her Discovery SUV was silent, though she couldn't say the same of the CD player. After hearing the word "bitch" for the tenth time in a one-block span, she raised an eyebrow.

"Do you actually listen to what these people are saying?"

Bailey took a deep breath as if searching for patience. "Don't start, okay?"

"Look, Bailey, as much as you'd like to believe I'm the enemy, I'm not. I don't want to start anything. I'm asking you a civil question and would appreciate a mature answer that shows some respect. In turn I'll treat you with respect. If you don't want to answer, fine, but I'd really appreciate it if you could lower the hostility a few notches."

Bailey glared at her for a long moment, though her brother cleared his throat in warning from the backseat. "You know what your problem is?"

"Perhaps, but I'm willing to bet you're going to tell me."

"You think giving us a few minutes of your time makes up for all the times you're not with us. If you want me to respect you, then treat me like I'm as important as your precious career."

For one so young, her argument was clear and to the point. What upset Tully was that she had nothing to counter it with. The truth, she figured, didn't always set you free; it only put more bars on the cage you carefully constructed for yourself with the choices you made.

Silence prevailed in the SUV as the private academy that Bailey and Ralph attended loomed in front of them. Tully turned into the main drive, stopped, looked at her daughter in the front seat, and could think of nothing to say, quite a feat for someone paid for her ability to articulately string words together.

"Have a good day." It was lame, but the best she could do.

"Thanks, Mom, you too. I have baseball practice tonight. Can you remember to tell Mama when you talk to her?" Ralph was trying to smooth things over from the backseat, a job he was taking on more and more.

"Thanks, buddy. You have a good day too, and I'll see you both tonight."

Tully drove away slowly, watching Bailey trudge into the building like she was entering a death chamber as Ralph patted her on the back as if trying to make her feel better. Being unable to talk to her daughter was starting to bother Tully in ways she couldn't explain even to herself.

Chapter Two

Tully left the suburbs and headed into the city for another day in the trenches, where she tried to find justice for those wronged by the medical industry. She used her background in medicine to help select cases in which she could improve the profession by removing a bad physician, intending to make sure that doctors earned the faith that people placed in them. With her reputation, she often heard the word "settlement" immediately from the people she was up against.

The elevator quickly reached the twenty-fifth floor of the Chevron Building where Barnes, Corey, and Badeaux had their offices. The other two partners rarely went into court anymore and had been more than happy to give Tully the large corner office with a beautiful view of the Mississippi River, downtown, and the French Quarter. She knew they had long ago nicknamed her the cash cow of the office and regularly congratulated each other for giving her a chance right out of law school.

"Are you mad at me or something?" Roxanne Lemoyne asked as soon as Tully stepped into the large office suite.

The tall, slender African American in her late thirties had been with Tully almost from the time she had become a partner. Roxanne had two assistants of her own, along with a handful of paralegals and junior partners who barely got them through when Tully was in the middle of a big case.

"Not that I'm aware of. Why? Did you do something to warrant my wrath since yesterday afternoon?"

Tully flipped through a slew of messages from potential clients, grateful that none of them concerned the Duplessy case, which they had just wrapped up. She grimaced at the memory of the surgeon who had mistakenly removed a young diabetic man's right leg instead of his left. To make things worse, he had then spent more than twenty hours trying to reattach the mistakenly amputated limb. The bungled procedure had further weakened a body already ravaged by a very unforgiving disease. Disgusted by the damage that one careless person could cause, Tully threw more than half of the message slips in the trash.

Tully wasn't, no matter what her partner Jessica's colleagues thought of her, an ambulance chaser. She accepted only cases of blatant medical malpractice, cases about which she usually felt strongly. After dropping her bag on the credenza behind her large desk, Tully took off her jacket and sank into her comfortable leather chair.

"What'd you do?" she asked Roxanne again.

"I didn't do anything, thank you very much for asking. I didn't get my usual seven thirty phone call, so I thought you ran away from home." Roxanne's face clouded over a bit when she took in Tully's appearance. "Are you okay?"

"I wish I could say I'm ecstatically happy, but I'd be a liar. Sorry for not calling, but I took the kids to school and got an earful of how I'm never around and what music they listen to is none of my business."

Roxanne scrunched her forehead. "Ralph told you that?"

"No. Those insightful words came from the next attorney in the family, Bailey."

"What did you tell her?"

Tully swiveled a little to the right, concentrating on the busy river traffic, and exhaled deeply before answering. "I wish I could say I came back with something really clever and insightful, but part of me knows she's right.

"My dad worked hard all his life, but I always knew in my heart of hearts how he felt about me. I understood that when he wasn't around, he was trying to make a living for my brothers and me." She took another deep breath and turned her head from the river to her assistant, who had long before become more of a caretaker than an employee. "Kids today, at least my kids, don't understand that concept. Or maybe I'm just an idiot. Whatever the answer, I'm doing a lousy job communicating with them."

"Honey, you are many things to many people, but an idiot isn't one of them." Roxanne strolled over and put her hand on Tully's shoulder.

"I know you just got here, but why don't you take off for a little bit and try to clear your head?"

"Maybe later, but now we've got a few other things to catch up on." Tully reached for the first file on her desk. Though the associates in the firm represented some of the cases they took, Tully liked to check their work before they reached an unsatisfactory settlement due to their lack of experience. "Why don't you set up the guys? We'll review files, then have a roundtable this afternoon. I want us to look at a couple of promising cases."

"You're on, boss." Roxanne moved back to the other side of the desk and jotted a few notes on the pad in her hand. "Want anything? Knowing you, you had Scotch for dinner last night and Pop-Tarts for breakfast."

"Those food items have all the vitamins and minerals growing bodies need, so don't knock 'em." Tully tried to joke off Roxanne's comment, but the night before that was exactly what she'd had for dinner, along with more than a few cigarette chasers.

Ironically, she'd started smoking several years before in the middle of a ground-breaking suit she'd led against the tobacco industry on behalf of the state. In hindsight, she should have paid more attention to the findings on how quickly you could become addicted. And they'd lied about the weight loss, she thought, and smiled at her perverse private joke.

The previous night she'd fully intended to go home and celebrate her victory in the Duplessy case with her family, but when she'd arrived she discovered that Jessica had taken the kids out to dinner. Later, when they got home, they'd all filed past the closed office door, not bothering to see if she was inside.

It was just one more night when she felt no longer a part of the family she loved so much. Bailey wasn't the only one who had grown sullen and distant. Jessica had put a barrier between them in the bedroom, and everywhere else, that was widening by the day. Tully was beginning to worry that Jessica found her touch repulsive.

"Well, you'd better start taking better care of yourself or I'm going to be having these morning meetings with you in the cardiac wing of the nearest hospital." Roxanne left without lecturing Tully any further.

She gathered the associates as Tully had asked and sat next to her, taking notes as they went through the files. In the end two cases caught Tully's attention, and they started to make plans and choose teams. The associates seemed thrilled since this time around Tully said she would let them all take the lead and fight the good fight while she sat on the sideline and did her best to coach them.

"That was different," Roxanne commented after everyone except her and Tully left the room.

"I want to have the young pups ready to venture out on their own by the time summer gets here. That way I can spend more time with Jess and the kids. What Bailey said this morning may be right. Sometime during the last year I started feeling it all slip through my fingers, and I want to stop the bleeding before it's fatal."

"Why don't you start now?"

"Start what?"

Tully was amused to see Roxannehold up her jacket.

"Get out of here and invite Jessica to lunch. When was the last time you did that?"

Tully furrowed her brow, and Roxanne laughed. "I thought so. Go on. I promise to keep the building intact in your absence."

❖

As Dr. Jessica Badeaux drove away from Children's Hospital, located at the end of Tchoupitoulas Street in New Orleans, toward home, she thought about the fact that she primarily treated kids with fevers and runny noses while many staff members were experimenting with cutting-edge treatments for a multitude of illnesses. She left the exciting medicine to others, content to deal with the mundane side of healing because her father had convinced her that was the best kind of practice for a woman with children to tend to.

On most days she compared this choice to the one she'd made in her personal life. She'd left her chance for excitement when she'd decided to settle down, and just…settled. Back in college, she'd thought the life she had chosen was what she really wanted—the family, the attentive partner. It was all a young girl's dream and what her parents had wanted for her as well.

Tully was still attentive, but lately Jessica really didn't want her attention, and eventually she'd have to explain her feelings in acceptable terms. She just wasn't ready for the turmoil that explanation would provoke. So for now she had to keep her desires under wraps.

She didn't know how she really felt about her family

responsibilities. If she were totally honest with herself, she'd admit that motherhood was starting to bore her. Most days she felt like an underappreciated chauffeur and tutor as she shuffled the kids to and from their various activities, then helped them with homework when she had the chance. However, she could only imagine what the world would think of her if she actually voiced her feelings. She wanted change, but hadn't yet found the courage to make it happen so that it didn't totally devastate the people she felt responsible for.

In the meantime, Tully strolled through the front entrance of the hospital and waved to all the volunteers manning the desk. They were blowing up balloons to hand out in the wards. If she had to guess, she'd say the youngest of them was seventy. She enjoyed seeing people almost at the end of their road help those whom illness had stranded at the side of it.

She waved one last time before she headed toward the clinic section, where Jessica's nurse recognized her and stopped to converse.

"Dr. Badeaux, have you finally come to your senses and decided to start practicing medicine instead of suing people?"

Cathy's remark had a bite to it that surprised Tully. "Come on, Cathy, you know how much I love suing people. You wouldn't want to take away my fun, would you?"

"Uh-huh." The nurse put her chart down and stood rigidly, as if impatient for Tully to get to the point.

Tully glanced at the rest of the people milling around, not seeing the one she was looking for. "Is Jess here? I thought I'd take her to lunch if she isn't swamped. Lately you all have been working her to death, so I've come to rescue her for a while."

Cathy's face remained neutral. If anyone in the hospital kept strict regular hours, it was Jessica. In by nine and gone by four. If Jessica was putting in extra hours, it wasn't here at Children's.

"It's about time, but you just missed her." She picked up her chart again, obviously avoiding eye contact with Tully. "Said something about getting a bite to eat. I just don't know where."

Tully was sure the portly woman wouldn't have held up under cross-examination. Years of courtroom work had taught her to read people and know with certainty when they were holding something back. "No problem. I didn't make an appointment, after all."

Though the sarcasm was hard to miss, Tully was sure the nurse didn't want to be put in the middle. After all, she worked for Jessica.

"I'll tell her you stopped by. I'm sure she'll be sorry she missed you."

Tully fought the urge to call Cathy a liar and left without another word.

Not wanting to go back to the office just yet, she headed to the coffee shop in the lobby of her building. An hour of reading the paper and enjoying a latte sounded like the best course of action. She was surprised to find Libby Dexter still behind the counter taking orders, since she usually knocked off by ten to attend classes. Tully had been coming in every morning for the last couple of years and had conversed briefly with Libby every time.

"Counselor, you're running late today." Libby pushed a stubborn strand of blond hair behind her ear and smiled.

"So you're still here on the off chance I'd stop by?" Tully teased in return. "I'm flattered." In truth she really was, since Libby always seemed happy to see her.

"How about a cup of coffee on me?"

"How about I pay for the coffee and give you a big tip, and you can ask for your bribe anyway?" A few weeks earlier, after one of their regular daily conversations, Tully had finally realized that she knew more about the young barista than she did about her own daughter.

Libby was a law student in her second year at Tulane, working as much as she could to cover what her scholarship did not. Their talks sometimes became a tutoring session when Tully came in and ended up helping Libby through a tough spot at school.

Tully always tipped generously, considering what she paid for the actual coffee, because she remembered how many peanut butter sandwiches she'd eaten during law school, not having the heart to ask her parents for one more dime. Every time Tully said to keep the change when she handed Libby a twenty, the young woman could eat a little better than Tully had when she was in college.

"Do you really have time to talk?" Libby fixed the coffee the way Tully liked it and smiled even more brightly before handing it over.

"I have as much time as you want, since it seems I'm not needed anywhere else at the moment."

"It's my contract law class. Professor Lange is a pompous ass who constantly tries to make me look like a buffoon."

"John Lange is one of those people who makes the old saying true, so I wouldn't worry too much about him. Just get through the semester and you'll be fine."

"What old saying?" Libby pulled her contract law book out of her ever-present bag, along with a list of questions.

"'Those who can't, teach.' John knows the mechanics of the law like no one else in the city, but what good are tools if you don't know how to use them? In the classroom he's a menace, but in the courtroom, *he*'s a buffoon. I took his class almost twenty years ago, and it sounds like he hasn't changed a bit." She threw her newspaper on the extra chair and examined Libby's notes.

During the next hour Tully explained the subject matter in a way that she hoped would teach Libby what she needed to know in a way she could remember, even under her professor's withering questioning. As she started in on the last question, Tully could feel herself blush when her stomach growled. The night and morning with no food was starting to catch up to her.

"Tully, when was the last time you ate?"

"Yesterday at lunch…I believe." Now that she thought about it, Tully couldn't remember exactly.

"That's it, come on. I'm treating you to lunch as a way to thank you for all this help." Libby closed the book and pried her notepad out of Tully's hands.

"You don't have to do that. I'll be okay, and we only have one more question to go."

Libby shook her head and had to retrieve a few stray locks when they came loose from her ponytail again. She really needed a haircut, but that wasn't in her budget for the month. "I think I finally have you figured out."

Tully's spontaneous laugh shed years of weariness from her face, and her eyes seemed to come alive, if only for a second. "I'm glad someone does, because lately I couldn't begin to explain what's going on with me."

"You focus on something and the rest of the world falls away, doesn't it?"

Tully didn't detect any malice in Libby's words, unlike Bailey's similar remark that morning, so she took the comment at face value. "I'm focused, so I guess your assessment of me is correct. Years ago, when I lived alone, it wasn't much of a problem, but I guess I should have paid more attention all this time, huh?"

"That's not a bad trait, Tully, but I want you to start taking better care of yourself. If something happens to you, who's going to help me through law school?" She put her hand on Tully's forearm and smiled again.

At times like these the walls in Tully's heart crumbled for the briefest of moments, and she felt lonely. "Come on, let's get something to eat."

Despite Libby's objections, they ended up in a nice restaurant with linens and fine china on the tables, since Tully insisted on treating. And after the waiter told her they didn't do takeout, Tully ordered five lunches. Libby walked out with dinner for the next three nights and told Tully that her inventive way of getting around firm, set rules was what made her a success when it counted.

After they parted, Tully called the office to inform Roxanne she was taking the rest of the afternoon off and headed home. Not much of a cook, she stopped and bought Chinese, making sure the selections included everyone's favorite dish. She changed into a pair of shorts, set the table, and looked forward to a nice family dinner once her wife and children actually arrived. She figured the only way to change things she didn't like was to start trying something different.

Four hours later, the back door opened and Jessica entered, issuing orders about homework and chores to Bailey and Ralph, who trailed her. They all stopped abruptly and stared from her to the table, since Tully didn't usually get home for another hour or so.

"I didn't know you'd be here." Jessica looked at the containers in the kitchen. "We stopped for something after Ralph's practice."

"I could eat again, Mom." Ralph winced when Bailey slapped him on the back of the head.

"Stop being such a suck-up," Bailey muttered before heading up the stairs to her room. A minute after the door to her room slammed, the music started.

"It's okay, Ralph," Tully said. "Go on up and do your homework. Just let me know if you need any help."

The hug her son gave her before leaving the room made her feel like crying for some reason, but she put the feelings aside and hugged him back.

"I'm sorry. If I'd known, I would've brought them home for dinner." Jessica had yet to put her bag down, but she looked like she wanted to bolt from the room. "Why don't you fix yourself a plate? No sense in letting it go to waste."

Something was different about her, but whatever it was hadn't jumped into Tully's focus. The woman standing fifteen feet from her wasn't the woman she'd fallen in love with, and hell if she knew when that had changed. She still loved Jessica, but plainly Jessica no longer felt the same.

"Is there something you want to tell me?"

"What do you mean?" The leather strap of Jessica's purse creaked from the pressure she was putting on it.

"I stopped by to take you to lunch today."

"Oh yeah, Cathy said she saw you. I was having a bad day and decided to skip out for a little while and grab something somewhere quiet."

Under Tully's scrutiny Jessica's intense focus on the stack of egg rolls gave her away. She was lying, but this wasn't the time to get into it. Their kids were upstairs, and Tully didn't want them growing up in a war zone. When she and Jessica had their talk, they would be alone, and she wouldn't give up until Jessica came clean.

As Tully rounded the breakfast bar wearing shorts and a T-shirt, she remembered her med-student days when Jessica had admired her tan skin, bare feet, and visible muscles from hefting nets from the water and carrying buckets of ice on her father's boat. In fact, Jessica had pursued her until Tully took an interest. Those long-past days had been full of love and affection.

She strode past Jessica and into her office, the food left opened and forgotten, her appetite lost to hurt feelings.

Chapter Three

The next morning Jessica was surprised when Tully didn't mutter as much as usual in the bathroom. And she didn't have to invent an excuse why she didn't want Tully to touch her because Tully made no move. She simply dressed, picked up her coat, and folded it over her arm before leaving. Jessica felt relieved in a way, but the new attitude told her that Tully had finally taken the hint and given up, which saddened her more than she would've thought. Now if Jessica wanted the situation to change, she'd have to make the first move.

Tully walked to Bailey's door first again and knocked loud enough to be heard over the music. When Bailey opened it, her hostile glare killed any greeting Tully might have offered. "If you want a ride I'm ready to go. I have court today, so I'd appreciate it if you meet me in the kitchen in five minutes."

Bailey opened her mouth, but for once the rude comment died in her throat. Her mother looked different and it wasn't a good change. Tully had been many things to her in her short life, from hero to punching bag, but one thing she never associated with her was defeat. Not the kind of defeat she was witnessing now.

"Ralph, you ready?" Tully called through his door.

In the kitchen she handed them what they had asked for the morning before and held the door open for them to head to the car. When Tully started the engine she turned on the music they had listened to the morning before and seemed to drive to their school on autopilot. She didn't comment on the language or attempt to make conversation.

"Have a good day," Tully finally said when she stopped in front of the school.

"You too, Mom," Ralph said. He got out and stood next to the car, waiting for Bailey.

With her hand on the door handle, Bailey stopped when Tully asked her the last thing she ever expected. "You don't like it here, do you?"

"It's not totally lame, I guess."

"Sometimes, Bailey, I ask you things because I really *am* interested in an answer and not because I'm setting you up for a lecture. What about this place don't you like? How about if I phrase it like that?"

Bailey's anger receded a bit and she stared at her mom. "Why do you want to know?"

"Because eventually you're going to see that high school is a blip on the radar, but when you have to live it every day, it's miserable if you don't like it."

Tully never took her hands from the steering wheel because she didn't want to set herself up for another rejection, but she ached to engulf Bailey in her arms and take the sad face away. "You don't have to tell me if you don't want, but if you ever do, I'll listen and try to come up with a solution that'll make it better."

"Thanks." Bailey hesitated before getting out. She didn't say anything else, but she smiled a little when Tully nodded.

"Anytime, Bailey Bean." The nickname made Bailey's smile broaden, and for once she walked away from the car as if she wasn't facing execution.

❖

"You were due in court in an hour, but Iverson's clerk called and said the judge had to move us back to tomorrow."

As Roxanne followed Tully down the hall to her office, Tully knew she was wondering why the front of her shirt and pants was covered in coffee and she'd been cursing under her breath from the minute she'd walked in.

"Lady Luck is smiling on you today," Roxanne continued, "so stop cussing before you work yourself into a coronary."

The closet in her office usually held a set of clean clothes, but when Tully opened it, the bar was empty. "Shit, I forgot to bring the damn things back after I took them to the cleaners."

"Go home and change and get back here as soon as you can. I just got off the phone with some potential clients I think you're going to want to take. They're coming in this afternoon at three."

"I'm already working two cases, Rox, so we wouldn't be doing them any favors if we stretch ourselves too thin."

"Just listen to their story, and if you don't want to take them, I'll find them a new attorney myself."

"All right, let me get out of this and I'll be back in an hour."

They headed back to the elevators.

Roxanne surveyed Tully's shirt. "How did that happen, anyway?"

"Some idiot elbowed me when I started to take a sip because he thought I was talking to the server too long. He was in a hurry, I guess."

"Were you?"

Tully punched the button for the elevator three times, though she knew it wouldn't make the cars move faster. "Was I what?"

"Talking to the server too long?"

"Libby was telling me how her class went last night after I gave her some pointers yesterday. She wasn't that long-winded." Spending time with Libby provided her a guilty pleasure every day, so an occasional miffed customer was a small price to pay. Libby fawned over her and seemed to enjoy her company, and, absurdly, Tully kept hoping that Jessica would feel the same way about her once again.

"You better stay out of coffee shops until you get back. We have a lot to do and you need to look the part."

Tully was still laughing about the comment when she turned into their driveway thirty minutes later. She had to slam on her brakes when she found a car parked in her spot. Her first thought was to call the police, but she decided to investigate the situation herself. Since the sticker on the front windshield read Children's Hospital, it was a safe bet that Jessica had invited a friend home for an early lunch.

The container of imperial chicken from the night before was sitting open on the bar with a spoon sticking out of it, as was the container of egg rolls. The only things missing were plates or any sign of Jessica. For once, Tully was glad their house still had carpet up the stairs and on the second floor. They'd meant to put down wood but never gotten around to hiring someone.

She walked down the hall to the open door of the master suite and, when she reached it, felt like someone had twisted a knife in her gut. What she'd found different about Jessica the day before hit her like a two-by-four across the forehead. The top two buttons of her wife's blouse were missing, probably because the redhead who was going down on her was too impatient to open them the old-fashioned way.

As Jessica's moan reached Tully's ears, an overwhelming wave of nausea hit her. Jessica had her eyes shut, obviously enjoying what her lover was doing so much that she didn't hear Tully. That changed in an instant when Tully grabbed the woman by the back of her head and jerked her off the bed.

"Tully, don't," Jessica screamed as she tried to cover her nakedness.

"Tully, don't?" she roared. "You fuck some piece of shit in my bed and I'm just supposed to walk out of here and let her finish?"

The naked woman cocked her fist back and connected with Tully's eye before she could complain about anything else. The blow was so hard that her eyebrow started to bleed instantly, but Tully wasn't about to retreat. She hit back, throwing the woman into the dresser.

"It's my fault she's here, so take it out on me if you want." Jessica held the sheet up around her. "Don't hit her again. Just tell me what you want and I'll do it."

"What I want?" The movement behind her made Tully turn around, only to get hit two more times. "What I want is to kill this piece of shit, but I'll settle for this." She felt some deep satisfaction when her blow connected, making the woman's head fly back. The redhead landed in a heap, in no shape to get up again.

"Tully, calm down before someone really gets hurt," Jessica pleaded, still making no move to get off the bed. She watched with a frozen expression on her face when Tully walked to the phone and dialed 911.

"Yes, Operator, I'd like to report an assault in my home." She paused, feeling numb as she looked at Jessica and smiled. "I came home unexpectedly and found what I believe was a woman trying to rape my partner." Jessica sat up, then rose from the bed. Tully watched her get dressed while she continued her report. "Yes, ma'am, the assailant then attacked me. I was able to fight back and she's momentarily unconscious. I've got a deep cut, I believe, but I'll have it looked at later. I just need you to send a unit out as soon as possible. Thank you."

"You fucking bitch." Jessica glared at her.

"No, darling, the only one doing any fucking here is you. I just laid the groundwork for the story your children will hear, which is the least I can do for you. If you choose to go another route, then tell the nice police officer your version of events." She didn't try to clean off her face or the shirt that now displayed a mixture of spilt coffee and blood. "I'll leave you two alone." Without another word she headed downstairs to wait for the police.

"You aren't going to get away with this, Tully," Jessica yelled after her.

Get away with what? Having some reaction to finding my loving wife with her legs spread for someone else? What a joke, Tully thought as she wiped the blood from her face.

❖

"Dr. Badeaux, your partner says it's an affair, not an assault," the police officer explained after talking to everyone involved. "Actually, both women say you mounted more of an assault than she did."

"Does my face look like the assault was my fault, Officer?" Tully removed the ice pack the paramedic had handed her and showed the man the damage.

"Tully, cut the crap and tell him the truth," Jessica demanded as she held another ice pack to her lover's jaw.

"Ma'am," the officer cut in. "Does this woman live here with you?" He pointed to the redhead sitting at the dining-room table.

"No, I share the house with her." Jessica pointed to Tully.

"My name is Dr. Kara Nicolas, not 'this woman,'" the redhead added.

"Is it fair to say that Dr. Badeaux knew about the relationship you have with Dr. Nicolas?" The officer added a bit of sarcasm to Kara's name, making Jessica realize where this was going.

"No, Officer, that's why it's called *an affair*."

"I understand that, ma'am, but you have to see the situation from my viewpoint. The person who lives here comes home and finds some stranger pinning you to the bed, the same stranger who then gets up and punches her in the face numerous times. Dr. Badeaux was well within her rights to protect herself and to file charges against Dr. Nicolas if she chooses to."

"It was a mutual altercation, not an assault," Jessica yelled.

"Do you have proof of that?"

"You have my word and Dr. Nicolas's word. What more do you want?"

"The word of someone not trying to cover up the existence of an affair, ma'am." He took his card from his breast pocket and handed it to Tully. "Don't worry, though, I'll include all of your statements in my report. The court system can work it out."

"This isn't the last of this, Tully." Jessica helped Kara out of the chair and headed to the door. It had been a bitch getting her dressed and presentable before the police got there, but now all she wanted was to get the hell away from Tully.

After Tully heard the engine start, she heard a crash and watched the remaining officers rush to the front door. Jessica had gunned Kara's car into Tully's vehicle and pushed it out to the street to get it out of the way. Before she could drive off, the same policeman stopped her and wrote her up for reckless driving, adding another report to give to Tully.

He stood at the door and gave her the incident number as well as the phone number of a wrecker service. "You sure look calm for someone who's just been fucked over, if you don't mind me saying so." He surveyed the wrecked car and shook his head. "I'd have expected this shit from you, not her. You're the wronged party here, after all."

"It may seem like I got fucked over today, but I do my fucking over in a different arena." When he cocked his head to the side, she added, "I'm an attorney as well, and this will eventually make it into court, sir. There you can really fuck someone over."

"Good to know. I'll call you if I ever have the need. Can't have too much luck or know too many good attorneys." He shook her hand. "I'll do this paperwork right away. And you might want someone to take a picture of your face for future reference."

"Thanks, I appreciate the advice."

❖

Though Roxanne offered to come over Tully's house to make sure she was all right, Tully made her promise to stay at the office and reschedule everything for the rest of the week until she was ready to return to work.

"I'll let you know if I hear anything from the police."

"I doubt if you will. Now I have to clean up a little and buy a new vehicle."

"Tully, I know you're probably not up to it, but I'm going to reschedule the couple that was supposed to come today for sometime tomorrow. I hate to push you, but I promised them that you'd see them as soon as possible, so if I have to beg, I will."

"Make it the late morning and warn them that their attorney might look a little worse for wear. The bitch was short but she packed quite a wallop."

After Tully finished on the phone she went up to take a shower. The rumpled bed made her skin feel even dirtier, but she could burn the sheets later. Now she needed to go talk to Ralph and Bailey before someone got to them first. As angry as she was at Jessica, she was just going to tell them they needed some time apart for now and let it lie.

The ever-efficient Roxanne had called for a tow truck and had a rental car delivered while she was getting cleaned up. Tully adjusted the seat of the Ford Explorer, thankful her car would be one less thing in the long list of humiliating things that had happened to her that day that she'd have to show the kids. She drove to their school and walked down the long corridor to the office, intent on checking them out for the day and sure that Bailey and Ralph would have more than their share of questions about everything, starting with the bruises on her face.

"I'm sorry, Tully, but Dr. Badeaux checked them out about an hour ago," the school secretary informed her. "Is there a problem?" The older woman stared at Tully's face.

"No problem. I'll just give her a call since it seems we got our wires crossed."

Not having the energy for anything else, Tully drove home to start making some calls to make sure her kids were all right. She didn't want Jessica to drive around with them, on the off chance she decided to ram someone else. She also didn't know who this Kara Nicolas was and how she would welcome a lover with two children.

Having no answers to the multitude of questions in her head, Tully felt lost. Aside from the kids, she was now alone, and having such solitude thrust upon her so suddenly and through no fault of her own left her wanting to hit something. She flexed her fingers, still feeling the soreness of hitting Kara earlier, but the memory didn't bring her any satisfaction.

Chapter Four

"No fucking way, Jess." Kara sat on her sofa and popped a few pills into her mouth before putting the ice pack back. "You can move in here if you need a place to stay, but I look at fucking kids all day long. I'm not coming home to any."

"You knew I had kids. And right now they're sitting outside the apartment building in the car and I'm sure wondering what the heck I'm doing in here."

"Your kids and her kids, not mine. This isn't up for discussion."

"What exactly would you like me to do with them? They're my children."

Kara glared at her from what seemed to be a pain-induced haze. "If they're that important to you, why don't you go find a nice hotel room for the three of you so you can play the doting mother. I don't give a fuck, but they're not staying here. I have enough shit happening in my life."

"All right, I'll be back in a little while."

After a silent drive from the apartment, Jessica and the kids parked in front of the house again, and Jessica wondered who the car in the driveway belonged to. "Something happened today, and I'm going to move out and stay with a friend."

"For how long?" Bailey asked.

"I don't think I can come back here, guys, but I want you to know I love you." She touched Bailey's cheek and sighed when she slammed against the car door to get away from her. Bailey apparently wasn't any fonder of her than she was of Tully, and Jessica figured this wasn't the time for total honesty on her part. "We'll work something out, but for now you're going to have to stay with your mom."

"That's all you're going to say?"

Jessica sighed. "This situation is between your mom and me, and not up for discussion."

"You pull this random crap and we're supposed to accept that it's 'not up for discussion.' That's not good enough."

"Bailey, I'd appreciate it if you didn't curse at me, and what happened was between adults. It had nothing to do with you or Ralph."

Bailey reached up and slammed her fist down on the dashboard. "My bad. I keep forgetting we're just the freaking last thing you or Mom are concerned about."

When Ralph opened the door and got out without saying a word or asking any more questions, Bailey was surprised, even though she wanted nothing more than to sit there and insist until she browbeat Jessica into answering. She followed him to make sure he was all right because he didn't beg Jessica to stay. She was even more surprised when she reached the back door and heard him screaming at Tully.

"Why did she leave? What did you do?"

"I didn't do anything, Ralph, and I'm assuming your mother told you why she left."

Tully was standing at the island in the kitchen with a Coke can in front of her, along with her car keys. Bailey wondered if she had been planning to run away too, or if she had intended to come try to find them.

"She just said something happened, but it isn't any of our business," Bailey said. She pointed to the large cut and bruise on Tully's face. "Is that part of what happened?"

"Your mom doesn't want to be with me anymore, guys, but I'd never lift a hand against her. You know that."

"Then what happened to you?" Bailey persisted.

"Her new friend and I had a little difference of opinion, but it's not as bad as it looks."

"That's all you're going to say?"

"Right now I can't think of anything else I can say that's going to make this any better or easier."

"Typical," was all Bailey said before she turned her back on Tully.

When it was clear Tully wasn't going to add anything new, she and Ralph went up to their rooms.

Tully left them alone, not wanting to push them into talking to her if they didn't want to. She sat outside on a chaise lounge with a pack of cigarettes. At nine that night she heard the back door open behind her but no footsteps, as if the person was hesitant to approach.

"You came home and found her with someone else, didn't you?"

"That isn't a question you should be asking me, Bailey."

"Why? You told me yesterday that if I answer questions in the most direct and respectful way I can, I'll earn the respect I think I deserve." Bailey even used the same inflection with which Tully had delivered the line.

Tully stubbed out the last stick in the pack and laughed so hard she started coughing. "So I did."

"So answer it."

"It's not that I don't want to, but right now the last thing I need is for you to blame me for one more thing. My face hurts, my head hurts, and I can only take so much in one day." The tirade sounded childish to her own ears, but she was tired, hurt, and shell-shocked, so in a way she couldn't help herself.

"What am I going to blame you for? You're still here, she's not."

"She left me, kid, and you're right about one thing—it has nothing to do with you." Tully sighed and stared up at the stars. In the dark backyard, they were vivid in the cloudless sky.

"The problem is, though, she left me and Ralph too, and I know you don't want…"

The unfinished statement made Tully swing around and face her daughter. "I don't want what?"

"You probably think we should be with her instead of here bothering you, but she didn't want us."

Not caring if Bailey pushed her away, Tully hugged her close and held her. "No, Bailey Bean, I *do* want you here with me. Your mom and I are having problems, but that has nothing to do with how I feel about you." She wanted to cry when her daughter slumped against her and accepted the comfort she was offering. "I love you with all my heart, even when you get really mad at me. Nothing you do in this life is ever going to change how I feel about you."

"You sure? I'm kinda buggin' about this, so you can imagine what

Ralph's going through. He won't talk to me and I'm worried about him. Usually I have to slap him to get him to shut up."

"I'm sure, baby." She moved them toward the door. If Bailey was feeling this undone, then she was right, Ralph was a wreck. "We're going to get through this just fine."

"But you don't know how to do anything." Bailey sounded almost as lost as Tully felt.

"As long as the grocery doesn't run out of Pop-Tarts we'll be okay."

She spent a good deal of time in Ralph's room with him and Bailey, reassuring them of the future but steering clear of any subject that would turn them against Jessica. As angry as Tully was now, Jessica was still their mother. All three of them cried together and went to bed with a new fragile truce in place. Tully hoped the kids were more certain that although their place in the world was changing, they wouldn't lose it.

❖

"Mom, where in the hell are you?" Bailey called from the kitchen.

The high-pitched, panicked voice made Tully pop her head up from the sofa. "What's wrong?"

"I went to your room looking for you and thought you'd left."

Running a hand over her face, Tully tried to think of a reasonable way to explain why she'd rather eat hot coals than sleep in her bed. "Sorry, I just sat here for a little while and must've fallen asleep."

"If you want I can get the guest room ready for you. I'm sure the maid put fresh sheets on the bed, but it's been a while since anyone's stayed in there." Bailey moved closer and sat on the other side of the sofa. She'd seen the way the bed looked when she went in to find Tully and figured her assumptions from the night before were correct. Contrary to what her parents believed, sixteen didn't equal stupid in some areas. "Until we decide what we're doing, I can do that if you want."

"You know something, kid?"

"If you don't want me to help you through this, that's just fine. I just thought you'd feel better if you talked about it." Bailey folded her arms across her chest so she wouldn't blow from anger.

"I was going to say that you're really observant."

"Maybe it's just that you and Mama think I don't have any brains for anything."

Tully shook her head. "I can't speak for your mother, but that's not what I think of you at all. And last night I decided to let the maid go." If Tully thought Bailey was going to object to the suggestion, the laugh she got instead surprised her.

"The drapes were Mama's idea too. Are we ripping those out?"

"The maid *was* your mother's idea, and the only time the woman can work herself up to talk to us is when it's time to get paid. Getting rid of her isn't going to be a real hardship, is it?"

Bailey poked Tully in the chest with her finger. "Not until you expect me to start vacuuming and cleaning up after Ralph in the bathroom. Get rid of her if you want, but we might need to talk."

"Can I ask you something else?"

Bailey's hair fell into her face when she nodded. "Whatever."

The answer didn't make sense to Tully, but she figured it was all right to ask her question. "Lately you're so angry all the time…can you tell me why?" She winced when she stretched her back out. "I know you think I'm never around, but I get the impression that even if I was here twenty-four/seven, you'd still feel the same way about me."

"I don't hate you…not really. It's just that…" Bailey's arms seemed to tighten against her chest as if to delay the words. "I don't want to talk about it."

"Want to make a deal?"

Bailey nodded.

"When you're ready to talk to me, and I mean really ready to talk, I'll answer all your questions truthfully until you tell me to stop. I'll do that if you'll do the same."

"Why would you agree to that?"

"Easy, because I love you. And if it takes laying myself bare for you to believe me, then it's an easy deal to make."

"I'll think about it, because I might want more stuff out of the deal."

"Ah, spoken like a true future attorney."

"Could we do one question now just for practice before we finalize things?" Bailey asked.

"Just one?"

"I think it's best to go slow."

"Then ask away."

"Mama told me that you never wanted to have children. Is that true?"

Tully was stunned to hear what Jessica was feeding the kids along with their nutritious breakfasts. "When your mother and I met, having kids had never crossed my mind," she started, as hesitantly as she ever spoke.

"So it's true?"

"Technically that's your second question, so let me finish answering the first one before we move on to your version of the truth." Tully helped Bailey off the sofa and led her into the kitchen. "When we met and started dating, I'd never considered having children. Later, I went along with the idea because she wanted kids so much."

"So it's true?"

Tully tugged on a strand of Bailey's hair and smiled, trying to keep her quiet until she was done. "I remember when I saw your mom's first ultrasound, then heard your heart beating. I fell in love with you right then. Once you were born I stayed up countless nights, without any sleep."

"I had a lot of colic?"

"That's four questions now, but that's not why I lost sleep. I'd just go into your room and watch you. You had this thick head of hair, and I knew right then that you were the best thing I'd ever done."

Bailey watched Tully as she spoke, especially the way her eyes were glued to the backyard as if she was trying to capture those memories.

"I never regretted having you or your brother in my life. You've always been my motivation to do good in the world so you'd be proud of me." She shrugged and didn't say anything else.

"Why haven't you ever told me that story?"

"I have, about a million times. Only then you enjoyed hearing stories from me, and the sight of me didn't repulse you like it does now." Tully's features relaxed. "Maybe you're right, Bailey Bean. We should talk more often. I don't want other people to tell you how I feel or don't feel about you. If you want to know, just ask—deal or no deal."

"You don't repulse me, you know." Bailey put her hands on the counter between them in an effort to stay calm, but she couldn't help shifting from foot to foot.

"It's okay to tell the truth, I'm not going to get angry. I haven't up to now, have I?" Tully reached across the space between them and put her hands over Bailey's. "I'm not very good at communicating my feelings, but that's not your fault. I just want to know why you're mad at me."

"You're never around anymore."

"I'm home every night, but you're right, I guess. I'm home, but I'm not really here."

"Why is that?" Bailey turned her hands so that their palms slid together in a more affectionate way. She had her mother talking and wanted to keep it that way.

"Because I came home to a family that didn't need me anymore, and I couldn't find a way to accept that reality. You always ate out with your mom somewhere, then came home and couldn't have cared less about talking to me." Seeming tired, Tully sat down and sighed. "I'm sorry. That sounds rather childish, doesn't it?"

"No, it sounds like you're talking straight. I know you talk to Ralph sometimes, but I felt the same way you did. You never seem interested in what I'm doing or what's going on in my life. I stopped talking to you because I thought you didn't care about me."

"Can I ask my question now?" The nod Tully received was so hesitant that she led Bailey around the kitchen counter and into the den. On the sofa she hugged her and just held her, expecting Bailey to withdraw quickly. The real surprise was that she didn't. "Why do you look so unhappy when I drop you off at school, Bailey Bean?"

"I'm not..." Bailey buried her face in Tully's shoulder in an obvious effort to keep from answering.

"It's all right. If it's too hard, don't answer. But tell me if you want me to do something to make it better."

"I don't have any friends. This girl has made fun of me from day one, and she's real popular so it stuck and everyone thinks I'm a total loser." The words came out in a rush, muffled since her face was still pressed to Tully's shoulder.

"There are plenty of good schools in this city, so if you want to transfer somewhere else we can start looking. I meant what I said about high school and being miserable. You should look back at this time with fond memories, not a sigh of relief that it's over."

"If I leave now that girl wins, doesn't she?"

"It isn't a contest, honey, but whatever you decide, you let me know."

"Aren't you supposed to make the decisions?" Bailey asked, sounding a lot better. It was the first time in forever that she had teased Tully.

"Tell your grandmother that when we visit her. I'm not young anymore, but she still feels it's her duty to tell me what to do. From now on I'm going to make an effort not to do that to you. That is, unless you want to run off and become a juvenile delinquent set on drugs and mayhem. Then I might be making plenty of decisions for you, starting with locking you in your closet until you come to your senses." She hugged Bailey closer, wanting to cry with joy because her daughter didn't hate her. "Give me time to think of a good solution that doesn't involve physical violence. Or I could come home early today and we can talk about it some more."

Bailey hesitated, then said, "Or you could take us to work with you today to help us get over the trauma of our parents splitting up."

"You know I haven't had time to think about that." *I suppose I should feel bad about the fact that so many years of a commitment are over.* "You won't be bored to death at the office?"

"I'll spend the day researching a paper due at the end of the month, and you can take us to lunch."

"Just for today. Then we go back to a somewhat normal schedule."

"Sure we will," Bailey said, sounding like Tully was spinning fiction.

CHAPTER FIVE

Libby was surprised when Tully came in with her two kids. Tully had often spoken of her family, and it was nice to put faces to the stories.

"Hey, Libby." Tully returned her greeting. "We thought we'd come by and let you help us with breakfast."

"Yeah, Mom couldn't boil water if her life depended on it," Ralph said.

"This would be my comedian." Tully put her hand on Ralph's head. "Libby, meet my son Ralph, and this is the family beauty, my daughter Bailey. Guys, this is Libby."

"Nice to meet you." Libby started on Tully's coffee while smiling at the good-looking group. "Your mom talks about you all the time, so I'm glad she finally saw fit to bring you in."

"She talks about us all the time?" Bailey asked.

"It's all good, so don't worry. You have a very proud parent. I wouldn't sweat being embarrassed. Well, unless praise embarrasses you." She handed Tully the cup and wiped her hands on her apron. "What can I get you two?"

Ralph waited while his sister made up her mind and ordered a latte and a blueberry scone, then he said, "Hot chocolate and a scone too, please."

He'd woken up that morning feeling as if his life had changed, but not because of anything he'd done. He lay in bed angry that everything would be so different but no one had bothered to ask for his input. His comfort had come from his sister, who had shocked him by taking

Tully's side on an issue for once when she came in to get him up for the day.

Libby interrupted his thoughts. "Go sit, and I'll bring all this out to you."

They picked a table next to the window, and since the morning rush was over, they had a bit of privacy. Tully put her cup down and turned her attention to Bailey and Ralph. "Guys, I think we need to discuss what happens now."

"We get to stay with you, right?" Ralph asked in a panic. He had felt sick the day before when Jessica dropped them off, basically telling them she didn't want them.

"Of course you get to stay with me, until your late thirties if I have any say in that decision, so don't worry about it. I'm talking about the fact that your mother isn't going to be staying with us, so we need to make sure we know what we're all doing so we stay on track."

"What do you mean?" Bailey asked.

"I mean your brother has practice on some days, you have stuff you do after school, we have to eat something, and we have a house to keep up. That's just for starters."

Ralph struggled not to cry. "Mama isn't coming back, is she?"

"Buddy, I'm going to do my best so that whatever the future brings, you and your sister will be happy. But no, your mom isn't coming back, at least to me. I'm sure she'll continue to be as big a part of your life as she's always been. What happened yesterday has everything to do with me and nothing to do with you."

She exhaled deeply, trying to curb the urge to light a cigarette. "I'll let your mom tell you about her new life and how it'll change your future, because that's not my story to tell. But for now we, the three of us," she circled her finger, "are going to do our best to get by."

"I just don't understand why she did this," Ralph said.

"Certain relationships are forever, Ralph. Like mine with you and your sister. What you mean to me will never change. Unfortunately, you can't say the same about the person you choose to marry. Sometimes those relationships don't work out, and no matter how much you try, you can't go back."

Ralph looked at Tully with eyes the same gray color and the same intensity as her own. "But if you really talked to her, I bet we could go back to being a family."

Bailey slapped Ralph's leg. "Mom, maybe you should go help Libby bring our stuff over."

"It's okay. He has a right to his opinion."

"And she might not be able to carry all that stuff, so go on." Bailey pointed to the counter.

"Do I look feeble?" Libby asked when Tully arrived at the counter and picked up a plate.

"You're more than capable, but my kids wanted a moment alone so they can talk about me," Tully said, her eyes never leaving the table. Bailey and Ralph had their heads together, and Bailey was doing all the talking.

"You okay?"

"My life is pathetic and I'm an idiot, but other than that I'm just great."

Like she often did, Libby put her hand on Tully's forearm and pulled a little on the jacket sleeve to get her attention. "I'm a great listener, you know."

"I know, but I have to wrap my brain around a few things before I'm ready to sit and talk." Tully helped put the cups and plates on the tray, then stood at the counter until it was safe to go back. "How was school last night?"

"Professor Lange was impressed with my newfound knowledge of certain concepts, so thanks. I owe you yet again."

"You don't owe me anything. Just knowing that pompous ass gets his comeuppance every so often is payment enough."

Libby's eyes strayed to the table where Ralph was now seriously shaking his head at whatever Bailey was telling him. "Will you at least remember that I'm here for you? After all the free tutoring sessions, I'd feel like I'm giving you something in return."

"How about you start by taking this over there before the drinks get cold, and I'll take this call." She picked up the tray and handed it to Libby, then pulled out her cell phone.

❖

"Ralph, if you ever repeat anything I'm about to tell you, I'll kill you in your sleep," Bailey said as soon as Tully started walking away. "I know you ace every test you take, but you're the biggest idiot sometimes."

"Just because I want them back together I'm an idiot?"

"Bro, I realize you got mad yesterday and blamed Mom for Mama leaving, but did you ask yourself why the queen of control had a black eye and a huge cut on her cheek?" She tugged him closer, not wanting anyone to overhear them. "You know how fanatical Mom is about not losing it. It makes her good at work and the best one to come to your room when you've done something wrong. Counselor Tully will talk you to death, then forget to ground you."

"When did you become Mom's biggest fan?"

"I feel sorry for her. She didn't exactly say it, but I think she came home and caught Mama in bed with someone else, which is so wrong on so many levels. I mean, step out if you want, but don't do it at home."

Bailey was still talking, but Ralph started shaking his head as if the last thing that had come out of her mouth wasn't true and couldn't be. "Shut up."

"Why?"

"Take it back. They're having problems, but Mama isn't like that." He balled his hands under the table, but since Bailey had her head down she saw the angry gesture.

"Did I say she was?"

"You just said she was screwing someone who wasn't Mom."

Bailey took his fist and did her best to coax the fingers loose. "They aren't getting back together, Ralph, and whatever you tell yourself so you can be okay with that is tight with me. And I'm sure it's going to be cool with Mom. Just don't keep telling her to go try to make things right with Mama."

Ralph screwed up his face and looked like he was going to say something loud, so Bailey shook her head to shut him up. It wasn't easy to say the words, but she had figured a few things out. "For once the work freak wasn't at fault."

"She was really with someone else when Mom came home?"

"I think so, but I don't know for sure."

Ralph gave her a pleading look. "Why didn't Mom tell me that yesterday when I yelled at her?"

"Dude, she'd run her tongue through the shredder before she'd try to turn us against Mama. As mad as I've been at her lately, I have to give her snaps for that."

"I feel horrible I screamed at her." He finally turned his attention to

Tully, who was near the entrance talking on her cell phone and pacing, which was normal when she was engaged in a conversation she didn't want to be a part of.

"You're the golden child, Ralph. I wouldn't worry about it."

❖

"You left yesterday, remember that?" Tully said.

"I want to see the kids before you poison them against me."

"You fuck someone where Bailey and Ralph could've walked in on you, and you accuse me of poisoning them against you? Have you started smoking crack on your lunch hour?"

Jessica ran her hand through her hair as she looked out the window of Kara's small apartment. The night before had been a nightmare of Kara screaming at her and taking painkillers, and it had left her head hurting. "I know you, Tully. When you're angry you'll take out your revenge in the courtroom, and I know you're mad at me. Since this won't end up in court, you have to take it out somewhere."

"Jessica, you don't know me at all. I want you to go back to your maiden name so that my family name doesn't get dragged down whatever road you've decided to take. I want you to reassure our kids that their mother hasn't gone completely insane, and I want you to leave me the hell alone. You make more than enough money to take care of yourself so forget about alimony, and I want the kids to stay with me."

"No fucking way."

"Agree, Jessica, or I'll take you to court, and when I'm done Jack the Ripper wouldn't trust you with his children."

"You're not a divorce attorney."

Tully's laugh made Jessica cringe. "Of course I'm not, but who do you think the best lawyer in the city will pick as a client when it comes to severing this relationship, you or me?"

"It depends on whether you've screwed over their family to make a buck, darling."

"Pick them up from school if you want, but have them home by seven or I'll come find you."

"That's all you have to say, Tully?"

"Not by a long shot. Months from now when your ass is puckering from the knowledge of what's coming, just remember one thing."

Jessica laughed and slapped her hand down on her lap to keep from yelling, "finally." This was the crude Tully who had spent summers working on her father's boat. The Tully who didn't know anything about picking a suit or using the correct fork at a formal dinner. The Tully who would be so easy to beat, because when confronted, she always returned to the old standards. She had been expecting this reaction from the moment Tully's fist connected with her new lover's jaw. It had taken a day, but here it was. "What's that, darling?" she said sarcastically.

"We could have done this the easy way or the hard way. You chose the hard way, and that road is paved with every misery I can think to pull out of my nice leather bag."

❖

"Thanks for everything, Libby," Bailey said. They'd had a great conversation while Tully was on the phone. The day was already educational in that she never would've guessed her mom had such a cool friend.

"Hopefully your mom will bring you in before school more often. I promise the extra shots will be on me, and they're guaranteed to keep you awake for the rest of the day." Over Tully's objections Libby had made her another latte to go and packed them all an extra muffin.

"Remember what I told you about being a good listener," she told Tully.

"Thanks for the offer, and remember to review chapter three for your quiz tonight. It's boring as hell, which is why the professor loves to take a majority of the questions out of there. See you tomorrow."

❖

Tully and her children rode up to her office exchanging small talk. In the waiting room, they passed a young couple that exemplified sadness, their shoulders slumped in defeat, each face a mask of grief.

When she walked through the office door, the woman immediately looked up and Tully noticed the glimmer of hope that crossed her dull brown eyes. The gaze told her that the woman believed that maybe she could tell her story to someone who would not only listen, but give her what she was looking for—justice.

"Come on, guys, let's get you settled," Tully said, ushering Bailey and Ralph into the office.

Roxanne was waiting in the corridor with three files in her hand. "Good morning, handsome family." She bent slightly to exchange hugs with the kids, who kept up a running dialogue as she showed them into Tully's office. "Tully, your nine o'clock is early, so if you want to brief yourself I'll get them some coffee."

"Give me about two minutes, then send them in. This time I want to hear from them before I read the file. Even if they don't have a case, I think it'll help them to tell their story."

Roxanne smiled and nodded before stepping back to her desk.

Tully focused on her kids. "How about you two go into the conference room, fire up the computers, and do your homework."

"Can I have your paralegals do my research for my paper?" Bailey asked.

"Can you pay them a hundred and fifty dollars an hour?"

"Like you're handing out that kind of allowance," she said with her hand on her hip.

"Then you'll be stuck doing your research all alone this time around. Save up my more-than-generous allowance and they're all yours."

With the kids actually talking to her and having work to keep her mind off things, Tully started to feel her world right a little. She had to be a successful parent and lawyer; Jessica had left her no alternative.

Chapter Six

"Tully Badeaux," Tully said, holding out her hand first to the young woman, then to her husband.

"Elijah and Simone Hebert, ma'am." Elijah gave a slight nod.

"My daddy always told me if you're going to trust me with something important, you're going to have to use my first name. Please call me Tully." She escorted the couple to the leather sofa in her office, taking the seat across from them. "Now, what can I do for you?"

"We talked to Roxanne," Simone started. "Her mama and mine go way back, and she told us you could help us."

"Just take all the time you need and tell me what the problem is."

"Elijah and me, we're simple people who wanted more than anything to have a family. We've been sweethearts since the third grade."

Elijah sat quietly next to his wife and held her hand. After telling the first part of the story, Simone paused and swallowed like she had a lump in her throat.

"We got married right out of high school and decided to wait a couple of years on those kids we wanted." Yanking a tissue out of her pocket, she held it to her mouth and shook her head, rocking back and forth as if some ailment had possessed her.

"Sorry, Tully, this is just hard for us," Elijah said, moving closer and putting his arm around his wife. "You want me to finish, baby?"

Because Simone didn't respond verbally or physically, he just started talking. "We were saving for a house, and those first couple of years were good fishing seasons. I know Gaston, your daddy. Always has been good to me, giving me tips, and taught me to get the best price for my catch, so Simone and me did good."

"If there's one thing Gaston Badeaux knows, it's getting a good price for shrimp." Tully stood up and took off her jacket. "Would you like to take a break before we go on? I really don't mind, and I want to make this as easy on you as possible."

"I figure the sooner we get this story told, the sooner you can start working on our case."

Tully rested the legal pad on her lap and picked up her pen. The next part had to be what was making Simone cry quietly into her husband's shoulder. "Just tell me if you need to stop."

"Four years ago, we bought our house and Simone got pregnant. A man couldn't have asked for more blessings, but I was wrong. When they laid that baby in my arms, I knew my life was rich even if my bank account didn't agree." His voice got softer, but he fought through the emotions. "We named her Evangeline and she was just beautiful."

"Do you have a picture of her?" Tully asked.

After the few minutes it took him to pull out his wallet and flip through the collection he carried with him, his eyes seemed clearer.

"She's beautiful."

"Thank you. Right after she was born they told Simone she couldn't have any more kids, but we were okay with that. Our dream had been to have a big family, but God had seen fit to give us just the one."

"Was it a health risk for her to get pregnant again?" Tully was taking copious notes.

"The doctor said something about her pressure and her womb being really thin."

It seemed rather strange to be talking about Simone like she wasn't there, but she did appear to be somewhere else, probably someplace where the pain wasn't crippling and she could hang on to the last shred of her sanity.

"I know my questions may sound strange, but I don't want to put you through this more times than I have to."

"It's okay, we understand." He wiped his face and brought Simone closer. "Things were great at first, but then right after her third birthday Evangeline got sick and we just thought it was the flu. Turned out she had bone cancer, and everyone told us to take her to New Orleans for treatment at Children's Hospital. The doctors there didn't sound real hopeful at first, but she responded well to the chemo they were giving her. She was a fighter like her mama."

"From the way you're talking, I understand Evangeline passed away from her disease."

Elijah stared at her blankly like someone who heard the words but didn't want to process them. "She died, but not from her cancer. She was in a lot of pain and they were having trouble keeping the IV in, so they told us it would be better to get something called a port." Big tears started to fall down his face, but he kept talking. "It was simple, they said, but she died in recovery. It was an accident, they said, but she was bleeding and no one noticed."

"What do you mean exactly by 'she was bleeding'?"

"When they let us see her, her stomach was swollen, and this nurse finally told me that it was her blood. She was bleeding inside, and it didn't have nowhere to go."

"Elijah, I don't mean to interrupt you, but could you hold on a minute." Tully held up a finger, stood, and walked to her desk. "Roxanne, please step in and bring Jo and Frank."

"You're not going to take our case?" Simone's voice sounded raspy from nonuse.

"The death of a child isn't an easy thing to cope with, and while telling your story will most probably get easier with time, there's no reason for you to suffer needlessly. Josephine Newmyer and Frank Tobias are my best associates and will be part of my team if we go forward."

As if finding a new source of inner strength, Simone sat up and stared Tully down with her brown eyes. "My little girl was sick, but she deserved better than she got. That woman killed her, and I want to hear her say it. This ain't about the money."

"Ma'am..." Tully started as the door opened and the people she'd invited entered. "If there's a case here, whoever is at fault will do more than just admit it, and it'll be more than just about the money."

"What do you mean?"

"It's simple. What was your daughter's life worth? What would she have become if given the opportunity to do so? To begin, how would you answer those questions? Then what's the answer to why her life was cut short?"

❖

Roxanne and the others sat down as they watched Tully weave her spell. She might have been born a fisherman's daughter, thought Roxanne, but Tully was smart *and* personable, unlike many other attorneys she had encountered. Her boss's ability to make her clients trust her integrity made all the difference in most instances.

Trials were usually won or lost not by the superior mind, but by who could reach the twelve people who mattered most. Tully had a way of getting into the hearts and minds of a jury like no one else Roxanne had ever seen work a courtroom. From her first trial, juries had warmed to her easy manner, razor-sharp wit, and warm smile and joined Tully's fight to vindicate her clients.

"Simone, lawsuits are more than just about money, at least for me. I went to medical school before law school, so I know what it's like to have to face people's expectations and hopes when it comes to their health." Tully sat again and looked Simone in the eye. "When you or your loved one is sick, you have to trust the person in the lab coat to make you better. I fight hard against those who betray that trust.

"So I try to prove they were wrong so convincingly that the district attorney has no choice but to pick up the torch and prosecute the offender. If that can't happen, then having to pay a lot of money makes the hospital be more careful the next time they hire personnel."

While Simone and Elijah nodded in approval, Tully got the others up to speed and had Elijah finish his story.

He described how they had seen their daughter in the recovery room after her surgery, minutes after she'd died. When he was done he sat back and waited, seeming to expect yet another disappointment.

"Rox, you have copies of the file for everyone?" Tully asked. She'd heard their side, so now it was time to fill in the gaps and try to separate grief from fact.

On the first line of the surgical report, flashing like a neon sign, was the name Dr. Kara Nicolas: Jessica's new lover and Evangeline Hebert's surgeon. Tully sighed and pinched the bridge of her nose.

"What?" Roxanne asked.

"We may have a problem." This was the first time her personal life had bled so profusely into her work.

"I checked the file, Tully. Jessica's not involved at all." Roxanne was about to flip to the pages again when Tully put her hand up.

"Her name isn't in there, that's not the problem." She turned her attention to her potential new clients since she knew her staff would keep her business confidential. "For me to be your attorney, you have to trust me just like those doctors I talked about."

"You haven't called us crazy yet, so I don't see a problem," Elijah said.

Tully started with her sexual orientation, which made Elijah shrug. She moved on to Jessica and where she worked, and again he shrugged.

"Believe me," Tully said, "I'm not boring you with all this to see how open-minded you are."

"You can sleep with sheep for all I care, just as long as you hand me that bitch's head on a plate."

"I want to thank all of you for being nice enough not to mention my face." Tully pointed to all the bruising. "Yesterday I filed assault charges against Dr. Nicolas."

"She beat you up?" Simone asked.

"Her face looks worse, believe me. We had a little disagreement yesterday when I found out that my partner of many years is having an affair with her."

The two associates didn't show any emotion.

"If you have a problem with that fact I can certainly recommend another attorney for you."

"Do you believe us?" Elijah asked. "That Evangeline didn't have to die so soon, I mean."

"I believe you have a good case, yes."

"Then I think, if Simone agrees with me"—Elijah turned to his wife, who nodded—"that we want you. You believe in us and you've got your own reasons to bring Dr. Nicolas down."

"Rox, get on the phone and drop all the charges I filed yesterday." Tully didn't raise her head from the file in her hand as she circled names and underlined facts. Before long she handed it to Josephine to kick-start her team's research. "Then get all the necessary paperwork for the Heberts to sign."

"When do we start?" Simone asked.

"Tully started the moment you walked in here," Roxanne said. "If you come with me, Frank and his guys will go through everything with you again so we can get your story into our files."

"It's important for you not to talk to anyone from the hospital or

Dr. Nicolas's office without one of us present," Tully advised, moving to her desk to get some cards and handing them to Simone and Elijah. "Here are all the numbers you need to get in touch with me, night or day."

Simone held it to her chest like it was a winning lotto ticket. "Tully, thank you."

"I've done this for years, but I can't imagine any other case that'll satisfy me more to win."

CHAPTER SEVEN

"Mom, can we go to lunch?" Ralph asked, and Tully lifted her head up from the file she was reading. The kids had stayed in the law library for the morning, and Tully had spent the time in her office starting on the Hebert case.

"What are you in the mood for?"

"A sandwich from Maspero's. Bailey said she voted for that too."

"Maspero's it is, then."

When they went to get Bailey and one of her paralegals handed Bailey a stack of papers, Tully looked at her watch, held up four fingers, and mouthed, "Four hundred dollars."

Libby was leaving work as they stepped out of the building, so both kids immediately flagged her down and invited her to join them.

"Are you sure?" Libby asked Tully. "I don't want to intrude."

"These guys are in charge today, so if they asked, I suggest you accept."

When Tully put her arm up for a cab, Libby had other ideas. "Come on, Counselor, it's only ten blocks. Let's walk."

"Yeah, Mom," Bailey added.

Tully mentally calculated the time such a trek would keep her out of the office, but weighed the lost work against how open her kids were to the idea. The peace wasn't going to last, her future fights with Jessica would guarantee that, so she decided to enjoy it as long as she could. Taking the heavy book bag from Libby, she waved everyone down the street, but by the time they reached the restaurant in the French Quarter, she was sweating and craving a cigarette.

"Explain to me why walking sounded so good to everyone?"

Bailey and Ralph took turns slapping her lightly on the stomach and laughing. "The extra set of tires, Mom. We gotta work on that," Bailey said. "And you can't puff in here, so chill."

Tully could feel her ears get hot and knew her face was boiled-crawfish red from the teasing, especially when the kids went in and left her on the sidewalk with Libby. "I raised two comedians, huh?"

"Maybe they're just concerned about you. It's good to have someone care enough to look out for you, so don't worry about it."

Something in the last statement made Tully stop Libby from going in. "You okay?"

"Just stuff you don't have to worry about."

"This morning someone told me she was a great listener. That offer cuts both ways, you know. I'm not only a great listener, but a pretty good problem solver too."

"With what you make, Tully, I'd certainly hope so," Libby teased.

"Yeah, but I do my best work when it's pro bono. I only put on my problem-solving hat and cape when the case is important to me."

Ralph stuck his head out one of the open doorways. "Are you coming in?"

"They're waiting," Libby said.

"You fed them well this morning, so they won't starve."

"It's too long a story to get into now, Tully, and you're busy later, I'm sure."

Tully opened the door to appease Ralph, but stopped Libby from going in. "I made a deal with Bailey and it's working out great for me, so I have a proposition for you too."

"Gosh, Tully, you're propositioning me?"

Her ears got even hotter as Libby put her hand on Tully's stomach, but the sudden heat had nothing to do with the extra weight she was carrying. "Uh-huh, funny girl. After lunch why don't you come back to the office with me and the kids and tell me what's bothering you."

"And what are you going to tell me?"

"If we have time, I'll recap the last twenty-four hours for you."

Throughout lunch Tully sat back with her burger, enjoying how Libby got her kids to open up. After the tremendous changes in their life they should have been sullen and depressed. However, Libby spoke their language.

As they walked back to Tully's office, Libby kept them talking while Tully gave her staff directions over the phone. They had worked through lunch and already gone over the file once after finishing the Heberts' statements. Now they were compiling their separate files so that Tully could use her medical background to decipher and add to them.

Libby and Bailey window-shopped along the way, but Ralph hung back and turned to Tully every so often as if willing to wait her out. "Just leave them on my desk if they're done and tell the team we'll meet later this afternoon." Tully cut her phone conversation short so that Ralph could talk to her.

"Big case, huh?"

"Could be, but the guessing part of my brain tells me that's not what you want to talk about."

Suddenly the hot-pink sweater set in the window of the boutique they were passing seemed to fascinate him. "I'm sorry I screamed at you yesterday," he said just above a whisper.

"You don't have to apologize, buddy." She stepped closer to him, not wanting anyone to overhear them. "When you protect your mother or your sister, you're just being the kid I hope I'm doing a good job of raising."

"Even if it's you I'm screaming at?"

"Even then. Just as long as you know I'm going to tell you when you're wrong about something." She stopped and turned him so they were facing each other. "No matter how upsetting any situation is in life, I hope you realize I'd never hit your mom or you."

"I know that. Why didn't you tell me I was wrong yesterday? Right away, I mean?"

"Because I was in shock. It won't rank as one of my most stellar memories, so I'm sorry for not explaining better."

"Are you okay now?"

From the corner of her eye she saw Libby and Bailey start walking again, so she jerked her head in their direction to get Ralph moving. "Not yet, but it has nothing to do with you or your sister. Your mother and I were together a long time, and it'll take time for me to be okay with the reality that we're not anymore."

"Are you mad at her?"

"Yes, I am," she said with no further elaboration.

"Me too." Ralph looked toward the windows again. "But I'm madder at myself for making you feel bad about what happened. That was my bad."

"You did what you thought was right in your heart, and that's what counts. Don't ever apologize for standing up for the people you love."

When they arrived at the building Libby rode up with them, with Tully still carrying her book bag.

"Mom, we're going back and I'm going to finish my term paper," Bailey said. "We're not going home real late, right?"

"Just tell me when you're ready, and I'll pack and finish up at home."

Libby followed her down the long hallway to the office at the end. Tully asked, "Want something to drink?"

"Maybe later. For now let me enjoy seeing the inner sanctum for the first time," Libby said as she turned full circle to take in all of Tully's office. "This great view encourages me to study."

"Once you're finished with law school, I want first crack at you."

Libby glanced back from the view to see if Tully was serious and noticed that Tully's head was down as she reviewed the stack of files on her desk. "Really? Do I give you the impression I'd make a good attorney?"

"You have the potential to be anything you want, and from our talks downstairs about law, I'd say you're going to be a fabulous lawyer. The added bonus, of course, is that you know how to use the fancy espresso machine we bought for the break room." Tully looked up after the jibe and winked.

"You're just hilarious." Trying to stay out of the way, Libby sat on the sofa. "If you're busy I can go."

"Not before you tell me what's wrong."

"I asked you first, remember?" She pointed to the other end of the couch. "So sit and tell me what's bothering you."

"I remember, but I don't want to dump my troubles on you, Libby."

She pointed to the seat again. "But you want me to dump mine on you? That hardly seems fair. Take a seat, Counselor. I asked because I wanted to help."

"Something happened after I left the coffee shop yesterday." Tully hesitated, then told the whole story, making Libby jump by smashing her fist into her other hand when she described briefly going home.

When Ralph had asked her if she was angry, Tully hadn't elaborated, but Libby was smart enough to hear the venom in her voice. Tully wasn't just angry, she was pissed.

"What happens now?"

"Great question, but I have no idea. I don't think I can go back after that. Walking in on that scene in our bedroom killed the part of my heart that belonged to Jessica, you know what I mean?"

"After being together all this time, you still loved her a lot, didn't you?"

Tully leaned forward and put her elbows on her knees so she could rest her chin on her hands. "Corny, I know, but yes."

Libby put her hand on Tully's back. "That's sweet, not corny. I've never met your partner, but she's a fool to have let what you two have go so easily over an affair."

"Ah, well, enough about my pathetic life. Tell me what's got you sounding a bit blue today."

"My roommate's getting married."

Tully moved back in her seat to give Libby her full attention. "And you were in love with the guy or something?"

"Oh, God, no. I'm upset about losing the other half of the rent when she moves out. Tracy wasn't the best roommate I've had, but she was quiet and seldom there. Studying at home was great." Libby raised her hands as if in defeat and smiled. "Oh well, I guess I have time to get another job."

"Libby, I don't mean to pry, but won't your folks help you out?"

"My mom and dad died a few years back, and not to complain, but all they left were a few debts." She gazed up at the ceiling as if trying to control her emotions. "Sorry, that sounded awful, I know."

"Don't worry about how it sounded. Just tell me how I can help you. I don't know your whole schedule, but how can you squeeze another job and school into your days?"

"I appreciate it, please don't think that I don't, but—" The intercom buzzed, interrupting Libby.

"Tully?" Roxanne's voice came through.

"What's up?" Tully pressed the button to respond.

"I hate to bother you, but Jessica's here and is waiting to see you."

"Keep her in the waiting room for a minute. I have to finish something first." Tully kept her eyes on Libby.

"There's nothing to finish, Tully. I'll go," Libby said as soon as Tully removed her finger from the intercom.

"You can go if you want, but I'd like for you to stay so we can talk about a few things." Tully didn't go back to the sofa, but did walk around the desk and sit on the edge of it.

"I'm not going to take a handout from you."

"I may only buy coffee from you, but somehow I knew that you wouldn't just accept money from me. That's not what I had in mind, so please stay."

"Okay, but if you want me to go and come back later, that's all right too. You have enough to worry about without adding me to the list."

"You're one of the few people in my life who's concerned about my stress level, which is refreshing." Tully picked up Libby's bag. "Come on, and I'll put you in the room with the kids. Just don't let Bailey talk you into writing her paper for her. The computers in there can access a couple of law libraries, so feel free to use one of them."

Tully suddenly started worrying about Libby and whatever was bothering her, which was better than concentrating on the mess her life was currently in.

CHAPTER EIGHT

The door of the office closed, and Jessica sat in the same spot Libby had been occupying. She rolled her eyes when Tully sat behind the desk, transparently trying to get her to jump through her hoops and to make the visit as uncomfortable as possible. If they were going to talk without screaming at each other, Jessica was going to have to move to the chair across from Tully's desk, which she conceded and did. After all, you didn't live with someone as long as she had with Tully and not learn just what made them tick and, in this case, what made her such a wonderful attorney.

"What can I do for you?" Tully asked.

"When I went to pick up the kids they weren't at school today." Jessica folded her hands on her lap and tried to stay calm. "It's not smart to give in to their whims, especially Bailey's."

"After you so kindly threw them out of your car yesterday, I thought a day off wasn't too much to give in to."

Jessica jerked her hands up and slammed them on Tully's desk. "That's not fair."

"Honesty isn't always fair, Jessica, so calm down."

It irritated Jessica that the more out of control she became, the more relaxed Tully seemed to be.

"The kids are here today catching up on some schoolwork, as well as coming to grips with what's going on in their lives. If you don't agree with how I handled the situation, sue me."

"Is that how you sold it to them?" Jessica almost screamed. She tried to calm herself by taking deep breaths but came close to hyperventilating when Tully went on.

"Why are you yelling?" Tully's voice was quiet. "I'm sure you'll disagree with me, but I'm the wronged party here."

"Stop talking to me like an attorney."

"I *am* an attorney, but I'll try and simplify my speech if necessary." Her voice was low but laced with sarcasm.

If Jessica prided herself on anything it was the level of her IQ, so she tried her best to let the comment go. "What I want is to talk about what happened."

"How long have you been seeing her?"

"Do you really want to get into that?"

Tully kicked back in her chair and sighed. "Then what else is there to talk about?" She put her hand up again when Jessica's mouth opened. "Wait, let me guess. You want me to tell you everything's going to be all right. How I should be okay with what you've been doing for probably over a year. That I shouldn't be upset that you were sharing a bed with me where your girlfriend had serviced you earlier."

Jessica's eyes dropped to her lap during the monotone delivery. "This isn't all my fault, Tully. I wanted you at home, but this office has always held more allure than your family."

"Stop before you drown in the bullshit you're spouting. What we need to work out is how to sever our lives with as little fuss as possible."

"We can do that, sure. I also wanted to thank you for taking the first step toward that peaceful split."

"Have I?"

"You dropped the charges against Kara. She told me this afternoon before I came over here. Just because we didn't work out doesn't mean we can't be friends."

"Jessica, we have children." Tully held up her index finger. "We are responsible for their welfare." She raised another finger. "Those are the only things we'll have to talk about from here on out."

"Then why the olive branch of dropping the charges?"

"Do you want to see the kids?" Tully asked, ignoring the question. "I can call them in if you do."

"Tully," Jessica said again.

"We're done unless you want to visit the kids." Tully pressed the intercom for Roxanne. "Could you come show Jessica to the conference room, please."

"What if I have more to talk about?" Jessica crossed her legs to imply that she wasn't going anywhere.

"I suggest you call Dr. Nicolas if you're feeling chatty. I really don't care."

Roxanne opened the door and stepped in without knocking. "Dr. Badeaux, are you ready?"

"No, I'm not," Jessica answered but didn't move.

"Jessica, you can follow Roxanne out of my office or I can call security and have them carry you out to the sidewalk," Tully said. "I do hope you go with curtain number two. So much more entertaining, if you ask me."

"No one's asking, Tully." Jessica stood up and walked past Roxanne, heading for the conference room.

"Thanks, Rox. Could you babysit for a second while I go get the kids?"

"Sure, just as long as I'm not expected to be civil by making small talk."

Tully laughed as she got to her feet. "That would constitute hazard pay, and we can't afford the rates."

❖

"Bummer, that's a crappy thing to have happen to you," Tully overheard Bailey say from outside the firm's law library. "I wouldn't worry about it. My mom will fix it."

"Why would you think that?" Libby asked her.

"You're friends, right?"

Libby nodded at Bailey's question.

"Then Mom'll fix it."

"Fix what?" Tully asked.

"Nothing," Libby said quickly.

"Uh-huh, we'll see about that later, but right now your mama's in the conference room, and she'd like to talk to you and Ralph." Tully put her hands in her pockets and rocked on her feet, an old habit that popped up when she lectured. Some people paced, but she rocked in an effort to stay on point and keep from yelling, a strategy that usually worked.

"What does she want?" Bailey asked.

"I didn't ask her, but I'm sure she wants to check and see that you're all right."

Ralph had clammed up and didn't let go of the book he'd been reading. When Tully came in she'd noticed him glance up every other word to participate in Libby and Bailey's conversation. Now he was obviously using his book as a shield.

"Ralph?" Tully called his name in an effort to lift his head. "You want me to go with you?"

"I don't want to see her."

"Buddy, she's your mom. Nothing that happened yesterday changed that."

"I know that, but I still don't want to."

"Okay, what about you, Bailey Bean?"

Bailey sat staring at her brother as if she didn't realize Tully had asked her something. When she did react, Tully caught a glimpse of the sweet baby girl she remembered hidden in the eyes so much like her own.

"Why are you being so nice to us?"

Tully stopped rocking and jerked her hands out of her pockets and to her sides. "Where did that come from?"

"I want to know."

"I'm not acting any different toward you, honey, and I'm not setting you up for anything. Why would you think otherwise?"

"I asked you a question first." Bailey was getting angry.

"Take a chance, Bailey, and just tell me." Tully put her hands on the table and leaned forward. "I'm not asking to punish you with the answer, but because I want us to be honest with each other. It's the only way we can move forward, and I won't let you down if you tell me what's bothering you."

"What do you care?" Bailey stood so fast her chair flew back. "When have you ever cared about me?"

"From the minute you were conceived. I know I haven't done a bang-up job of listening lately, but that doesn't mean I don't love you." She knew her soft response sounded tired.

"You let Mama take us to that school because it was a status symbol," started Bailey. "You let her make me go to parties because you knew the kids' parents, not because anyone wanted me around. They wouldn't have invited me otherwise. You never opened your mouth to take up for me, and now you're just lying again."

Tully was stunned at the river of words that had finally poured out of Bailey and how much baggage the kid was carrying. "What do you think I'm lying about?"

"You buttered us up today just so you could dump us the first chance you got."

"I don't understand, sweetheart. Why would you think that?"

Bailey pointed to Ralph. "He said he didn't want to go, and I don't either, but you're going to make us so she'll take us away."

"Okay," Tully said, stretching out the word. "If I leave for, like, five minutes, do you both promise not to go anywhere?"

Both kids nodded.

Tully walked out, leaving a thick tension behind her, then endured the screaming that erupted in the conference room. Jessica made numerous threats before she slammed out of the front door.

When Tully stepped back in, both kids opened their mouths to speak but she beat them to it. "I want everyone to be quiet. I have a few things to say." She handed them and Libby her business card. "For the rest of today I don't want you to think of me as Mom or coffee buyer, but as your attorney."

"Why?" Ralph asked.

"When you have a problem, it's good to talk to someone like me. You lay out your grievances and it's my job to fix them. So, who wants to go first?"

No one volunteered, so Tully took Bailey by the hand and escorted her out, waving good-bye to everyone else.

When they were back in her office, Tully dropped onto the sofa. "I'm sorry, Bailey."

"For what?"

"For letting you down in every way possible and for not doing anything about it sooner." Taking a legal pad from the coffee table, she found her pen and wrote a few lines. "We need to agree on some things, okay? Okay?" she asked again when Bailey just stood there with her arms crossed.

"Okay."

"First, your mama and I are probably going to have a lot more of those screaming matches you just heard, but at no time should you think that any of what's going on has to do with you."

"What does it have to do with, then? You keep saying it has nothing to do with us, but you don't say what it does have to do with."

"My relationship with your mother ended yesterday afternoon. I know you want the gory details, but as a favor to me and my ego, could you just let me stop there for now?"

Bailey nodded and Tully took a deep breath and kept going. "I plan to keep you and Ralph with me no matter what your mama decides to do in the future. It's not always going to be easy, and I'm sure we'll disagree on more things than we agree on, but I'm not ever giving up when it comes to you and your brother."

"More dialogue would be good here. The lawyer-speak is lame, so spell it out for me."

"I love you, Bailey, and I want you in my house, in my life, and in my heart. So promise me that from now on when someone tells you something, and I don't care who tells you otherwise, you come ask me before you take it for the truth." Tully waited for Bailey's tension-filled body to relax, but she showed no sign of calming down. "The next thing we have to talk about is this—you have to be in school."

Bailey threw her hands up and yelled, "Weren't you listening to a damn word I said?"

"I think we can manage this discussion without cursing at each other, so listening before attacking would be helpful. I said you have to be *in* school, not necessarily the one you attend now. All right?"

"Do I get to pick?"

"We'll get to that, but I want to talk to you about something else." She patted the cushion next to her. "I look at you and see a beautiful young woman who's smart and kind. Why don't you have any friends?"

"Because of Liza Williams."

"Victor and Joyce's kid?" Tully scrunched her brows together. "What does she have to do with it?"

"She's the one who made sure everyone in school knows Ralph and I are the kids of the gay couple. If anyone's our friend it means they're gay too, so we don't have a lot of those."

Tully snapped the pencil she was holding. "Did you tell your mother all this?"

"I did a couple of times, but she told me it'd get better and to not fight back."

She snapped the piece of pencil that remained in her hand. "Why not fight back?"

"Because it gives you a bad reputation," Bailey said, doing a good imitation of Jessica.

"I want you to give me a day, okay?" Tully dropped the splintered pencil and stood up.

"For what?"

Tully put her hands on Bailey's shoulders and squeezed gently. "I have an idea, and I need a day to set it up. All I ask is for you to consider what I'm thinking and not just blow it off because you're mad at me."

"What about Mama?"

"Leave your mother to me. You just worry about you and I'll take care of the rest." She didn't let go of Bailey, just pressed her closer. "I'm sorry I've been too self-involved to do something about this sooner. I'll do better, but if I'm falling down on the job, let me know, okay?"

"What about Mama?"

"What about her?"

"Are you going to force us to see her if we don't want to?"

"How about you wait until tomorrow so you can see I'm working in good faith, as they say. Then we'll talk about seeing your mom."

Bailey raised her head and looked at her without blinking. "Do you swear this isn't just a bunch of bull?"

"I don't blame you for not trusting me, but I'm asking for one more chance."

"Okay."

Tully sighed in relief, then walked Bailey back so she could have the same talk with Ralph. As successful as she'd been in her professional life, just one afternoon convinced her how poorly she'd done with her family. For so long, she'd thought she was contributing by making a living. That philosophy had cost her children in ways that sobered her.

❖

After Tully finished with Ralph, Libby walked into her office to find her lying on the sofa with an arm over her eyes. "Rough day?"

"I just found out I have kids."

Bypassing the chairs, Libby chose to sit on the coffee table. "Don't beat yourself up too much. They're great."

"Not because of too much input from me." With a grunt she sat up and took a deep breath. "But there's no reason to burden you with all my problems."

"Why not? Like I said before, that's why you wanted me to stay, isn't it? So I could burden you with mine."

"I have a feeling your problems are a little easier to solve, so let me ask you something. I know you work downstairs, then somewhere else, and you squeeze school in between. Are you really fond of the two jobs?"

Libby laughed and moved to the sofa. "The coffee gig is great because it includes health insurance. The warehouse job is mindless and physically hard, but in a way it gives me a mental break." She combed a strand of hair behind her left ear. "Why do you ask?"

"How would you like to come work for me?"

"Doing what? Making coffee?" Libby put her hand on Tully's shoulder. "I appreciate everything you've done for me, but I can't accept."

"You're beginning to remind me of Bailey. Quick to jump to the final answer before you've heard all the facts. Once you graduate, you need to lose that habit in a hurry. Clients have a way of not liking their attorney to decide certain things about them before she gathers all the facts." Tully sat back and put her feet on the table, trying to make the pain in her back go away. "You've got a year and a half left before you finish, right?"

"If I survive, yeah."

"You need the degree, but where do you think you'll learn the most law? With Lange or with me?" She smiled, but she was so tired her lips barely moved. "I had an internship like I'm offering you when I was in school, and it was invaluable when I started practicing law. It's just an idea, though, not an ultimatum. Don't worry about saying no."

"Please don't think I'm not grateful. Can I think about it?"

"There's no deadline attached, so ponder all you want." Tully stood and offered her a hand up. "You have class tonight?"

"At six, but just the one." Libby glanced at her watch and grimaced. "I'd better leave so I can finish my reading."

"Thanks for listening to me and for having lunch with us. The kids really enjoyed it."

As if on impulse, Libby hugged her. "Thanks for caring."

She walked out right afterward, leaving Tully feeling lonely. She hadn't had physical contact with another person in so long that she didn't realize how much she missed the closeness.

When Jessica had started to drift away, Tully hadn't bothered to notice how long their separation had lasted until she realized the gulf between them couldn't be breached. Especially when someone else who obviously seemed so much more exciting and fresh was ready to take her place.

"You're an idiot, Tully, and that girl thinks you're desperate for friends." Tully stared at the closed door as she spoke out loud about Libby.

CHAPTER NINE

Mom, you have to stop falling asleep down here," Bailey said the next morning.

Tully was on the sofa again, fully dressed except for her shoes, the ever-present ashtray overflowing on the coffee table. She and the kids had gone out for Chinese, then she'd worked from home until they went to bed.

Piles of paperwork had appealed to her far more than facing what was behind the closed door of the master bedroom. "Are we selling the couch or something?"

"It's not good for your back, so cut it out. Should I get Ralph up for school?"

"One more vacation day, sort of, then back to the grind on Monday. I want to show you something, so it's not a total day off, okay?" She had to raise her voice for the last part because Bailey was already running up the stairs.

Tully followed at a slower pace, heading for the shower. When she finished and walked into the bedroom, she stared at the bed with its rumpled sheets and missing pillows. It was a shrine to what she needed to fix in her life.

A knock on the bedroom door broke though her stupor, and she moved to the closet for her robe. When she opened the door, Bailey stood there, still in her pajamas.

"Do you want to use our bathroom?"

"Who are you and what have you done with my surly kid?" Tully teased, then hugged Bailey. "Thanks for looking out for me."

"I'm tight with the fact that we'll be better off with you."

The honesty made Tully laugh. "Don't worry, Bailey Bean. I'll try my best not to crack up on you."

"If you do, Ralph and I will do our best to keep you glued, even if you require heavy medication."

"Go on, comedian, so you can beat Ralph into the bathroom."

Bailey's eyes strayed to the bed like they had the day before. "Can I tell you something else?"

"Sure, what?"

"When we get back from wherever we're going, can we talk some more about what happens next?"

"We have plenty of time to talk about anything you want, honey." Tully put her hand on Bailey's chin and gently tilted her head so their eyes met. "It's really going to be okay." She figured the kids would get tired of hearing that line before things returned to normal.

❖

Tully parked in the first space she found around Tulane University's main square. Bailey and Ralph flanked her as soon as they stepped out, their heads like oscillating fans, trying to figure out where they were headed.

The building at one corner differed from the rest in that small children were playing in the fenced yard. Tully started in that direction.

"Two years ago, Tulane started an experiment to give their education majors a good training ground by establishing University High." She pointed to the large building.

"But it's full of little kids," Ralph said.

"It's preschool through high school, buddy." They arrived at the gate where a woman in her late thirties was waiting. "I'm just asking you to take the tour, okay?"

"Good morning." The woman held her hand out to Tully first, but didn't ignore the kids. "I'm Kim Paler, the administrator. Welcome to our campus."

Though the first large building housed the elementary classes, it was part of Kim's tour. A slightly larger building next door housed the high school, which consisted of grades seven through twelve. Throughout the tour a few students came up to talk to Bailey and Ralph and offered to answer any questions.

Kim finished her tour and walked them back to their meeting place; then, after a few more pleasantries, she excused herself.

"Let's go to the student union for something to drink," Tully offered.

Once they were seated at a table she waited for one of them to ask questions, and Bailey didn't disappoint.

"Why are we here?"

"Even before all our family drama started, I noticed you weren't exactly thrilled to go to school most mornings, so I did a little homework on alternatives. I want you to get a good education, but I don't want you to get beaten down in the process, so I thought you might consider giving this place a try."

"Why this place?" Ralph asked as he played with his mug.

"Because unlike the kids you go to school with now, the students here at U High have much more diversified social backgrounds. That means—"

"We know what 'diverse' means, Mom," Bailey said.

"Some of the kids come from families with two dads or two moms. When you aren't the only two in school with that distinction, you usually aren't a novelty." Tully held their hands. "I'm not forcing this change on you, but I want you to think about it."

"You'd really let us switch?" Bailey asked.

"That's why we're here, but it's your decision." She turned to Ralph. "What about you, buddy?"

"Do I have to?"

"Of course not. If you're happy with school now, then so be it."

"Ralph, who are you kidding?" Bailey wore an incredulous expression.

"Okay, Bailey, he gets the same consideration you do, so don't pressure him."

"But he's as sick of that place as I am, so why be an idiot now?"

Bailey stopped talking when Tully raised her hand.

"Ralph, I want you to be honest with me, okay? I'm not going to lie to you—our future is going to be different. You're going to have to spend time with your mom and me separately, and that might not always be great."

"I said I didn't want to go and see her."

Tully leaned back in her chair. "She's your mom, son, and you can't avoid her forever, but I'm not going to force you until you're ready. However, you should have one place in your life where you aren't completely unhappy." She wrapped her hands around her half-full cup of coffee. "I thought U High would be a good fit for you, but you don't have to go if you don't want to."

"I do," Bailey said. "And I want you to think about it, Ralph. You know you want to." When he shook his head, she tried another tactic. "Mom, could you get us some donuts?"

From the Krispy Kreme display Tully watched the exchange that ensued. Bailey had spent most of Ralph's life teasing him unmercifully, but she was very protective of him when anyone else tried to give him any grief. No way would she desert him.

"We both want to switch," she said when Tully returned. "I explained that if we come here, we aren't admitting that we give up and letting the buttheads at our school win. But we also figure there's no way Mama's going for this."

As if Bailey's words had conjured Jessica up, Tully's phone rang. She glanced at the caller ID before flipping it open, and at first Tully said nothing.

She flipped her hand over and studied her fingernails before she stopped Jessica's tirade by saying, "We're on Tulane's campus touring University High, so no, they're not in school today either."

Jessica began screaming and Tully stood and moved to an empty table, not wanting to let the kids hear their mother so out of control.

"Jessica, this has nothing to do with you or who you're sleeping with. It has to do with what the kids want. They won't get a great education if all they can concentrate on at your alma mater is how they don't want to be there."

"Switch them and I'll make you pay."

"Then send me a bill." Tully hung up.

When they finished enrolling, they drove back to her office, and as she turned into the parking garage, Tully remembered she hadn't heard from Libby. Considering it was almost lunchtime, she'd have to wait until Monday since Libby didn't work on weekends.

Tully fully intended to keep her promise to herself to spend more time with the kids, and an idea started to germinate. She and the kids could get away somewhere this weekend, if they agreed to it. It would also give her a respite from everything that was going wrong in her life.

"How about a trip to your grandparents' place this afternoon? I'll take you fishing if you want."

"Really?" Ralph asked.

"I thought you had to work?" Bailey followed up.

"Can't I do both?"

"Since when?"

"I'm trying, Bailey. You were right that I spend too much time here and not enough time with you. Maybe we can experiment, try some new stuff so we all get what we want."

"And fishing is what you came up with?"

"How about this, we go fishing today and tomorrow, then Ralph and I will sit at the mall and I'll give you some money for some fishing of your own."

Bailey folded her arms and pouted slightly, appearing to rebel. Visiting her grandparents usually bored her, since she wasn't into fishing, but she wanted attention.

"Okay, I'm in," she told Tully, and Ralph pumped his fist.

As they entered the lobby from the parking garage, Tully glanced into the coffee shop and was surprised to see Libby at a table behind a pile of books. "You guys go on up and I'll be there in a minute." As she spoke, Libby's head came up and she turned in their direction.

"Did you help Libby yesterday with what she has going on?" Bailey asked. "She's really nice, really cool, and she actually likes you. Try not to screw it up. You don't have many friends either, and you could use some. And Libby's really cool with me and Ralph, so everybody wins."

"I'm really trying to get the humanitarian of the year award—no problem's too small for me," she teased. "Go on up, and try not to harass the staff by telling them we're related to get them to do your work for you."

When Ralph appeared to be rooted in place wanting to see Libby, Bailey grabbed him by the back of the collar and dragged him off.

"Are you trying to avoid me today?" Libby asked as she walked outside to join Tully.

"I was stepping out on you, getting coffee over at Tulane this morning."

She laughed at Tully's attempt at humor but kept her eye on her table, not wanting someone to walk off with her notes. "That's an unforgivable offense in the world of baristas, Counselor." After punching Tully on the arm, she rested her hand on Tully's bicep. "I was hoping you weren't mad at me for walking out on you yesterday after you offered me a job."

"I'm not mad at you, and I won't be if you turn me down. Did you at least think about it?"

"Actually, last night as I was trying to stay awake at my second job, it's all I thought about. I bombed my latest quiz because work has been taking up so much of my time, but I can't afford the rent without it." Libby let go of Tully's arm, and for a long moment she felt lost. "I've been on my own for so long now that it's hard to accept when someone is trying to help me out just for the sake of helping me out. Know what I mean?"

"I know exactly what you mean. Come on upstairs."

As she had the day before, Tully carried her bag of books like an interested suitor. "I did a little bit of thinking myself last night," she said once they were inside the elevator.

Libby kept her eyes on the buttons, not trusting herself not to cry. "You changed your mind? That's cool."

"I'm more of a nerd than cool. I hope that doesn't disappoint you in a boss."

Tully lost her balance and fell into the wall of the elevator when Libby threw herself at her in a bear hug.

"I didn't change my mind."

"What were you thinking about, then?" Tully asked as the doors opened and they moved away from the elevators.

The office was much livelier than the day before; the associates were hard at work at their computers and only glanced up briefly as Tully and Libby walked to her office.

"What's going on?" Libby asked.

"We picked up a new client yesterday, which usually fires up the staff. But this one has them more than energized." Tully gestured to Roxanne to stay seated. "They want to win this one as a favor to me."

"Should I call you the Gipper?"

"Not unless you want me to put you on bathroom cleanup duty." She opened the door to her office and put her hand up, stopping one of the associates from coming any closer. "This one is a little different, even for me. I'd thought I'd experienced every kind of case in my field of law, but this case comes with a list of complications that started me thinking last night."

"Anything I can help you with?"

"This is a good case for you to begin on, and we'll get to your duties after we get you squared away. As a free bonus you'll learn an invaluable lesson from this case once we're done. A lesson we'll both learn together, the more I think about it."

Libby helped herself to the legal pad Tully kept on the coffee table and flipped it to a new page. If Tully was willing to take a chance on her, she wasn't going to disappoint. "I thought about what you said too and realized the practical experience would be invaluable."

"You have the job, Libby, no need to suck up," Tully joked. "The experience is just one aspect, but it's not the lesson I just mentioned. That deals with how to keep your personal life separate from your job for the good of your client, even when the two collide in ways you couldn't imagine even if you were a fiction writer."

Though Libby usually found Tully's pacing distracting, she now focused more on the part of the story Tully hadn't told her. "Does that happen often? Keeping them separate, I mean."

"I've practiced for years now, and this is a first." Tully described the case and its players. From what she'd read, the Heberts' account of what had happened seemed accurate, and it was backed up by the medical records.

Evangeline had gone into surgery for the placement of a port just below her rib cage. Kara Nicolas was the surgeon on hand who'd performed the routine procedure, and by all accounts that was exactly what it should have been—routine. But what had happened to Evangeline Hebert, what had really happened, was missing from the record. After the surgery notes, the attending in recovery had made just one entry.

Patient expired at 2019 hours.

A life so new and fragile ended in one short sentence, with no explanation why. Tully told Libby that after reading the first part of the report and seeing Kara Nicolas's name, she had flipped to the very back, looking for the ending of Evangeline's story. Like reading a novel, she could peruse the middle at her leisure, but the end drove Tully to see if there was a tale at all. And incredibly, by some convenient mix-up at the hospital morgue, Evangeline's body had been sent off for cremation. Whatever secrets her body held were lost forever in an urn of ashes.

Libby glanced down at the notes she'd taken, wondering why cases like this one were never in the books she had to study in school. "Let me see if I understand you."

"My ex's new plaything performed a procedure on this kid and she died," Tully said succinctly.

"Do they know about your relationship with this woman?"

"Relationship? I'm not screwing around with her. Jessica is." Tully sounded glib, but her tone still had a bite. "Sorry, I'm trying to be nice, but my face hurts too much to pull it off."

"Is it even ethical for you to take this case?"

Tully ran her hands over her face and sighed. "If the world were fair and I'd married Jessica and the state recognized our union, then I'm sure they'd do everything they could to have me removed. Even if our relationship was sanctioned, I'd still fight to stay on, though. I'm suing the hospital for something Kara Nicolas, not Jessica Badeaux, did. Also, this incident happened before I became aware of Nicolas's existence, but I'm sure they'll still try to have me removed."

"I want in, so where do I start?"

"Roxanne will do your internship paperwork and show you your desk." Tully summoned Roxanne, who entered a moment later with some forms.

"You need to sign these papers, Tully, so we can start on discovery." Roxanne handed Tully an official-looking folded paper. "This request arrived this morning while you were out."

Tully scanned the document briefly. "Jessica wants to come get her clothes." She took out a cigarette by rote to calm herself. The building had a no-smoking policy, but she ignored it on occasion.

"Do you want Libby to start with anything in particular?"

"Put her with Jo first. She's working on Dr. Nicolas's background."

"I'll do that, and you put that cigarette down."

Tully glanced down at the unlit cigarette.

"Do it, or I'm calling your mother."

Libby laughed at the banter before she followed Roxanne out with a small wave. Her afternoon passed quickly, broken only by a late lunch with Tully and the kids in Tully's office. Later, Tully surprised her by taking away her files and pointing to her book bag.

"Your workday's done, but I expect you to study from now until five." Tully stood by Libby's workstation. "I'm sure Rox pointed out that clause in your job description."

"You're going to pay me to study?"

"You may think you're getting a lot of money now, but when you're an associate here after you pass the bar, you'll think you sold your soul for it." Tully spoke with a serious tone, but Libby could tell she was joking by the wink at the end.

An hour later, Libby raised her head from her book to see Roxanne lift her phone, then slam it down with a little too much force. "Something wrong?"

"Nothing having a bus hit Jessica wouldn't cure." Roxanne stood and smoothed out her skirt. "Sorry, she's just not one of my favorite people at the moment, and she's back."

Within seconds, Tully stormed out of her office, so focused that she didn't even glance in Libby's direction.

Libby could see by the set of Tully's shoulders that she was upset. In the two years since she'd first encountered Tully, Libby had come to notice a lot of things about her, and not just how she liked her coffee. How her face came alive when she explained certain concepts of the law and saw that Libby understood what she was saying. How she used her hands when she talked, and how very generous she was, not only with her money but with herself. And how her smile widened every time Libby found some excuse to touch her. Tully was in a relationship and would've never have pursued anyone, but Libby could tell she liked the closeness. It might not come to anything, but with Jessica's colossal screwup, Libby felt like fate had handed her a beautifully gift-wrapped chance at a life that up to then had been impossible.

As Tully slammed the door, Libby promised herself that in the coming months she would try to support Tully. "You deserve to be happy, Tully, and I'll do my best to see that you are," she said softly to the empty room. By helping Tully, she figured she might find happiness. She was tired of being alone.

CHAPTER TEN

Before you say no, I want you to listen to me," Tully said with her hands up. "Your mother's here and asking to see you again."

"And what part of no didn't she get yesterday?" Bailey asked.

"Guys, I know she upset you with how she handled things, but I'm asking you to just meet with her for a few minutes."

"Why are you being so nice to her?"

"This has nothing to do with nice, Bailey. It's got to do with simplifying our lives." She put her hands up again when Bailey started to ask something else. "You can't go the rest of your life without seeing her."

"Until I'm eighteen and I can do whatever the hell I want."

"True, but you have another couple of years before that magical birthday, so please do me this favor since I'll be paying for your tuition and the apartment you hope to have once you turn eighteen and only want to talk to me about money." Tully dropped into an empty chair and rubbed her temples. "You know how much I love going to court, but I want to come to some agreement without someone in a robe making us."

"You think Mama would take you to court?" Ralph asked.

"Eventually, if I keep saying no, but even then, don't worry about it, buddy." After leaning forward and placing her hand on Ralph's shoulder, she turned to Bailey. "You don't have to talk or act like everything's okay. Just let her see that I'm not beating you and am actually feeding you on occasion."

"That's it?" Bailey asked.

"That's it. Then you can go home, lock yourself in your room, and listen to music I find objectionable."

Bailey cracked a smile. "Can we leave when we're done?"

"Sure, I'm sure your grandmother will be thrilled to see us early." Tully squeezed Ralph's shoulder, then stood up. "Just remember that I'm a call away if you need anything."

"We'll be testing that claim, trust me," Bailey said as they walked to the conference room.

❖

Jessica Badeaux sat alone in the firm's expensive-looking conference room and stared through the wall of glass across from her. Tully had always joked that the opulent furnishings were intended more to intimidate than to make a fashion statement. Sort of a message to visiting attorneys that the firm of Barnes, Corey, and Badeaux made a living by eating the competition before they even realized they were on the menu. Their high success rate allowed them to afford the trappings.

That conversation felt like a lifetime ago, a lifetime that had included her perfect family and loving partner. A lifetime she'd traded so easily for a chance with Kara Nicolas, but she wouldn't change what she'd done. For once she felt like the rebel her parents never allowed her to be, and forgetting that perfect life had made her skin tingle when Kara peered at her with such desire in her eyes.

Sitting there alone, Jessica felt as if the trade-off that had jump-started her libido would reveal the true meaning of this room. The Tully who had served her strawberries every year for Valentine's Day would be replaced by the Tully who strove to win. This room reflected her competitive nature, and nothing in their past would make a difference.

"Mama?" Ralph stood at the door with his hand on the knob, obviously waiting for Jessica to acknowledge them. Bailey shoved him inside.

Seeing only the two of them, Jessica relaxed and stood with her arms out. Both children rebuffed her silent request for a hug and just sat.

"Where's your mom?" she asked.

"If you want to meet with her, I suggest you get Roxanne in here,"

Bailey said, taking her usual combative pose, arms folded across her chest.

"I came to see you guys, so please give me a chance, Bailey, before we waste our time together."

"We had time together two days ago." Bailey snapped her fingers as if suddenly remembering something. "Oh, wait, you threw us out at the curb."

"What I did was a mistake on so many levels. You're right. I'm sorry for that."

Ralph leaned forward like he'd suddenly taken an interest in the conversation. "You're coming back?"

"Not anytime soon." Jessica shook her head. "I just meant that I should've told your mom sooner that I wasn't happy with our relationship."

"Yeah. I'm sure that whole girlfriend situation was a real drag when you're supposed to be faithful and all." Bailey wiped her palms on her jeans in a gesture that made Jessica know she was nervous and trying to control the urge to get up and leave. "You've seen us and I'm sure we'll hook up whenever Mom says we have to, but right now this is a waste of time."

"I've been here less than five minutes."

"Look, Mama, I'm sure you're here to make things right and to make yourself feel better, but you don't have to worry." Bailey stood up. "Everything's fine, and we'll see you when we do. If that's all you wanted, we're done." She left, glancing at Ralph as she stalked out.

"Ralph, I'm sorry." Jessica tried one last time to salvage something.

"Like Bailey said, no problem." His departure wasn't as smooth as Bailey's, but he followed her quickly.

When they were done, Tully walked in and leaned against the door.

Jessica stared at her, trying to remember the very last time they'd been intimate. However, she couldn't see past the haze of passion that Kara induced in her.

"Tully, listen—"

"I need to know when you want to get your things out of the house." Tully's voice was devoid of emotion. "This weekend might be a good time. I'm taking the kids to see my parents."

"Alma will be thrilled to hear about my fall from grace."

"Have whoever is going to represent you contact me about separating our assets." Tully ignored the shot at her mother. "This isn't a divorce in the eyes of the law, but we do have a partnership of sorts that needs to be dissolved."

"What about the kids?"

"I've enrolled them, at their request, at University High. They start Monday. As for their care, I'll take full responsibility for the time being."

Jessica closed her eyes long enough to center herself. She didn't want to lash out and make things worse. "Whatever happened between us, we need to make our major decisions together. I don't think changing something as important as their school is the right thing to do right now."

"The only other matter we need to discuss is how Dr. Nicolas will fit into my children's lives when they spend time with you. Once you have the particulars on all that, call Roxanne and schedule an appointment."

After the slam of the door left her alone, Jessica let the tears roll. She wouldn't be able to return to the safety she'd known for so long.

CHAPTER ELEVEN

Alma Badeaux wiped her hands on the bottom of her apron, emblazoned with "Kiss the Cook or Else." She'd just finished preparing her chicken stew in her favorite pot and was studying the long driveway from the road as if she could make Tully and her grandchildren materialize sooner.

Tully and the kids hadn't come for a visit since the holidays, but she understood how busy everyone was. Something had changed in those sixty days, though, which made her anxious to spot Tully's car. She was so intent on seeing the white Land Rover that she almost didn't recognize the driver of a Ford Explorer.

Though Bailey was usually reluctant to spend time in the small town of Montegut, she fell easily into Alma's arms.

"We thought we'd surprise you by being early for a change, instead of three hours late," Tully said when it was her turn to hug Alma.

"Your father's going to be upset he isn't here to meet you."

When Gaston came home with an ice chest of jumbo shrimp they were having for lunch the next day, they repeated the whole exchange of hugs. Alma didn't get Tully alone until the dishes were done and the kids were in bed.

"What's wrong?"

"It's not too late for you to go to detective school, you know," Tully said. Since they were sitting outside, she took out her pack of cigarettes and lit one.

Just as quickly Alma snatched it away and put it out. "You don't need to imitate a chimney to tell me about what's going on."

Tully laughed before she leaned forward and rested her elbows on the tops of her legs. Though she left out the part about *how* she found out Jessica was cheating, she did tell Alma why they were separating.

"My mama always preached to me about how God closed some doors in our lives only to open certain others," Alma said. "You might take that message to heart, my love. Just remember to look for those new doors."

"I won't miss them." Tully kissed her mother's cheek. "Now go on inside and get to bed." That was the only way she'd get to smoke the cigarette she craved.

Later, sitting on her father's dock across the road from the house, she propped her feet against the hull of the *Alma Mae*. The old boat creaked as it gently bobbed with the outgoing tide, but the cypress it was constructed of felt solid.

"When I was little—" The sudden sound of Bailey's voice scared Tully so badly she fell out of her chair. "Sorry."

Tully watched her cigarette roll off the edge of the dock and figured she was the victim of a conspiracy. "You're supposed to be in bed, not crossing the highway by yourself." She straightened her lawn chair and unfolded another for Bailey so they could sit side by side. "You were saying?"

"I remember you holding me when Granddad took us out fishing. You told me stories about the stuff that lived in the water and how, if I looked hard enough, I'd see mermaids." Bailey sat and expelled a long sigh. "They were only dolphins."

"But wasn't it nice to pretend, just for a little while, that mermaids existed? Bailey Bean, I told you things like that to fire your imagination. You might not think it's important, but having a good one can make you a success at whatever you do. I want you to find a little of that imagination you had when you were small enough for me to hold." She tugged their chairs even closer and put her arm around Bailey. "Life is hard enough. You need to have a little fun and just take some things on faith."

"Is that why you're out here, trying to find your faith?"

Tully thought maybe Bailey's question showed she missed times like this with her mom.

"I'm out here trying to relive my youth, thank you very much. Those days when I stepped off this boat and could see my feet." She patted her stomach to finish the joke.

"Stop making fun of yourself to make me feel better." Bailey bumped shoulders with her and stayed close. "Are you going to tell me what exactly happened with Mama?"

"Why do you really have to know?" Tully held tight when Bailey started to turn away. "I'm not trying to blow you off, honey. But it's like you're looking for a reason to hate your mother and want me to hand you one."

"I'd've thought you'd jump at the chance."

"Then I'm sorry for giving you that impression. I may not want to live with your mom, but I'd never go out of my way for you guys to hate her." She paused to try to erase the mental image of Kara Nicolas with Jessica. "If I did, I'd be cheating you of an important relationship, even though it doesn't seem like that right now."

A faint splash came from the other side of the boat, and Tully pulled Bailey up to investigate. Something seemed to be trying to break free of the water.

"What is it?" Bailey asked.

"I need to get you out here more often." Tully retrieved something out of one of the storage boxes on the boat. "Every Cajun kid can spot shrimp feeding on the surface just from the noise."

With balance Bailey didn't realize Tully had, she stood on the rail of the boat with a cast net in her hand. Completely open, the circle of net was about eight feet across, with a row of weights tied along the bottom. She held the top rope in one hand and grabbed just a bit of the bottom with her other. Bailey thought about holding Tully when she started swaying, but she was just building momentum for her throw. When she released the net, it resembled a large cobweb heading for the water.

It hit with a small splash, and Tully yanked on the rope to make the weights come together and close the bottom. She dumped out a small bucketful of shrimp captured inside. "Big enough for bait if you want to go fishing with me," she offered.

"Can I try? Will you teach me, I mean?" Bailey asked, referring to the cast net.

It was late before she finally got the hang of releasing the net so that it would open and not just hit the water and sink. The shrimp had fled by then, but it didn't matter. As they walked back to the house with the shrimp Tully had caught, Bailey basked in the attention her mom had paid her, which beat the hell out of catching any bait.

❖

They drove back early on Sunday morning loaded with fresh fish and shrimp Alma had packed. The kids hadn't had the heart to tell their grandmother Tully would probably just freeze the stuff since she didn't know how to cook.

They were kidding about her lack of culinary skills as they drove up to their house, and Tully threw Ralph the keys to unlock the door while she walked to the mailbox. When Bailey screamed, Tully dropped the mail and ran to the back door.

"Mom, we've been robbed."

The dining room table and chairs were gone, as were a few more pieces of furniture the kids always remembered being in the house. They were all family heirlooms that Jessica had inherited from her favorite grandmother.

"More like your mama coming by for her stuff, babe." Hands on her thighs, Tully was bent over trying to catch her breath. "This gives us a good excuse to go out and eat."

Ralph stood next to his sister, his eyes riveted to the empty spot where the table had been. "I guess she was serious about not coming back."

"Buddy, when she gets a new place, she'll need all this stuff you're missing to make it feel like home."

As soon as the words left Tully's mouth, Ralph ran to his room and slammed the door.

"What?" she asked when Bailey shook her head and rolled her eyes.

"Thank God you aren't this clueless at work or we'd starve. Saying that to him is like packing our bags and shipping us off."

When Tully tried to defend herself, Bailey held her hands up. "I know you won't send us away, but Ralph obviously doesn't, so I suggest damage control."

It took Tully over an hour to get Ralph to the same level of enlightenment as Bailey, and when she stepped out into the hall she smelled dinner. If Bailey cooked this well, maybe the kid was correct that she was totally clueless. Tully heard conversation and was surprised to enter the kitchen and find Libby not only talking to Bailey, but also cooking. "So coffee isn't your only specialty, huh?"

"Bailey said it'd be all right." Libby stopped chopping broccoli to answer.

"Then Bailey gets a raise in her allowance for being so astute. Were you out looking for a downtrodden family to cook for?" Tully popped a broccoli floret into her mouth.

"I was making a delivery for Josephine, and your ice chest of fish inspired me," Libby retorted. "I really am sorry if I'm intruding. My kitchen is so tiny this was a treat for me."

"You're not intruding, and you're more than welcome to cook for us whenever the mood strikes you." Another piece of broccoli disappeared before Libby moved the cutting board out of Tully's reach.

"Bailey mentioned another table outside." Libby pointed to the empty space, having heard the story earlier.

Considering it was her house, Tully took the dismissal well and called Ralph to help her wipe down the lawn furniture. It was a little warm outside, but everyone was too busy enjoying the broiled fish topped with shrimp cream sauce to complain about the heat.

Without thought at the end of dinner, Tully produced the pack of cigarettes from her shirt pocket and was about to light up when Libby blew out her match and said, "I'll make a bet with you."

"Why do I feel this cigarette isn't in my future?"

Libby laughed and moved closer to nab the cigarette. "Not necessarily. If you can walk around the block at a fairly good pace and not cough once, it's all yours."

"A block?" Tully snapped her fingers. "That should be a cinch."

After telling the kids where they were going, Tully bowed and let Libby walk ahead of her. They turned left at the end of the drive, wanting to enjoy the slight breeze that was keeping the mosquitoes at bay. Tully started wheezing before they reached the corner, and at the stop sign she started coughing.

Libby stopped and waited until the fit subsided, then pointed back to the house. Not only had they walked less than a block, they weren't even four houses from where they'd started. "Learn something, Counselor?"

"This street seems a lot shorter from behind the wheel of my car," Tully said, knowing she sounded rather pathetic.

Libby tugged on her hand to get her moving again. "I tell you what. I'm going to return the favor of you giving me a job."

"How's that?" Tully was enjoying the hand in hers more than the walk.

"By helping you quit smoking, as well as a few other things."

Tully almost stopped moving. "Other things?"

"A little exercise isn't going to kill you, and you can start by helping me move next weekend."

"Move you? Don't you have a gaggle of friends lined up dying to help out?"

Libby tugged on her hand again and quickened their pace. "I don't have a gaggle of anything, but I don't want you to feel obligated."

"Never mind about that." Tully had broken a slight sweat, but she felt good. "Where are you moving to?"

"I've got it narrowed down to a couple of places. I just need to make a decision."

Tully noticed that something in Libby's voice sounded a little off. "How many classes do you have tomorrow?"

They were nearing the house again, and turning in meant their night was ending. "Two in the morning, then nothing until tomorrow night. Why?"

"I want to go see which place would be the easiest to move you into," Tully said as they passed her driveway. "Another block?"

"Can we talk about civil litigation?"

"Can I smoke while we do?"

The glare Libby shot her way made her laugh.

"Kidding." Tully put her free hand up.

They walked around the block four times before they'd finished their conversation, then Tully put Libby in her car for the night. "Call me when you're done, and I'll swing by school and pick you up."

"You're responsible for two people now, Tully. You don't need to take on any more."

Tully laughed and bent closer to the open car window. "Remind me to invite you the next time I go visit my mother. She'll be happy to explain responsibility until you understand what it is."

"What is it?"

"Some land on your doorstep." She pointed to the files on the seat pertaining to the Hebert case. "We're responsible for getting those people justice for their little girl. Then there's responsibility you seek." Tully turned and pointed to the house. "The kids I sought.

Maybe I haven't done such a bang-up job up to now, but they're my responsibility."

Libby leaned forward and rested her head on the steering wheel. "Where does that leave me?"

"In neither category."

"Is that good or bad?"

Tully laughed again and suddenly realized how long it had been since she'd felt like this. Talking to Libby made her feel young, happy, like what she had to say mattered. The most absurd thing of all was that she felt desirable to another person, but she wasn't about to dwell on that lest she lose the friendship she shared with Libby.

"You ask so many questions that it's a good thing you're going to law school. You're in neither category because you didn't land on my doorstep and I didn't seek you out. You're someone I want to help simply because I want to, Libby, but only if it's agreeable to you."

"It's so very agreeable," was the soft reply. "And it makes me feel like someone cares about me. I haven't had that in a long time."

❖

The next morning the first thing Tully noticed was the smell of brewing coffee.

The first thing Bailey noticed when she handed her a cup was that the ashtray was empty.

"Thank God Mama didn't take the couch," Bailey said before turning and heading for the stairs.

By the time they were all showered, dressed and ready to go, Tully would've traded her car for a cigarette. She fidgeted so much that on their way to school Bailey called Roxanne and sent her out for some nicotine patches.

"Make sure you slap one on her the minute she gets there," Bailey instructed. "Or someone might sue her for crabbiness before lunch."

"Funny girl," Tully said. She pulled up and parked the car, wanting to walk them to the gate on their first day. "I'm not going to embarrass you if I tag along for a bit, am I?"

"You're not going to cry, are you?" Bailey asked in a teasing tone.

"I'll try to hold myself in check."

They were halfway there when Tully heard someone call her name and turned to find Libby. "Hey, guys, I came to wish you luck and bring you lunch." She held up two bags and joined the laughter when Tully snapped her fingers at having forgotten.

"Thanks, Libby. And don't worry, Mom. We would've hit you up for some cash," Ralph said. "But this is going to be better." He held up his bag.

"Good luck, buddy, and call me if you need anything." Tully gave him a hug, but made sure it didn't last too long. "You too, Bailey Bean. Just remember one thing, okay?"

"To be good?"

"To have fun, baby girl. I bet some kid in there is waiting for a new friend today."

"You make me sound lame."

Even Tully could sense that Bailey was nervous. "No one this beautiful, smart, and outgoing can be lame. I've known that about you all your life, and today, so will the rest of the world."

With a piercing gaze that begged for reassurance, Bailey stepped closer. "Why do you think so?"

"Find your niche, darlin', and you find your stride. Once you do, nothing can stop you." Tully pivoted her so they were facing the front of the school. "In there's your niche, and the rest is up to you, but I have faith in you."

"Thanks, Mom." Bailey initiated the hug this time.

"Anytime." Tully handed them some money anyway and waved one last time before she mock-reprimanded Libby. "And what are you doing skipping class, young lady?"

"I finished my first and the second got cancelled, so no lectures, thank you."

"Thanks for remembering their lunches. You may spoil them."

"Your kids are easy to spoil, so it wasn't any trouble. Do you still want to go apartment hunting with me?"

"If you don't mind being constantly interrupted by Roxanne and her barrage of phone calls, I'd love to."

"If you're busy—"

"I'm kidding, and if Roxanne needs me she won't hesitate to call, believe me. Besides, I cleared my schedule to go with you this morning." Tully opened the passenger side and waved her into the vehicle. "Where to first?"

In the first apartment a set of pipes came up through the floor in the corner of the bedroom and extended into the place upstairs. While they stood there a rat climbed one of the pipes as if he often used the water main as his personal stairwell.

"How about we try the next place?" Tully suggested.

After she shivered, Libby nodded.

They looked at four places, and Tully found something wrong with all of them, with good reason.

Sitting together outside the last place, Libby just stared out the window, appearing depressed. "I know what you're going to say," she told Tully.

"You do? That the Cubs have a decent shot at the pennant next year? You should be on the psychic hotline." Tully put her hand to her chest and tried to look shocked.

"Stop it." Laughing, Libby slapped her arm. "You were going to tell me I need to look in a higher price range. I know these places are pathetic, but they're all I can afford right now." Before Tully could even think to offer, she added, "And you're not giving me a raise. You're paying me way too much now for the amount of work I do."

"Okay, I'm not giving you a raise, Scouts' honor." Tully felt almost docile as she answered, her fingers up in the correct position to make a Scout oath.

"You're not?"

"You just told me not to."

"Good." The agreement sounded less than enthusiastic.

"I want you to look at one more place. Think you can handle it? I swear it won't have anywhere near the number of roaches we saw at the last place when I switched the lights on."

"You aren't going to make the landlord lie about the rent, are you?"

Instead of answering, Tully started the engine and took a call from Roxanne, who asked her a number of questions. As they neared their destination, Tully gave her assistant the names of the people she needed appointments with.

"Did you forget something?" Libby asked when Tully stopped the car.

"I'm highly organized, so I seldom forget anything," Tully joked. "Take a walk?"

After they entered the gate at the side of the house, Tully circled the pool and paused by the deep end.

"Did you want to take a swim break?" Libby asked.

"You may be doing just that if you don't get over here. Before you say no, I want you to look at the pool house." Tully opened the door to a large open area with a terra-cotta tile floor. At one end was a bedroom and bath, at the other, a kitchen. The small place was clean, full of light, and tastefully decorated.

"We started with a pool house that morphed into a guesthouse, that eventually Jessica wanted to convert into a home office," Tully explained. She opened the refrigerator to an assortment of beer and sodas. "I think it's a hell of a lot better than all those places we saw today."

"This is generous..." Libby stood in the middle of the open space, light coming in from the wall of glass that faced the pool. "I love it. Are you sure?"

"The only question is—do we store your furniture or all this stuff?"

"It's a deal only if you'll tell me if it becomes a problem." Libby imitated Tully by putting up her finger as if she were getting ready to rattle off a list. "You also have to promise to take a walk with me when you have time, and let me pay rent."

"Okay to the problem and the walks, but no deal on the rent. Come on, Libby, don't argue with me. I'm an attorney who thrives on arguing, and you know that the fewer expenses you have now, the quicker you'll be debt-free after law school. Besides, it's a pile of bricks in my yard, and maybe you'll get the urge to cook a few more meals for me and the kids."

The small house was anything but a pile of bricks, and Libby took the hand Tully offered. "Deal, then."

CHAPTER TWELVE

Are you learning to relax?" Roxanne asked as soon as Tully walked into the office, Libby at her side.

"It would seem I've quit smoking, so I'm anything but relaxed."

"That reminds me." Roxanne ripped open the box in her hand. "Lift your sleeve for me." She held up one of the patches Bailey had called about. Her eyes slid by Libby and she made no comment about her presence.

"Unless you can roll that up and light it, I suggest you stay away from me."

"Uh-huh." Roxanne just handed the patch to Libby. "Pasco got here a few minutes ago. I put him in your office."

"Pasco?" Libby asked, poring over the instructions on where best to put the patch.

"Pasco St. John," Tully said. "I use him to do all my investigative work."

"I'm sure he can wait a few minutes." Libby held up the patch. "I'll be gentle, and it'll make you feel better."

Once inside her office, Tully made the introductions and asked Pasco to step out briefly so that Libby could minister to her. Wishing she'd kept her New Year's resolution to work out, Tully rolled her sleeve up as high as Libby needed.

"Thank you," she said as Libby's warm fingers smoothed the small square flat against the back of her bicep. She couldn't determine whether she was tingling because she'd bared her arm to Libby, because Libby had touched her so gently, or because she needed a cigarette.

"I'll be out at my desk if you need anything." Libby stopped at the door and added, "Thanks again for the pool house."

"Get to work," Tully ordered in a joking tone and laughed. "Rox, send Pasco back in, please."

Tully thought about the man she would be working with on this case. Pasco St. John hailed from a long line of law-enforcement professionals, but had chosen to follow his father into his private investigating firm. Tully had known the nearly sixty-year-old jokester almost from her first day at Barnes, Corey, and Badeaux.

He had let her know that he enjoyed working with her because she knew exactly what information she was after and provided enough of a starting point to help him find it. And he loved to win as much as she did.

"Tell me you have something exciting for me to do. I've been nothing but bored out of my gourd lately," he said in lieu of a greeting.

"I've got sex, betrayal, murder, and intrigue, bored man."

He rubbed his hands together and settled into the chair across from her desk. "Whatcha got?"

Tully handed over the Hebert file, along with everything she knew about Kara Nicolas, then waited. Since Pasco was a voracious reader with close to a photographic memory, it wouldn't take long.

"Sounds like a fairly common procedure, nothing the kid should've been dying over."

"Give me the usual workup on Dr. Nicolas. I'm talking from the time the doctor slapped her ass to what she had for breakfast this morning."

His eyebrows spiked. "You sound mad as a wet hen. Are you not telling me something?"

The nagging want for a cigarette was abating, and Tully expelled a sigh of gratitude that Bailey had thought of the damn patch. "We've worked together long enough for you to realize that some cases affect me more than others. I want to win this one for the Heberts. But you're right, there's something more."

With a clear detachment from her feelings, Tully told him about Jessica's new relationship with Kara. She still couldn't talk about how she knew for sure just how close they were. Pasco listened, nodding every so often.

"I'm surprised you aren't frothing at the mouth. You want to bring this woman down because you want Jess back?"

"Not even if she came with the ability to spit gold out of her ass." Tully let some of her control go. "Once you meet Elijah and Simone Hebert, you'll know why I want to win."

"But bringing this bitch down will satisfy that part of your soul that wants to skin her slowly, am I right?"

"There *is* that." Tully laughed as she found a copy of the file she'd given him in the pile on her desk. They spent the rest of the morning mapping out a course of action for gathering all the information Tully wanted. She gave Pasco a final set of directions and shook his hand as she showed him out. He had only been gone for a few moments when Libby stuck her head in and asked if she had plans for lunch.

"Not at this time." Tully sat on the edge of her desk and smiled at her. "The staff treating you all right?"

"I was helping Jo and Frank with some research. They just left for lunch."

Tully knew Frank and Josephine weren't rude, so their not inviting Libby to go with them surprised her. "Were they meeting a client?"

"No, they're just going down to the deli. They invited me, but I, uh, decided to see if you were free. If you have other plans—"

"Do I get to pick the place?" Tully noticed Libby blush, and the redder she flamed, the wider Tully smiled.

"Sure." Libby's voice broke.

Tully left her jacket in the office and walked Libby down the street toward the river. She rarely left the office to eat, but something about Libby's innocent air was hard to say no to. Four blocks later they were approaching Magazine Street, and Tully grabbed Libby's hand before she could cross.

"We're going this way." She pointed to the left.

Liborio, a Cuban restaurant a block down, was one of her favorites, and Tully had been hoping she could introduce Libby to it as a way of thanking her for all of her support. They blended in well with the rest of the lunch crowd, mostly from the nearby federal building and other area firms.

"I'll have the Cuban sandwich, please," Tully said, handing the menu back to the waiter.

"She'll actually have the roasted chicken with a side salad, and

I'll have the same." Libby smiled sweetly at the guy who was busy scratching out what he'd written and waited patiently for the blowup from across the table.

"Are you going to cut up the chicken when it gets here too?"

"That sandwich is, like, a gazillion calories over your limit," Libby replied evenly, "so just accept the fact I'm looking out for you."

"Uh-huh, and why does that sound like I'm going to be on a diet for the rest of my life? And don't think I forgot the bit about me having a limit."

Libby decided to change the topic. "Are the kids going to be okay with me living so close by?"

"I'm sure Bailey will love having you there to talk to, and Ralph is as easygoing as they get. I'm sure it won't be a problem. If that's your only concern, then feel free to move in whenever you like."

Libby slowly stirred sweetener into a large glass of tea and felt the tightness in her chest loosen. She'd been on her own for so long that she constantly worried about the unknown. She worried about financially making it so that she had a place to live, about getting sick, about school, and about the future in general.

Tully seemed to be her exact opposite in that she didn't act like she worried about too much. "I just don't want to add any more to what they're going through."

"I want you to repeat after me." Tully leaned closer and smiled. "Everything is going to be okay."

Libby laughed but dutifully repeated the mantra. "The best thing that ever happened to me is that you love coffee."

"Thanks, but you don't have to flatter me. I've already told you the place is yours," Tully joked. "But if you must, then go on. I'm not going to argue about how wonderful I am."

The days Libby worked in the office, they followed the same lunch routine. Libby usually tried to get Tully to actually leave the office, but sometimes they sat on Tully's sofa and ordered from the deli downstairs.

❖

When Roxanne came in with the day's mail, she said, "Libby just got here, if you're interested."

Tully whipped her head up from her reading so quickly that, forgetting she was holding the pen so close, she drew a yellow highlighter line along her face. “Is it her birthday or something?”

“No.”

“Then why the announcement?”

Roxanne turned back to the door to make sure it was closed. “She looks like she’s been crying, and she didn’t come in and tell you hello like she usually does. I just thought something was wrong.”

“Order that veggie pita thing she loves from downstairs, and tell her I need to see her.”

When Libby stepped in and closed the door, her eyes did appear red and a bit swollen. “Have a bad morning at school?” Tully asked.

Libby shook her head and just leaned against the closed door.

“Anyone in the office giving you problems?”

Again Libby shook her head. “Sorry, I’m not usually this morose, but today’s my dad’s birthday, or should I say used to be my dad’s birthday.”

“It still is, no matter that he’s not here to blow out some candles. I’m sorry I haven’t asked before now, but could you share with me what happened to your parents?” Tully asked.

“When I was Bailey’s age, my grandmother died.”

“Were you close?”

When Tully took Libby by the hand to the sofa, she went willingly. “Not really. We didn’t see her that often, and my dad was always working, but she made the best peanut butter cookies.”

“Sounds like something you aren’t going to let me eat anytime soon.”

When the tease made Libby laugh, Tully felt like she’d finally accomplished something.

“They left to go to the funeral, and because I didn’t feel well, my mom let me stay home. On the way back, driving through a bad storm, an older man lost control of his car, crossed the center line, and hit them head-on. Neither of them survived.”

When Tully wrapped her arms around Libby, she sobbed into her shoulder.

“Sometimes their birthdays and the anniversary of their deaths blindside me. I always thought that if I’d been with them my life would be so different.”

"Oh, Libby, don't do that to yourself. If you'd been with them you might have died too, and I'm glad you didn't." Tully pulled back enough to wipe away Libby's tears. "What happened to you after that?"

"Since I had no other living relatives, the state had to put me in foster care until I turned eighteen. I went to five families in that time, and then I started working so I could go to school."

The knock on the door stopped Libby from saying anything else, and she seemed embarrassed that anyone else would see her like this.

"Hang on," Tully said, loud enough so whoever it was could hear her. "Do me a favor, okay?"

Libby nodded.

"Take off your shoes and get comfortable. I had lunch ordered for us, and I have a lot of reading to do today, so we're going to stay in here and take it easy."

While they ate lunch Libby told her the rest of the story. Her time in foster care had left her heart broken, but she never lost hope that if she was patient enough she'd connect with someone like her parents had.

After lunch Tully picked up her file and started reading as Libby stretched out and closed her eyes. Putting her head in Tully's lap and squeezing one of Tully's hands between both of hers, Libby fell asleep.

CHAPTER THIRTEEN

Once Libby moved into the pool house, she rode in to school with Tully and the kids most mornings, then caught the streetcar to work. Things had changed after that day in Tully's office: Libby approached Tully more easily with different concerns, and Tully reciprocated.

Every evening except the two nights Libby had class, they walked and discussed whatever came to mind, if she didn't need help with her homework. Other than the one night a week that Jessica spent with Bailey and Ralph, taking them out to eat and then dropping them off without getting out of the car, Libby had time to get to know the kids when they helped her cook dinner.

While Tully never replaced the dining room furniture and other pieces Jessica had taken, she did move into the guest room to sleep. Initiating other changes, Bailey and Ralph had set a new rule that Tully was happy to go along with: from six to eight every night no one would work. As a family they'd taken up biking, and when Tully bought Libby a bike, she joined them.

Tully was sure pedaling around the neighborhood would kill her, just as she'd thought walking with Libby would. But with every mile they covered, she began to discover her lost stamina as well as a closer relationship with the kids. What she was having a harder time ignoring was just how big a part Libby had become in all their lives. She knew instinctively that no matter what, Libby would never turn her back on Bailey and Ralph and the bond they'd formed, but something much larger did make her fear for the future.

No matter what Jessica thought about her being an idiot when it came to feelings and what it took to be an exciting partner, Tully was smart enough to know just how wonderful Libby was. Libby's life had been more than difficult, but she'd come through it with an incredible insight into people and a rosy outlook on the future. It was only a matter of time before those attributes, along with her beauty, would attract someone's attention and she'd move on to the kind of relationship she deserved in order to be happy.

The day that happened, Tully was sure that the pain of losing Jessica would pale in comparison to watching Libby fall in love with someone else.

❖

"Can I tell you something without sounding rude?" Libby asked Tully after they had dropped the kids off at school. During the ride, she usually read something for school and Tully talked on the phone with Roxanne, but today Libby caught her before she could dial.

"Sure, what's on your mind?"

"Those pants look horrible on you."

Tully whipped her head around and stared at her. "Excuse me?"

"You've lost a lot of weight. You have to have noticed that your pants are getting baggy." When Tully stared at her until the light turned green and the driver behind them sat on his horn, Libby started to get nervous. "Never mind. Forget I said anything."

"No. What else about me needs fixing?"

"New pants, new shirts, and new suits are a reward, not something that has to be fixed about you, Tully."

"Shopping for new clothes is more of a penance than a reward," Tully said, and visibly shivered.

"I'll make you a deal."

"Our last deal involved a lot of exercise, sweat, and giving up cigarettes."

Libby laughed and leaned closer in. "That was a bet, not a deal."

"There's a difference?"

"Of course. Finish up early today, and I'll take you shopping and help you get some new things."

"You're buying me some clothes?"

She pinched Tully's side. "As if I could afford them, even if I don't pay rent. No, I'm picking things out and you're paying. I'll be your personal shopper."

"I see." Tully grabbed Libby's hand before she could pinch her again, and didn't let go. "And what's this service going to cost me?"

"Dinner at Le Jardin." *And one of the most romantic restaurants in the city, so hopefully the candlelight will make you notice I'm alive.* Libby kept that thought to herself. "You know you want to, and the kids are having dinner with Jessica tonight so you don't have an excuse."

"Sure," Tully said, blushing when her voice cracked on the word.

That afternoon the salesman at Brooks Brothers smiled broadly when Libby handed him Tully's suit and pointed to a few more things for him to bring in to Tully, who was busy complaining in the dressing room. Unless she wanted to stroll out of the mall in her underwear, Tully would have to try on everything Libby picked out.

"How about this one?" He held up a navy pin-striped suit. "It should fit perfectly to wear out."

"Good. She has a dinner date after this," Libby said, loud enough for Tully to hear.

"Is this the last one?" A slimmed-down, tailored Tully stepped out.

As Libby looked her up and down, she was sure her feelings were written all over her face. This new Tully was a walking fantasy. Not that Libby hadn't found her attractive before, but the weight loss had taken years off her face.

"Wow." Libby couldn't think of anything else to say.

"We'll take all of it, I guess," Tully told the hovering employee, who clapped his hands. "Come on, personal shopper, let's take these to the car." She bent her arm and offered her elbow to Libby.

After stowing their purchases they strolled through the French Quarter, since it was too early for dinner. When they were close enough Tully recommended the bar at the Bella Luna restaurant, and Libby agreed. Located in a large veranda to the side of the restaurant, it had a perfect view of the river. People talked softly and listened to the three-piece jazz band playing slow songs for their enjoyment.

"I've never been here," Libby said after Tully handed her a glass of wine. The women at the table next to her had kept their eyes glued on Tully the whole time she'd been at the bar, and Libby was about to throw peanuts at them to make them stop.

"We're breaking new ground together, then, because I've never been here either." Tully sat next to her, her back to her admirers. The band swung into a familiar piece. "Do you dance, Ms. Dexter?" She put her drink down and held her hand out.

"Not well, but I think I can handle the slow ones."

Libby followed Tully's lead and spent the next four songs enjoying the feel of Tully's arms around her and the sound of her heart beating. They swayed in place for the next song, still not talking as they watched the sun make its final descent.

"Your table's ready, Ms. Badeaux," said the host, sounding almost loath to disturb them.

"Thank you." Without losing contact Tully stepped back a little so she could see Libby's face. "How about dinner here, and I'll take you to Le Jardin next week?"

Libby nodded and had to rein in the temptation to kiss her.

They fell into a more comfortable and normal conversation at the table, but as they walked back to the car Libby was sure of one thing. That night, both of them bathed in candlelight and enjoying good food, she had seen something new in Tully's gray eyes—a little wanting and a lot of fear, which gave her enough hope to try.

When they arrived home, she helped Tully carry everything in from the car, then they walked together to the pool house. Tully kissed her forehead as they stood at the door and waited until she had let herself in locked up. But Libby didn't move once the dead bolt slid into place. She wanted to watch through the French doors as Tully walked to the back door of her house, and was ready to come out again if she turned around.

"You might not be ready yet, but don't run from me, Tully," she whispered.

Tully made it to the house without turning back. With the summer break approaching for Bailey, Ralph, and Libby, and the information gathering for the Hebert case coming to an end, she was ready to draw her line in the sand. After only three short months she felt like a new person, ready to face her demons or slay them, depending on how others interpreted her actions.

With all she had going on, the one thing she strove for above all else was willpower. Young women like Libby didn't fall in love with single parents in their forties, so Tully was determined to control her feelings. Libby deserved someone young and full of life to build a future with, not a cradle robber.

But Libby made it hard. Those blue eyes just about did Tully in every time Libby turned them her way.

“Be strong, Tully, or you’ll lose a good friend,” she said to herself.

Chapter Fourteen

A week later Libby walked into the kitchen in the main house and found Tully standing at the counter drinking a cup of coffee and reading the paper. Tully had gotten her hair cut shorter, a new style that curled slightly at the ends.

"Good morning, Counselor. New suit?" Libby accepted a cup, smiling at Tully's obvious pride in her new coffeemaking ability.

"You should know, since you and Bailey are the ones who talked me into it. I wanted to look the part since it's time to let our opponents know there's a battle abrewing. I couldn't go in there with baggy pants, especially after someone mentioned them."

Libby smiled. The more weight Tully lost, the flatter her butt got, but Libby secretly thought it was adorable. She had started to notice all sorts of new things about Tully, such as her favorite dishes and how Tully seemed to enjoy doing things for her.

Libby had a new desktop computer and a laptop to make her schoolwork easier, as well as a password to the online law library the firm used. She and Tully lunched together at least twice a week, and Tully indulged her when she continued to order healthy meals for both of them. In fact, if Libby mentioned that she liked anything, it magically appeared.

"The great pinstripes will dazzle them," Libby teased. "But shouldn't you wait until Monday?" It was Friday, the last day of class for Bailey and Ralph.

"I love having these initial meetings on Friday."

Libby turned from the open refrigerator to Tully. "And that's why?"

"I can lower the guillotine just enough for them to know what's coming, then leave it hanging over their necks for the weekend. Frazzled nerves make for great negotiations."

Libby put the fruit salad she had made the night before on the counter. It was one of the only breakfast choices, other than Pop-Tarts, that all of the Badeauxes enjoyed. "You're going to settle?"

"I will for fifty million dollars."

Libby laughed so hard she almost snorted as she handed Tully a bowl. "Tully, no one's going to give you that kind of money."

"Then I guess that answers your question. I'm not settling."

"I think you're spoiling for a fight."

Tully put her hand up to her chest and gasped, "Who, me?"

They both laughed at the blatant lie.

"Contrary to what you may think, I *am* able to put my personal feelings aside when it comes to this case. But a good fight never hurt anyone." Tully offered up a strawberry and smiled when Libby snapped it from her fork with her teeth.

"Remind me never to get on your bad side," Libby said after she swallowed.

"I wouldn't spend a whole lot of time worrying about it. I know for a fact that you don't have a bad side," Tully said, sounding surprisingly flirty. The rumble from the stairwell cut their banter short as the kids ran down for breakfast.

"Ah, release the beasts from captivity for the summer and they show signs of life!"

In reality, Bailey and Ralph had blossomed at their new school, as proven by their constantly ringing phone. Kids now called the house all afternoon and night, but Tully was just happy that her kids had become typical teenagers.

"Nope, you're wrong, since we volunteered to work in the school's summer camp for the young students. We're going back in a couple of days," Ralph said, bumping shoulders with Tully.

"I know, buddy. I'm pretty excited about that myself."

Bailey's head popped up from her bowl of fruit. "Why?"

"Because of all the valuable experience you're going to get."

"And?" Bailey smiled through her menacing glare.

"And the allowance break I'm going to be enjoying over the summer."

"No reprieves to be had, so stop your daydreaming."

"One day you'll have children of your own." Tully playfully grabbed Bailey in a headlock and rubbed the top of her head with her knuckles.

"I know, and you wish they'll act just like me." Bailey tickled Tully's side and tried to squirm away.

"That's a given, but not my point." Across from them Libby and Ralph were laughing. "You're going to have kids and still be calling me to demand an allowance."

"Well, hey, if you want to see your grandkids."

"Get in the car, funny girl," Tully said, shaking her head. Bailey had lost a lot of her surliness, but not her wit.

❖

After they dropped the kids off, Tully and Libby rode into the office together. Law school had ended for the session two weeks earlier, and Libby had decided to take the summer off.

For once, Roxanne didn't phone, and during the comfortable silence Libby stared off into space, deep in thought.

When Tully stopped at a light, she gently ran her thumb over the small crease along Libby's brow, apparently not wanting to mess up her makeup. "You okay?"

In that one instant Libby felt her feelings coalesce and focus. Tully had long before stopped being her savior and become someone she truly cared about. Every moment Tully had spent with her had made her fall that much harder, and Libby suddenly feared that Tully would never return those feelings, that after everything that had happened, Tully wouldn't want to risk her heart and try again.

"Nothing's wrong," she whispered. Her eyes filled with tears when Tully pulled over to the curb.

"You can tell me, Libby. I'll listen and we'll fix whatever it is together." Tully cupped her cheek. "I thought you knew by now that you aren't alone."

The statement made Libby's tears fall, and she felt foolish for not being able to control her emotions. "Maybe later, okay? We don't have time for my issues right now."

"The rest of our day can wait. All you have to do is ask."

"I appreciate it, Tully, but come on before we're late." She reached up for Tully's hand and with regret rested it in her lap, needing some contact with her. How could she not have figured out the depth of her feelings before now, when she had no place to hide from Tully's eyes?

"If you change your mind, you know where to find me," Tully said once they'd driven to her office building.

Upstairs, Jo and Frank were waiting in Tully's office, and Roxanne started filling her in on what calls had been made so far. The Heberts had finally accepted the invitation for the meeting the hospital administration had been pushing for since the day Evangeline died.

Normally, Tully would have preferred to go with the Heberts for the initial contact, but she respected Simone's wishes. The grieving mother had wanted to see for herself just how honorable the hospital was willing to be. More than money, she just wanted Kara Nicolas to admit she'd done something wrong and apologize.

"Did Elijah or Simone call yet? I'm willing to bet the administrators are putting the velvet screws to them, trying to make them think signing is the best choice they can make," Tully said as she took a seat next to Libby at the table in her office.

"Not unless they're willing to give her Nicolas," Jo said. "I'm sure they'll be fine until we get there."

"Did Pasco finish his report?" Tully asked.

"He's scheduled to come in this afternoon," Frank said, "because he's still trying to run down one thing."

"Let's get going. The details will have to wait for later." Tully stood, an action mimicked by everyone but Libby, and told Jo and Frank, "I'll meet you at the elevator."

Roxanne followed the others.

"Don't you want to go to the hospital with us?" Tully asked once she and Libby were alone.

"Do you want me to?"

"I didn't think I had to ask. You've been here working almost every day on this case, so I figured you'd want to be there once we actually start." She sat back down and rolled the leather conference chair closer. "You even wore the nice suit," she teased.

Tully wasn't flirting like she had in the kitchen early that morning, but the fact that she had noticed what Libby was wearing was a good start.

"You mentioned you liked it."

"You could have smacked me if I hadn't. Come on. We don't want to be late."

❖

Jo and Frank were waiting in the main lobby when Tully and Libby arrived, Tully carrying only a small leather portfolio and the organized case file.

"Let's make this quick, people." She led them toward the west wing, acknowledging almost every employee they passed, most of whom knew her by name.

Libby just smiled at the easy manner until she saw Tully's back stiffen ever so slightly. She was about to ask what was wrong when an attractive brunette walked up and put her hands on Tully's forearms.

"My God, you look fabulous!" Jessica said. Her quasi embrace kept Tully from moving forward. "I mean really fabulous."

With an almost disgusted expression, Tully forcefully stepped back and stared at Jessica as if questioning her sanity. She noticed that Jessica had changed too, and not for the better.

"Don't be like that, Tully. There's no reason we can't be friends," Jessica continued, not yet noticing Tully wasn't alone. "Do you have time for coffee?"

Behind them, Libby couldn't hear what they were saying and couldn't see Tully's face. All she could see was the big smile on the woman's face as she gazed up at Tully.

"Boss, we're running a little late," Jo said, glancing down at her watch. Beside her, Libby was strangling the handle of the bag she was carrying.

Just then Jessica looked past Tully at the rest of the group. "Here to ruin someone's life?"

"Merely doing my job, so I'll have to pass on the coffee," Tully said civilly. "The kids are expecting you this afternoon after school. Just remember to do something special. It's their last day."

"You're the neglectful parent, not me."

"You're also the tooth fairy. At least if you keep telling yourself that, you might convince yourself it's true."

When Tully laughed, Jessica's face twisted into something ugly. "This is why I left."

"You left because some piece of ass made you forget your commitments. Let's not fool ourselves, darlin'." Tully's voice had dropped to a whisper, but it still carried menace.

"That was Elijah, Tully. We have to get going," Frank said.

"Then let's do it." They continued down the hall, all of them trying to keep up with Tully.

"Who was that?" Libby asked Jo in a whisper. In a strange way she felt better when the talk had obviously turned bad.

"You haven't met Jessica yet?"

"That was Jessica Badeaux?" Libby whipped her head back to Jessica, who was still standing in the hallway.

"That's her, and if you ask me, she hasn't improved with the breakup."

Any other questions would have to wait as Tully opened the door to the conference room without knocking. "Neil, nice to see you again." She held her hand out to the hospital administrator while smiling at Victor Williams and his associate. Neil never stepped into these meetings without his in-house pit bulls.

"What are you doing here?" Neil Davis frowned momentarily. "Never mind. I don't think we'll need you. We're just about to offer the Heberts a more-than-generous settlement." He shook her hand, then sat in one of the two chairs across from himself and the hospital counsel. There was room for only the Heberts, and he obviously intended to keep it that way.

"What does that mean—more than generous?" Tully asked, content to stand.

"That's between the hospital and the Heberts."

"I'm not talking numbers, Neil. I meant the expression."

She glanced at Simone, who nodded in return.

"If it's already generous, how can it be more than that? It's an oxymoron, don't you think? Sort of like jumbo shrimp."

Tully heard Jo, who was partially hidden her from view behind her, laugh at the comment. They hadn't had many cases at Children's Hospital, but when they did Tully couldn't help but needle Neil about his height. He was solidly built, a bit overweight, but height evidently didn't run in his family. When he'd reached five feet two inches, his growth spurt had fizzled out, a reality that had left him with a severe case of short-man complex.

"So, Neil, what's the offer?" Tully asked.

"Two hundred thousand, plus we'll reimburse any funeral expenses and cover the hospital bill."

"What about the doctor that operated on my baby?" Simone asked.

"Dr. Nicolas? What's she got to do with this?" Neil stopped talking when the attorney sitting to his right put his hand on his forearm.

"What are you asking for here, Tully?" Victor Williams, the hospital's lead counselor, locked eyes with her.

"For the truth. This was a routine surgery."

"You're a doctor, for God's sake," Neil said. "No operation is routine!"

Victor squeezed his arm and Neil stopped talking again.

"This was routine and Evangeline bled out, so we have twenty minutes of mystery, but you can fix that. Fill in the blanks for us and we'll be reasonable." Tully stated their position in as few words as possible, then waited.

She knew Neil Davis would no more admit fault than he would strip naked and stroll through the lobby. No, it would take putting a gun to his head, and Tully was in the process of loading hers.

"Mrs. Hebert," Neil said with sincerity, "what we have here is an unfortunate incident. There was no medical mistake, no negligence—just a procedure your sick child's body couldn't handle."

Simone stood. "Tully, call me when you're done," she said before she left, her husband close behind her.

"Mrs. Hebert? Mr. Hebert?" Neil yelled after them.

"See you in court, Neil." Tully pointed to Frank, who produced the suit for wrongful death. "You should've paid attention to this one. Your first offer with the explanation I asked for would've done the trick."

"You want me to serve Dr. Nicolas up to you for what happened? And I'm not talking about Evangeline Hebert."

"That's going to cost you, shrimp." Tully didn't intend to tease her opponent any longer. "My private life has no bearing on this case or any other one I'm working on, so kindly limit your remarks to why we are here."

"We all know what a bitch you can be, so what's it going to take to make this go away?"

Victor and the woman next to him rolled their eyes.

"The thing I love about you is your consistency, Neil." Tully dropped her portfolio and leaned over him with her hands pressed to the table.

As Neil craned his neck up, he lost any advantage he'd had from the seating arrangement.

"You're a bean counter with the compassion of a shark, shorty,"

Tully said. "I just told you what it would take, but it's evidently not in your nature to admit fault of any kind, even when it would be cheaper for you in the end."

"A number, Tully, not a lecture."

"More like a date, Neil. I'll be happy to get Mrs. Hebert what she really wants, and that's justice for her only child. She wants to know what happened and for others to know that as well. In this case it'll be jurors, and once they're finished listening, I'll leave it up to them to give you a number."

She faced Victor before standing straight. "See you soon." They made a quick exit after that since everyone was already standing.

Tully kept her hand on the small of Libby's back until they reached the car. Seeing Jessica again and having to deal with Neil and Victor hadn't upset her as much as Libby's sad look. Tully was confident she could deal with the first two annoyances, but Libby was still an unknown factor in her life.

Chapter Fifteen

The ride back to the office was again silent, but Libby noticed how tightly Tully was gripping the steering wheel. The meeting and Neil Davis's reaction to it weren't a surprise, so this was something else, and if she had to put a name to it, it would be Jessica. The way her face had softened when she saw Tully had been hard to miss. It spoke of their history that she felt comfortable enough to walk up to and put her hands on Tully.

The more Libby thought about that history, the harder she pressed her fingers into the armrest, squeezing with so much force that it squeaked. Instead of heading for the office parking garage, Tully put her turn signal on and parallel parked on the street near the park across from the federal building. When the engine stopped, Libby let go and shook out her hand, not realizing she was tensing her fingers to the point of pain.

She watched as Tully walked in front of the car and headed to the passenger side, opened the door, and held out her hand. "This place isn't very big, but it's quiet."

"Do you need to think?" Libby took Tully's hand but didn't get out. "Because you have a great quiet office upstairs if you do."

"What I want is for you to talk to me and tell me what's wrong, but I can't force it out of you." Tully let Libby's hand go, and Libby got out of the car. "It's really okay if you want to pass."

Libby took a deep breath before walking to the nearest empty bench. It was early, but the heat was already stifling in the humidity the region was famous for. Beside her she heard the slight crackle of the starch in Tully's shirt as she sat down, something that would definitely disappear if they stayed out here too long.

"Can I ask you something, Tully?"

"You have the right to ask me whatever you like."

Libby combed a strand of hair behind her ear as a delay tactic. Having this conversation was a huge risk. "Why is that? Why do I have the right to ask you whatever I like?"

"Simple. I trust you with what's in here." Tully tapped her temple. "You're my friend. So ask whatever you like."

"Do you want Jessica back in your life?"

"Why would you ask that, of all things?" Tully leaned forward and rested her elbows on her knees in the very familiar pose she struck whenever she was troubled about something.

Libby could tell from the answer that she was avoiding the issue. "I'm sorry, it's not my business."

"No, I'm sorry. Really, I didn't mean to snap at you. It's just that a real answer to that question might make you think less of me."

"She's your partner and you're willing to forgive her. I wouldn't think less of you for wanting her back."

"She *was* my partner and now she's not. A small part of me wants to hurt her the way she hurt me, but I'm not going to give in to that. I can forgive some offenses, but I can't recover from others." Tully's voice had risen a bit, but she was far from yelling. "This is something I can't recover from."

"Then why do you think I'd be upset with you?"

"Because I want nothing more than to put her through the same hell I went through when I found out what she'd been doing. I hit that bitch she was with so hard I thought it would make me feel better." Tully sighed again before scrubbing her face with her hands.

"Did it make you feel better?"

"Momentarily, but now I could give a shit."

Libby put her hand on Tully's back. "You were together a long time, so of course you care."

"That's just it, Libby. I don't. That's why I can't recover. My heart can't and I certainly can't wrap my head around the betrayal. Jessica isn't even on my list of things to worry about. She made her choices and I can live with that. Hell, even if she hadn't slept with Nicolas, it would only have been a matter of time before we got to where we are now. We both changed over the years, but not in the same direction." She took a deep breath and blew it out slowly. "But enough about my problems. Tell me what's wrong."

Libby still had her hand on Tully's back, but she couldn't get the words out. She wasn't willing to give up times like these when she had Tully's complete attention and concern. Telling her the truth might sever their connection. "I don't know if I can."

"You can trust me, Libby. We can work it out just like we did with the job and your apartment." She stretched her arm along the back of the bench. "No matter what it is, I promise to help you through it."

Libby leaned back and looked into Tully's eyes. In the sunlight they appeared clear, a true window to her soul. "This time a job and a place to stay aren't going to fix what's bothering me."

Tully curled her arm around Libby so she'd come closer. "Why not?"

"Because you said your heart couldn't recover." The comment slipped out almost without permission, but Libby knew she needed to cure her own heartache. "Look, just forget it."

Tully put her fingers under Libby's chin and gently coaxed her head up. "I'm not blind. You're hurting and I want to know why. Please don't shut me out."

The compassion always on Tully's face gave Libby courage. They were so close that she had to take the chance. Slowly Libby moved forward and Tully didn't back away, even though her eyes were wide with what looked like fear.

Libby released a small moan when she realized that Tully's lips were as soft as she'd imagined them and that she felt as solid as she appeared. The kiss started slowly, then Libby deepened it, overjoyed Tully hadn't pushed her away.

When they parted, Libby followed Tully back and pressed one more chaste kiss on her lips. "That's what was bothering me, and I'm sorry."

"Sorry for wanting to kiss me?" Tully's arms were still around Libby.

"Sorry that I couldn't hide my feelings from you anymore. You just said your heart won't recover, so I guess it doesn't matter anyway."

"I didn't mean forever, Libby. Just when it comes to Jessica."

She did lean her head back this time when Libby tried to kiss her again. "That doesn't mean I'm the right person for you."

"Shouldn't I get to decide that?"

"Your feelings probably come from all the help I gave you. I did that because I care about you, not because I wanted you to think you owe me something."

Tully appeared stunned when Libby stood up and slapped her on the head. "Is that what you think of me?" She stood in front of Tully with her hands on her hips. "Do you?"

"Libby, be reasonable. You're twenty-four, with a bright future ahead of you, and I'm forty-two."

Reasonable arguments as defined by Tully made Libby slap her head again. "This has nothing to do with favors, age differences, or any other lame excuse you come up with, you idiot."

"It doesn't?"

"No!" The yell frightened a flock of pigeons off the benches nearby. "It has to do with what I feel in here." She placed her hand over her heart. "It has to do with the fact I've never felt like this about anyone."

She turned, not wanting Tully to see how vulnerable she was. "I've been on my own since I was sixteen, so I'm not some young idealist who's confused gratitude with love."

Tully stood at the word "love." It was a word uttered lightly by some, but she didn't think Libby would use it that way. And her apparent rejection had crushed Libby's hope.

If she was honest with herself, she had felt a spark of interest from the first time she saw Libby in the coffee shop. She would have never acted on it, but it had lowered her defenses enough to lead to their friendship. And after all the time they'd spent together recently, Tully couldn't imagine not having Libby in her life.

"I only said it because I want the best for you." Tully put her hands on Libby's shoulders from behind.

"Why can't you believe that it's you?" Libby put her hands over Tully's. "Don't you trust me enough to believe I know what I want? What I need in my life?" She let go of Tully's hands, turned around, and wrapped her arms around Tully's neck. "How about we try something new?"

Tully laughed but didn't move away. "This is about as new as I can think," she said, indicating their position.

"I'd start getting used to this, but that's not what I'm talking about. You look me in the eye, Tully, and tell me you don't care about me."

"Are you joking? A woman who's hit me on the head twice,

kissed me, and called me an idiot in less than two minutes has more than enough potential to run away with my heart." Tully gave in to the pressure of Libby's soft hands and brought her head down. This time she allowed herself to enjoy the kiss. She moved her hands to the small of Libby's back and pushed her tongue gently into her mouth.

"All I'm asking is just a chance," Libby said, so close that Tully could feel her breath against her lips. "And you can trust me with your heart. If you do it'll be safe for a lifetime."

"My heart feels fabulous already," Tully said with a smile. "Thank you for taking that chance. We could've been dancing around our feelings for a very long time. If I'm honest with myself I'd say I feel the same way about you, but would've never admitted it."

"You big argumentative types just need a kick in the pants sometimes."

"Yes, but once you get us going, we can make it so you can't live without us."

With just a light tug, Libby pushed her head down and kissed her again. "Oh, honey, you're way too late. I'm already there."

❖

Kara Nicolas stalked out of Neil Davis's office, so furious her hands were shaking. He had just finished briefing her on that morning's meeting with the Heberts and their lawyers. After hearing Tully's name again, she wished she'd hit her harder the first time she'd laid eyes on her.

She headed for the doctors' atrium at the back of the hospital and lit a cigarette before the door had a chance to close. When it opened again, she almost flicked her smoke at her visitor. Giving in to Jessica's itch was going to set Tully on her heels like someone possessed, and Kara could ill afford to be under the spotlight. She wanted to be alone.

"Maybe you should get back to work, Jessica."

Jessica ignored her curt tone and cut the distance between them by half. Ever since she'd met Kara, with her cocky personality and deep brown eyes, she hadn't been able to stay away. Kara was Tully's exact opposite, except that both of them were very sure of themselves. Jessica had never thought she'd find someone worth gambling so much for. "Not before you tell me what's going on."

"That bitch you used to live with is gunning for me because

of what happened to Evangeline Hebert. You'd think those people would have gone back to their little fishing village and left me the hell alone."

"Honey, they lost their child. It's only natural that they're still upset."

"You're taking their side?" Kara stepped forward and jabbed her index finger close to Jessica's face. "A fucking fisherman and a housewife have the right to judge me? Is that what you're telling me?"

Jessica knew Kara wouldn't be saying things like this unless the stress of her job was getting to her, so she changed her approach. "You know I'm on your side, so calm down." She took Kara's hand and kissed her palm. "I just want you to concentrate on some upset parents who've talked Tully into representing them. This is important, so listen to me. Maybe you should change some things until all this is over. If Tully can find anything wrong, or anything that can be conceived as wrong, she'll use it against you. It's what she's good at, and I don't want you to suffer."

Kara jerked her hand away from Jessica's. "Maybe the first thing I should change is getting you out of my apartment and out of my bed. What do you think?"

"How can you even say that? I'm just looking out for you."

"You're either with me the way I am or you're not. You try to change me and there's a hospital full of women in there who would love to take your place."

Jessica stood still for a long while, wondering where her pride had gone. When had it become all right for someone she loved to talk to her like this? "I love you and I'm going to stand with you. That's all you need to know."

She glanced at her watch as Kara pulled her forward and kissed her. Though there was no gentleness in her kiss, it still ignited Jessica's libido. She would just take a few minutes to reassure Kara, then pick up the kids from school. She'd been anticipating their tradition of going for beignets and coffee at Café du Monde, which they'd done from the time the kids had started school.

"You have some place you need to be?" Kara asked when Jessica glanced at her watch again.

"Just here in your arms, baby." A few minutes wouldn't hurt. The kids would be outside waiting.

❖

"Tully?" Roxanne's voice came over the intercom. "I hate to bother you, but Bailey's on line one."

The request broke through Tully's stupor, and she realized she hadn't heard a word of what Jo had been saying. Her mind was squarely on the outer office, wondering what Libby was doing.

"Hey, babe, what's wrong?" It was close to four in the afternoon, so she was ready to listen to some grievance Bailey had with her mother. Ever since they'd started on a visitation schedule, Bailey or Ralph would find some excuse to call her when they were spending time with Jessica.

"Nothing's wrong, except for the fact we're sitting out here in the heat."

Tully pinched her left brow, trying to decipher the bit of information. Café du Monde was open-air and hot this time of the year, but it wasn't like Bailey to complain about that. Both kids liked their annual end-of-school-year tradition. "Where exactly are you?"

"Outside of school, and Mama isn't here and didn't call."

"Do me a favor and go sit in the library, and I'll be there in a few minutes." She was standing, already having gone from a long stretch of daydreaming to total alertness. "I'll call you when I'm outside."

"Don't sweat it, Mom. We'll be waiting."

"Trouble, boss?" Frank asked.

"Not anymore. Jessica's somebody else's problem. Finish up and make sure you get Pasco's final report."

She stopped at Libby's desk on the way out, not wanting to miscommunicate this early in their relationship. Some of her anger toward Jessica evaporated when Libby smiled up at her.

"Do you want some company?" Libby asked.

"Sure. We can take them out for something to celebrate their last day."

Libby packed her things and followed Tully to the elevator. When the doors closed and they were finally alone for a few seconds, she hugged Tully. On the drive they didn't talk, but Tully had a hard time keeping the smile off her face as Libby stroked her open palm with the tips of her fingers.

The kids were waiting outside when Tully drove up and waved.

Neither mentioned Jessica or her absence, which Tully had confirmed with the hospital as being just that. She and Dr. Nicolas had checked out earlier, the receptionist had informed her, and they hadn't returned. Tully's anger returned at Jessica's callous behavior toward Bailey and Ralph. Because Jessica had repeatedly told Tully over the years what a negligent parent she'd been, Tully was appalled that she would abandon the kids for Kara Nicolas.

"Feel like Café du Monde?" Tully asked.

"No," Ralph said, and Bailey agreed. "You can just take us home if you're busy."

"How about a new Badeaux family tradition for the last day of school?" Tully met their eyes in the rearview mirror before she took her foot off the brakes. When they didn't argue she headed toward City Park.

Behind the New Orleans Museum of Art, at one of the main entrances, sat one of the city's oldest establishments: a playground with equipment fashioned after nursery rhymes and an amusement park.

"Mom, this place is lame," Bailey said.

Tully paid for four admissions and a handful of ride tickets. "You're here to amuse me, Bailey Bean, and you know how easily bored I get, so we shouldn't be here long."

She remembered the first time she'd brought Bailey here. Bailey had just turned three, and it had taken them forever to get from place to place since she had wanted to walk and explore. Tully wondered where the years had gone. The young Bailey was now almost a woman. Watching her leaving the trappings of childhood behind, Tully felt a sense of loss. She had missed out on a lot because of work. She couldn't change the past, though, so she wanted to seize the last days of her daughter's childhood now, before the chance was entirely lost.

They all followed Tully to the back of the place and entered the old wooden structure that had been lovingly restored thanks to patrons of the park. "The first time I brought you here," she told Bailey, "you pointed to that big fella there and asked if you could take him home." She indicated a black stallion, his mouth open permanently as if he was running somewhere and was breathing hard.

She walked Bailey to the carousel horse with a brass plate on his chest that bore her name. "They wouldn't let me take him home for you, but because of you he still looks great after all this time."

"Why didn't you tell me?"

"Because my little girl started to grow up and didn't want to ride wooden horses anymore, so I was selfish and kept a bit of her alive on a brass plate." Tully put her hands on Bailey's hips and lifted her into the saddle. "I knew eventually she'd think this guy was cool again."

She walked Ralph to the tiger he'd fallen in love with when he was four, and he hugged her when he saw his nameplate.

Because of Tully's sizable tip and the vacant park, the operator let them go around for forty minutes. They used the rest of the tickets on the Tilt-A-Whirl and the roller coaster. The kids kidded around with Libby, laughing when Tully came close to making her sick on the Tilt-A-Whirl.

"How about a chili dog?" Tully asked, directing her question to Libby and laughing when she raised her head slowly with an incredulous expression.

With one hand on her stomach and the other on Tully's arm to steady herself after all the twirling, Libby took a deep breath. "Do you like the shoes you're wearing?"

"They're some of my favorites, actually. Why?"

The kids were wiping their eyes from laughing so hard.

"Then we're definitely skipping the chili dog." She leaned farther in until she realized where they were and who they were with. "In fact, maybe I should go splash water on my face. Wait for me?"

"They'll wait, Libby. Come on, I'll go with you," Bailey said, pointing her toward the nearest bathroom.

"How about one more ride on the carousel, Mom?" Ralph asked.

"Not without us, shrimp, so park it on the bench over there," Bailey warned.

As they walked to the bathroom, Bailey took note of how often Libby glanced back at the bench. She was sure Libby wasn't afraid Tully would leave them behind.

"You feel okay?"

Libby laughed when she stood before the bathroom mirror. "By the looks of my hair I'd go with no, but I was just teasing your mom. I had a great time with you guys today." She put her hand on Bailey's shoulder. "Thanks for letting me tag along."

"We may do things like this a lot in the future, don't you think? Have you told her yet?"

Libby glanced from Bailey to the door with an almost panicked expression until Bailey covered her hand with hers and smiled reassuringly.

"Would you be mad if I said yes?"

"That depends."

"On?" Libby asked.

"My mom's right. You do ask a lot of questions," Bailey teased. "It depends on how she reacted to the news that you're in love with her. She's my mom and I love her, but she can be quite the bonehead sometimes."

"You figured it out, I take it."

"I'm sixteen, not stupid, and you're too old for a crush, so I went with the next thing on the list."

"Does it bother you?" Libby leaned against the sink and folded her arms over her chest.

Bailey just stared at her, thinking of the best way to answer. In reality, the conversation was surreal to her, but then so were the past few months. "Just don't hurt her. She's had enough of that lately." She imitated Libby's pose. "It doesn't bother me, just as long as you take care of her. I'll talk to Ralph too if you want."

"Thanks, Bailey, but I'll do it. And don't worry about your mom. Her heart is safe with me."

❖

Jessica peered over Kara's naked shoulder and grimaced when she saw the time. The red digital readout on the alarm clock was flashing 6:45, meaning that she was three hours late to pick up the kids. When Kara had suggested they go home for the day, Jessica forgot about her clinic, knowing her nurse would reschedule most of her patients. After Tully's stunt that morning, she figured she owed it to Kara to go along with her wishes and provide an outlet for her frustrations.

She rolled out of bed and placed her pillow next to Kara so she'd stay asleep. In the small den next to the bedroom she pushed aside an overflowing ashtray and a stack of old magazines to pick up the phone, then slowly dialed the number to her house, dreading what would come of the call.

This wasn't the first time she'd blown off her family to make Kara happy, and she was ashamed to admit to herself that it wouldn't be the last. Kara Nicolas had become her addiction, and she had proved repeatedly that she was willing to sacrifice plenty to get her fix. That all-consuming feeling was new, and still thrilling.

Jessica thought about her conservative family, who hadn't taken the news of her sexuality well until she'd brought Tully home. Her father, an orthopedic surgeon and workaholic, had found he had a lot in common with her new love.

From the beginning of their relationship, Tully had been easy to love. She was kind, outgoing, generous, and thoughtful—all the attributes any woman dreamed of. Only one thing was missing, and Jessica hadn't realized what it was until she met Kara. She realized she had loved Tully but never craved her, craved her in such a way that her desire consumed her soul. Tully was comfortable, but Kara ignited her blood.

Jessica awoke from her musings and released a long breath of anticipation as the phone rang for a third time. Two more rings would engage the answering machine. Her family was either screening calls or not at home. Neither possibility gave her peace of mind.

"What are you doing?" Kara asked from the doorway. She'd thrown on jeans and a T-shirt. A pair of old tennis shoes completed her studied casual appearance. "I asked you a question," she said.

Jessica hung up the phone, not wanting to leave a message after all. "I was calling the kids since I'm running late."

Kara glanced down at her watch. "It's not even seven. How late can you be?"

"I told you last week, today was their last day of school. They got out before three today, so I'm running really late."

"Hey, if it was that important to you, you should have said something." Kara picked up her wallet and keys.

"I did say something," Jessica said in the direction of the front door. From the sound of Kara's footsteps she was already on the first floor. The silence that ensued closed in on her, and for the first time in her life she felt totally alone.

Chapter Sixteen

"Can we go in with you in the morning?" Bailey asked. They were on their way home after having dinner at Port of Call. The thick burgers and baked potatoes the restaurant was known for, on top of their active afternoon, had left them all listless.

"Did they hand out book report assignments for next year already?" Tully teased.

Libby laughed and pinched Tully's side after her comment. "Behave."

"Ralph and I wanted to help you with whatever you're working on. It's got to be better than sitting by the pool all day while we wait for summer camp to start." Bailey yawned as she stared out the window through half-closed lids. "And the pay should be better with you than the summer camp gig."

Another round of laughter came from Libby. "She's got you pegged on that one, boss."

"You be quiet or I'm naming them your new assistants."

Tully put the car in park and turned off the ignition. Glancing in the rearview mirror, she could see Ralph's head resting peacefully against the seat. Bailey jerked Ralph awake, and Tully had to laugh, remembering her own relationship with her brothers.

Groggy, Ralph slowly climbed out of the car and kissed Tully's cheek, then Libby's before he headed to bed. Tully followed him up so she could talk to him.

Libby and Bailey stayed downstairs, and half an hour later Bailey told Libby good night when Tully called her from the top of the stairs.

"How'd he take the news about Libby?" Bailey asked as she opened the door to her room and waved Tully inside.

"You know your brother. He said 'cool' and shrugged."

"He was still hoping things would work out and we could go back to the way things were." Bailey pointed to the desk chair.

"Is that what you want?" Tully looked around the neat space. Aside from a few scattered CD cases, the room was orderly, nothing she'd expected from a teenager with an independent streak as wide as the Mississippi River.

"I didn't tell you that because I want you to go back or because I have a problem with you seeing Libby. Jeez, you'd be totally miserable if you went back to Mama." Bailey plopped down on the bed and grabbed a worn stuffed bear Tully had given her years before. "Ralph's bummed about stuff because he doesn't like Mama's new girlfriend."

"When did you meet her?"

"We haven't officially." Bailey made air quotes with her fingers. "We've just run into her a few times, and she calls a lot when we're spending time with Mama. She talks loud enough for us to figure out she's a butthead."

Tully picked up a pen from the desk and twirled it between her fingers. "I'd talk to her, but that isn't my business anymore."

"I know that, Mom. It's like you tell us all the time, everything you do affects your life. Mama's old enough to know that." Bailey stretched out and stared at the ceiling as if putting her thoughts in order.

"When I met your mom and we started building a life together, I never considered what it would be like if we started over with other people."

Bailey laughed. "Who goes into a relationship thinking that?"

Tully chuckled. "I should have, since we've become a cliché, and I'm sorry for that. Having to spend time with both of us and having new people thrust into your life without your say-so can't be pleasant."

"This is about Libby, isn't it?"

"Maybe."

Bailey laughed again and sat up. "This is a change, all right. You're looking for our blessing, aren't you? Ralph's and my permission to see her?"

"It's not that, exactly." She scrubbed her hands over her face.

"Then what?"

"I want you to be honest and tell me if you have a problem with it. This isn't just about me."

"Do you care about her?" Bailey got up and put her hands on Tully's shoulders.

"I really do."

"Then go for it. Mama's already building a life that doesn't include you, so don't try to make everyone but you happy by letting Libby go."

"Thanks, Bailey Bean. I'm glad you're willing to support me. Dating at forty-two makes me feel kind of silly."

"Hell, Mom, you've lost weight and look totally hot. Just relax and get down there before she decides to find somebody else."

❖

"Did they talk some sense into you?" Libby asked.

"Bailey did, anyway." Tully leaned against the entryway of the kitchen and crossed her arms over her chest.

"So I guess I should get going, huh?"

That afternoon when Libby had admitted how she felt, something in Tully's heart had opened up. Even if things between her and Jessica had worked out, she would've never been happy. With a little time and perspective she easily realized just how bad things were between her and Jessica, even if she put the cheating aside. Life was fleeting if you let it slip through your fingers just trying to survive it, and she was resolute on stopping her negative behavior. From that moment on she wanted to enjoy her children, her success, and her life with someone who really wanted to stand by her side.

Before Libby could move, Tully lifted her and sat her on the kitchen island. "Actually, I'd rather you stayed for a while. We really do have a lot to talk about." She kissed Libby's neck until she reached the underside of her ear.

"You're interested in a long conversation, are you?" Libby bent her head back and anchored her fingers in Tully's hair.

"Oh, yeah." Tully bit down gently on the very tip of Libby's earlobe, liking the moan it produced. "A long talk so you'll have no doubt about how I feel about you and what a brave genius you are. If you'd left it up to me we'd have been flirting in the kitchen for the next twenty years." She framed Libby's face with her hands and gazed at her before she kissed her. Libby wrapped her legs around her waist, her lips parting slightly to invite Tully in.

They leisurely kissed until they either had to slow down or strip, so Tully put Libby on her feet and offered her hand, then they strolled to the pool house through a light fog.

"One of the last things I remember my mom telling me before she died was to wait for someone who understood my secrets."

Tully put her arms around her when they reached the door, smiling when Libby rested her head on her chest. Having Libby this close made her hopeful for the future. "I don't think you've had a secret from the moment I met you."

Without moving, Libby decided to see if her mother had been right. "Tell me what you know about me."

"All I need to."

The answer made her gaze up at Tully. "What do you mean?"

"That you have a good heart, a true spirit, and no secrets. They aren't necessary, because secrets stem from fear. My feelings for you are genuine, and you have nothing to fear from me no matter what." Tully met her eyes with an openness that made Libby wrap her arms around her. "And I'm going to try to make sure we never have any secrets between us."

"If I didn't know better, I'd say you knew my mom." Libby stepped closer into Tully. "You're right. You're the only person I've trusted with who I am, and you not only understood me, you accept me."

"Libby, that's been the easiest thing I've done in a good long while. Just remember you're in good hands."

Libby reached for her hands and placed a kiss in each palm. For an attorney Tully's hands were callused, a lasting testament to where her road had started. "I know that, and I'll try to make you want to stay. Do you want to come in?"

"I really want to, but I don't want to leave the kids too long. And when I do stay, I want our first time together to be special. When I come in it's because I won't be leaving you."

"I'm keeping you to that, and thanks for taking a chance on us. Your heart—it's in good hands too."

After their last kiss Tully stayed by the door until she heard the dead bolt slide into place. Now her nights were going to be long for a completely different reason.

When she settled into the chair in her office, she set the Hebert case aside and started on a different set of legal papers. It was time to pay the toll of the past so she could start over. She finished just before midnight, but made a call despite the late hour.

"Are you free for coffee tomorrow morning?"

If she was expecting a fight, she was pleasantly surprised.

"Good. Nine o'clock at the Bluebird Café."

❖

"Just remember to keep your cool," Libby said the next morning. She wished there was some way she could be there to watch out for her. Of course, Tully didn't need anyone else to fight her battles, but Kara Nicolas was obviously not the most stable person, and Libby hoped she only fought with her fists and nothing worse would happen to Tully. Her black eye had long since faded but the cut had left a little scar, and Libby worried what would happen if they set Tully off again.

She stayed quiet about her fears, though, and kept her eyes on Tully's butt until she disappeared behind the gate. She could feel her ears get instantly hot when she turned and found Bailey and Ralph standing at the back door.

"Is that what people are talking about when they say breakfast of champions?" Ralph asked innocently, getting a slap to the back in congratulations from Bailey.

"No, that would be gruel they're talking about, which I could whip up for you if you don't behave," Libby shot back. The sound of the engine starting made her send a silent prayer that things would go well.

Tully drove down the oak-lined avenue of St. Charles and studied the sky. It was dark gray because of a thick cloud cover that would probably bring rain before too long. She never really thought about the weather, but now she could imagine spending the afternoon with Libby on the sofa watching television.

Jessica's Lexus was parked close to their meeting place, and Tully took the space in front of it. She had made one stop at the bank before getting there, which had made her ten minutes late. It didn't matter what came of this meeting; she had made up her mind to keep her cool and just move on.

Jessica put her coffee cup down and her hands flat on the table when Tully walked in. She took in the pressed chinos, dark blue polo shirt, and polished loafers. Tully resembled the young college student Jessica had first spotted one afternoon walking on the sidewalk in front of Tulane. The weight loss and the new clothes had definitely changed Tully since the last time she had seen her at their home.

"Good morning. I'm glad you called."

The only thing about Tully that hadn't changed was her laugh, and when it came out it was genuine since the skin around her eyes crinkled.

"I'm sure spending time with me was at the top of your list of things to do this morning, Jessica."

"Are you going to be hostile the whole time we're here?"

"It depends."

"On what?" Jessica leaned back and let the waitress refresh her coffee.

"If your girlfriend is in the bathroom warming up. Though she might not want to take a swing at me with so many witnesses around."

"Okay, what do you want? If it's just to give me a lot of shit, I'd rather leave now."

"Calm down." Tully nodded when the girl held up the coffeepot. "I wanted to go over a few things. First off, I figure you're living with Dr. Nicolas, so I'd like to buy you out of the house." She took out the first set of papers from the file she'd brought in.

"Always the organized one, aren't you?"

"Let's just say I *now* know who I'm dealing with. It's best if we do things in the most straightforward way possible."

Jessica thrust her head forward a little and let some of her anger out. "What's that supposed to mean?"

"That I don't want you coming back telling me how unfair I was, so just listen to what I'm saying before you start attacking, okay?" She laid three separate sheets in front of Jessica. "I had the house appraised by three separate firms. They were within ten thousand dollars of each other, so I went with the highest value. I'd like to offer you half of that appraisal."

"What if I want the house?" Jessica picked up the cashier's check that Tully had also put in front of her.

"Then I'll need a check in that amount from you by the end of business next Friday."

Jessica cut her eyes up to Tully after the quick, calm comeback. Tully wasn't exactly known for giving in so easily. "What's the catch?"

"None. I want the house because the kids are comfortable there, but if you want it, I'm sure they'll enjoy hunting for a new one. Hell, that might even be for the best, for all of us." She reached out and snatched the check out of Jessica's hand and put it back in the folder.

"What if I want to keep the house with the kids in it?"

"Then pick a court date and let me know when to show up. If you insist on a fight that doesn't involve fists, I'll be more than happy to oblige you." She didn't raise her voice or show any emotion that would hint that she was upset. With the first issue out of the way, she laid out another set of papers. "Have we decided that you'll keep the house?"

"I don't want the fucking house, Tully."

"Okay, I see your new acquaintances have improved your vocabulary immensely." She handed back the check and summoned the waitress to witness Jessica's signature on the receipt. "Next we'll move on to the joint accounts."

That took two hours, and when they were done, Jessica asked, "Is there anything else?"

"Not that I can think of, but you'll be the first to know if I do. Good luck to you, Jessica. I don't really expect to talk to you much unless it has to do with the kids." Tully paid the bill in cash. "Whether I like it or not, you're their mother and we'll be forever tied because of that."

"Do you really hate me that much?"

"Hate you? Not really. You wanted something new and I wasn't it. I can live with that. How you got there is your business, and you'll have to live with where you've ended up. All I ask now is that you don't let many days like yesterday happen. Bailey and Ralph were really hurt, and there was no excuse for it. No piece of ass is worth bringing pain to your children."

"I have no response to that."

"Good, then we're done." Tully stood and had just reached into her pocket for her car keys when Jessica's reaction stopped her. Tully turned and looked at the door to find Kara Nicolas. She appeared to have slept in what she was wearing, and she scanned the room rapidly. Despite all the things that were obviously wrong, it was the sweating that captured Tully's attention. Granted, it was noon and May in New Orleans, but unless Kara had run over to the café, there was no reason for her to be that drenched.

"Are you going to be all right?" Tully asked Jessica. She balanced her weight over her feet and waited. Kara appeared a bit crazed, and Tully was ready for anything after what had happened the first time they'd met.

"Are you trying to say something?" Jessica asked in return. "Just because I'm sleeping with her there has to be something wrong? Get on your white horse and ride away, Tully. I'm fine."

"You got it, babe."

Kara's nostrils flared at the endearment Tully had used. It seemed to make her lose what little control she was displaying at the door.

Even if Tully thought she was ready there was no way to defend herself from the running start Kara took from the door. One moment she was standing at the table ready to leave, and the next second she was falling over the table and the elderly woman who had been sitting behind them now sat above her, holding her fork close to her mouth. The Mexican omelet she had ordered was splattered all over the front of Tully's pants.

At the bar the waitress was dialing 911.

"What exactly is your problem?" Tully asked Kara as she wiped a blob of black beans off her forehead.

"You may sit back and let someone take your woman, but that's not my style," Kara announced. "And I don't give up easily."

When Jessica smiled, Tully vaguely wondered if she found Kara's antics romantic. She certainly didn't. "Trust me, I'm willing to give you a set of checks too if you keep her, you moron." Tully laughed hard as she stood up and shook herself off. "You're going to make the next few months easy, aren't you?"

Kara stood close by opening and closing her fists. "What do you mean?"

"The courtroom loves people who like to put on a show." She laughed harder when Jessica jumped up and held Kara back. "Oh yeah, they're going to love you."

Chapter Seventeen

Man, Libby, you make the best waffles in the world," Ralph said.

"And you have the table manners of a slob," Bailey said as he shoved another portion into his mouth.

The kids had helped Libby mix up the ingredients and spent their time talking and teasing each other. Libby had worked hard to achieve the relaxed atmosphere, and she was enjoying spending time with them alone. If her relationship with Tully was going to work, it would only happen if these two Badeauxes accepted her place in their lives.

"My mom used to say that if someone eats like that, it's a compliment to the chef," Libby said.

"Then your head should be as big as the house by the time he's finished," Bailey teased. "Hurry up and stuff your face, slobbo, and we can go sit by the pool for a little while." Despite the morning cloud cover, the sun had finally broken through and the temperature had started to rise.

Ralph helped with the dishes after he'd finished eating, then went up to change into his bathing suit. He returned with his Nintendo DS Lite, and Bailey had her MP3 player and towel.

Libby, lounging near the pool in a conservative one-piece suit, glanced up when she heard them whispering but pretended not to see them.

"I can't wait to get a load of Mom's face when she sees how good Libby looks in that."

"If it was a competition then I'd say Mom won hands down," Ralph said. "She's a lot better than that biatch Kara."

"Spoken like a true dog."

"Hey, Mom said it was all right to be a dog if you aren't married, you aren't obnoxious about it, and you don't make any promises you aren't going to keep. I'm going to make the most of that while I can."

"First you have to get girls to realize you're alive and breathing. Then you can go on and start your dog career, Casanova."

"I'm sure you're doing so much better," he said as he bumped hips with her.

"Maybe I am."

They sat on either side of Libby, Ralph engrossed in his game and Bailey moving her foot in time to the music playing in her ear. Libby smiled at their conversation and resumed reading the files on her lap. Pasco had finished his report with one piece still missing. After searching for weeks, he still couldn't find any information about a six-month span in Kara's history.

Libby was now finalizing a roster of the names of people working in the surgical ward the day that Evangeline had died. They were beginning depositions in the coming week, and Tully wanted to make sure to talk to everyone who had been even a mile away from Kara's suite.

"Hey, Libby, can I talk to you about something?" Ralph asked when she put her stuff down and reached for a soda.

"Sure, whatcha got?"

"Bailey and me, we've been talking."

"Should I be afraid?" Libby asked with a smile.

"Things are like way different now, so we decided that if we're going to make changes, they should be radical. Mom'll probably be cool with what we want, but we thought if you were on our side, it'd be that much easier to talk her into it."

"Talk her into what exactly?" Libby asked, her eyes on Bailey, who had removed her earpieces and gave her a smile that could only be described as sweet and innocent.

"We want you to help us convince Mom to sell the house."

"Would you like me to convince her to shave her head while I'm at it?" Libby asked incredulously. "Why would you two want to move?" she asked Bailey this time.

"If you and Mom are together, I'm sure you have to know how you got here. What you may not know is where she's sleeping at night."

"Explanation, please."

"She treats the master bedroom like it's radioactive, so don't expect her to go all goony on you in there. If you want a legit shot at making this work you'll agree with our plan."

"Guys, you have to know how much I care about your mom, but do you think a move this big is any of my business?"

"If you want to stay with her, then you'd better learn to jump in and speak up. Mom won't put up with you letting her make all the big decisions," Ralph said. "We're a team. Don't you want to be a part of that?"

A moment later Libby heard Tully's car screech into the driveway and the door close just a little too hard.

"Are you in?" Bailey asked.

"Sure. It sounds like she had a great breakfast meeting, so this would be a good time to spring this on her. I'm sure she'll be easy to talk into packing up and moving." Libby reached over and knocked the front of Bailey's baseball cap down before doing the same thing to Ralph's. "I promise I'll talk to her about it if you two really want me to, but let me find out what happened this morning."

As Tully walked through the gate, the outcome of her meeting was obvious.

"This might be a guess on my part, but I'm thinking it didn't go well. How about you stay put and I'll go calm her down."

"Oh, man, if there was a food fight I would have loved to be there to see Mom's face when those pants got messed up. She hates spilling stuff on her clothes," Bailey said when Libby stood and tugged her bathing suit down in the back.

"Okay, guys, you may hear a little screaming, but don't send in reinforcements unless I ask for them," Libby said.

As she headed upstairs she heard Tully muttering and stepped into the guest room to see her taking off her shoes and tossing them onto a towel in apparent disgust. Her sock and left loafer were soaked with what appeared to be syrup. Without a word Libby went into the bathroom to get another towel for the rest of Tully's clothes.

"Should I even ask, or would you rather stew?" she asked as she threw the towel next to Tully and stood in front of her.

Tully laughed when Libby picked a piece of tomato from the front of her shirt. "You're just a riot, darlin'."

"It appears like *you've* been in a riot, sweetheart." She pulled the polo shirt out of Tully's pants and kept going, removing it and throwing it onto the towel. "I know she was mad at you, but this is ridiculous."

Tully had to laugh at the methodical way Libby was working on getting her undressed. "No, she gave in to everything I asked. The new additions to my wardrobe came when the crazy bitch she's sleeping with joined in the fun."

"Kara showed up? Why?"

"Not because I invited her, I can assure you."

Tully explained what had happened, and they were both laughing as she described Jessica's demeanor when the same police officer that had written up the report at the house the day she'd caught them in bed showed up at the café. When Tully passed on the chance to press charges again, Jessica had paid for the damages in an effort to get them out of there before anything else happened.

"Can you handle the pants by yourself or do you need help?" Libby asked.

"Ooh, my day's improving by the second with offers like that. Let me get my suit on and I'll join you outside." Tully started for the master bedroom where she still kept her clothes.

Libby followed her and leaned on the dresser while she was in the closet. "Honey, why haven't you moved back in here?"

"Because I haven't been able to convince our parish priest to come over and perform an exorcism on the bed."

From the way she said it, Libby didn't think she was kidding.

"I know it makes me appear weak, but I can't just forget."

"Do you trust me enough to tell me what exactly happened that day you came home?"

After a few minutes Tully had changed clothes, and she came out with a T-shirt over her bathing suit. With her eyes on the bed she told the story for the first time, leaving out no detail. Though the mess had been cleaned long ago and the rumpled sheets thrown away, from the way Tully described the betrayal in vivid detail, Libby could tell it was etched into her mind.

"It makes me sound like a pansy, I know, but I'd rather do my next opening statement in a thong than sleep in here."

"Now that you've put that image in my head, I really need a swim, sexy." Libby moved closer and put her hands behind Tully's neck. "I have a solution for your problem, if you care to hear it."

"It isn't you and I making love in here to dispel the bad memories, is it?"

Libby dropped her head to Tully's chest, knowing from the familiar heat that she was blushing. "Behave or else. The kids are right outside."

"If that's what you had in mind, I'd rather go back to the guest room to try it out. It's stupid to hate a room, but I hate this one."

"The kids mentioned this little problem, and after listening to your story I have to agree with them. We think you should sell the house."

"I just paid for half of it *again*. Couldn't you and your partners in crime have mentioned that before I had the check drawn up?" Tully kissed the top of her head and pinched her butt. "And where do you and the geniuses outside think we should move to?"

"I think we should go about it the same way I found my great new place."

"Look at rat-infested dives, then all decide to move into the pool house?"

"Something like that, smart-ass." Libby could understand what Ralph had said about speaking up and giving an opinion. Tully seemed to want and expect that from a partner. If the Badeaux family was indeed a team, Libby really wanted to join it.

Chapter Eighteen

"Are you sure this is a good idea?" Libby asked for the fourth time.

The kids had returned to their toys and music, only now they were enjoying them from the backseat of the Explorer, oblivious to the conversation going on in the front.

"I'm positive this is a good idea. It has to happen sometime, and today's as good a day as any," Tully said. "Trust me, honey, they're going to love you."

After Tully had changed they had talked to the kids together about what they wanted, then spent the rest of the afternoon by the pool, grilling burgers before the sun set. They were cleaning up when the phone rang, and Alma had invited them to Sunday lunch. Before she said yes, Tully talked it over with Libby, trying to convince her to join them.

When Tully called her mother back and told her to set another place at the table, she sat back and answered the litany of questions that arose from having someone new in her life. Alma seemed satisfied when Tully finally explained that Libby was as different from Jessica as a trout was from a catfish.

"If it helps keep your mind off it, let's talk about something more important," Tully said.

"Meeting your mother ranks up there, if you ask me." Libby smoothed down her simple sundress with her right hand and clutched Tully's hand with her left.

"Not as important as what I'm thinking about."

Libby swiveled in her seat so she could study Tully's profile, enjoying her relaxed smile. "What are you thinking about?"

"Our first date. It should be something memorable, don't you think?"

"That's true." Libby lifted Tully's hand and kissed her knuckles, laughing when she heard retching noises coming from the backseat. Bailey had obviously spotted what she'd done. "We've been to dinner and lunch a bunch of times, but that was before you really noticed me." She kissed Tully's hand again.

"You must be delusional if you think I never noticed you. You're like a triple chocolate sundae someone places in front of you. The willpower not to take a bite might last longer than you think, but hell if you don't notice it sitting there."

"Nice way of putting it. I don't ever think I've been compared to ice cream before."

"I was talking more about the temptation, but back to what we were discussing. For what I have in mind for our first date, I'm glad we're headed to my parents' place today." Tully turned into her folks' long drive and stopped in front of the house. "Libby, would you like to go out with me next Saturday night?" Tully put the truck in park and leaned closer to her.

"I'd love to." Libby gladly accepted the sweet kiss that Tully placed on her lips, then just as quickly groaned.

"Ooh, Gran saw that one," Bailey said a bit too gleefully.

"Just remember something, Bailey Bean," Tully said.

"What, that I'm going to enjoy the teasing that's about to begin?"

Tully turned fully in her seat and smiled. "Not by a long shot, kid. You should remember that, at sixteen, your first date shouldn't be too long in coming. Unless I'm wrong, Libby and I'll be there to greet this lucky person, and today will be in the forefront of our minds. Right, darlin'?"

Libby kissed the side of Tully's head before looking back at Bailey. "Count on it."

"Ralph, we should've thought this over before we told them how we didn't mind them going out."

He laughed as he opened the door and jogged up the stairs to greet Alma.

Until then Alma had been content to stand and watch what was happening in the vehicle. Libby certainly seemed more affectionate than Jessica. The size of Tully's smile when Libby kissed her temple released the knot of worry Alma carried around for her. From the time she was born, Tully had been extremely giving of herself. When she'd brought Jessica home, the first thing that jumped out about her was how standoffish she was. Life was too short not to enjoy the simple things like holding someone's hand.

When Tully walked around to the passenger side and opened the door for Bailey and Libby, Libby immediately reached for Tully's hand.

As Alma hugged Ralph she smiled, relishing her feeling of joy. She had always wanted Tully to have as much happiness as she could cram into her life, and her daughter hadn't seemed very fulfilled while she was with Jessica.

Then Alma opened her arms to Libby and hugged her. "I've been waiting for you for a very long time," she whispered in her ear. She held her just long enough, then moved to greet Bailey and Tully.

"Mama, you jumped a little ahead of me here, but this is Libby Dexter. Libby, my mother Alma."

"Sometimes if a woman has to wait on you, Tully Badeaux, the world could come to an end. Am I right, Libby?" Alma laughed at the cute blush that colored Libby's face. "Tully, why don't you show Libby around the place, and Ralph and Bailey can stay and help me. Your father's across the street fixing something, so make sure to stop and tell him to get up here and clean up."

"You want me to do that, Gran?" Ralph asked.

"Sure, take Bailey with you and make sure to watch out for cars on that road."

"If you need help with lunch, Mrs. Badeaux, I'd be happy to pitch in," Libby offered.

"I'll get you all to myself soon enough, honey, so enjoy some time with Tully. Take a walk and I'll be happy."

Tully took Libby's hand and headed to the row of oak trees in the backyard, where she pointed out the large bayou across the main road into town and the lake out back. The large violet water lilies scattered across the surface gave good cover to the fish Gaston had stocked the shallow lake with for his grandchildren to enjoy. A swing that he had made when his children were little hung from the tree closest to the water.

"See, you were worried over nothing. My mother loves you already, I can tell."

"She's really sweet."

After they'd settled on the swing, Libby gazed out at the water, thinking that although she was happy Alma liked her, she really wanted someone else to love her.

Not too much time had passed since they had admitted their feelings, but Libby already knew how strongly she felt about Tully. She wondered how Tully would react when she revealed the depth of her feelings.

Tully stretched her arm along the back of the swing, then moved closer to Libby. She remembered sitting here alone with Bailey about a month after she was born. Jessica had stayed in the city, not liking the country, much less her family. Tully had first talked to Alma about her sexual orientation here and had held her children in this swing to talk to them about their futures for the first time.

"I'm glad you came with me today," Tully said.

"At the risk of sounding totally sappy, I'm glad for every moment I spend with you." Libby pulled Tully's hand over her shoulder and kissed the palm. "It's beautiful out here. I can see why you like coming."

"That it is, but that's not why I wanted to bring you."

The swing swayed gently as Tully pushed them with her feet, Libby having folded her legs under her so she could lean farther into Tully.

"Why did you, then?"

"I've done some of the most important things in my life right here." Tully moved Libby so she was almost resting across her chest. "I've learned that life consists of certain moments. I tell the kids all the time that how you handle those moments produces everlasting consequences."

"Do you think overall you've handled those moments well?"

"Obviously they couldn't all be good, but most of them turned out for the best. I have the love of my parents and family, I have my children, and because of you, I have the opportunity for a second chance. It's maybe too early to say this, but I love you."

"Could you say that again?" Libby pressed her lips to Tully's neck and seemed to stop breathing.

"I love you, Libby. You might have been alone for a long time now, but you never will be again, if you don't want to. If you're not ready, I'm not going to push."

"Oh no, you can't take it back now." She raised her head and quickly kissed Tully. "I may be your second chance, but you're mine too. I've been waiting a long time to hear you say that. I love you too."

"I'll have to add to my list of firsts out here," Tully said before she kissed her again.

"What do you mean?"

"My first kiss."

"I would've thought—"

Tully kissed her for a long sweet time. "Nope. I always thought the first person I kissed out here should be special. And you are."

"Thank you for sharing that with me, but I don't understand why Jessica wasn't that person."

"That's easy to answer. Though we were together for a long time, she detested spending time out here with me." She waved to encompass the area. "Not out here, but coming out to visit my family. Granted, she and my folks are worlds apart, but she never really tried to build a relationship with them."

"I've only spent a few minutes with your mom, but I don't think you're going to have the same problem with me. Any woman who raised you has to be special enough for me to want to get to know her," Libby said before she moved back to Tully's lips.

They sat and swung together until Alma came out to find them for lunch.

CHAPTER NINETEEN

Talk to me, Pasco," Tully said as she propped her feet on the coffee table in her office and leaned back with the file he'd put together so far. Three months of digging and he still hadn't finished.

"You have everything we've got so far," he said. "There are still some holes, which we're working on. You know me well enough to know we won't give up until we get you the timeline you're after."

Her office door opened and she laughed as Libby walked in carrying a mug. In fact, she chuckled every time Libby came in with coffee, because it reminded her of the day she'd showed Libby the break room. Tully really hadn't been kidding about the espresso machine.

"Thanks," she told Libby for the latte she'd handed her.

"So the hole comes in college?" she asked Pasco.

"Beginning of her senior year, to be exact. It's weird that she went from superstar student to thin air." He flipped to the section of the report that documented Kara's college days in Texas. "She skipped two semesters, then went back and finished. Her grades and her entrance exam got her into medical school right after that." He flipped to the back and ran his finger down the page. "Like you already know, she came to New Orleans last year. According to hospital gossip, she started her affair with Jessica not long after she arrived."

"Any other suspicious cases?" Tully asked, ignoring the comment about Jessica. She realized Pasco hadn't meant to embarrass her, just to complete the picture she was asking him to paint.

"We're digging, but the staff is tight-lipped. You should know that from your hospital days. These guys are worse than cops when it comes to not flipping on each other."

"Attorneys aren't much different. No one wants to be the one to turn on their own. You do, and the gloves come off when it's your ass in the vise." She sipped her coffee and slowly took in the information. Something was off, but it wasn't jumping out at her yet. "We'll assume that there've been some close calls, but Evangeline has been the only patient she's lost to suspicious circumstances."

"Why are we assuming that?" Libby asked. She was sitting at Tully's desk updating some information on the computer.

"Because a surgeon that something like this happens to is either unskilled or has some other factor impeding her skills. You don't get to Children's Hospital or any other hospital with questionable skills. Medical school has the best possible vetting system. Those who don't belong with a scalpel in their hand are weeded out there."

Libby stopped what she was doing and put her elbows on the desk so she could look at Tully. "Then how do you explain Dr. Nicolas?"

"I can't…not yet, anyway."

The answer to that question resembled wisps of fog as the sun started to burn through. Tully was positive those missing months would eventually snap into place. That time was the key to the present, and that truth would give the Heberts peace.

"All these new privacy rules slow us down, but I'll keep in touch and let you know how it's going," Pasco said as he got up and gathered his papers. "Nice seeing you again, Libby."

"You too, and take care."

After he left, Libby stepped behind the sofa, put her hands on Tully's shoulders, and kissed the top of her head. "Are you just having coffee for lunch?"

"It's nutritious, and from what I hear, the milk does a body good."

"What'll do this body good is to join Bailey, Ralph, and me for lunch."

Tully tilted her head back and laughed. "And if I say no?"

"Then this body will be busy tonight when you want to watch television on the couch after the kids go to bed," Libby teased. "Come with us, because I know you're planning to work late this afternoon, and I worry about you skipping meals."

"I have some other cases to get up to speed on, but I'll try not to be too late. And since I'm dying to watch TV tonight, let's get going."

Libby kissed her forehead this time. "Is something good on?"

"The best show in town," Tully said. "A little romance, a little kissing, and a lot of holding the girl."

"Sounds like must-see TV, honey." Libby moved away reluctantly. "Let's go so we can get you back early. Tonight I'll cook and stay until you get home. I e-mailed the list of realtors you asked me to compile, and the kids and I started looking at properties on their Web sites."

"I should've offered you a job the day I met you."

"That was two years ago, and you wouldn't have given me the time of day. That's why I love you."

"The same applies now," Tully said. "I'm with you now, and no one's going to come between us. You know that, right?"

"I know that. Jessica was a fool, but I'm not going to be."

Tully laughed. "You're so much more diplomatic than me. A lot of words pop into my head when I think of Jessica, but 'fool' never makes my list."

"I'm hungry, guys," Ralph said, walking in without knocking.

"What's on the menu today?" Tully asked.

"Debris po-boys at Mother's, but Libby said you guys are having a salad."

He turned around to get Bailey, leaving a smiling Libby behind.

"A salad?"

"Honey, we want to keep those pinstripes looking good," Libby said, pinching her on the butt. "Have the salad and I'll make it worth your while."

"I'm counting on it."

❖

At lunch as Tully methodically worked through her salad, she thought about Kara Nicolas. Their two very brief meetings had left an impression, but nothing she could use to build her case.

"Either that salad is that good or you need a bite of my sandwich to bring you back from the coma you're about to go into," Bailey said. She waved her roast beef po-boy under Tully's nose.

"I'm thinking about something that's bugging me, sorry."

"Why don't you tell us, and we can help you with whatever it is," Ralph said.

"That's the problem, buddy. I'm not sure what it is, and that's what's bugging me."

"It has to do with the Hebert case, huh?" Bailey asked. "Did Mama's girlfriend really kill that kid?"

Tully put her fork down and wiped her mouth as a delay tactic. "Where did you hear that?"

"We overheard Frank and Jo talking about it, but we got most of the details from Mama."

"Guys, I trust you, so I'm not saying this because I don't, okay? You can't discuss this case or anything else you see or hear at the office with anyone, especially your mother." She took a deep breath, trying to squash her dread that she had inadvertently opened an information leak. "This is important to our clients."

"She asked us, Mom, but we didn't tell her anything," Ralph said. "Roxanne told us about confidentiality when we started."

"I think Mama was trying to find out if we knew anything," Bailey said, "and I meant to tell you that, but then she didn't come get us, and I got mad and forgot all about it." She put her po-boy down and shook her head. "That woman killed some kid, and Mama's protecting her? She keeps preaching to me about my behavior, so how screwed up is that?" She looked Tully in the eye. "It's true, isn't it?"

"The truth is what I'm looking for, Bailey Bean, so I can't answer that for you."

"What do you think happened?" Ralph asked.

"Just go with your gut, Mom," Bailey said.

"When I finished medical school, do you know what I liked best about being a doctor?" All three of them shook their heads.

"The exactness of the discipline. A patient comes in with certain symptoms, you use your skills to find what's wrong with them, and you treat whatever it is. It's like putting together a jigsaw puzzle. It might look impossible when you start, but if you put the pieces together right, you end up with a clear picture."

"Then why'd you quit?" Ralph asked.

"Because the law offered me the same opportunity, and it's where I thought I could make the biggest impact for good. You can't make up the law as you go along, and you always have to find all the facts before you can do something about the problem."

"I get you, but why are you telling us this stuff?" Bailey asked.

"Because right now, I know only the basic facts. A sick little girl had surgery and died. Kara Nicolas did the surgery, and Evangeline's parents blame her for their daughter's death. It's not enough for me to answer your question and tell you what I think happened. A good attorney understands there are three cardinal rules of success, and the first is to know the answer to every question before you start asking them." She picked up her fork and speared a piece of chicken from her salad. "When I start asking questions, it's because I can answer them all as well."

"What if we ask Mama if we can meet Kara? We might be able to find out something to help you," Ralph said.

"If you want to meet her because you think your mother has a future with her, then sure. But don't ask because of my work." She pointed her fork at Bailey, then Ralph. "Promise you won't."

"Scouts'," Bailey said.

"Honor," Ralph finished.

"Keep an eye on the Eagle Scouts," Tully told Libby when they got back to the office. "We already have an investigator on this case."

"They just want to help."

"Libby, you haven't had the pleasure of meeting Kara. For a surgeon she's a little unhinged, and I don't want my kids on the receiving end of her temper."

"I'll keep my eye on them, don't worry. I'm not going to let anything happen to them."

"We're all lucky you found us, especially me," Tully said with a warm look.

CHAPTER TWENTY

The week was ending, and during another meeting with Pasco, Tully made one more request. After listening to something Bailey said, and her own gut, she was willing to pay for this item herself.

While Tully worked, Libby accepted the assignment of putting the house up for sale, using a realtor who also supplied a list of potential properties for Tully to buy. She'd recruited Bailey and Ralph for that part of the deal.

After the third day of summer vacation both kids had told her they wanted to spend the summer with her instead of working at the summer camp, and because they had found their own replacements, she agreed, glad she had done so because they worked diligently filing and doing other tasks.

She didn't really expect them to become attorneys, but she liked that they were focusing on something constructive instead of getting into trouble. She realized that most kids changed their minds dozens of times before they knew what they wanted to be.

"Is everyone packed and ready?" Tully asked Friday morning during breakfast. "I want to leave from the office, so throw your bags in the truck."

"Aren't you supposed to be taking Libby out on a first date tomorrow?" Bailey asked.

"I am."

"Then why are we going to Gran and Pop's place? It's taken you forever to get moving on this, and you know we're going to the most boring town on the planet, no offense, with no nice restaurants." Bailey rolled her eyes and sighed. "You want the girl to like you, clueless."

Ralph jumped in. "Mom knows what she's doing." He glanced at Tully with a question in his eyes. "You know what you're doing, don't you, Mom? Bailey's right. You want her to like you, and we want her to keep cooking for us."

"Thanks for the confidence, dating professionals, and Libby isn't just here to cook."

"We know that, but we like her, so please tell me you put some thought into this," Bailey said.

"I've put plenty of thought into it. Don't panic thinking you're going back to daily Pop-Tarts."

"If I find those things in the pantry again, Badeaux, there'll be hell to pay," Libby said as she entered the kitchen. "Just so you know."

"We're eating the bran muffins you made last night, and our colons thank you," Tully said before she kissed her. She waved the kids out of the room to the pool house to help with her surprise.

"Why do I smell a conspiracy?" Libby asked when they broke apart and she noticed they were alone.

"Such paranoia, pretty lady. The kids just know how much I want to spend time alone with you. I'm sure they think they'll get a raise if they vamoose every so often." Tully pulled her closer and kissed her with a little more passion. "Thanks again for agreeing to reschedule our date."

"It's your mother, honey. Of course I don't mind. What exactly is the problem again?"

"They got some legal papers and she's not sure why. If it's nothing, I'm sure we can make it back in time to go somewhere."

Though Libby was a little disappointed, she understood how important Tully's family was to her. "There's always next weekend, so if we have time we can take the kids to a movie or something."

Libby turned around when she felt Tully's hand come off her back. Bailey was standing in the window waving for no apparent reason, but she didn't ask and just followed Tully to the door. "I'm confident we'll get to do something," Tully said as she started the car.

She drove toward the office, but when they got to the interstate she turned onto the up ramp. Libby just looked at her, then back at the kids, and sat back in her seat, silent. She was just going to trust Tully since she'd never been given a reason not to.

At the speed Tully was going, they soon left the city behind. The marsh, its huge cypress trees draped in moss, dominated the scenery, and the white cranes napping in the morning sun provided the only color in the deep green of the tree canopy. As Libby slipped her hand into Tully's lap, she tilted her head to the side so she could enjoy the landscape.

Gaston was loading the *Alma Mae* with supplies when they arrived, and Tully drove up to the dock instead of turning into the drive. She was surprised to find both her brothers coming off the boat after her father, both with huge smiles. While Tully had excelled in the classroom and in her career, Jerrold and Walter Badeaux had wanted to stay home and continue the family tradition on the water. Both had graduated from college with business degrees and with Tully's help now ran a seafood processing plant not far from their father's dock.

"You guys got everything ready?" Tully asked as soon as she opened her door.

"We're set, but we aren't going anywhere until we meet your new friend," Jerrold said. He and Walter had missed Sunday dinner the week before to attend a boat auction.

"Libby, these two overgrown troublemakers are Jerrold and Walter, my brothers. Try not to embarrass me now," she said to the boys as she put her arm around Libby's shoulders. "This is Libby Dexter."

Once the men had said hello, they greeted Bailey and Ralph by picking them up and tossing them around like they had since the kids were born.

Out of the corner of her eye, Libby noticed Ralph load two bags onto the boat and vaguely wondered what he was up to, but she was distracted when Gaston approached her.

"It's nice of you to come out here today, Libby," he said. "Alma and I realize that y'all are busy, but sometimes you just got to put all that aside and have a little fun."

"That's true, sir, but we're here to go over some papers she received in the mail."

"I'm sorry, honey. I was just trying to help my little girl plan something nice for you," Alma said as she walked up. She handed Jerrold a covered dish, and he jumped on board to put it away. "You best get on that boat before she leaves without you."

Everyone except Tully and Libby got into Tully's Explorer, Walter and Jerrold slapping Ralph and Bailey on the back after they hugged Libby before leaving.

Libby watched the vehicle cross the road until it disappeared around the slight bend. Only then did she turn and put her hands on her hips as she faced Tully.

"If you say so, we'll go back to town and go with plan B," Tully said.

"What's plan B?"

"We drive back and go to the restaurant that I made a reservation for tonight."

"And plan A?" Libby smiled and walked toward her like a woman who really wanted to go on a boat ride.

"I get you alone for the night on the water, catch you dinner, and show you how bright the stars look when you don't have anything around you but fish."

"And you thought I'd pass that up to go with the second choice? Shame on you, Badeaux. I get you alone for the night someplace where I really get you alone, and I'm going to want a dinner in the city instead? I think not, baby."

"Then step aboard and I'll cast off. I just thought this would be a memorable first date."

With the ropes clear, Tully started the engines and turned the wheel to head down the bayou. The usual four-hour cruise into the open Gulf of Mexico would take just a little longer with what Tully had in mind. Once underway, she went into the cabin and changed, and when she came out in shorts, an old T-shirt, and bare feet, Libby went in search of her bag to change too.

❖

The trawl net was dragging behind them when Libby emerged in an outfit similar to Tully's, and she listened, apparently really interested, as Tully explained the process of catching shrimp. The local fishermen trawled in the bayous close to the Gulf for brown shrimp, which most cooks believed had more flavor, but which didn't sell as well. The white shrimp most diners were used to seeing on their plates were found in the Gulf, but Tully had grown up in her mama's kitchen with big pots of wonderful dishes that centered around the browns.

Her months of working out and dieting made it easy to lift the nets up when she was ready. While they were culling their catch, Libby laughed and shrieked a few times as a few crabs scampered along the box Gaston had set up to use when they separated what was in the net. Afterward, Tully sat with a beer and a bushel of shrimp and started peeling while she told Libby which direction to steer the boat in.

Soon the dark waters of Bayou Terrebonne started to clear as they entered the Gulf of Mexico, and the birds that had been feeding off the shrimp shells that Tully was throwing overboard flew back to their perches in the trees. With enough clean shrimp, she took the wheel and headed east. The longer they traveled, the fewer boats they saw, and most of the owners called out to Tully in French to welcome her back to the water.

"Hungry?" she asked Libby when the sun was directly overhead.

"You're going to cook?"

"I'm going to cheat a little, but if you make yourself comfortable I promise I won't make you sick." Tully went into the small galley, found the bowl in the refrigerator that contained their main course, and set it on the counter.

Taped to the top were directions written in Alma's hand. Tully put a little butter in the bottom of the pan, along with some minced garlic, and added the brown shrimp. When they turned pink she added the sauce her mother had made and stirred until everything was hot. The other bowl Alma had included went into the microwave, and when the buzzer sounded, she was finished.

"Lunch is served." She handed Libby a plate and laughed at the accusatory glare she received. "I haven't been holding out on you, honey. I had a little help from my mother."

"We might have to spend more time here so I can learn to make this Creole sauce. She's a miracle worker."

After they washed the plates together, they settled into the back of the boat in the chairs the boys had set out for them. In the distance was a small barrier island with a few gulls on shore, but aside from that they were alone.

"Did you spend a lot of days out here like this?" Libby asked.

"Not like this, no. I experienced a lot of days doing what we did earlier, only we started at dawn and worked until sunset. This is a working boat, and we only made money when we were trawling.

Pop used to joke he had a built-in crew, and growing up we spent our summers out here learning what he liked to call 'earning a good living.'"

Libby moved from her chair into Tully's lap. "It sounds like you didn't agree."

"No, he was right about that. I love my father and my brothers, but this wasn't the life I wanted. I earn a good living too, and while my family likes to hear about some of our more interesting cases, I don't think they really understand what I do."

"You might be wrong on that one, baby. My afternoon with Alma last weekend after we had that nice time on the swing makes me think they not only understand, but they're extremely proud of you." She took Tully's baseball cap off and ran her fingers through her hair until they landed on the nape of her neck.

"That I do know. Funny thing is, for as much as I tried to outrun this life, I love being out here now. That's why I wanted to share it with you. This is where I came from, love, and you're where I'm going."

Libby moved so that she was straddling Tully's legs and pulled her into a kiss. "I love you."

"Say it again."

Libby put her lips right by Tully's ear. "I love you, and I want very much to have a future with you. I want to be the one who comforts you." She placed a kiss just below her ear. "I want to be the one you turn to when you need anything." She moved to Tully's jaw. "And the one you want to make love to." She ended at Tully's lips and gave her a kiss that drove Tully's passion to the point of no return.

Libby's T-shirt felt soft in Tully's hands, but she was more interested in what it covered. Without losing eye contact, she lifted it slowly until it cleared her head and dropped it to the deck. She scanned the area one more time, not wanting to share this view with anyone else. Libby leaned back, keeping her hands on Tully's shoulders as an obvious encouragement for her to touch her.

Every other woman Tully had ever been with melted from her mind when she dropped her eyes to the pink, very alert nipples. She had figured Libby wasn't wearing anything under the T-shirt, but this was proof. The last thing she was expecting was a finger to the forehead when she moved to wrap her lips around the closer nipple.

"You don't want me to?" Tully asked, figuring she had a long swim in her future.

"I want you to in the worst way, but you have to take your shirt off first. In the interest of time, why don't you just stand up and take everything off, because once we start, we aren't stopping."

Tully stood and placed Libby on her feet before removing her own shirt. "Do you want to go inside?"

Libby helped her take her sports bra off and popped the button to her shorts. "I fell in love with a fisherman who happens to be an attorney, so I want my first time to be out here on the water and under the sun that make up a big part of who you became." She unzipped her own shorts and let them drop to the deck with the rest of the clothing and stood before Tully, not making another move.

"My God," said Tully in awe.

"What?"

"You're beautiful."

Libby laughed before pushing her back into the chair. "Yeah, yeah, you can slap yourself on the back later. The way you're looking at me makes me believe you, though."

They both moaned when they touched for the first time with nothing between them, and Tully just put her hands on Libby's back and held her. Libby was so close Tully could feel how wet she was getting since her sex was pressed up against her lower abdomen. Wanting to go slow and savor the moment, she leaned Libby back a little and headed back to the hard left nipple. When she sucked just hard enough to feel it on the roof of her mouth, Libby moved her hips closer.

After that nipple turned deep pink, Tully moved to the other one and gave it equal treatment until Libby grabbed her hand and pushed it toward her center.

"Let's take our time, baby," Tully said, but Libby didn't let go of her hand.

"Just not too much time, okay?" Libby's skin felt like it was on fire, which was caused not by the sun but by the calluses on Tully's hands that made her hyperaware of where she was being touched, accentuated by how maddeningly slow Tully was going.

Libby tugged on her hand, and for a second Tully gave in and ran her fingers through the wet heat, but only for a second. She moved from there to Libby's butt, then down her thighs to behind her knees. Just when Libby thought Tully would quell some of the throbbing between her legs, she headed back up to the undersides of her breasts.

Libby felt worshipped and devoured all at once, and her senses were shifting into overdrive. She sank her fingers into Tully's hair and pulled hard when she sucked on her nipple again, wanting to keep her in place. The pressure was building, and as much as Libby wanted to turn the release valve, she waited. The only way she could think to describe it was a delicious torture.

Tully moved to the other breast, and when she sucked, Libby felt as if a live wire ran from her nipple to her clitoris. The sensation made her moan so loudly that Tully let go with a pop.

When Tully leaned back, she watched Libby take some deep breaths as if trying to regain control. But that was the last thing Tully wanted her to do. She wanted Libby wild and desperate for her touch, to lose some of that control that had helped her survive the deaths of her parents and the loneliness that followed. She also wanted Libby to crave this experience and the commitment it implied as much as she did.

This time Libby didn't have to guide her hand. Tully put just her middle and index fingers between Libby's breasts and dragged them down her body until she dipped them into Libby's wetness. She smiled at not only how turned on Libby was, but also how hard her clitoris had gotten. If Libby got any relief from the touch, it was fleeting.

"Please, baby, don't go," Libby said when Tully took her hand away again.

"Just one…little…taste." Tully pinched Libby's right nipple between her fingers before she painted it with the wetness she'd collected. "I just want a little taste, but I like having you this close to me and don't want to let go."

She finished by taking her prize, and this time she moaned when the sweetness that was so purely Libby exploded against her tongue.

In that moment her resolve to go slow shattered, and she slid her hand back down to make love to Libby. She felt Libby's fingers wrap around her wrist, but this time it wasn't to encourage her to keep going; she was making her stop.

"Did I do something wrong?"

Libby shook her head and seemed a little shy despite what they'd just been doing. "I just—"

"Honey, you can tell me, even if you want to stop. It'll be okay." She swept back Libby's hair and tried to get her to raise her eyes.

"I don't want to stop, but could we trade spots? I've thought about this for so long, and I just want you over me, making me feel safe and like I'm yours." Libby laughed when she finished, her blush adorable. "It's stupid, I know, but…"

Tully slid down to the end of the lounge chair and very lovingly lowered Libby. "How you want me to touch you will never be stupid, love. Because you're mine, I'll always take it very seriously." The feeling of desire sprang back instantly when she stretched out over Libby, careful to keep her weight off her. "I love you."

"I love you too, and I've waited all my life for you."

Libby spread her legs and took Tully's hand, not resisting when she moved it down. To rebuild their passion, Tully wet her fingers again and rubbed from the opening of Libby's sex up and gently over her clitoris. The sweep from bottom to top was so soft that Libby seemed to be chasing her fingers by tilting her hips up with every pass.

"I love you," Tully whispered in Libby's ear again. She sped up just slightly and felt Libby dig her fingers into her shoulders.

"Please go inside." Libby had tensed every muscle in her body and appeared to be willing to beg for release.

Holding herself up with one hand, Tully looked down as she eased her fingers in, only to whip her eyes back up when she felt a barrier she didn't expect. "Honey?"

"Don't stop—I want it to be you. I meant what I said. I've waited all my life for you." Libby laid her hand on Tully's cheek and kissed her. "I wanted our first time to be special, and because it's you, it's going to be."

"Are you sure?"

"I've had some opportunity if all I wanted was sex, but I wanted to hold off."

Tully just gazed at her and smiled.

"I wanted it to be with someone who cared about me, and who meant something to me." Libby kissed Tully. "I waited for you."

Tully resumed her sensual massage, wanting Libby to be as aroused and open as possible. Slowly, never taking her thumb off Libby's clitoris, she slid a finger in just enough to feel the top of Libby's sex, then pulled out again. When she went back she pushed a little deeper until she had broken through the last of Libby's innocence.

They stopped moving as if by mutual consent to allow Libby to grow accustomed to the fullness. When Tully pressed her thumb down, their dance began again. She sped up, feeling Libby clutch her fingers in the most intimate of ways, all the while continuing her stimulation.

"That's it, baby. Let go for me," she said, not knowing if Libby heard her over her moaning.

Libby felt like she was falling, but she wasn't afraid. Tully was there for her to hang on to, so she opened herself up and gave in to the overwhelming sensation of her orgasm. It came in one life-changing moment, and she welcomed it by tightening her body in an arc before slumping like a rag doll. She had no doubt because it forever bound her to Tully in a way no one could ever share.

"You okay?"

Libby nodded against Tully's shoulder, still grasping her until Tully moved and held her close. The boat drifted around the anchor, with only the sound of the water lapping at the hull and the cry of gulls in the distance.

"Are you sure you're okay?" Tully asked again some time later.

"I'm fabulous, actually. I was just wondering about something."

Tully stopped running her fingers along Libby's spine and made eye contact with her.

"When can we do that again?"

"In about two minutes, sweetheart."

"Then what?" Libby propped herself up so she could see Tully's face. "This isn't a fling for you, right?" She tried to sound like she was joking, but even she could hear the slight desperation in her voice.

"I have to marry you now, huh?"

"It hasn't been that long—" Libby didn't know how to finish.

"When my parents met, my dad said it took him one afternoon to know how long he'd be with my mother. True love doesn't need time to grow. It just needs a heart to take root in." Tully wiped the tears from Libby's face. "And it needs its other half to flourish." She tapped over her heart. "You've taken root in here," she tapped Libby's chest, "and in here is where it will flourish."

"I love you so much."

"Enough to want to make this permanent?"

"Are you asking because I need reassurance, or because you want to?"

"Remember how I told you the first of the three cardinal rules of being a good attorney is never ask questions unless you know the answer?" she asked, making Libby nod. "The second rule is that we sometimes ask blindly because we really want to know something that we don't. Libby, will you marry me?"

"Over and over again."

Tully rolled them over slowly, never letting go of her. "Just once is all I'm asking. I love you so much that once is all it'll take."

"Do you think the kids will be okay with this?"

"Bailey and Ralph wanted to make sure I didn't screw this up, so they gave me a good grilling on how much thought I'd put into our first date. I'm sure they didn't think a first date would turn into a proposal, but I'm sure they'll be happy for both of us."

Libby laughed as she started to run her hands up and down Tully's back. "Didn't want to go back to Pop-Tarts, huh?"

"There was that and the reality they'd have to go back to crabby Tully, who was more than happy to hand out groundings." Tully stopped her teasing to kiss Libby until they had to pull apart for lack of oxygen. "And I should've mentioned there was an additional clause to my proposal."

"If you want a prenup , that's all right, baby."

"I don't believe in those, so no. My terms are that you never mention to our grandchildren that I proposed to you naked."

"But I accepted when I was naked too. What's wrong with that?"

"Because when it's Bailey, Ralph, or any Badeaux's turn, I don't want to have to listen to how they were naked when the big question was popped. There are just some things I don't want to know about our kids."

They laughed, but Libby locked away exactly what she'd said. Ralph and Bailey were already in her heart, but the mention of future children won her over completely. As an only child she had often wondered what it would be like to have someone to turn to like the Badeaux kids did when they experienced heartache.

"The other thing I should've done—" Tully said.

"You did everything perfectly, honey."

"Was get a ring before I asked."

"There's always time for that." Libby tried to bring her head down close enough for another kiss. "Where are you going?"

Tully had not only not met her lips but had gotten up and was headed into the cabin.

"I'm going to teach you the third and final rule to what makes a successful attorney. Care to review?" She stood just out of Libby's reach with her hands behind her back.

"Never ask a question you don't know the answer to." Libby held up one finger.

"Very important number one rule."

Another finger went up. "Ask even when you don't know the answer when it's important enough to you."

"Number two should be used sparingly, but can be rather effective." Tully dropped to her knees and put her fists on the edge of the cushion. "The third is the most important, though. Three is what will guarantee your success every time."

"Does it have to do with questions?"

"It's more of a statement than a question, love. Prepare for everything. I asked you, not knowing what your answer would be, but the hopeful soul in me remembered the third rule."

Libby sat up and framed Tully's face with her hands. "What do you mean?"

"I asked myself, what if my girl says yes?" She opened her right hand and in her palm sat a ring. "So I came prepared. Are you willing to say yes again?"

"You can ask all day long and my answer's always going to be yes."

Tully took Libby's left hand and slipped a ring, a large sapphire flanked by two equally sizable diamonds, onto Libby's ring finger. When it was in place she lifted Libby's hand and kissed it.

"There's just one thing left to do," Libby said.

Before Tully could think of an answer, Libby's hands were between her legs, and still turned on from their afternoon, she never made it off her knees before a strong orgasm shot through her.

"If I lose my mind and tell the story to our grandchildren, I wanted to make sure they didn't think it was all one-sided," Libby said as she bit down gently on Tully's earlobe.

❖

After a swim Tully started the engines and moved them closer to the island where she planned to anchor for the night. She brought out a few rods from the cabin and baited the hooks with some leftover shrimp.

"What are you doing now?" Libby asked. She had rinsed off in the small bathroom and thrown on a fresh pair of shorts and a T-shirt. Her hair was slicked back and starting to dry at the ends in the warm breeze blowing from the south.

"I was planning to fish for dinner, but I got a little sidetracked." Tully's first cast landed well away from the boat, and she settled the rod in a holder in the rail before casting the second line.

"You call it sidetracked and I call it wonderful. Whatever you decide is fine, as long as you know that we'll be doing it often."

Tully had to laugh at Libby's infectious giddiness. They'd been pretty much glued to each other since the first item of clothing had come off, and their closeness hadn't changed now that they were dressed again. Libby was so different from Jessica. Not that Tully wanted to compare, but it was difficult not to. She could feel the genuineness of Libby's feelings in every touch.

"Are you happy with our first official date so far?" She took her eyes off the fishing lines and concentrated on Libby's face.

"I'm comparing it to my first first official date."

"My competition, huh?" The cork bob she'd put on the line sank suddenly, so she turned Libby around just in time to see the other one follow. "Start reeling in slowly."

Libby's face was the picture of concentration as she copied Tully's actions. When their catch was close enough to the boat, Tully spotted a fish on each hook of the double-rig lure.

"You're a natural, sweetheart," she boasted as she kept her catch a little farther away so their lines wouldn't tangle. She put her rod back in the holder and reached for the net to bring in Libby's catch.

"It's my day to try new things." Libby's blue eyes sparkled in the waning light as her two speckled trout landed on board.

"A fisherman and lover—sounds like my luck is changing." With the net in one hand and the rod in the other, Tully brought in two more trout. "This is going to be the quickest fishing trip in history, since four should be enough. Or did you work up a voracious appetite today?"

"Just promise me we'll do this again."

At the boat's small cleaning table, Tully unsheathed a filleting knife and made fast work of their dinner, throwing the scraps back into the water. "Whenever you want. You were right. This is a nice way to spend time with you with no interruptions."

"Can I ask what happens now?" They hadn't really talked about anything serious, but Libby looked scared.

Tully read the directions taped to a cabinet in the galley and coated the trout fillets in mustard before dredging them in Alma's fish fry. "What do you want to happen?"

"Once we eat tonight I want to go to sleep in your arms and wake up there tomorrow. When we get home I want to know we're moving toward that being a normal occurrence."

"Today was all about that, Libby."

She washed the mess off her hands so she could put her arms around Libby. "You made me believe in second chances, and I'm not going to squander the opportunity."

"No more doubts about anything?"

"You love me and my kids. You want to build a life with us and I want the same thing, so no. No more doubts about any of it."

"Good." Libby slapped Tully on the butt and kissed her chin. "Get back to work."

After they ate, Tully sat with Libby on her lap and just enjoyed gazing up at the stars until they went inside to a bunk. It was tight, but Libby got her wish of being held all night.

The smell of breakfast woke Tully the next morning, and she shook her head when she spotted a very naked Libby sliding a shrimp omelet onto a plate for them to share. She continued to watch as she thought about how much her life had changed in the span of a day.

"Did you have a good sleep?" Libby asked when she turned and found her awake.

"Not only that, but I'm having a really good morning too."

"I was just trying to prolong our first official date." Libby put the plate down and walked back to the bed, climbing in until they were pressed together from shoulder to feet. When their lips parted, Libby rested her left hand on Tully's shoulder and gazed at the new adornment on her ring finger. "Thank you for yesterday and for giving us a chance. I realize how hard it must've been for you to try again, but I promise you won't be sorry."

"Darlin', you were the easiest decision I've ever made, because loving you was something I could've no more stopped doing than breathing." Tully kissed her again before putting a T-shirt over Libby's head. "Let's go out and eat."

❖

They were back in the bayou and would be back at the Badeauxes' dock in a few hours. Libby had stood with her arms around Tully's waist the whole time, resting her head on Tully's shoulder.

"Something I can help you with?" Tully asked.

"Sorry, what?"

"You're lost in thought, so I'll be happy to help you work through whatever's bothering you."

Libby kissed the soft cotton of Tully's T-shirt. "I wasn't thinking about a problem, honey."

"What, then?"

"If we get a boat, can we get one with at least a double bed?"

Tully was still laughing when they tied up to the dock. She didn't have clue as to what the future held for them, but after spending the night with Libby she really didn't give a damn. Having Libby with her would make even the plague bearable, she was sure.

Bailey and Ralph were standing, having put down the cast net they'd been practicing with. When Bailey gave Libby a hand down from the boat her eyes fell instantly on the new ring and on the finger it sat on. Its ramifications meant drastic changes for not only Tully, but for her and Ralph as well.

"I have to give you snaps," she told Tully.

"For?"

"You really did know what you were doing. I didn't think you'd actually get it right this fast." In Bailey's opinion, it was all that needed to be said on the subject, and Ralph obviously agreed since he was nodding. "Congratulations."

Chapter Twenty-one

"You have depositions at two on the Tucker case. Opposing counsel is coming here, so you have plenty of time to get up to speed if you need to." Roxanne put the appropriate folder in front of her with a sticky note showing a time. "Since they're coming in at one, I pushed Pasco back until four."

"Anything?"

"He has more background, but not what you're looking for yet."

"He's been at it almost all summer and he still has nothing? He must be losing his touch."

"Some people hide their tracks better than the average Joe. Give him a chance and he'll get you what you're looking for." She stopped to answer Tully's phone, handing it over after a brief conversation. "It's Libby."

"How goes it with the three great house hunters?" Tully asked.

"It'd be easier if you hid a penny in town and told us to find it with no clues," Libby said. "I'm standing in line at a coffee shop with Bailey and Ralph, taking a break before our next appointment. What isn't totally disgusting needs major repair or updating. With all the time we've put in on this, you'd think there's at least one decent house out there."

"Why do I get the feeling you'll be saying the same thing about me in a couple of years?"

"I've seen your foundation timbers, honey, so I seriously doubt it."

"You're just a sweet-talker." Tully swiveled her chair to the side and stared out the window. Since the kids and Libby had spent the first part of their break mainly working in the office, the place was quiet now that they were playing real estate agents. "Happy hunting, darlin'. Call if you need anything."

"Try and make it home by seven. The kids and I are cooking, so you don't want to miss out."

Ralph pulled Libby forward by the hand, since she hadn't noticed the line moving.

"If you let Ralph or Bailey cook anything, I demand fair warning."

"Smart-ass." Libby pointed to what she wanted and Bailey ordered for her. "Just one more place to see, then your loyal staff will be reporting for duty. Oh, before I forget, the Land Rover dealership called and said your vehicle is finally in. He suggested the next time you just pick something on the lot."

"I'm sure he's thrilled that he won't have to take anymore annoying phone calls from me demanding to know where the damn thing is. Swing by and pick it up for me if you don't mind, and I'll make arrangements for the rental."

"After you painstakingly picked everything in it, you don't want to drive it first?"

"You can tell me all about the new-car smell when you get back. Love you, baby, but Roxanne's giving me the evil eye."

"Love you too." Libby snapped the phone closed, and as she bent down to find her wallet in her purse, both Bailey and Ralph moved closer in.

"Ralph? Bailey?" Jessica wore her lab coat and a pair of large sunglasses that hid most of her upper face. "What are you guys doing here?"

"It's a coffee shop, we're getting coffee," Bailey said, not moving from Libby's side.

"Try to be nice—just a little bit," Libby said.

"Why?" Ralph asked.

"For your mom's sake, to keep the peace, and because Jessica's your mother."

"I think I can handle my own battles, thank you," Jessica said. She pointed to a table, clearly expecting the kids to follow her.

"Libby, we're going to be late," Ralph said. He moved—to pick up their drinks.

"Tully hired a sitter for the summer, how sweet." Jessica crossed her arms over her chest and smirked. "If you spent more time with me, you wouldn't have to suffer the humiliation, Bailey."

Bailey said in a hopeful way, "Could I come over and watch television with you and your new girlfriend?"

Both Libby and Ralph stared at her like she'd lost her mind.

"I suppose, if you want."

"Yeah, right. Like that bitch wants us around. I'd rather stay home with Mom and Libby. They're not trying to ditch us every chance they get a better offer, like you do."

"Who's Libby?"

"That would be me." Libby put her hand on Bailey's shoulder in an effort to calm her down. Given all the time they'd spent together, she was familiar with the kids and their emotional triggers. "We'd love to stay and visit, but we have an appointment we need to get to." She put some money on the counter and started to walk out.

Jessica was about to move aside for them to pass, but something made her stop midstep. Libby noticed that both kids had followed Jessica's line of sight and ended up at her left ring finger.

"What exactly do you do for Tully and my children?"

"Don't answer that," Bailey said. She grabbed Libby's hand and tried to force her toward the door.

"Can I remind you that I'm your mother, even if we don't live together anymore."

"I told her not to answer because it's none of your business." Bailey stopped, but she didn't let go of Libby's hand. Behind Jessica, Ralph had the tray in his hands and kept looking from Bailey to Jessica. "If you want to know something about us, have the guts to ask Mom."

"You're going to lower your voice and treat me with respect, young lady. If these are the kind of manners Tully's teaching you, then perhaps it's time to make other arrangements for you two, especially if she's got some slut living with you."

Noticing all of the patrons in the café avidly listening to the argument, Libby encouraged Bailey to leave when Jessica's voice started to rise with her anger.

"I'd rather be sent to a boarding school in hell than to live with you," Bailey screamed back, then started crying and ran out the door.

"Ralph," was all Libby said to get him to put the tray down and go after his sister.

"Not so fast," Jessica said, grabbing Libby's bicep. "You're not going anywhere with my kids."

"If you have a problem, either call Tully or a lawyer. Now move." When Libby made it outside, Bailey and Ralph were leaning against the car crying.

Jessica watched as Libby did something her children didn't want from her anymore. She hugged them and they accepted her comfort before they all climbed into the Explorer and drove away.

Jessica was infuriated because, while her life was open to Tully's scrutiny, her ex had carefully moved on under her radar, obviously with Bailey and Ralph's blessing. Not once in all the time she'd spent with the kids had they mentioned anyone in Tully's life, and Tully had probably ordered them to keep their mouths closed on the subject.

She forgot about ordering anything and gave in to the pent-up feelings that had been brewing since her breakup with Tully. She was determined to regain control of the areas of her life that had slipped away from her.

❖

Tully leaned back in her chair and closed her eyes, though she still paid attention to the droning that had been going on for the last thirty minutes in the meeting she'd been dragged into.

"Why the hell did you take this case, Tully?" Dr. Nelson Kramer's attorney slammed his hand on the conference table, but the only one who jumped in surprise was the stenographer. "This is a little lower than your holier-than-thou caliber."

"I didn't take this case. My associates, Hank and Sheila here, did." She waved her hand to the two young associates sitting on either side of her. "I read the file and agreed that the case has merit."

"Bullshit." The attorney slammed the table again.

"Do that again and I'll make the same noise with your head when I slam it into the table," Tully said calmly. She opened the file, flipped through a few pages, and pulled something out. "My opening argument before the jury." She glanced up at the lawyer and his poor excuse for a client. "And yes, there'll be a trial and a jury. My opening argument will ask them to look at this." She threw the picture to the middle of the table. "As a matter of fact, I think that'll be my whole case."

Dr. Kramer briefly gazed at the picture, then sat back in his chair and stared at the ceiling.

Tully had purposely picked the most gruesome photo taken of his patient the night she'd arrived at the emergency room. The close-up of her chest showed that her left nipple was missing and a light bloody discharge seeped from where it had been right before the patient had run her hand over her breast in the shower. After her breast-augmentation surgery the month before, her nipple had simply rotted off because the bag had ruptured after the doctor had placed it in her chest.

"Mrs. Mailer complained to you about the clear discharge leaking from the nipple a week before this picture was taken, and you ignored it, as you did the multitude of symptoms she complained of following the surgery. From the look of that picture, you can't deny that she had a problem." Tully slid the picture back across the polished oak surface and placed it in the file. "Open and shut, if you ask me."

"Give me a minute to confer with my client."

Tully slammed her hand down on the table and laughed. "I see why you like doing that—real attention-getter."

When her hand hit the surface it finally had its desired effect, and both the doctor and lawyer jumped in their seats.

"We'll be right outside, so take your time."

"You bitch!" All heads turned toward the door as Jessica walked in and disrupted their meeting, with Roxanne right behind her trying to restrain her.

Before she could get out another word Tully grabbed her by the arm and practically carried her all the way to her office. "Do that again, and I will have your ass, you get me?"

"Get off that white horse of yours and stop fucking threatening me. I just ran into your slut with my children. She's living with you, isn't she?"

"If you're talking about Libby, might I suggest *you* stop referring to *her* as a slut. On the day I come home and she's sleeping with someone else in the bed we share together, you can call her a slut. But right now, there's only one person in this room who can claim that little stunt—you." Tully let her go as soon as the door was closed and kept walking until she reached her desk and her calendar. "You're going to get your wish, though."

"What wish?"

Tully was thankful there was a piece of furniture between them, because she'd never in her life wanted to choke the life out of someone as much as she did right now. Stabbing the air in Jessica's direction, she said, "We're going to court. I'm going to ask for full custody of the kids and supervised visits when you do get to see them."

"In your dreams, lover."

"I wouldn't touch you now if my life depended on it, so refrain from the cute nicknames. When we started this, I promised you it could be easy or it could be hard. Today you definitely picked the hard road." She flipped through the pages of the calendar, then pressed the intercom to Roxanne. "Get a court date for the last Friday of this month."

"What case?"

"Badeaux versus Badeaux."

"You got it, boss."

"You don't frighten me," Jessica said. "I lived with you too long not to be able to tell when you're bluffing."

"Jessica, listen to me. I lived with you a long time as well, and it still amazes me how much I don't know you. Whatever you choose for your life now is fine with me. I really could give a shit." She sat down, put her hand behind her neck, and squeezed. "If you want to live your life with this woman you've found, then I say go for it, but you're not going to take Bailey and Ralph down with you."

"Why do you think Kara's going to take me down?" Jessica's pose didn't change, as if she was waiting for an attack. "You moved on. Why not give me the same opportunity?"

"I'm telling you I don't care what you do with your life. You do what you want, with whomever you like, and you leave me the hell out of it." Her cell phone started ringing. It was Libby, so she answered the call.

"I know it's important," she said after Libby launched into a description of what had happened. "But let me get rid of something first."

Jessica gave her an indignant look.

Tully shrugged and said, "We're done, Jessica. I just want to start my life over and make Bailey and Ralph happy. One of my people will serve you with papers as soon as I draw them up."

"Why do you keep running away from me?" Jessica asked when Tully moved past her.

"Because you give such compelling reasons. Like I said," Tully opened the office door and waved out to the hall, "we're done."

❖

"I figure you can guess who we ran into today?" Libby asked, sitting in the car dealership. The kids were already sitting in the new Land Rover pressing buttons.

"Maybe I should start with I'm sorry. You shouldn't be stuck in the middle of this."

"I'm not." Libby balanced the phone while signing the papers the guy handed her. "I'm stuck on you, so I'm more front and center than I am in the middle. Hell, I've never been called a slut in front of total strangers before."

"What?"

"Calm down, baby. I'll tell you about it tonight, but I need to ask you a favor first."

As she listened to Libby's request, as well as what had happened and how the kids had reacted to it, Tully picked up her jacket and followed Roxanne to the elevator. Before the doors slid closed, Roxanne handed her a list of the meetings she'd rescheduled and the offer the guys in the conference room had tallied up. "This is a joke," Tully said.

"What's the multiplier?" Roxanne asked.

"Let's start with six and we'll go from there."

When Tully was in the elevator alone, she sighed and, before she hung up, agreed to take the afternoon off and meet Libby and the kids.

❖

Libby parked in front of Tully's office building and climbed into the passenger seat. As much as Bailey and Ralph had complained they wanted to go home, they seemed relieved to see Tully heading for the driver's side door.

"I want everyone to listen to me before you complain about anything that happened today." Tully merged into traffic and took a right, headed for uptown New Orleans. When they passed Napoleon as they were driving down St. Charles Avenue, she knew they all probably thought they were going home, until she turned down State Street.

The house she stopped in front of stood on the corner, with crape myrtles full of white blooms planted between the street and the sidewalk. Ten steps led to a front porch with eight large rocking chairs and a swing hanging on the end. Black shutters contrasted well with the house's white paint, and the six windows across the front opened from the floor so they could double as doors.

"When we went through all the changes during the last few months, I promised myself not to make any major decisions without you." She twisted in her seat so she could see the kids. "I got an offer on our house today."

"We haven't found a place to live," Ralph said.

"The lady who offered talked more about a trade, buddy, so we'd have a place to live, but only if you want."

"What kind of trade?" Bailey asked.

Tully noticed that her eyes were still a bit red from recent crying, and the sight made her want to break the car in by running over Jessica at the first opportunity for using the kids to try to make the situation worse.

"Our house for that one." She pointed to the house they were parked in front of and held up a key.

"This one looks bigger than ours," Bailey said, sounding doubtful. "What's the catch?"

"She gets our house and some money from a doctor I met with today. There's nothing wrong with the place. She just has bad memories of the shower."

"Did she see a snake or a ghost?" Ralph asked. Unlike Bailey, he looked thrilled with the prospect.

"Sorry, buddy. No slimies and no ghosts. She just had a little personal problem she'd like to forget." Tully held up the key to the front door. "I know you three have been house hunting for days now, but I think this might be a good place for us."

"I say we do it." Ralph grabbed the keys and pushed Bailey out the door.

"What kind of personal problem?" Libby asked when they were alone.

"Her nipple fell off in the shower."

Libby shuddered and raised her hand to her chest. "Honey, that's disgusting."

"I'm sure she wasn't thrilled with it either, but don't sweat it, darlin'. You've never going to have that problem." She leaned over the center console and kissed Libby on the cheek.

"I'm not, huh?"

"Nope. If you want, I'll personally take a shower with you every morning and keep my hands over your nipples the whole time to make sure nothing happens to them."

"We'll see about that, Counselor." Libby peered out the window. "Come on, Bailey's putting her finger in her mouth and gagging herself. We're being too mushy again."

"Just as long as you tell me how today really went later on."

"I will, but I think everything considered, they did great."

"Bailey and Ralph are important to me, baby, but so are you," Tully said. "Our talk is going to be about that too."

They joined the kids on the porch as Ralph unlocked the front door. Tully had always thought formal living rooms, like the first room they entered, were wasted space since they were seldom used, but this one opened to another large room through some pocket doors. In the back were a large kitchen and the master suite, both with an excellent view of the large yard. Bailey and Ralph headed up the stairs, talking about seeing what the rest of the bedrooms looked like, leaving Tully and Libby alone downstairs to explore.

From the way Libby was walking around seeming to study the space, Tully could tell she was already decorating it in her mind. When she had come alone to see it, the one picture she had in her head was waking up in this bedroom with Libby every morning.

"Can we get a new bed?" Libby asked.

"We can get whatever you like."

"No, I want to shop for this place, but with you, especially when it comes to the bed."

"Why?" Tully held out her hand to Libby. "With all the other stuff we have to worry about I'd be happy with whatever you pick."

"Because it's the one place in this house that will be strictly ours, and I want you to pick it out with me. Call it strange, but that's what I want."

"We'll go this weekend."

"You've made up your mind, haven't you?" Libby asked. They stepped out of the bedroom and headed to the kitchen, then stood together at the windows looking out at the yard.

"I came and checked it out a few days ago after my client and I discussed it as a possibility. It's not that I decided on this particular place, but you and the kids were right. We need a home that doesn't have a lot of baggage associated with it, someplace we can make ours, with our own memories." Tully rested her chin on Libby's head and enjoyed having her close.

"You three have been doing a great job trying to find something, so our being here isn't a reflection on the effort. To answer your question, I haven't made up my mind. That's why we're here. It's a family decision."

"You want us here too, right?" Bailey asked.

Because Tully and Libby had been facing the wall of windows, they hadn't seen Bailey and Ralph in the middle of the next room.

Tully raised her head at the question, but remained quiet when Libby squeezed her hands.

"Will you guys show me the upstairs?" Libby asked. "We started the process together, and this place shouldn't change how we go about our plan."

The room at the end of the hall on the right overlooked the blue-tiled pool, which was about the same size as theirs at home but ringed by more trees. There was no furniture left in the house, so after glancing out the window Libby sat on the floor and patted the space beside her.

"I think it's time we had a talk." When they joined her she reached for their hands. "Change is tough, I realize that, especially when it isn't your idea."

"It sucks," Ralph said. "You've been great, but sometimes I don't know for sure where we fit."

"I know, buddy." She called him by the same nickname Tully used without realizing it, and when she did he moved closer to her. "Before we make any other changes, even if they're your idea this time, I wanted to make sure we're clear about a few things."

"Getting together with somebody with kids is a bummer too, huh?" Bailey asked.

"I love your mom very much. That's the first thing I want you to know." For the moment she ignored Bailey's question. "In the years I've had her as a friend, I knew something about her even before I knew what she did for a living. From her stories of you guys I realized she was a parent to two wonderful people. Sometimes she felt lost as to how to reach you, but I could tell she loved you. You don't worry so much about people you don't love and care about."

"We know you love her, but what's it got to do with us?" Ralph asked.

"It has everything to do with you and Bailey. I wanted you to hear how I felt about your mother so you'll understand how you fit here. I want us to be a family. I'm not here to replace Jessica, and I'm not telling you all this so you'll like me. Blowing smoke so that it'll earn me points with your mom isn't what I'm about. After getting to know me I hope you realize that. You just need to remember that I love you, and I'm here for you."

"Thanks. We want you to be happy, but Ralph and I didn't want to get in the way of you and Mom getting together."

"You're stuck with me and your mom." Libby opened her arms to both of them, and that's how Tully found them a few minutes later, still in a tight embrace.

"So? What's the verdict?" she asked.

"Can I paint my room black?" Bailey asked.

"We'll start on that right after we get home from getting that forehead tattoo you've always wanted."

"I'd take that as a no, honey," Libby told Bailey.

"When do we move in?" Ralph asked.

"In a couple of weeks, once we finalize the paperwork. That gives you some time to go through your stuff and hide any girlie magazines you have stashed in your room. But we should be settled right after you start school."

Tully took a seat across from Libby, glad she was able to make them laugh. She felt certain there'd be more bad days like this one for them until she was legally done with Jessica, but as long as she and Libby kept them talking and made them a part of every major decision, Ralph and Bailey would be fine.

"Your mother came by the office after she ran into you today."

"She was, like, totally beezy," Bailey said, and Ralph nodded at the assessment.

After spending more time with them Tully knew this was teenage speak for Jessica being a total bitch.

"And she called Libby a slut. Sorry," Bailey said to Libby.

"I scheduled a court date for the end of this month, but I think we'll push it back a few more weeks."

"'Cause you're busy?" Ralph asked.

"When it comes to you two, I'll never be too busy again. I'm going to wait so we can put together a good case as to why you guys should live with Libby and me." Tully took their free hands so they were all connected. "That's what I want for us, but I want to make sure that's what you want too. This isn't about me trying to bend you into doing something you'd rather skip. But I want you to consider one thing. As much as I want us to start over, I want you to have a relationship with your mother."

"You're clueless sometimes, Mom, but I always felt like you were interested in what happened to us," Bailey said. "Like all you want is for us to make good decisions."

"I still want you to do that, Bailey Bean."

"The difference is, Mama wants to make the decisions for us."

"The court will make the ultimate decision unless your mother changes her mind and adheres to your wishes. No matter if we get everything we want, you'll have to have a relationship with her."

"I don't hate her, but I'm still upset by what she did. I don't know about Ralph, but I need more time."

"Me too, Mom," Ralph said.

"That's good enough for me, then."

"You're really happy about all these changes too?" Bailey asked, waving her hands around the room.

"You can tell us if you're not," Ralph added.

"Just as long as I have the three of you in my life, I'll be happy in a cardboard box on Canal Street."

"Tully's right," Libby said. "It could be any house, anywhere. Just as long as we're together it's going to be fine."

"Because if you weren't here, with all the trees out there, who'd skim out the pool?" Tully's joke broke the tension, and her children's laughter was one more brick on the repaired road between them.

Chapter Twenty-two

"How can you have nothing?" Tully sat back in her chair at home later that day, facing Pasco. Jo and Frank had come over with him to work on the Hebert case, and she could hear them helping Libby and the kids fix dinner. "We've been digging for how long now?"

"She, or someone in her life back then, did a good job of covering her tracks, but we'll keep at it. No matter how hard you try, you always leave a trail."

"We need something before we can move forward. Neil smells only speculation on our part, and he's moving for a quick trial. You know how those hospital administrators are, and Neil Davis always tries to protect his own."

"You're sure your attitude toward Kara isn't blinding you on this?" Pasco raised his hands. "I know it's probably not, but I had to ask."

"When I was doing my residency, the head of emergency services warned me that losing a patient was inevitable, no matter how hard I tried, because death was something you couldn't defeat. Outrun it at times, but never really beat it." Tully dug through the bottom desk drawer and found an old photograph that was yellowing around the edges. "I started his rotation hoping to prove him wrong, even if I was being naïve."

"Caring about people isn't naïve."

"The third week I was there, Billie LoGreco came into the ER two hours before my shift ended. The loser who dragged her in was kind enough to tell us her name and that she'd been popping pills and drinking peppermint schnapps all night and most of the morning. That was all he said about her."

"He just left her there?" Pasco frowned.

"She was probably some street kid he'd picked up, or at least that's what she looked like. I worked on her for about forty minutes before having to call it." She stopped when Libby walked in and took a sip from the drink Libby handed her, then scooted back so Libby could sit in her lap. "Billie LoGreco was my first loss." The autopsy photo showed a small, pale child of about sixteen.

Pasco shook his head. "Thanks for sharing that, but what's it got to do with Kara Nicolas and this case?"

"That doctor was right. Death *is* inevitable. Sometimes people invite it in, like Billie did by foolishly taking drugs and drinking in either a desperate attempt to fit in or because she trusted someone she shouldn't have. But other times, through no fault of our own, death is thrust upon us too early. If that's what happened to Evangeline Hebert, I want the person accountable for it to stand up and take responsibility."

Tully took the picture back from Pasco and carefully slid it back in the file folder. "Evangeline might have had only a few more days on this earth, or years, but whatever time she had was stolen from her and her parents."

Pasco stood and left the room, and as soon as they were alone Libby initiated a passionate kiss.

"If he doesn't find something she's going to walk, isn't she?" Libby asked when their lips parted.

"I can spin a good tale when I need to, but yeah, we need some reason for this to have happened. If not, the case'll never make it past the medical review board." Tully rested her head back and enjoyed the sight of Libby with a smudge of flour on her forehead. "How's it going in there?" she asked as she reached up to rub it off.

"Jo and Frank were catching me up on the office gossip, and Ralph's learning to peel things."

"There's office gossip?"

"The juiciest thing is that the boss is hooking up with the law-student intern."

"Do they think I'm a letch who went for the young and beautiful intern?"

The door to the office was open, so Libby chose not to tease her too much. "Actually, Jo wanted to know my secret, since I scooped you up so easily."

"I give up. What's your secret?"

"I told her," Libby bit down on Tully's earlobe, "my secret is," she traced Tully's lips with her tongue, "my coffee."

Bailey suddenly appeared in the doorway. "You guys ready to eat, or should I tell everybody you're in here making out?"

"It's called an appetizer, wise guy," Libby said. She stood up and offered Tully a hand. "I'm sure it's something you've thought about when your friend Chase calls over here about fifteen times an hour."

"Libby," Bailey said in a warning tone.

"Chase?" Tully asked. "Why haven't I heard anything about her new friend Chase?"

"Libby," Bailey repeated.

"Honey, she's a great kid, and she's taking Bailey to the movies tomorrow."

Tully crossed her arms over her chest. "Home by ten, right?"

"Home by ten thirty." Bailey mirrored her pose. When Tully didn't back down she added, "Mom, the movie ends at ten. You want me to look like some hella dork when I have to leave early?"

"This kid coming here to pick you up?"

"Libby volunteered to take us and pick us up, since she didn't think you'd have a problem with it."

Libby didn't remember saying the last part and figured the sweet smile Bailey shot her was a dare to contradict her.

"You do realize your mother is expecting to see you tomorrow," Tully said. "It's her Saturday, and after today you might want to reconsider turning her down."

"Again, why are you being so nice to her?" Bailey put her hands out to her sides, appearing equally confused and disgusted. "You don't have to anymore."

"Honey." Still holding hands, Tully and Libby moved closer and they each put an arm around Bailey. "I'm going to fight and keep fighting anyone who tries to take you away from me. I'm going to do that until the day you voluntarily walk out our front door and start a wonderful life on your own. Even then, I'll be there to make sure nothing or no one harms you."

"That goes for me too, Bailey," Libby said.

"I know that you and Ralph don't want to live with your mother, and I agree with you. And I'm going to court fully armed to make sure she doesn't gain custody. The most important weapon I have, though," she put her hand on Bailey's cheek, "is allowing Jessica access to you and Ralph."

"What do you mean?"

Libby answered, not thinking Tully would mind. "She means Jessica's representative can't argue that Tully has denied her liberal visitation. That, along with your and Ralph's wishes, should make it easy for all of us to get what we want."

"Can we make it early so I can go to the movie?" Bailey grinned.

"Sure," Tully said before kissing her forehead. "Why don't you call Chase and invite her over for dinner, just in case your mother brings up the subject tomorrow. That way I won't look like a hella dork when I don't know what I'm talking about."

"This isn't an excuse for you to give her a hard time, is it?"

"Libby, after all the fun Bailey's made of us, would I use this as an excuse for revenge?"

"Of course not." Libby let go of Tully and put her arms around Bailey. "Go on and call her, and I promise I'll make your mom behave."

"You're cool that it's a girl, right?" Bailey asked Tully over Libby's shoulder.

Libby moaned when Tully grabbed her, bent her back, and delivered a long, hot kiss.

"I'm cursing the gods as we speak," Tully teased when she let Libby up.

❖

Libby's jambalaya didn't taste quite like Alma's, but she had come really close. She stood back with Tully as everyone took a turn filling their plate from the large pot she'd made.

They were both watching the interaction between Bailey and Chase, and Libby couldn't help but echo the large smile splitting Tully's face. Bailey had come a long way from the kid she'd met in the coffee shop months before. The surly young woman was laughing and actually flirting with the tall redhead who had rushed over after her call.

"You ready for this?" Libby asked Tully.

"Hormones run amok, you mean?"

She turned so that she was facing Tully, moving closer when Tully's gray eyes focused on her. "Something like that, yes."

"I'm having trouble keeping my own hormones in check when you're this close to me, looking at me like you want to chew my clothes off, so I can't blame her for enjoying this kid's company." Tully pressed her closer and whispered in her ear. "Of course, if Chase hurts her or tries to remove any article of Bailey's clothing, the new backyard is big enough that they'll never find her."

"Spoken like a true mom."

"Will you guys give it a rest," Bailey said.

"I didn't think you'd notice after all the—"

"Mom, just grab a plate and eat," Bailey said, obviously panicked.

They headed outside to the table by the pool, Tully making a mental note to put a dining table on their shopping list. When the kids joined them, they set aside business for the moment and just enjoyed the lively conversation. From the sound of it, Ralph had teased his sister so much he was going to have to sleep with one eye open.

"You guys weren't at school long enough last year to appreciate how good this is," Chase said to Ralph and Bailey. She'd been filling them in on some of the kids at school, while Libby had been telling Jo and Frank about the new house. "Jake Porter's in rehab."

"Is that the big kid who thought he was hot stuff?" Ralph asked.

"One and the same," Chase confirmed for him while she never took her eyes off Bailey.

"What was he into?" Bailey asked.

"He totally freaked on crank."

"This kid a friend of yours?" Tully asked.

"Jake doesn't need friends, Ms. Badeaux. He's a legend-in-his-own-mind kind of dude."

By the way Chase tripped over some of her words, Libby thought Tully was probably making her nervous, but having Bailey's hand on her thigh evidently gave her the confidence to go on. "I just heard about it today from a friend. You don't have to worry about me chillin' with Bailey—I'm not into the drug scene."

"You wouldn't be here if you were."

"Mom," Bailey dragged out the word. "Please, you promised."

"I just mean you've got good judgment about people. You telling me you don't?"

Libby pinched Tully's side to make her stop laughing at Bailey's blush.

"You play any sports, Chase?" Tully asked, changing the topic.

"Softball and soccer, ma'am."

"Shit," Tully whispered in obvious disgust before standing up and heading inside.

"She have an aversion to balls or something?" Chase asked.

"Weird question when asked about Mom, but no," said Bailey, and everyone but Chase laughed. "That's Mom's usual reaction to thinking of something she should've figured out weeks ago." She gently patted Chase's leg.

"Thanks for sharing with all of us non-Tully experts, Bailey," Libby said as she stood to follow Tully inside.

When Libby walked in, Tully was pacing behind her desk, twisting the phone cord into a mess. Libby just leaned against the doorway of the study and watched. While she loved the softer side of Tully, who was a good friend, lover, and parent, she enjoyed this straight-edged side that made her such a successful attorney.

"If we go now, Calvin, no one's going to find out. Your office runs those queries at all hours," Tully said, before reversing and heading in the opposite direction. "Okay, I promise I won't forget, so call me when you get there."

"Problems?"

"Not if I can deliver clubhouse tickets at LSU's opener later this year." She seemed distracted as she flipped through a stack of papers on her desk.

"Not what I meant, Counselor. Who was that on the phone?"

The phone rang and Tully mouthed "I'm sorry" before she picked up the receiver. "Punch in a travel query for the entire year of 1993." She flipped the pages to the very front and spelled out Kara Nicolas's name. "If you don't find anything from our research, go back and forward a year, but you should find it in 1993."

Pasco joined them, still taking bites from the plate he'd brought with him.

"Who's Calvin?" Libby asked.

"A college friend of Tully's who's a customs agent now," Pasco said after rinsing his jambalaya down with a big swig of beer. "His kid brother was one of the few criminal cases she ever took on."

"What'd he do?"

Pasco moved closer to her and continued in a low tone. "Went for a joyride with a friend who ended up robbing a convenience store and shooting the store clerk. The guy who did the shooting fingered Calvin's brother when they got caught."

"Did he kill the clerk?" Libby asked.

"He lived, but it took him a while to heal. Calvin drove straight to Tully's office after seeing his kid brother in central lockup." He put his plate down and blew out a long breath. "I don't know how he talked her into it, but it was one of her best closing arguments. After that, Calvin's brother went on to college and did well."

"Did he know what the guy was going to do the night they went for a ride?"

"If he did, the only person he told was his attorney."

When she glanced at Tully, Pasco asked, "Does that bother you?"

"Even the guilty deserve a defense—that's what they teach us in law school."

"You sound like you don't agree with that philosophy."

"I'm not supposed to question the difference between right and wrong. I'm there to represent my client." Libby patted his hand and briefly made eye contact. "That's what Tully has stressed in our study sessions together, and that's probably why she's so picky about what cases she takes."

"And when they're not of her choosing?"

"I think they're *all* of her choosing. You said so yourself. It was one of her best closing arguments. The kid didn't know what he was getting into, and if he did, his attorney was the first person he lied to."

"Good point." He stopped talking when Tully slammed the phone down. "What's up, boss?"

Tully put her finger up as she sat down and began an Internet search. "Hacienda del Lago," she said, pointing at the screen once she found what she was looking for. "I'm willing to bet that's where our bird flew off to when she disappeared."

"She went to a spa?" Libby asked. "At least that's what it sounds like."

"It's a treatment center for drug addiction. Dr. Nicolas landed at Guadalajara International Airport two days after you lost her trail. She didn't return to the States for six months and then started back at school for the fall semester."

"So why are you so sure that she was at this Hacienda place?" Libby asked.

"Twenty minutes from the airport and on a lake where you're sequestered as well as secluded—call it a hunch. A vacation spot this is not." She checked travel information next. "What Chase just said made a few things click in my head. Something's off about Kara Nicolas, and her behavior as well as some of her physical oddities are characteristic of an addiction. Let's keep an eye on that possibility."

"That's a leap, honey." Libby folded her arms over her chest. "Granted, Kara sounds paranoid, but that doesn't mean she's hooked on something."

"If that was all, Pasco would still be chasing down those missing months, but add to that the hyperalertness, sweating, chapped lips, and rapid speech pattern, and I'd guess she's not only hooked, but hooked on crystal meth." She steepled her fingers together and sat back in her chair. "I should've thought of it sooner, but because of her profession, I didn't consider the possibility."

"Wow." Libby dropped her arms to her sides. "A surgeon hooked on drugs? Of course, with all that access—"

"It would explain what happened to Evangeline, wouldn't it?" Tully picked up the pen she'd been using to take notes, and just as quickly it snapped in her hand. "And this is what Jessica wants to expose my kids to."

"Let's verify your theory before you make any rash decisions," Libby said.

"Don't worry. I'm going to be incredibly thorough, but if I'm right, I'm going to bury Nicolas and plant Neil Davis alongside her. If he knew and is trying to cover for the hospital in his capacity as administrator, I'll have his ass."

❖

Taking Libby's advice to go slow, Tully scheduled one last meeting with Neil Davis and the hospital's counsel, Victor Williams. With the

Heberts' permission to negotiate on their behalf, she set out to get as much of what they wanted as she could.

"Come to our senses, have we?" Victor asked. "Neil's original offer was more than generous, and we're still willing to stand by it."

"On behalf of my clients, we decline that offer. This is what we want for starters: reimburse their funeral expenses, give them a reasonable settlement for the loss of their daughter, and waive all the expenses still pending from Evangeline's treatment." Tully lifted out the first page in the file that listed everything she'd just mentioned.

"This amount seems reasonable," Neil said as he read over the document. "What's the catch?"

"The apology they want from Kara Nicolas and an explanation as to what happened to their daughter. A detailed explanation backed up by at least two other people who were in that operating room."

Neil tossed the page back to her and stood up. "The kid was sick, and sick kids don't do well in surgery sometimes. That's the best and simplest explanation I can give them. It's tragic, but it isn't liable."

"I don't agree with their wishes either, Neil, so calm down and sit."

Tully never raised her voice, but Neil dropped back into his chair. "Finally you're being reasonable."

She shook her head and smiled. "I think the settlement they're asking for is way too low, but that's their prerogative. But this is the last time I'm coming here and trying to work this out among ourselves."

"Don't try to bullshit a bullshitter, Tully. You're bluffing because there's nothing to this case. Neil's right. It was a tragic accident, but in reality it brought the little girl's death a couple of weeks sooner than had nature taken its course." Victor smiled and transparently tried to sound as compassionate as he could muster. "If you don't take this offer," he showed her his own sheet, "then I'll have no choice but to fast-track this in court."

"Go ahead." Tully ripped the page he'd handed her in half and placed it on the conference table. "Like you said, I've got nothing, and by bringing this case to trial soon, you can only vindicate your side that much quicker." She pushed her chair out and stood up, taking her time to button her jacket and collect her files. "Just so we're clear, you're turning down our offer, right?"

"If that's all you have, Tully, you're wasting our time," Neil said.

"See you in court, Victor."

Her laugh as she headed to the door made Victor twitch in his chair. It wasn't the usual merriment of a woman who had nothing.

"Neil, now's the time to tell me what's going on with her." Victor quickly dragged Neil's chair closer and glared at him. "God knows I'd love to wipe that condescending smirk off her face, but I can't go into court and have her blindside us with something you've kept from me and the hospital board. I'll be the first one to make them sign a waiver of liability if this thing goes wrong, because I'm pinning it on you and whatever you withhold from me."

He knew that legally he couldn't do this, but hoped he'd rattled Neil enough to bluff him. Ignorance wasn't a defense.

"There's nothing to talk about, so clear this as soon as you get a court date. Tully's got her ass in a twist because Kara's screwing Jessica, nothing more." Without another word Neil got up and walked out.

❖

"Mom, you can't go and leave us here," Bailey said in the biggest whine she'd used in forever. "We're in this with you and we can help." She stomped for emphasis.

"Bailey, school's already started, and your mother already gives me enough grief about any day I let you stay home. If I could've gone sooner I swear I would've, but sometimes the world doesn't stop on a dime just because I want it to. I had court, and unfortunately some of the things couldn't be continued. I'll just be gone two days, tops. Remember that it's a business trip, not a vacation."

"We'd only miss Thursday and Friday. Big deal." Bailey was arguing with the top of Tully's head, since her mother was busy searching through some of the boxes in her office for a file. They'd started the packing process so they'd be ready to move into the new house the first of September.

"It's not like I'm sending you to your mother's. Libby's staying with you guys until I get back." Obviously having found what she was looking for, Tully faced Bailey. "You can help her plan our commitment ceremony."

Bailey had opened her mouth to give her next reason for going with Tully when Libby placed her hand over it. "The phone is for you," she said softly in her ear.

"We're not finished yet," Bailey said to Tully.

"Excuse us a minute, honey, but don't go anywhere." Libby pointed at Tully to keep her from wandering off.

After a quick conversation with Bailey in the hall, she returned and closed the door before sitting on Tully's lap. "I want you to take us all with you, no matter how much school the kids miss."

"Baby, you can't give in to her on every little thing," Tully said about Bailey.

"This isn't about Bailey or Ralph. Well, it is, but it's mostly about me."

"Something wrong?"

"Nothing being with you all the time won't cure." She tried to sound teasing, but when Tully put her fingers under her chin and made her look up, Libby knew she'd failed.

"Just tell me, darlin'."

"There's a storm in the Atlantic and it scares me. Bad weather always makes me remember my parents and how I lost them. If you go and we stay behind and something happens to you, I don't know how I'd handle it."

Tully drew her closer and rested her cheek on the top of Libby's head. "It's headed for Florida and I'm going in the opposite direction, and I saw the news this morning. It's just a small thing that will probably blow apart before it makes it across the state, if in fact it hits Florida at all. You know how unpredictable these things are. They haven't even named it yet, so it might fizzle out before it turns into a hurricane."

"I'd just feel better if you took us with you, even if it's a stupid request."

Without displacing Libby, Tully leaned back, grabbed the phone, and punched in the number to her travel agent. "Three more tickets. Just have them delivered to the office in the morning."

"Thank you," Libby said before kissing Tully in a way that conveyed how she felt and what kind of future they'd have together.

"Nothing to thank me for, and nothing that you feel so strongly about is stupid to me. Try to remember that."

❖

"Neil called me in today," Kara said. She turned her head so that Jessica could hear her. They had left the hospital early and spent the afternoon in bed. Kara was enjoying having Jessica lying on her back. "He said your ex came in to see him and Victor again."

"For what?"

"Something about it being his last chance to take some chump-ass offer. He said it was a really low number, so he figured she was up to something."

"Tully's always up to something. You just have to figure out what it is so you can turn it around on her and beat her at her own game. If she bid a settlement low, then she's definitely up to something." Jessica kissed her shoulder. "Why did he turn her down?"

"Part of the deal was handing my head over on a plate to make those hicks happy." Kara laughed, knowing she didn't have anything to worry about. "Neil just couldn't figure out why she didn't flinch when Victor talked about going to court as soon as possible so we can all show our cards."

"She wants to fast-track this with what she has?" The way Jessica posed the question sounded like she didn't really expect an answer. "You told Victor everything, didn't you?"

"Not this fucking shit again." Kara pushed Jessica off her, disgusted.

"Listen to me, Kara. I lived with Tully a long time, and while she's cool under all kinds of pressure, going to court just for kicks isn't in her. If she didn't try to talk Victor into slowing things down, then she has something."

Jessica sat up and took a deep breath, clearly not trying to appease Kara for a change. "How much money did she want in the settlement? Did Neil tell you that?"

"Five thousand. It was what it cost to bury the kid." Kara stopped talking and watched Jessica massage her forehead as if trying to erase any unpleasant thoughts from her head.

"She's willing to let the hospital off the hook for five thousand dollars? Doesn't that seem odd to you?"

"You said so yourself, she's an idiot. How do I know why she asked for so little?"

Jessica grabbed Kara's arm. "The night before I left her to come here, Tully was celebrating her latest win. In that case the patient survived but lost a leg, I believe. She's won so many cases like this that

I stopped listening to the details a long time ago. Between the doctor and the hospital, the guy ended up collecting close to two million dollars."

"See, that's what's wrong with health care today. Fucking vultures like the bitch you lived with are sucking us all dry."

Jessica squeezed Kara's bicep. "Focus, honey. It was a leg, and she raked them over the coals she lit, fanned, and got red-hot. In this case I would've expected her to come out with something so outlandish that two million would've sounded like small change. Five thousand tells me something is very wrong."

"If I had any secrets, I buried them a long time ago on the shores of a lake no one here has ever heard of, so stop worrying."

"It's not the secrets from your past that'll sink you, honey. She'll just use anything like that to start the bleeding before she throws you into the tank and releases the gators. It's the secrets you have now that Tully will use to gut you."

"Are you going to share anything with her?" Kara didn't move away as her anger started to take over. She slitted her eyes and came close to laughing at how quickly Jessica let go of her.

"I'm telling you this not because I admire Tully, but because I want to help you."

"If you want to help me, then don't mention her name to me again."

Chapter Twenty-three

"When's your flight?" Pasco asked.

"Tomorrow at six a.m. We should be in Guadalajara in plenty of time to drive down to the clinic and gather some information." Tully yawned and stretched.

They had been trying to find their way back into the routine of having Bailey and Ralph in school again. With Libby still in the pool house but attending the same campus as the kids, she was in their kitchen every morning fixing breakfast so they could all ride together.

"I figure by Friday afternoon we should have discovered plenty, so we can head back into town."

"I'm not up on the privacy laws in Mexico, but hopefully they'll be a tad bit more relaxed than they are here. Just to catch you up on the other thing you wanted, in my latest report I added some details on our twenty-four-hour surveillance. So far, nothing."

"You can say it again, if you want."

"That you could be wrong?" Pasco asked. "You could, but in this case I'm praying a novena that you're not. I want to see this bitch go down more than anyone. I'll get in touch if I find anything."

"Thanks for all the time you're putting into this one, pal."

"My youngest needed braces, so it was a godsend," Pasco teased. He stepped out, waving to Roxanne as he left.

Roxanne, in her ever-efficient manner, laid a few folders on Tully's desk. "The doctor settled in the case where our client lost her nipple and had to have all that leftover goo scraped off her chest. He wasn't happy about the check he had to write, but I'm sure she wasn't real happy with the fact her nipple fell off in the shower. Jo took care of the house papers for you, so when you get back we can confirm with the movers."

"I'm sure the esteemed doctor would cringe at your 'goo' word, but thanks. And thanks too for setting up the movers. Since that's not in your job description, I appreciate you lining up all this stuff for me."

Roxanne punched Tully's shoulder softly. "You just seem so happy lately, and I'm enjoying it. Call me selfish for wanting to keep you that way."

"Every so often I have to pinch myself to make sure I'm not conjuring up Libby and my new relationship with the kids. It hasn't been that long, but so much has changed." Tully leaned back and sighed as she turned her eyes to Roxanne. "I don't consider myself a superstitious person, but lately I keep waiting for something to go wrong."

"She loves you, Tully, so unless you lose your mind, nothing bad is going to happen."

She took Roxanne's hand for a second and squeezed her fingers. "From your lips to God's ear, as my mother always says."

The day had gone by quicker than they had anticipated, and Tully had to put in a long night with the associates to make sure all their other cases were on track and covered. Libby and the kids let her sleep during the flight the next morning, shaking her awake when the wheels of the plane hit the tarmac in Guadalajara.

❖

After clearing customs, Tully watched the crowd around the luggage-retrieval area as the kids scanned the conveyer belt for their luggage. Most everyone on the plane with them were locals returning home from a visit in the States, she imagined, but now in the airport some other sights captured her attention.

Two couples stood out from the rest, and without much effort she started to formulate a plan. A middle-aged woman and a surly-looking teenager with his hands buried so deep in his pockets that Tully thought he might pull his pants to his ankles stood off from the crowd. Not far from them was an older gentleman with his hand wrapped firmly around the bicep of the woman standing next to him, and she was doing her best to pry his fingers open.

When a group of men walked through the main entrance wearing white pants and navy blue golf shirts with a logo stitched on the right breast, Tully surmised where they were headed. The Hacienda del Lago clearly sent guys big enough so the reluctantly sober wouldn't have a chance to relapse before their true sobriety began.

"Something wrong?" Libby asked.

"I'm thinking of a way into where we need to be." She discreetly pointed to the boy and woman, who were now arguing loudly with their companions and fighting the workers by kicking, biting, and throwing a punch whenever they could get their arms loose. "Call me a betting woman, but I'm willing to wager those two are the newest visitors to Lake Ajijic."

Ralph and Bailey joined them, pushing a cart with all their luggage on it. "Are you planning on sightseeing in the airport while we do all the work?" Bailey asked.

"That's why we brought you, so don't complain." Tully guided them out of the terminal and into a cab. Once they were in their hotel suite, she sat Libby down to ask a favor.

"You want me to do what?"

"I want you to delve deep and channel a sarcastic and moody kid. If you could appear like you're in a drug-induced haze, that would be good too."

"I'm beginning to think *you're* on something," Libby said as she put her feet up on the sofa and laughed.

"That isn't going to work, you know," Bailey said as she stepped in from the balcony.

"Why not?"

"Libby's way younger than you are, but no way are they going to believe she's your daughter. You two have a vibe going, and it doesn't scream mother-and-daughter affection. If you looked at me the way you do Libby, trust me, you'd be checking me in here for real. You can try getting lucky with this scam, but I'm telling you the people in charge over there are going to know you're bogus right off. If you want authentic, you need to take me."

"No way." Tully put her hand up and stopped any other plans Bailey had. "I'm not putting you in that kind of situation."

"But you're willing to put Libby in that kind of situation?"

"I think she knows I can handle it," Libby said.

"So can I, and I want to help. What's the worst that can happen—they throw us out for impersonating a crankhead?"

"Bailey Bean, this is important, and I want you to think about what you're asking. If you decide you can't do it, just tell me and I'll go with my original plan and take Libby with me. We shouldn't be long, and you guys can relax by the pool."

"Just answer one question for me," Bailey said, shaking her head.

"Shoot, kid."

"Do you think Kara's still on drugs? Or was it something she kicked here?"

"I'm going to answer your question, so don't start arguing just yet," Tully said holding up a finger. "But can I ask why you want to know?"

"It's not because I feel sorry for her and think you're going to bring her down for what happened, if that's what you're worried about." The way Bailey dragged her hand through her hair was a sure sign she was frustrated. "I'm just having a hard time wrapping my head around the idea that Mama is with someone who would've cut some kid open while she was high. It doesn't fit, you know?"

"I don't know if Kara's still on anything, honey."

"Then why are we here?"

Tully leaned forward and placed her elbows on her knees, but maintained eye contact. "I'm guessing that Kara Nicolas went through this program when she was in college."

"I get that, Mom."

"To me, if she was, that tells me something about the kind of person she is, or at least what she's capable of. I know as well as the next person that addiction is an illness, not a choice, but what happened to the little girl in the picture her parents showed me when they came to me for answers deserves an answer. A lot of people think I'm doing this because of what happened between me and your mother." She reached out, but before she could put her hand on Bailey's leg, Bailey grabbed her hand and held it between hers.

"I know it might have something to do with that, but that's not why you're doing it."

"Why, then?" Tully asked.

"Because you're so good it's sickening sometimes. Even if the first time you'd heard of this woman was when the Heberts came in, we'd still be here."

Tully moved from her chair to sit next to Bailey. "Something happened, and I think we'll start to find the answer here. Once we do, I can add that to what we already know, and we can move forward to the trial the hospital is dying to have."

"Count me in, then. If you want bitchy, I can do bitchy."

"It's good for us, then, that that Bailey doesn't live here anymore," Tully teased.

❖

The grandmotherly woman doing their intake information acted as if Bailey wasn't rapping her knuckles against the glass door in her office rather loudly, stopping only a couple of times to try the lock. "And how long has Pearl had a dependency problem?" she asked Tully in a thick Spanish accent.

"We started seeing changes about seven months ago, but I had hoped she'd show improvement after we placed her in the program near our home back in Texas," Tully said before pivoting in her seat and looking back at Bailey. "Pearl, could you come over here and sit down. This is for your own good."

"Kiss my ass," Bailey said without turning around. She sounded sincere.

"It's okay, Ms. White. Paying attention and participation aren't necessary just yet."

"Thank you. It's just been hard on the whole family, but we've heard you can just do wonders in getting kids back on track."

The woman stopped writing and glanced up at her. "So you were recommended?"

"The Nicolas family said you worked with their daughter Kara, and she went on to become a doctor. We just want the same opportunity for Pearl."

"Kara Nicolas…yes, she was one of the first patients I worked with here." Her voice faded away as she punched some more information about Bailey into the computer. She scanned the screen before taking her glasses off and turning her attention to Tully, as if she didn't realize what she'd just said. "It was the beginning of the ecstasy craze, and we caught her just in time. Kids don't always realize the long-term effects of some of these drugs." Grabbing her clipboard, she stood and waved to the door. "Would you like a tour?"

Tully's cell phone rang as she was about to answer. "I'm so sorry." She flipped the phone open as she stood, trying to appear ready to join the tour. "I have to get this, since my son is still back at the hotel." Tully pinched the skin on her forehead between her fingers. "I see. Try and make him comfortable and I'll be there in thirty minutes."

"Something I can help with?" the woman asked.

"I'm sure it's from drinking the local water, but my son's taken ill and I have to go back and check on him." Tully copied what the man at the airport had been doing and grabbed Bailey by the bicep.

"You could leave Pearl with us so we can get started."

"I'd like to take the tour first just to ease my mind about leaving her here. You understand, of course."

"I'll call you later on this afternoon at the hotel, then."

"Please do, and I have a good feeling about this," Tully said as she shook hands with the woman without letting go of Bailey.

"Pearl? That's the best you could come up with?" Bailey asked when they were driving out the gates.

"I thought it was a great name, and you never even asked what your middle name is."

Bailey turned in her seat, obviously so she could more effectively glare at her. "I'm almost afraid to ask."

"Well, Pearl Lee, you should be." Tully couldn't help but start laughing.

"You wrote down Pearl Lee White, and that woman didn't figure out we were totally bogus?"

"I'm sure she figures that's why you're taking drugs."

They both laughed.

Tully kept to the speed limit as they drove back, making a call to Libby. "I promise to take all three of you on a vacation in Mexico during your first school break, but we need to head back as soon as we can get a flight."

"Pasco called while you were over there, so I already booked it."

"We're almost back, so save it." Tully hung up and handed Bailey the phone. "Sorry this was so short, but I'm glad you came. I don't think me going in there alone and asking about Kara would have had the same result."

"Just remember you promised a vacation."

"I'm sure after the next couple of weeks and the work we have to do on this case, we could all use one. Oh, by the way, Libby told me that Hurricane Katrina just made landfall in Florida."

CHAPTER TWENTY-FOUR

"Judging from the amount of product Kara's buying, she's got a pretty strong habit," Pasco said. He had been waiting for them at the airport on Friday afternoon to give her a complete report and them a ride home.

"What in the hell is going on?" Tully asked as she looked around the terminal, still packed with people despite the late hour.

"Florida slowed the storm down, but it's in the Gulf, and a few of the models have it coming our way. I guess these folks want to get home just in case the majority of forecasters are wrong. It's a shame that it's cutting their vacations short, but most of the weather guys have the storm heading to the panhandle of Florida in the next couple of days. We all know how wrong they can be, though."

"Honey, should we stop for some stuff?" Libby asked.

"If it's for storm supplies, you're about to find out you're marrying the most anal person alive when it comes to preparation," Ralph said. "Mom's got enough water, food, and gas to start her own city, believe me."

"Pop-Tarts don't count, buddy," Libby said.

"Nah, it's more like canned ravioli."

Libby grimaced. "Okay, a trip to the grocery before we go home, and we'll be set."

"We do have a lot of stuff," Tully said as she picked up their bags.

"Honey, if the electricity goes out we're not eating pasta out of a can for days on end. I'm sure Pasco has to get a few things. If not, he can drop us off at the house and I'll go."

"Let's go grocery shopping, boss," Pasco said, grabbing half of the luggage from her.

After Pasco had given Tully a complete update, he went for other supplies with Libby and the kids, but Tully stayed home and prepared her case alone. She wanted to call in her associates but didn't want to take them away from their families for the weekend as the paranoia about the upcoming storm began to grow.

After a few hours, with Libby and the kids safely home, she checked the generator and supply of gasoline. Ralph had joked about how anal she was, but having been raised by a couple who made their living on the water, she had taken their lessons on survival to heart. And after she'd had kids, her desire to prepare for every situation had only grown, even as Jessica's mocking laughter at her axe, life jackets, and box of supplies in the attic rang in her ears.

Libby spent time in the kitchen making a huge meal while Tully went over her class assignments with her. Having a live-in tutor was cutting down Libby's study time and helping her keep her mind off the weather. When they finished eating and putting away the leftovers, Libby followed Tully upstairs to the guest room.

They never undressed, but lay down together and enjoyed the utter silence outside the window. After seeing how freaked Libby was, Tully didn't want to leave her alone.

"We'll be okay, right?" Libby asked.

"I'll do everything in my power to make sure that we are."

❖

The scenario that the forecasters had predicted changed on Saturday. The models had the storm coming ashore anywhere from the Mississippi line to Florida, but with each passing hour the lines drifted farther west.

As Bailey, Libby, and Ralph sat in the house watching the Weather Channel, Tully stepped outside and studied the sky. She couldn't see a single cloud, and the blue expanse appeared as if someone had painted it. The only uncomfortable thing was the temperature. The heat was stifling, seeming to suck the oxygen out of the air.

"Honey, don't you want to come in here and take a look at this?" Libby asked from the back door.

Tully held up her hand to request a few more minutes as she took out her phone. "Rox, call the staff together and have them meet me at the office in thirty minutes. I don't care what they're doing, tell them to be there."

"What's wrong?" Libby asked when Tully snapped the phone closed.

"What did your father do for a living?"

Libby appeared confused. "He was a train operator for big freight. Why do you ask?"

"My dad and a lot of generations before him were fishermen."

Libby could feel the sweat dripping down her back, the drops losing their battle at the waistband of her shorts. "You okay? I know what your dad does, but what does that have to do with anything?"

"It's just that I often wonder how many people died years ago when things like this happened and they ignored the more-than-obvious signs. If you didn't live on the water and know what to look for, something like Katrina could catch you unawares and with little time to get out of the way."

"You're starting to scare me," Libby said as she put her hand on the side of Tully's face and tried to get her to focus. "What are you talking about?"

"Two hundred years ago, if we'd been standing here looking up at this sky, would you have guessed a killer was churning through the Gulf?" She waved her hand toward the south. "Without the radar images and the television coverage, how would we have known?"

"I guess we wouldn't have, so it's a good thing we're not living two hundred years ago."

"But even though this is just like so many other summer days, there would've been a sign if you were looking, even without the benefit of the Weather Channel. Tell me what you see."

Libby turned in a slow circle and did as Tully asked. She mentioned all the things that Tully had noticed when she first walked out there, like the lack of clouds. She guessed Tully would eventually let her in on why she was doing it.

"Now tell me what you don't see," Tully said.

Libby made the same slow circle, but nothing was jumping out at her. Everything in the yard and beyond looked the same. "Nothing's missing."

"I don't see or hear one bird out here. It's the middle of the day, without a lick of wind or a cloud, but don't you find it strange there isn't a bird anywhere around?"

Tully was right. The house was situated in an older, established neighborhood with plenty of big shade trees that were a haven for birds. Now that Tully had pointed it out, the silence of nature was so overwhelming that it became instantly conspicuous to Libby.

"What does that mean, exactly?"

"Mom, the news just said Katrina became a category three," Bailey said from the back door.

"Honey, talk to me."

Libby grabbed two fistfuls of Tully's T-shirt.

Tully could tell Libby was truly scared from the way she was shivering when she wrapped her arms around her.

"I'm not going to lie to you. This isn't good. I really thought this thing would blow apart after crossing Florida, but the hot water in the Gulf is fueling it, and I don't see it slowing down any. If the news is right, a jump from a tropical storm to a cat three in a day doesn't bode well for us."

"But the forecasters still have it going toward the Alabama/Mississippi border."

Tully sighed and nodded. "That they do, but in this case I'm going with what I've been taught. And from what Gaston Badeaux beat into my head, I don't think this is going to turn out well."

"We're leaving, right?"

Tully held Libby tightly against her chest. "You have to calm down and know that I'm not going to let anything happen to you or the kids. I may take chances every day at work to get the best outcome I can, but I'll never gamble with your or the kids' safety." She put her fingers under Libby's chin so she would look up. "I need you to start packing the essentials and get organized."

"Where are you going?"

"I have to go pack the files at the office, back up the servers, and make copies of those tapes to take with us. We have a responsibility to our clients. That shouldn't take more than an hour. Then I want my people to get out with their families, and when I get back we'll leave." She framed Libby's face with her hands and kissed her. "You're not alone anymore, sweetheart."

"I know I'm acting insane, but stuff like this really scares me."

Tully kissed her again. "Understandable, but go ahead and get the kids ready. Once people realize and accept what's coming, the traffic is going to get crazy."

Because Tully had taken Libby's small car, the SUV was packed and ready when she returned from the office. Before they left, she opened her home-office safe and took out all the available cash she had on hand and the sidearm her father had given her years before. As the hysteria rose, so did the feeling that all hell was about to break loose within the part of society that never followed the rules anyway.

Tully sat them in the kitchen for a serious talk before they left. "Guys, I've been listening to the news and they've started contraflow on the interstate, so everything is heading out of here. From the sound of this, we could come back to a very different city, so I want you to walk through the house one last time and take anything, within reason, that's important to you."

From what Tully could see going and coming from the office, the public was starting to panic. Every market and pharmacy had lines out the door of people trying to buy last-minute supplies, and others were trying to find a way out of New Orleans.

"Just don't take too long, okay?"

They waved to their neighbors as they backed out of the driveway, but instead of heading toward the interstate, Tully turned in the opposite direction. She suspected that her passengers knew exactly where they were going, but none of them said anything. Despite what had happened between them, Tully still felt some obligation to Jessica.

❖

"I won't be long," Tully said as they stopped in front of the hospital.

"Take all the time you need," Libby said.

Ralph piped up from the backseat. "She really amazes me sometimes."

"Yeah, most people would've let Mama rot," Bailey agreed.

"If you ever wonder why I love her," Libby pointed to Tully as she walked through the front doors, "this is why. Her relationship with your mother might be over and beyond salvation, but she's still your mother, and that's why Tully's here. It takes someone special to put her personal feelings aside."

Luckily, Jessica was standing in the lobby directing some of the personnel who had been called into work. Since the nonessential surgeries had been called off, Kara wasn't too far away, leaning against the wall with a sullen look on her face.

"What in the hell do you want now?" Kara walked toward Tully with her finger up, her wrist captured in a vise grip before she touched Tully's chest.

"I'm not here to see you." Tully squeezed hard before letting go and continuing on to Jessica. "The kids are outside, and if you want, you can come with us. Neil should understand you want to be with your family."

"I can't leave, you know that, but I would like to know where you're taking the kids."

"I'm going to get on the road and start driving until I find a place that's well out of the path of this thing. Don't worry. I'll call you as soon as we get settled."

Tully lifted her hand, but before she could put it on Jessica's shoulder, Kara's fist connected with the side of her face.

"What in the hell did you do that for?" a police officer standing close to them asked. "You all right?"

"I'm fine, Gus," Tully said, reading his name tag, "and your memory isn't going to go bad on me, is it?"

"I work for the city, not the hospital, so look me up when the time is right. My memory will be just fine. I'd offer to bring her in, but in this mess I think that's going to be impossible."

"Don't worry about it, Officer." She accepted a tissue from Jessica for the blood and pressed it to her cheek. "Last chance, Jessica."

"Stay here, Kara. I'll be right back," Jessica said.

"You walk out and you'd better keep on walking."

For once, Jessica let go of the fear of losing her new lover and let some of her ire show. "I'm going to talk to my children, so calm down and go do something useful." Once they were outside she stopped and turned to Tully. "I'm sorry for what happened. It was uncalled for. But please, no more lectures, okay?"

"I'm here because of the kids and the kind of example I want to set for them. What you do with your life is your concern now. I just hope you don't allow her to do this to you just to keep her around. No one's worth that, Jessica." Taking away the tissue, Tully showed her the forming bruise so Jessica would know exactly what she was talking about.

"You just worry about your life and the child you've chosen to become a part of it, Tully. That's another issue we'll have to deal with eventually, once all this craziness is over."

Tully motioned for the kids to get out of the car and kept walking to the driver's side without another word. Libby was waiting with a makeshift ice bag and a sympathetic smile. "What is it with that woman and your face?"

"How'd you know it was Kara?"

"Just a wild guess, since you seem to trigger her violent streak every time you meet."

"Maybe she thinks if I look bad enough you'll leave me so she can start an ex-Tully harem," she joked.

They spoke softly to each other, not looking to see what was happening outside as Jessica and the kids stood talking. It didn't take long for them to finish, and Bailey and Ralph didn't say anything when they got back in the car. In her rearview mirror, Tully noticed that Jessica stayed outside watching them leave until they turned the corner.

After they crossed the Huey P. Long Bridge over the Mississippi River, Tully stayed on the small country roads as they called to arrange for lodging and to find where her parents and brothers were going to ride out the storm.

Finally Libby and the kids found the whole Badeaux clan rooms in Lafayette for as long as they needed. But since ninety percent of the city was trying to evacuate, they had no idea how long the drive, usually two hours, would take.

Along the way they saw old cars, unable to sit in traffic for hours, parked on the shoulder with their hoods up. To be stranded now would truly be a nightmare if the storm came farther west. Alongside the folks trying to get their cars started were the pet lovers who'd brought their furry family members along for the ride. Bailey and Ralph spent some of the time pointing out playful dogs in the median.

Everywhere they stopped, those fleeing from the storm had become like an extended family. They offered conversation as well as luck whenever Tully stopped for gas or for something to eat, and when they arrived at their hotel she shook her head at how many folks were out in the parking lot grilling, offering to share with whoever passed by.

"Why are they cooking all that stuff?" Libby asked as Tully drove around searching for a parking spot.

"For something to do to forget what we're facing, and it's better to cook it than to bury it in your yard when you get home."

Ralph stuck his head up front. "What do you mean, Mom?"

"If we're out of town for a few days and the electricity goes out, all that stuff in everyone's freezer will go bad, so why not enjoy all those shrimp people were storing for gumbo instead of throwing them out? You were too little to remember the last time we had to leave for one of these things, but the atmosphere was pretty much the same. This is a good example of why the rest of the country thinks we're a breed apart, but if the damn boat's going to sink, then why not go down with a beer in your hand and the band playing," Tully joked.

One of Tully's classmates from law school was cooking a huge pot of jambalaya, so they accepted his invitation instead of trying to fight the crowds at the local restaurants. They set up a few more pots in the parking lot when the rest of the Badeauxes arrived so Alma could start frying the fish and shrimp she'd brought with her.

For once, patrons in the sport bars and at every available television were glued to the Weather Channel instead of ESPN. The later it got, the more it seemed that the doomsday scenario the forecasters had predicted for years was about to materialize.

When the wind started to pick up, everyone retired to their motel rooms, but the kids wanted to stay with Tully and Libby. Sitting together on the king-sized bed, they watched television to pass the time. At one in the morning on Sunday, Tully held Libby and her children and watched as Katrina was upgraded to a category four, then six hours later to a five, with winds of 165 miles an hour. The record-setting pressure readings being reported filled her with dread.

The talking heads kept showing the progression from the time the hurricane left Florida and now marveled at the intense and well-formed storm. It was a killer, but the satellite photos showed a huge, perfectly shaped storm with a compact eye. Though it might kill hundreds of people, some of the announcers seemed enthralled with the power of Mother Nature.

Tully closed her eyes to shut out the screen and ended up taking a twenty-minute nap. When she woke up the satellite images showed the edge of the storm making landfall in Buras, with the outer bands already reaching New Orleans. The eye and its more devastating winds were headed for the Mississippi coast, but at eight in the morning Katrina arrived in the Crescent City.

The rest of her family was awake when the storm moved northeast just as quickly as it had hit land, and Tully released a deep breath of relief. All the planning, worry, and running had been for naught, but she was glad that they'd left.

After merely an hour she realized she had made one of the wisest decisions of her life. Tears streamed down her face and none of them said anything when, a little after nine o'clock Monday morning, most of New Orleans and the surrounding suburbs were full of water.

Hell had begun for those who had stayed behind either by choice or by circumstance.

❖

Three days later as they rode to a local bakery to pick up breakfast Ralph asked, "Do you think our house is full of water?"

"If it is, there isn't much we can do about it, buddy. In the end it's just some stuff we can replace." Tully put her hand on the back of his neck and squeezed gently.

"Do you think Mama's okay?"

"I've been trying to reach her but haven't had any luck. You have my word that as soon as we can head back, she'll be the first person we'll go and see." She turned the ignition off and looked him in the eye. "She's at the hospital, so I'm sure she's fine. You saw how many police officers they had stationed there keeping an eye on things."

"It's just that I was so mad at her, and all that stuff they've been saying on TV didn't sound good."

Ralph was right—the picture the media had painted of what was happening in the city was in some cases horrific, and the cavalry was mired in bureaucratic red tape.

"Your mom is going to be fine, and I'm sure she knows that it was just going to take you a little while to get over the hurt of everything that happened. She's not going to hold anything against you."

"I hope you're right."

"Like I've told you, buddy, we're your parents, and no matter what, we love you. Just remember that I'm here if you need to talk about anything. What happened between your mother and me didn't affect just us. You and Bailey are in this too, whether you wanted to be or not. Things may be different now, but how I feel about the two of you is as constant a thing as you'll ever find."

❖

At Children's Hospital they had barricaded the doors to keep out those needing a fix and wanting to raid their medicine supplies. Katrina hadn't just washed away homes, trees, and parts of history, but also the dealers who stood on the street corners peddling their shit. Those who visited often in sunny weather with sweat-soaked dollar bills hoping to score a few rocks of something were beyond desperate.

Stressed by the inability to move critically ill patients and the heat of the locked-up building, Kara Nicolas had finished her hidden stash, and her hallucinations were worse. With no phone service and no way of knowing when help was coming to evacuate them from the facility, she'd just wanted an escape, even if it was into the drugs that helped her numb the pain of life. By seven Monday morning, as the storm raged outside and she became convinced the halls were full of snakes, the staff had had to subdue and sedate her.

Despite the pandemonium around him, Neil Davis gave thanks that Tully wasn't there to witness the drug-induced breakdown. Before help arrived they had to break up some of the desks and nail them to the windows and doors to keep the violence that had broken out in the city from overrunning the hospital and those trapped inside.

The generators had been running the equipment for their critical patients, and he was sure they would soon start losing the weakest among them. While they had plenty of fuel, the back of the hospital where the generators were located had been flooded, so they were starting to shut off one by one.

"What's she taking?" Neil asked Jessica when he took a break from the chaos around them.

Not since her residency had Jessica felt as tired as she was now. As the systems of the hospital had broken down, she'd been running from one patient to the next, making sure they were stable until the evacuation teams arrived. In this helpless situation, caring for her patients was the only thing keeping her going.

"I really don't know, and I'm not sure I'd tell you if I did," she said softly. She had taken a few minutes to sit and regroup and decided to spend them with Kara.

"You know what this means, right?" Neil said. "If, once this is over, someone in the hospital tells Tully about what happens?"

"Tully isn't going to find out a thing unless you or I tell her, and I'm not about to do that."

He laughed and slapped his hands together. "You can't be that naïve. Gossip spreads as fast as flood waters around here. Of course she'll eventually hear about it. As soon as we're out of here and back to some sort of normal situation, I'm going to have to go to the board and decide what steps we should take in giving Tully and the Heberts what they want."

"You can't take someone's career away over a moment under pressure and unusual circumstances, Neil." Jessica sat on the end of Kara's hospital bed. "Especially if she's a brilliant surgeon, so stop asking me to help you strip her of something she loves. In my heart I can't believe that she'd endanger a child's life."

"Bullshit, Jessica. Tully was right, wasn't she? You knew about this and said nothing. Do you know what kind of position you put the hospital in?" The stubble on his chin felt rough against his hand as he massaged his face in an effort to stay alert. "Victor and the board will think I knew about this, and I'm not going down for you or her. Especially her, if she put me in a position to be ripped to shreds."

"I lived with her and didn't realize she had this kind of problem, Neil. She had it that under control."

He laughed again. "Yeah, right. Is that the physician in you talking, or her girlfriend? You know damn well this is a huge cluster fuck."

"Both." She tugged on her hair before sitting up and pinning him with tired eyes. "What happened to that kid was an accident. For God's sake, what kind of monster do you think I am that I'd let her kill a child? She told me it was an accident, and I believe her."

"An accident? What exactly does that mean?" he rasped, haunted by the sound of Tully's laugh as she left the hospital after offering him what seemed like a gift now—a chuckle that said, "I know how this happened and I'm just the windshield that's going to teach you a lesson, you little bug of a man."

"Just forget I said anything."

He stood up, grabbed her by the arms, and shook her. "No, you tell me what you meant by that."

"Mr. Davis." One of the security guards walked in breathing hard from the obvious run he'd taken to get there. "Two armed men just broke through the back door and are demanding oxycodone."

"Shit." He let her go and began to follow the guy out. "This isn't over, Jessica. I know how you feel about her, but she's not worth throwing your career away for."

When she was alone, Jessica slid her hand into one of Kara's, unable to lift it very high since the orderlies had tied Kara down for her own safety. For some reason she thought about the birth of her children and Tully sitting much like this on her bed holding her hand. Next to them had stood the bassinet they put the baby in, and while Tully had never left her side, her eyes never left the tiny life peacefully sleeping beside them.

The day Bailey was born had been gray and overcast, very similar to the sky Jessica imagined was overhead right now. Only then, her future had seemed brighter. Now she wasn't so sure what it held and how Kara would fit in her life if she were stripped of all the things that defined her as a person.

Chapter Twenty-five

Tully finally got them back into the city two weeks later, using some persuasion at the police checkpoint. Driving down some of the city's most famous streets was like maneuvering an obstacle course of trees, electrical wires, water, and general debris. She kept turning down different streets, taking a circuitous route to the house since she didn't want to accidentally injure any of them.

The word "surreal" echoed continuously in Tully's head. Some flooded parts of the city had been burnt beyond recognition by looters. Yet some people were sitting on their porches rocking and telling stories, most likely of what they had lived through, though most of them were wearing pistols in holsters in a very visible warning.

"Mom, we're going to have to get out. Mrs. Foret's tree is blocking the road," Bailey said, as if Tully hadn't noticed the two-hundred-year-old oak lying across the street like someone had shot it. Its massive root system had taken part of the street and the sidewalk with it, the cement slabs tangled and hanging in the gnarled wood twenty feet in the air.

"Be careful where you step," Tully said before she turned the ignition off and opened her door. The heat was overwhelming, as was the quiet once the echo of the slamming car doors ceased. They were only a block from their house, but they couldn't see it yet because of the fallen vegetation.

"I always wondered how old that tree was," Tully said as she finally stopped in front of their house.

The huge pin oak whose age Tully had just commented on had taken up a good portion of the corner of their front yard. It now rested in the master bedroom, the storm having pushed it over like a twig even though it was larger than the one they'd had to climb over in Mrs. Foret's yard.

"I guess we'll find out when they cut the damn thing out of there." Finally fully realizing that the master bedroom was now part of the first-floor den area, she couldn't help but laugh until tears fell from her eyes.

"Honey, you all right?" Libby asked.

Tully kept laughing. "I'm fine," she said, glad she didn't see a waterline on it. The Army Corp of Engineers was reporting that the most severely flooded sections of town would take about a month to dry out. "I'm not laughing at the new owners' misfortune, but I was just thinking. Somebody gave us a pretty clear sign that we need to move out of this place. The room that got destroyed was the place that brought about all these changes in our lives to begin with. It's truly over now, don't you think?"

"Let's go see what else is wrong," Bailey said, holding her hand out to Tully.

The front door opened easily, but Tully made them all wait outside until she could check to see if it was safe. Upstairs she got as far as Ralph's bedroom door before she started to see daylight from the hole in the ceiling. The massive tree limbs had stabbed through the floor, creating an indoor jungle effect in her office as well. After a quick walk-through, she discovered that only the pool house had escaped unscathed.

"I want to wait for someone to check and tell me it's not going to collapse on us if we try to take anything out. It's a good thing we were already packed and ready to go. Most of the boxes seem okay."

"What now, Mom?" Ralph asked.

"Let's go check out the new place and see if all those trees we thought were great a few weeks ago are still standing. Then we'll probably have to go stay with your grandmother until the mayor's office reopens the city for good."

"What about Mama?" he asked.

"The police officer told me they evacuated them all, so it's just a waiting game now. We'll have to sit tight until she gets in touch with us from wherever she ended up, and that could be anywhere from Houston to Atlanta."

"Mom, do you think Chase and her family are okay?" Bailey

stopped walking before they reached the car and glanced in the opposite direction. Her friend's home was about three blocks away.

"You guys up for a walk?" Tully asked.

It took them more than an hour to reach Chase's house, and when they did Tully let go of Libby's hand and grabbed Bailey before she made a run for it. All that remained of the two-story house was a pile of ash with a few wall timbers.

"Do you think they stayed?"

"I'm sure they got out, but I can't let you go in there." Tully held Bailey and tried to turn her away from the destruction.

"I can't just leave, she might be hurt."

"Promise me you'll stay here, and I'll go see." Tully motioned both Ralph and Libby to hold Bailey. "I mean it, Bailey. I'll be right back."

Tully walked the property until she reached the back fence, which had held up surprisingly better than the house. The only other structure left standing was a utility shed with a barbecue grill in front of it.

"Hello," she called, hoping someone wouldn't shoot her because they thought she was there to steal something.

"Ms. Badeaux?" Chase emerged from the shed, shielding her eyes from the bright sun. "How'd you get here?"

"Bailey walked me over." Tully walked closer and clasped Chase's shoulder, ignoring the fact that she was sweating profusely and appeared a little shell-shocked.

"Bailey's with you?" Chase ran her hand over her unwashed hair and blushed.

"She is, and I'm sure she's going to think you're as cute as the day you came to our house for dinner, so stop worrying." Tully glanced past her to the door of the shed. "You aren't here alone, are you?"

"My mom's with me."

"Where's your dad?"

"In Arizona the last time he called, I think. My parents are divorced."

"Uh-huh. What happened to the house?"

"Lightning is the best we can figure," an attractive brunette said from the door. "Are you a friend of Chase?"

"I'm the mother of Chase's girlfriend." Tully stuck her hand out. "Tully."

"Dana." The woman took her hand.

"Were you two able to salvage anything?"

Dana sighed. "Just the stuff we evacuated with, but we'll manage."

"Mom?" Tully heard Ralph scream from the front.

"Everything's fine, Ralph. Just give me a few minutes," she yelled back. "Come on, then. I brought backup with me."

Dana took a few steps from the door and shook her head. "That's really nice of you, but we'll be fine."

"The way I see it, you have two choices here." Tully motioned Chase back to the shed for their things. "You can either leave with me willingly or I'll carry you out of here. But there's no way in hell I'm leaving the two of you here alone."

"I'm sure you have enough to worry about." Dana wiped the sweat from her forehead, appearing aggravated with the heat.

"Chase, pack up what you have," Tully said when she just stood there. "You can carry the bags and I can carry your mother."

"Okay, we'll come with you, but only for a few days." Dana threw her hands up. "I can't believe it's this bad," she said as they walked past the burnt-out shell of the house. "I've been sitting next to my lawnmower for the last couple of days because I couldn't bring myself to look at it."

"I wish I could make it better, but I can't think of anything to say except that you and Chase are fine," Tully said. "You're here together, so the rest will take care of itself."

Chase broke out into a run when she saw Bailey, obviously overjoyed and yelling, "I've been so worried about you."

Bailey drew back from the hug and examined Chase's face. "Are you sure you're all right? I've been trying to call, but once we left Lafayette, the phone was as useless as a rock."

"Don't look too close. The shed didn't have any running water. Not that it's running anywhere else."

"My mom always says looks are only skin deep, babe. Of course, she's dating Libby, so she can make cute comments about people's looks since beautiful doesn't begin to describe her." She rolled her eyes and laughed. "Being a little funky isn't going to turn me off, unless you're going with this look once we get to my grandmother's and you decide to take a pass on the working shower."

Tully drove Libby's car through more than one yard to make it around the fallen trees. She figured ruts in the landscaping would be the least of people's problems. She let Dana drive the Land Rover and take the kids with her so she could lead them all out.

On the way to the Badeaux home, Libby asked her, "Are we stopping by the new place before we head out?"

"I guess we should, since we'll probably be having houseguests for a while. We can offer the middle bedroom upstairs to Dana and Chase, if you don't mind."

Libby reached over the center console and took Tully's right hand. "You're a nice person for doing that, honey."

"I figure it'll keep my mind off all the hurricane damage and the other problems I'm going to have."

"I don't think they're going to be that big a problem. Do you?"

"Not a problem having another two people in the house, no. But worrying about Bailey having sex before I think she's ready will keep my mind humming for months to come."

With a slap to Tully's arm, Libby laughed. "You're telling me that if we'd been dating at their age and were living under these circumstances, you'd be able to keep your hands off me?"

"Baby, I'm over forty living in these circumstances, and I can't keep my hands off you. I saw the way that kid looks at my little girl." She stopped at the corner and peered in the rearview mirror to make sure Dana was still with her. "Do you know any more about Chase and her mother than I do?"

"Think I'm keeping secrets from you, huh?"

"More like I think Bailey sees you as someone to confide in more than me with stuff like this."

Libby slapped her arm again, then pinched her. "And you want me to tell you if she did? Shame on you, Counselor."

"Not tell on her. More like drop a few major hints."

"Before I give you anything, tell me what you were like in high school."

"My mother used the word 'driven' a lot. I got good grades, played sports, and read for fun whenever I had time."

"You've just described the kid riding in the car behind us, and she's crazy about your daughter." Libby lifted Tully's hand and kissed her knuckles. "You may not be ready for Bailey to be seriously dating someone, but you couldn't have picked someone better for her to start off with. Chase will respect her and know what her boundaries are." She kissed Tully's hand again and bit gently on the tip of her index finger. "And more importantly, she'll know what your boundaries are."

"My boundaries involve a two-by-four to the head if she hurts Bailey. But I really am glad Bailey's opened up like this. It's nice to see her socializing after the rough time she and Ralph had at that damn school Jessica insisted on."

"Speaking of, have you heard from her?"

"I tried the hospital a few times before we left Lafayette but didn't have any luck, and now the phones are so sporadic that I'm really not getting through. We need to get in touch with her so Ralph and Bailey will stop worrying about her. They say they don't care, but I know better."

They drove down St. Charles Avenue, taking to the sidewalk every so often to avoid the streetcar lines that had snapped under the pressure of fallen trees. Because most of the city was still without power, Tully didn't think anything would be hot, but she went slowly anyway.

The block where the new house was had lost a lot of old trees too, but the water hadn't reached there either. The kids jumped out of the Land Rover before Tully had the chance to turn off the ignition and say, "Everything looks okay here."

"Come on, Mom," Ralph said, rapping his knuckles on the window of the car.

When they opened the front door, they could smell the musty air that came from the lack of ventilation, and from the kitchen window Tully could see a huge pine standing almost perfectly straight in the swimming pool, as if someone had come by and purposely planted it there.

The rooms were still empty, except for the master bedroom where the new bedroom furniture they had picked out and ordered was waiting for them. When Tully turned the faucet in the bathroom, the ferocious gust of air that had been trapped in the pipe made her jump back. Having no running water would keep them out of the city that much longer. If they couldn't brush their teeth, the fire department couldn't put out fires either.

"Looks okay in the attic, Mom," Ralph reported. "We can move in if we want, huh?"

"Eventually, buddy, but until the utilities come back we might be out for a while." With one last glance at their new bed, she pointed them to the door. "Let's just hope it's not a long while," she whispered as she locked the front door. "I have a life to start on, and I want to get to it."

CHAPTER TWENTY-SIX

Tully shifted and sped up as they reached the Mississippi River bridge. The conversation Libby had kept going since they'd left the house was taking her mind off the empty streets. Considering it was just past noon, normally the streets would be filled with traffic and the sidewalks with tourists and locals. She couldn't help but think what the lack of activity foretold—the wounded city would take years to heal.

Once they were over the bridge and out of the city, Libby finally contacted Alma, after fifteen minutes of trying. The state roads were just as empty as the city's, so she told Alma they would be there soon and were bringing guests. The rest of the Badeaux clan had returned home at the first opportunity to check on their boats and property, so Libby had caught Alma in the kitchen preparing dinner for them, as well as her sons and their families.

"I'm sure she has enough for the whole town. Don't look so worried," Tully said when Libby hung up and started tapping the phone on her chin.

"That's not what I'm worried about. I just want to help her out."

Tully tugged her closer and kissed her temple. "The fact you're with us is making her happy. You don't have to do another thing."

"Have I told you again how much your love of coffee changed my life for the better?"

They reached the overpass that would take them to the small fishing town that was located on the highest point for miles, and the spot at the top before the off-ramp was one of Tully's favorites. Every time she had left home to drive back to college, she would stop and admire the sugar cane growing in the fields as far as she could see.

"Something wrong, Mom?" Bailey called from the window of the Land Rover.

"Just showing Libby something. Keep going to your grandmother's if you want, and get everyone settled." They waved as Dana drove by with Ralph in the front seat giving directions.

"The first time I left for Tulane I reached this spot just at sunrise. It was late August and the cane was almost ready for harvest. I sat on the hood of my car and just enjoyed the way it waved in the breeze." The storm had flattened the crop so that only a few stalks were standing.

"We'll have to come back so I can see that."

"After that day I stopped here often and saw it as the part of the small-town girl I brought with me on the way to the life I've built." Tully moved behind Libby and rested her chin on her right shoulder. "When my heart found you I realized something fundamental about myself."

"What's that, my love?"

"The part of me that wants nothing more than to leave here and conquer the world needs and wants the dreams of the kid who stood here years ago."

Libby turned around and put her hands behind Tully's neck, tugging her down. After what they had just lived through, they took their time and enjoyed the kiss until a truck driver speeding by blew his horn in obvious endorsement.

When they broke apart, Libby rested her hands on Tully's shoulders just under her shirt. "Tell me what you need and I'll try my best to give it to you."

Tully sighed. "When I started my career I wanted more than anything to be successful, but I worked so hard at achieving my goal that I lost sight of my family." She uncharacteristically felt tears swim in her eyes, though they didn't fall. "Now I see that I'll never find fulfillment at the office, but with you, Bailey, and Ralph. So all I need is you and them in my life, and I'll be happy."

"Don't waste your wishes on things you already have." Libby kissed the part of her chest she could reach through the opening of her shirt. "And you have me."

❖

The kids, Dana, and Alma were having iced tea on the front porch when they drove up, Libby laughing when Alma hugged and kissed her hello before Tully. "I have your rooms ready for tonight, and there are fresh towels in the bathroom."

"Rooms?" Tully asked.

"Rooms, Tully Gaston Badeaux. You're bunking with Ralph in your brother Jerrold's old room at the end of the hall, and I put Libby in with Bailey. I don't care how old you are, there's things you have do besides give the girl a ring." Alma had her hand on her hip and an expression that defied Tully to disagree with her.

"Honey, go take a shower and I'll help your mom finish up," Libby said with an affectionate rub to the small of Tully's back.

"Before you make fun of me, kid," Tully said to Bailey, who had her mouth open poised to make a comment, "I'm betting she put you in my old room."

"So?"

"So, it has about five loose boards by the door. Just think about that if you're contemplating sneaking out of there tonight for any reason." Her eyes came up and met Chase's. "And the fact that your grandmother sleeps like there's a serial killer on the loose in the house and she has to be vigilant." Tully ruffled Bailey's hair and headed in for her shower and a restless night's sleep, she was sure, in her brother's old room.

The next morning Tully and Ralph joined her father and brothers as they inspected the boats and the canals they navigated to get out to their fishing grounds. It gave Libby the opportunity to spend time with Bailey and Alma as they prepared a huge family dinner. Around the table that night the rest of the family entertained Libby and their other guests with fishing stories from their youth. As they laughed and reminisced, Tully noticed how Libby glowed and realized that this was probably the first time since her parents' deaths that she had been included in a family like this.

"You fell in?" Libby asked, wiping her face, which was wet with laughter after Walter Badeaux's amusing story. She was sitting on Tully's lap with her arm looped around her neck.

"More than once, if you believe these goons." Tully glared at Walter and Jerrold, but promptly forgot about them when Libby kissed her. "Walter, how about you tell them about the time you dragged poor Jerrold back to the house in the shrimp net?"

"Not that one again," Jerrold said with a bit of a whine.

"But when we finally fished you out, you looked so good wearing all that squid," Tully said.

Their father laughed the hardest as he shook his head at some of the memories they were reliving, but he left them to their fun when someone knocked on the front door. "Stay put, Walt. It's probably just Jimmy from down the way wanting me to square up my fuel bill before things get any crazier over this damn storm."

Before he made it to the door their visitor started knocking again, louder this time, as if using a fist to pound on the door. "Hold your water, I'm coming."

Judging from Gaston's surprised expression, Jessica figured she was the last person he expected to see standing on his front porch. She stepped back when Gaston's face registered a slight grimace. She, along with everyone else who had stayed behind at Children's, had been literally trapped inside the hospital for just under a week without running water. Things hadn't been much better when they returned to Kara's apartment, but they didn't have any place else to go so they'd stayed there until Kara was stable enough to travel. Jessica couldn't blame Gaston for noticing their less-than-perfect living conditions.

"Is Tully here?"

"Come in." He held the door open and waved her in.

"I just need to talk to her."

Jessica turned to see what Gaston was looking at, but he obviously couldn't see Kara, who was still asleep in the front seat, not moving.

"I know you do, but it appears as if you might need a shower and some of Alma's chicken stew. Come in and join us, Jessica. I promise it'll be all right."

"You might want to check with Alma first." Jessica twisted her hand in the bottom of her scrub shirt as she laughed.

"Gaston is smart enough to know that I'd skin him if he sent away someone in need of some comfort," Alma said from behind him. "So why don't you take that shower before you go in and see the kids. You remember where everything is upstairs, don't you?"

"I didn't come often, but yes, I remember. Thank you, Alma." Jessica stepped closer and put her hand on Gaston's arm. "Thanks, Gaston."

She climbed the stairs, holding the small of her back with one hand and clutching the rail firmly with the other. After driving out of the city and leaving that chaos behind, Jessica felt the stress drain from her body, leaving her just bone tired.

"It's been forever since she's seen the kids, and she asked for Tully first?" Alma said.

"How about we wait and see why she's here, honey, before we go making judgments."

"It's a question, not an accusation." Alma backhanded Gaston in the belly softly, her eyes still on the stairs even though Jessica had made it all the way up.

"Mom's right," Tully said from the doorway that separated the front foyer from the living room. "After this long, I should've been the last person on her mind."

"How long you been standing there?" Gaston asked.

"Long enough, but you were handling things so well I decided not to interrupt." Sensing Libby behind her, Tully lifted her arm up so that she could press against her side. "Is the party moving in here?"

"It would seem that way," Libby said. "Everything okay?"

"Jessica just got here and is upstairs taking a shower."

"Bailey and Ralph will be thrilled. I know they try to blow it off, but they've been worried."

Tully sighed and nodded at her parents as they left to join the others. After they were alone, she didn't say anything for a long while, content to just hold Libby. "She didn't ask about them, though. She asked to speak to me."

"You're not surprised by that, are you?" Libby was obviously trying to sound incredulous, but Tully noticed the haunted look in her eyes. "Of course she'd ask for you first."

"You think she's back here for me?" Tully was surprised. "I love you, darlin', but that's nuts."

"Nuts was leaving you in the first place."

Just then Jessica emerged from the bathroom. Her hair was wet and slicked back, but she still wore a rumpled scrub suit. "Everyone does nutty things in their life—the real pain comes from not being able to change or take them back," she said as she made her way down the stairs. After a moment's hesitation she took another step toward them. "Hello, Tully."

"Jessica, I'm glad to see you made it through the storm all right."

It was the first time she had looked at Jessica and felt nothing. This woman who had given her a family and shared so many years with her had always evoked some emotion, but now Tully felt no love, no anger—not one thing.

"Could I talk to you alone for a minute?"

Tully tightened her hold on Libby, who tried to move away. "You do remember that the kids are with me, right? I'd think you might want to talk to them. They've been worried about you, so I'll get them if you want me to."

"Please, Tully, just a few minutes."

Libby stood on her tiptoes and kissed Tully's cheek. "Honey, you just sit in here, and I'll go stay with Bailey and Ralph. Just call when you're done."

When Libby was far enough away that she couldn't overhear, Jessica said, "You've finally found the one who's going to adore you, haven't you? I always thought that's what you wanted from the person you'd end up with."

"Am I supposed to respond, or was that just an oversimplified observation on your part?" Tully pushed off the doorway and moved to take a seat. "Libby is many things, but an overzealous puppy isn't one of them."

"I'm sorry, that was out of line. She just seems too good to be true."

"Why are you here, Jessica? I'd love to sit and…" She put her hands up and shook her head. "I take that back. I don't have time for this anymore, so just say what you have to and be done with it."

"I have to leave for a while, and I want to know that you'll take care of the kids."

"Where are you going, and why?"

"I don't really want to talk about it, but I have to leave." As Jessica let out the breath she was holding and sat next to Tully, she almost relaxed as she felt Tully's body heat. "I know I hurt you, but I need more time before we can start over and move on."

"Start what over and move on to where?" Tully sounded as if someone had woken her up out of a deep sleep and demanded she do calculus in her head.

"Given our history together, we could eventually repair the damage we've done to our relationship by messing around with Kara and Libby and begin again."

"Sure we can, but I really need to know where you're going." Tully was trying to sound sympathetic, but the only conclusion that made any sense to her was that Jessica had started taking drugs with Kara. It was the only plausible explanation for the way Jessica was talking.

Libby, coming to offer Tully some coffee and Jessica something to eat, couldn't help but overhear Tully's last remark, which stopped her cold. She leaned against the wall in the hall and willed herself not to cry. As Jessica started talking again, Libby quietly returned to the kitchen and sat silently next to the kids.

"I need to head to Texas with Kara for a while. It's nothing serious, but this hurricane and the stress of the hospital have really taken their toll, so she wants to go home for a little while and regroup."

"I see." Tully leaned forward and pressed her fingers together in front of her lips. "This is how I see our future. You can take all the time you need, wherever you need and with whomever you need to make your life complete."

"But you just said we could go back." Jessica reached out to touch her, but the expression on Tully's face made her drop her hand to her lap.

"That would be the definition of sarcasm in its purest form. I'd rather fill in the Mississippi River with a spoon and a pile of sand than to try and go back to something that was broken long before Dr. Nicolas ended up in our bed. I won't keep you from Bailey and Ralph, because I think keeping you out of their lives is wrong, no matter how I feel about the subject on a deep personal level. But I won't agree for you to take them out of the state, not now, and not while you're with Kara."

"What you mean is that you can have someone in your life, but not me. She's a child, for God's sakes, compared to you, and she's really involved with our children. But the high-and-mighty Tully won't extend me the same courtesy because it's your ego we're talking about. I slept with someone else. Get over it."

"You want to compare our lives now, Jessica? Is that what you really want?"

The tone Tully was using sent warning bells off in Jessica's head. "What are you talking about?"

"I promised you a court date, and I'm planning on delivering. It's time we finish our business. When that day comes I'll be happy to have Libby sit next to me and explain exactly what she means to me and how she fits into my life. I don't care why or how our relationship ended, but because it did, I had a chance to truly be happy. Feel free to do the same, but I'm going to make Kara answer for Evangeline, so tell her not to get too comfortable wherever it is you're going."

Jessica laughed until she was holding her sides and crying from the humor she found in what Tully had said. "Have you been back to the city? While you've been here in Alma's special little world, New Orleans has been destroyed. As sad as that is, I'm rejoicing over the fact that you and your ilk are out of business for a long time to come. No more destroying lives, no more parading and performing for the juries you love so much, Tully."

"According to the courts, it shouldn't take more than two weeks for business to resume in Baton Rouge. If that's accurate, then I'm going to fast-track both court dates." She stood and glared down at Jessica. "Since Dr. Nicolas is so tied up in both issues, I'll need to know where in Texas you two will be. I'm sure neither one of you is going to extend me that courtesy, so I'll be contacting the hospital to make sure I know exactly where Kara Nicolas is."

"She needs to rest," Jessica said softly.

"She needs to be in court when she's summoned. Beyond that, I could give a good goddamn what she needs. I'm going to get the kids so you can talk to them before you leave. Your priorities are obviously with Dr. Nicolas and getting her to a better place, but for twenty minutes why not pretend you give a shit about the kids."

Jessica grabbed hold of Tully's wrist before she could move away. "That's not fair."

"Tell me honestly that you stayed behind because of your job, and I'll apologize."

"Not totally for my job, no, but I won't feel guilty for my choices. I knew the kids would be all right with you." Jessica let go of Tully and fell back in the seat.

"Then I think I'm being more than fair. Just stay put and I'll send them in. Take all the time you need. They've been worried about you, so it's good that you're here."

❖

She stepped into the hall to find a visibly red Libby, clearly embarrassed at having been caught since she'd gone back to see if Tully was all right. Instead of saying anything where Jessica could overhear them, Tully just took Libby's hand and led her to the back of the house where the kids were watching television with their cousins.

"She's waiting up front for you guys," Tully said after she told them that Jessica was there but had to leave. "Take it easy on her, okay? She's had a rough couple of days."

"That was generous of you," Libby said, as if fishing for something to say as Tully led her to the swing by the water. "I'm sorry I was out there listening."

"Don't apologize." Tully raised her finger in a request for Libby to stop talking. "It's time you realize just where you stand in my life, what rights you have when it comes to everything."

"You don't have to do that."

"It has nothing to do with Jessica, my job, the house, or anything else you think is important to me." Tully sat back and put her arm around Libby, still maintaining eye contact. "We've been watching television for days now, digesting just how much our lives will change if we decide to go back to New Orleans the way it is now."

Libby pressed her hand to the side of Tully's face. "I've been thinking about that myself."

"All those people, Libby, standing on their rooftops waiting to be rescued because they either didn't have a way out or refused to leave made my heart ache. It hurt me to see so much suffering, but it also made me start thinking."

Libby kissed her. "Just tell me what I can do to help you process all this."

When their lips parted, Tully reached for Libby's left hand. "It's a weird analogy, I know, but I've been living my life like those poor souls trapped in something not of their own making, but trapped nonetheless by their inaction." She kissed the skin just under the ring she'd given Libby. "I don't want to spend another night without you because someone doubts my commitment to you, especially if that person is you. If you're willing, I want to have a ceremony, even if it's small, and make this permanent."

"You just tell me when and where, and I'll be there." Libby gently let go of Tully's hand and put her arms around Tully's neck. "I'll be there because you've given me a chance at the life I've always dreamed about. You talk about me being your second chance, but in reality that's what you are to me. You love me and gave me a family."

"Then let's start this rebuilding together."

❖

"Tully?" Alma called from the back porch of the house. "Jessica's ready to go and wanted to speak to you again before she leaves."

"We'll be right in." After one last kiss Tully helped Libby up and they walked to the house hand in hand.

"Did you have any ideas of what type of ceremony you'd like?" Libby asked.

"Actually, I do, and considering some of the things we've been through, I thought it might be appropriate. After we finish dealing with Jessica, let's sit with the kids and talk about it. If you're not okay with the idea, then we can do whatever you have in mind. It's a day I want you to remember as special, so we'll do whatever you want."

"I spent more time dreaming about the woman standing next to me than the actual ceremony, and if you ask me, I've got that pretty well covered," Libby told her before she let go of her hand when they entered the kitchen. Ralph and Bailey were sitting at the table having a Coke, appearing drained after their visit with Jessica. "You guys want something else?"

"When you're done with Mama, can we go down to that place you like and have pie?" Bailey asked Tully. "I need to get out of here for a little while."

"If you can convince Libby to let me have a piece, then sure."

Jessica was standing at the front window looking out at the yard and only partially turned when Tully came into the room. "If you need me I'll be on my cell. I realize it's not working at the moment, but once we're farther away from the damaged areas we should get decent coverage. I'll call and check in when that happens."

"Jessica, we can't go back to the way things were, but do you need my help in any way?" Tully stepped closer but stopped short of touching her. "No matter what, we have a history and a lifetime connection because of Bailey and Ralph. If you need my help, all you have to do is ask."

"Don't be so patronizing. I'm sure you're just waiting for me to crash and burn, but I'm not giving you the satisfaction."

"That can't be further from the truth," Tully said, trying to find some of the compassion she once held for Jessica and hoping to reach her.

Jessica clenched her fist and jerked around to face her, making Tully think she was about to hit her. Instead Jessica shook her head and opened the door. "I'll call when we get there." Once she was outside, she practically ran to her car and left.

"What's made you so angry, Jessica? And whatever or whoever it was, before you pass the point of no return I hope you realize how close you are to losing all you held dear." Tully whispered the sentiment to the wind before she went back in to her family.

Chapter Twenty-seven

The diner Bailey had wanted to go to was two miles farther south. The owner was a great cook, but the only thing she bragged on were her three types of pies.

"What's good?" Libby asked as they sat in the booth closest to the kitchen. She was still smiling that as they came in, more than half the people dining told Tully hello, and Tully had introduced her to every single one of them.

"The coconut cream," Ralph said.

"The pecan," Bailey said, while she put her hand in Ralph's face and pushed him into the booth first, making room for herself and Chase.

"The apple, hands down," Tully finished.

When the waitress came to the table to take their order, Tully introduced Libby and Chase, then ordered three pieces of each kind. "You are not eating more than one piece of pie," Libby said to Tully when the waitress left.

"Don't worry. You don't have to stab me with a fork. I just thought you and Chase should try each one so you'll know what to order the next time you come in."

"Who says that's the only reason I'd stab you with a fork?" Libby asked with a smile.

"Ah, an optimist, I see," Tully said jokingly. "I'm sure once we've been together for a while you'll have a list and then some when it comes to reasons not to."

"Who's being the optimist now?" Bailey asked before sticking her tongue out at Tully.

"Bailey Bean, would you like to be grounded in front of Chase?" Tully asked in return.

"Change of subject, then. Did Mama tell you she's moving to Texas?"

After Bailey had brought up Jessica, they all leaned back so the waitress could put their food down. "Something about needing to forget the horrors of the storm."

"You don't believe her?" Libby asked.

"Could we not talk about her now?" Ralph said. "If she wants to go, then let her. But I'm tired of it." He jabbed his fork into a piece of coconut cream pie and took a huge bite.

"Okay, buddy. That's not why we're here anyway." Tully took a large sip of the milk she'd ordered with the pie. "How'd you like to help Libby and me with our commitment ceremony?"

"Cool," Ralph said, brightening. "When?"

"Tomorrow, if I can get the girl and your grandmother to agree." Tully opened her mouth and accepted a piece of Libby's pecan pie.

"If you're going for that, you might want to tell Grandma tonight so she can start cooking," Bailey suggested. "But if you hold it so soon, we won't have many people there."

"I'll take care of your grandmother, don't worry. Tomorrow should be about how I feel about Libby, not what we're serving or who we're entertaining."

"Good answer, sweetheart," Libby said.

"I've never done this before, and this time around I wanted to share with my family how I feel about you." Libby leaned over and kissed Tully's cheek.

"You and Jessica didn't have a ceremony?" Libby asked.

"I said I didn't want to talk about her," Ralph said.

"It's okay to be mad, buddy, but it's not okay to be rude," Tully told him in a way that didn't sound like a reprimand. "And to answer your question," she told Libby, "no, we didn't. We cared about each other enough to want a family, but the idea of something like a commitment ceremony was something we really didn't talk about."

"What changed your mind?" Bailey asked.

"I loved your mother."

"I'm not questioning that, Mom."

"I just didn't want you to get the wrong impression about why I want to do things differently this time around. I loved your mother, and when we got together we had goals we set for what we wanted. There were careers, kids and a house, and we got so busy wrapped up in all that, that I think we forgot to enjoy it. Now that I have Libby in my life, or should I say now that we have Libby in our lives, I wanted a great memory of how we started on that new life."

"So what'd you have in mind?" Bailey asked.

"I was telling Libby earlier that this storm has changed our lives a lot, but in some ways they've stayed the same." Tully reached across the table for both Ralph and Bailey's hands. "No matter what you two decide to do with your lives, and no matter who you decide to share it with, I'm always going to be on your side. It's my responsibility to protect you from as much harm and hatred as the world can throw at you, but some things are going to take time."

"Like what, Mom?" Ralph asked.

"Like what happened to you at your old school when people knew that you were the kids of the gay couple. No matter how much the world progresses on a lot of things, some people will react negatively because of what Libby and I feel for each other. I can't change that, but I'm going to spend my life trying. Right now, though, we can't formally marry in the eyes of the law."

"That doesn't matter to me, baby," Libby said. "It doesn't change how I feel about you."

"It doesn't change how I feel about you either, but now we're like so many people before us who the law didn't recognize at one time or other."

Bailey reached for Chase's hand under the table and leaned slightly into her. "I sense a Mom special-learning story."

"I like those," Ralph said.

"I do too, so be quiet."

"I'm not going to pretend that anyone alive today has suffered as much as the slaves who once worked on the plantations around here. But when they were stolen from their homelands and shipped here, many of them brought their traditions." The way her children were hanging on her words reminded her of the time in their lives when a good story was all it took to cajole them out of a bad mood.

Tully continued her explanation. "Since the law didn't allow them to marry, they had a ceremony where they jumped the broom."

"I've heard of that, but I don't know what it means," Libby said.

"It means different things to different people, but the definition I like best is that it's a symbol of sweeping out the old and starting on a new path. The person you jump the broom with is the one who agrees to walk that road with you."

Libby smiled. "That sounds beautiful to me."

"Yeah, Mom, it does. Just tell us what you want, and we'll do it by tomorrow."

The genuine way Bailey said it and the size of her smile made Tully's eyes water.

"I'm happy for you," Bailey told Tully, then turned to Libby. "She's a real pain at times, works too long most of the time, but overall she's really great, so take good care of her."

"I promise, and that taking-care job goes for you and Ralph too."

"Compared to Mom we're low maintenance."

"That, Bailey, is the true definition of optimism," Tully said with a laugh. "You're so cute, though, that we don't mind how high maintenance you are."

They all laughed when Bailey smeared coconut cream pie on Tully's nose.

❖

At sunset the next day, the whole Badeaux family, Chase, and Dana, wearing light-colored shorts and white shirts, stood around Libby and Tully, who stood by the swing they both loved, holding hands.

"Libby, I stand here with you and it makes me feel complete. How could I have not noticed that I've been waiting so long for you and what you bring to my life? You're the woman who has healed what I didn't know was broken and opened my eyes to the possibilities of what's to come." Tully lifted Libby's hand and kissed the back of it. "I promise you here in front of our family that I'll try always to give you more than you give me, that I'll love you, cherish you, and take care of you no matter what we face in a lifetime."

When it was Libby's turn, she took a deep breath. "I've been alone since I was sixteen, and it would've been so easy to settle on just anyone to fill the void of my loneliness. But I couldn't. You may have started as a good customer who came in for coffee, but you ended up being the one thing that makes my life complete. You, Ralph, and Bailey are my family now, and I thank God I waited for my soul mate."

From her pocket Libby produced a gold wedding band that

appeared to have scratches and writing along the sides. "This was my father's and my grandfather's before him. The writing is ancient Gaelic and translates as 'a long life to thee if only so I can enjoy the years as your wife.' I love you, Tully, I cherish you, and I'll stand with you for as long as I have life in me. Becoming your wife is the answer to every prayer I have ever offered up to the heavens. I want you to wear this"—she slipped the ring onto Tully's finger—"not only to show you how much I love you, but because I think, had my parents lived, my father wouldn't have had it any other way. We are the next generation he dreamed of."

Tully nodded and gazed down at Libby's extraordinary gift. She had only one thing left to do, and in her mind it would make this ceremony as legally binding as if they'd stood in front of a judge and signed a license. Holding hands, she and Libby jumped over the broom the kids had decorated with white ribbons and flowers, sharing a long kiss once their feet hit the ground.

The family congratulated them, Tully smiling when Bailey and Ralph gave Libby a bear hug to welcome her officially into their lives. Closer to the house Alma had set up tables, and the boys' wives were busy bringing out the feast they'd thrown together.

They stayed long enough to cut the small cake Alma had baked and to enjoy a few toasts, but Libby readily accepted when Tully held out her hand and asked, "Take a walk with me?"

"I realize a honeymoon might have to wait, but as long as I get you in the same room with me, I'll go wherever you like. It's going to be a little awkward with so many people in the house to…well, you know."

Tully waved over her shoulder as they started down the long drive to the road. "Baby, you're crazy if you think we got married and we're not going to…well, you know," she whispered back. "Come on. I have a surprise for you."

Libby smiled, since Gaston's boat was the only logical place they could be going, but the smile dimmed somewhat when Tully stopped before they boarded. "Forget something?" Libby asked.

"Granted, we had a great time on Dad's boat, but the last time we went out you asked for one thing that I couldn't figure out how to request without everyone teasing me from now until the end of time."

"I made a request the last time?" Libby stared at the boat as if it would give her a clue as to what Tully was talking about.

"A double bed. Does that ring any bells for you?"

"Ah, thanks, honey, for not mentioning that to your father." Libby laughed and buried her face in Tully's chest.

"Since I didn't ask him but still wanted to fulfill your wish, I had to go ahead and get a bed."

"How'd you do that?" Libby asked.

"I bought the bed and a boat to put it in." She pointed to a shrimp boat moored a few hundred yards away. "Nice big bed for us and a set of bunk beds for when the kids come along, and when you think of a name we'll paint it on."

"I love you," Libby said before she pushed Tully to get her moving.

When they boarded, Libby could see the nets were sitting neatly folded on the back of the boat. The fiberglass hull was white and pristine, which could only mean that since they'd gotten home, Gaston, Jerrold, and Walter had been busy cleaning anything the storm blew onto the boat. Inside, the generator was working to cool the big open one-room cabin and keep the lights dim. The two other doors led to the head and to a pantry and storage closet.

"It's ours?" Libby asked.

Tully let go of her hand to start closing the window blinds to give them some privacy. "It's all ours. A friend of Dad's built it for someone else who decided it against it for financial reasons, so I told him if he could put a bed for two in here, we'd take it. I thought you'd like the large kitchen too."

The cooking area, located in the corner in front of the closet and bathroom, had a full-sized stove, oven, and small freezer. "Just tell me you're not hungry right this minute?" Libby stood in the middle of the cabin with her hands on her hips.

"Starving, actually," Tully said. When the last blind was closed she picked Libby up and dropped her gently in the middle of the bed. With quick fingers she unbuttoned Libby's shorts and pulled them and her underwear off in one quick motion. "Only it's you that's on my menu."

Libby lifted her shirt over her head and tried to work open Tully's shorts, but it was difficult when Tully popped her bra off with one hand and squeezed one of her breasts with the other.

"Take these off and lie down, baby," Libby said, tugging on the top of Tully's shorts. "No, on your stomach," she added as Tully complied.

"I think it'd be better if I could touch you."

"You're crazy if you think you're leaving here without touching me, but I want you all to myself right now. I want you on your stomach so I won't have any distractions."

With one more kiss, hoping Libby would change her mind, Tully rolled onto her stomach and rested her head on her folded hands. Her head fell to the side when Libby climbed over her and straddled the small of her back, the brush of Libby's pubic hair branding her skin as if she'd used hot oil.

"I've thought of one thing all day. You'll belong to me for the rest of my life."

Tully tried to stay focused on what Libby was saying, but when she added her hard nipples to the sensual massage, Tully almost lost it. "I'll belong to you as long as I live, considering the differences in our ages, sweetheart."

"Doesn't matter how old you are or how much time we have." Libby moved from left to right, pushing her hips against the curve of Tully's butt. "I know we'll live our time together well. It's that life that I'm looking forward to."

"Keep telling me things like that and I'm going to have to turn around and prove how much I love you," Tully said. She arched her butt up just a little, hoping Libby would ask for just that.

"Not yet, baby. I want to tell you a few things, and if you're looking at me I'll cry." Libby stopped moving and lay down so that they were touching the entire length of their bodies. "I'm glad today wasn't fancy and just your family was there. It's been so long since I've belonged anywhere. Thank you for giving me that back, but also for opening your heart to me." She kissed Tully's shoulder and hugged her. "I love you so much."

Not thinking she'd get reprimanded for turning around, Tully did so slowly, not wanting Libby to move off her. She opened her arms and held her, liking the slow, even pace of their passion. Because of the storm, they hadn't had many chances to be intimate, but Libby had awakened in her a need to touch and be touched that rounded blind corners and swamped her at times, so she wanted to make this moment last.

"I may have been alive longer than you, and I may have more life experiences, but you have an old soul, honey." Tully ran her hands down to Libby's bottom and just as slowly dragged them back up and around to the sides of her breasts. "My mom says that all the time, and now I know what she means. I promise that for as hard as your life has been, I'm going to spend the rest of our days trying to show you just how cherished you are."

"You don't have anything to make up for."

"I'm not making up for anything. I'm reveling in the things I know for sure," she whispered in Libby's ear. "The things I don't have to ask or try to learn about you."

"What things?"

"That for all my mistakes," she rolled them over, but kept her weight off Libby, "I've been blessed to woo a girl who not only has an old soul, but a beautiful one. And the true blessing is that she wants to be with me." Her fingers found Libby's nipples, which were still hard. "She fills a hunger in me, and for the longest time I didn't even know I was not only hungry, but I was starving." Not wanting to wait anymore, she moved her hand down and ran her index and middle finger through Libby's sex, finding it as hot and wet as an August rainstorm in New Orleans.

"Do you belong to me?" Libby asked. She spoke quietly, but her tone was filled with the authority that demanded an answer.

"I belong to you—" Tully wanted to tell Libby all the things she felt, but all that came out was a moan when Libby pressed her hand between them and pinched Tully's clitoris. Because of their height difference she couldn't reach any farther down, but Tully's hips jerked to meet her fingers, the movement pushing her fingers all the way into Libby's sex.

"Then prove it and come for me," Libby said before she moaned.

The slow pace Tully had been enjoying disappeared when Libby squeezed her fingers. She could feel her own orgasm forming and stroked faster, wanting Libby to come with her, wanting their first time as a committed couple to be a mutual experience. Just before she felt like she was going to explode from the inside out, Libby grabbed the hair at the back of Tully's head with her free hand and brought her down for the most passionate kiss they'd shared yet.

Unable to help herself, Tully gave in to what her body was craving and let go. From the way the walls of Libby's sex clutched her fingers, Tully could tell she wasn't too far behind. The orgasm was so hard that Tully slumped bonelessly into Libby, unable to move.

"Think you can manage about ten more of those tonight?" Libby asked as she outlined Tully's ear with her index finger and laughed.

"Maybe, if there's an ambulance handy." Tully found the strength to move and rolled off Libby, liking that Libby rolled with her. "Happy wedding day, baby."

"Can I make one request?"

"I think you're in a good position to request whatever you like," Tully said drolly, since Libby had her hand between Tully's legs again.

"I want to take a long honeymoon, maybe to Mexico, like you promised the kids and me."

"If you want to take Bailey and Ralph on our honeymoon, you're opening yourself up to teasing."

"It won't matter what we're doing from now on, honey. We'll have to be doing it with Ralph and Bailey. I don't feel right about leaving them behind if we don't have to."

"Right here, right now, I'd rather leave them behind," Tully said as she lifted her head to meet Libby's lips. "And you can have a honeymoon wherever you like and invite whoever you want to go."

"I want the kids in a suite where their rooms are about three hundred feet from ours."

If Tully thought to ask why the odd request, the grunt Libby was able to get out of her was answer enough. By the time they gave in to sleep, they hadn't done it ten more times, but Tully was sure she'd have a hard time getting up the next morning.

CHAPTER TWENTY-EIGHT

The next morning they almost had to crowbar each other out of the small shower, but they managed. By the time Bailey, Ralph, and Chase arrived to bring them breakfast, they had changed the sheets and were having coffee on the boat's deck.

"Mom, you go, girl," Bailey said as she sat on Tully's lap.

"Go where?" Tully asked, and everyone laughed.

"It's an expression that means you did good, goober," Bailey said with a roll of her eyes.

"I knew that. I was just testing you."

"Sure you were, and I was talking about the hickey on your neck," Bailey said, making Libby and Tully blush.

"Don't get any ideas, Chase," Tully said, adding one more blusher to the crowd. "I'm going to start doing thorough examinations of Bailey's neck." She held Bailey to keep her from getting up. "Just kidding, Bailey Bean, so wipe that scowl off your face."

"Can we go fishing today, Mom?" Ralph asked.

"Sure, we can take the boat out, just not too far. I'm not sure what kind of debris is out there and don't want to sink on my first trip out. That would give your uncles fodder for years to come."

A car door slammed behind them as a deputy who appeared to need a diet got out of the driver's side.

"Tyler, how's life treating you?" Tully asked, letting Bailey up. The visiting officer was her cousin Tyler, but she hadn't seen him in a while.

"Can't complain much except for the size of my waistline." He took off his sunglasses and put his boot on the side of the boat. "Got a minute, cousin?"

❖

Tully leaned against the squad car and after some conversation said, "Part of me wants to hear that you're kidding." She rubbed her chin and released a long breath. "And part of me wants videotape."

"That's part of our procedure now." Tyler wrapped his fingers around his utility belt as if it was getting ready to fall off. "That's not the reason I'm here, though."

"Of course not." Tully laughed. "I figure my mother's been filling you in on my personal life lately, and you sound like you're just getting started on your story."

"Aunt Alma told me just a little of what's going on with you. That's why I figured you'd want to know Jessica was in the car with this woman."

"Okay." Tully dragged out the word. "Once more from the top."

"The car was doing ninety on Highway 1 along Bayou Terrebonne, which is just crazy. We fished the Cheost boy out of there last month after looking for him for a week."

Tully laughed again. "Let's focus, buddy."

"Sorry. It took us about ten miles to get the driver to slow down and another ten for her to pull over. Herby thought the woman was intoxicated, so he tried to administer a sobriety test."

"You've been practicing, I see." She raised her thumb in approval. "If you were testifying in court, I'd say you did your job or, I should say, Herby did his job. What was his basis for the field test?"

"This woman"—he flipped through the notebook he took out of his shirt pocket—"Kara Nicolas fell out of the car when Herby opened her door after she refused to get out. He said he thought she would've gotten violent if Jessica hadn't been there to keep things calm."

"Did she pass?"

"No, and she refused the breathalyzer test so we had the right to take her in. From what Herby said, she couldn't walk a straight line if her life depended on it."

"I doubt you would've found something even if she'd agreed to it. Drinking isn't her problem. Where is she now?" Tully fell back against the car feeling as if she'd run a mile as fast as she could.

"Down at the local lockup. The sheriff is about to ship her off to the middle of the Gulf if she keeps on threatening to sue everyone in sight." He was close enough to Tully that their conversation stayed private. "I offered to call you for Jessica, but she turned me down."

"Imagine that. She would've probably rather run her hand through a table saw than have you call me. Where is she now?"

"Down at Mrs. Robichaux's bed and breakfast place. She's been trying to find an attorney, but she hasn't had much luck with everything going on. We didn't have the damage that New Orleans did, but the farther south you go the worse it gets." He glanced down the waterway at Gaston's boat. "How'd Uncle Gaston and the boys make out?"

"They lost all their nets and some rigging on their boats, but mostly okay." Tully smiled at Libby but didn't move. "Think you can arrange for me to see Kara? You can even call Jessica to be there if you want."

"You thinking of representing her?"

"Right after I join a cult that worships buffalo that wear leis made out of artichokes."

Tyler almost pushed Tully over after he started laughing. "Still a smart-ass, I see."

"It's part of my charm."

"I'll head back to the office and see if the queen of whine is up for visitors. If you're part of some lawsuit against her, I can't imagine she'd be up for it, but I live to be surprised."

"What's going on, honey?" Libby asked when Tully joined them again.

Tully gave her the rundown on what Tyler had said and finished by telling her she wanted to visit Kara. Libby didn't agree with the idea of Tully going alone, but nodded anyway.

"I'll be back in an hour or so once I leave, but I have a couple of phone calls to make first," Tully said.

"To whom?"

"It might be a problem, but I need to see if I can get in touch with Neil before I do anything about Kara. As the administrator of the hospital, he should be informed about what's happened and know that I'll have a videotape before the end of business today."

"I thought the phones weren't working."

"They're not, but I want to try. It's time to finish this." Tully moved closer and put her arms around Libby. "You don't agree with me?"

"I'm more than ready, but I don't see how you're going to go to court anytime soon. From the news we're getting out of the city, and after seeing it firsthand, we won't be back to normal for a long time."

"Let me start with going to see Kara Nicolas. After that, things should just fall into place."

Libby kissed her over her heart. "That's what I love about you, baby. Your optimism."

"I'm really optimistic about getting lucky when I get home," Tully said softly.

"That's not a real stretch, Counselor."

"Mom?" Bailey put her hand on Tully's back. "They didn't put Mama in jail too, did they?" Bailey had obviously overheard most of their conversation.

"Just the driver, babe, and in this case it was Kara."

"Where is she, then?" Bailey asked in a tone tainted with disappointment.

"She's staying at the bed and breakfast down the road," Tully said.

"When were you planning on telling us?" Bailey sounded like she was starting to get angry.

"Didn't you see me over there talking to Tyler? I just found out and I'm telling you." Tully let Libby go and took Bailey in her arms. "Tell me what's wrong."

Bailey didn't have enough strength to get away from her and began to cry.

In a show of support Ralph came up and put his arm around Bailey's waist. "I think I know what's wrong, Mom."

Tully started walking backward, not letting go of Bailey until the backs of her knees hit the chair they'd been sitting in. The sudden outburst of emotion from Bailey took Tully by surprise since she thought they had created a relationship that had lifted Bailey's spirits along with her self-esteem.

"What's wrong, buddy?" Tully asked.

"If Mama stayed, why didn't she stay with us?" Ralph appeared as broken as Bailey. "It's like her new girlfriend is more important than anything or anybody in her life."

Ralph had uttered the truth that Tully had tried to ignore. She had dealt with Jessica's abandonment in her own way, finding her second chance with Libby, but had glossed over what it had done to her children. As much as she wanted to be enough for both of them, she knew they missed their mother. Jessica's actions had cut deep, and Tully felt she hadn't done enough to make up for that loss, especially at this difficult time in their lives when love had to be proven over and over again, like the simplest tasks being taught to an addle-minded person.

Tully had to tell them the harsh truth, because Jessica refused to. "Is that what's wrong?" she asked Bailey, who nodded. "I don't know why your mama did what she did. Leaving me was one thing, and I somewhat understand her motivations there, but honestly I don't understand when it comes to you two."

"She doesn't care, she never did," Bailey said.

"Bailey, you know that's not true, and I know this is going to make you angry"—Tully glanced up at Ralph so he'd know she meant him as well—"but you need to wait on that judgment."

"I don't need to wait to figure out what I already know," Bailey got out between sniffles. "Some crankhead is more important than me and Ralph. Those are the facts, as you love to say."

"Okay, I'll concede that point because I don't have a counterargument, but I want you to promise me something."

"What?" both Ralph and Bailey asked.

"Right now you have every right to be angry, and no one should try to convince you otherwise, but one day you might want to listen to her side of the story. That might be tomorrow or a couple of years down the line. Whenever it might be, don't let your anger get in the way of a relationship that could be important to you."

Bailey sat up and wiped her face with the tissue Libby handed her. "You're not going to make me change my mind?"

"Honey," said Libby, "I think your mom knows she'd have better luck trying to get you to join a convent than change your mind about something like this. If you were about to do something harmful, then she'd pull out all the stops to get you to reconsider, but not on something like this." Libby put her hand on Bailey's cheek and wiped away the last of her tears. "Just try to talk to either of us before it eats you up inside. Because by now I hope you know, when it comes to you and Ralph, neither of us is going anywhere."

Bailey pointed at Tully with her thumb. "Just remind her of that when she tries to make me do something I don't want to."

"Sometimes I wish I had that luxury," Tully said. She kissed Bailey's forehead before opening her free arm to embrace Ralph and repeating the action. "The last thing I want to do is waste my time visiting Kara Nicolas, but that's exactly what I have to do so let me get going."

❖

PLEASE KEEP ALL YOUR CLOTHES ON WHEN VISITING THE INMATES! The sign in the waiting room of the local jail always made Tully laugh. She could only imagine what the guards had seen to make them put it up in the first place.

"Tully, she's in room three," the guard behind the Plexiglas window said before pressing the buzzer that released the door lock.

Being in this confined space, though it was cleaner than most jails, made Tully glad she hadn't picked criminal practice. She could still count on one hand the number of times she'd had reason to visit places like this.

"You woke me up from a nap for this?" Kara asked when she stopped in front of the glass. "I thought the idiot was kidding when he said you wanted to see me." She pointed at the guard.

"You don't have to talk to me if you don't want to. As a matter of record, I need to inform you that you should actually have your counsel present before we exchange another word."

"Hell, you're the first attorney who agreed to come, so why the hell not. It's not like I'm going to suddenly break down and confess to something I didn't do." Kara dropped into her seat and casually lounged back.

"You do realize I can't represent you. If you've forgotten with all the trouble you've gotten into since the storm, I'm suing you on behalf of the Hebert family."

"Still don't know the definition of 'accident,' do you?" Kara pressed her fist against the glass. "Considering how Jessica talks about you, I wouldn't hire you to represent me for the traffic ticket this is going to result in."

"It's my understanding it's a little more complicated than speeding, but no matter. I don't see Jessica whipping out any miracles for you. Don't believe everything someone tells you just because she's willing to sleep with you."

"She couldn't have been that bad if you're still wearing your wedding ring." Kara's eyes dropped down to Tully's hand.

Tully glanced down as well. The gold of the band felt warm

against her thumb. "I met Jessica in college and thought for the longest time that she would help me improve those parts of myself that refused to let go of the kid raised by a hardworking fisherman and a housewife. I believed I had to abandon that part of myself for her to be proud of me."

"Should I have tears in my eyes by now?" A laugh dripping with sarcasm bubbled out of Kara's chest. "When I started tapping Jessica, I'd feel sorry for you sometimes. You think us fucking on your bed was a mistake?" She laughed again. "She did it because she knew you'd never figure it out. And here you are still pining away. Jessica was right, you're pathetic."

"Thanks for sharing. I see that this is a complete waste of my time."

The policeman sitting with Kara stood when she punched the glass hard enough to make it rattle as Tully rose to leave. "Hit too close to home?" she taunted.

"I didn't come for you to try to provoke me on dead subjects."

"What's that mean?"

"To the Hebert couple you'll always be the person who killed their child." Tully leaned forward and pressed her fists into the small counter. "No matter what I think of someone personally, professionally before I move ahead with my plans I like to see if they still have any redeeming quality, any remorse for the misery they've brought other people. I came to get a sense of where I need to head next."

"Does that road lead you to hell?"

"When the Heberts came to me, at first I thought of them as grieving parents who couldn't accept that their child had lost a fight to cancer and that this was just a senseless tragedy."

Because Tully was still standing and the guard had forced Kara back into her chair, she had to crane her neck up. "That's all you'll ever have because that's what happened. You're only pushing this case because of Jessica."

"If anything, I'm willing to cut you some slack because of Jessica. Not because of what you think, but because I owe you my thanks for putting that last much-talked-about nail in the coffin of the relationship we had."

"You think I'm falling for this?"

When Tully placed her hand against the glass, the ring Libby had given her clicked against it. "Jessica gave me twenty-two years of her life, and two children. And she and the Heberts brought you into my life. But she never gave me a ring. That came from the woman who I plan to spend the rest of my life with."

Tully laughed when she saw the shocked expression on Kara's face, but shook her head when Kara balled her hands into fists. Since she knew that Kara's first response to anything was violence, Tully looked forward to getting her out of their lives as soon as possible.

"I wish you the best when it comes to Jessica. If you need my blessing, you have it. Turns out the best thing I could have changed in my life to be happy was the girl."

"You aren't kidding, are you?"

"I only tell tales when I come home from fishing."

"Wait!" The chair scraped a little wax off the industrial tile when Tully pushed it back into place, but Kara kept her seat. "What are you planning to do?"

"So many things that I don't have time to list them all. If you're worried I'll forget you, you're definitely in the top five of my things to do." At a nod from Tully, the guard moved to the door to unlock it for her. "Enjoy your stay and I'll see you soon."

"The sheriff's ready to see you," the guard said as he showed Tully out.

Walking across the waiting room toward the sheriff's office, Tully slowed only when she saw Jessica sitting under the only window staring down at her shoes. Her wrinkled blue scrubs appeared to be the same ones she'd come to town in.

"You need a minute, Tully?" the patrolman asked.

"Just with Carl." Tully kept walking.

A huge moose head hung over the sheriff's desk with a plaque that proudly announced where and when Carl had killed it.

"How in the hell did you find a judge in New Orleans to sign this?" Carl asked, holding up a court order. "And in less than twenty minutes after you found out about it?"

"You always told me when you have your prey in the scope, don't hesitate to pull the trigger." She picked up the videocassette he slid over. "This isn't the kill shot, but it's good bait to line up my trophy." She pointed up to the moose head.

"This going to put an end to Evangeline's case?"

"With any luck, yes."

"Herby will be ready if you need him to testify. Those folks have suffered enough, and they deserve the justice you're going to give them."

"You got it, Sheriff." She tapped the tape. "And thanks for this."

"Does this mean you won?" Jessica asked as Tully headed for the exit.

"The sad thing is that you're the only one who doesn't see that she needs help." Tully stopped with her hand on the doorknob.

"Just let it go, Tully."

"For old times' sake, huh?"

"For once, prove to me that you have a heart."

"My proving days are over, and you lost the right to ask me for anything a long time ago."

Jessica stood up when the guard called her name, but her attention stayed on Tully. "You bitch."

"When it comes to certain things I guess you're right, but you knew that already. I haven't changed all that much since you left or from the time we met." The heat from outside warmed Tully's legs and side as she opened the door wider. "I just had a conversation with Dr. Nicolas, and I'll tell you what I told her. If you need my blessing for a life together, you have it. I really do want you to be happy, Jessica, no matter what your opinion of me is. If it's with Kara Nicolas, then so be it; only find the strength to help her make the hard decisions."

"There's no going back for you, is there?"

"You taught me something with all this, so no."

Jessica put her hand up to her forehead and shaded the sun streaming through the door Tully was holding open. "You're going to tell me I taught you how to hate me?"

"You taught me that you weren't enough for me anymore, and that's okay because I wasn't enough for you either."

"Of course *she*'s enough for you. She's, like, ten years old. How hard is she to keep happy?"

"Libby isn't up for discussion. Not now and not ever, so try and remember that. I realized I had only so much time to make up to Bailey and Ralph what I had neglected for too long." She paused as if to let her words sink in. "I don't want them to think they were an afterthought in both our lives. They deserve better than that."

"I'm sure you've had ample time to warp their feelings for me."

"You can't have forgotten that much about me already. Your relationship with them will have nothing to do with me."

Jessica let out a short laugh. "Just like everything in my life, what I make of it will have nothing to do with you."

"Finally we agree to agree on something. You're on your own, darlin'. Try and make the best of it."

With that final bit of advice, Tully walked out and left Jessica to her visit. Tully was sure that Jessica felt the storm surge had washed away any concerns and consequences resulting from Kara's arrest and disrupted law enforcement to the point of chaos.

And she was partially correct. Tully was a good lawyer, but she knew the rules had changed in this post-Katrina world. She had lost her arena. The courthouse at Tulane and Broad Street where she had slain her dragons had been deluged by six feet of water.

CHAPTER TWENTY-NINE

Tully smiled when she recognized two of the newly arrived cars in Alma's driveway. The vehicles were bug- and mud-splattered, but the fact that they were there at all made her hope their occupants had fared better.

Roxanne's husband and her teenage son James had been at the office when Tully had called everyone in to prepare for their evacuation. James had talked about the upcoming football season as his mother made backup disks for her and Tully to take with them. Tully wondered now what would happen to the school year. The flooding had damaged much more than the homes and businesses.

The other car belonged to her junior associate Josephine. Jo was single and had headed up to Baltimore to stay with her parents, but in her few telephone conversations with Tully she'd said she was coming back to her newly adopted home. She said she had heard from the nightly news that cases were still pending and clients were waiting to be represented.

"Carrying on the fun without us?" Roxanne asked from the porch.

"Some fun is hard to resist, and then there's the kind that's like having your wisdom teeth removed without meds."

"Which one were you out having?" Jo asked as she appeared next to Roxanne.

"I just had a short visit with Kara Nicolas. She's in jail in an attractive orange jumpsuit with a Plexiglas window separating us." Tully rocked on her heels and laughed. "I haven't had that much fun at work in a long time."

"If you'd said in a long time, period, I'm thinking of someone who'd have knocked your head back a few pegs." Roxanne pointed behind her at Libby, who was walking out of the house carrying two glasses. "Congratulations, by the way. Your mother and I had every faith in you to finally get it right. And this time around you got it right." She put her arm around Libby's shoulders and kissed her on the cheek.

"Thank you from both of us," Tully said. She accepted a glass of tea and a kiss from Libby. "I see you all made it okay. How did your homes fare? Have you had a chance to make it back to the city yet?"

"My house in Lakeview got about twelve feet of water," Jo said. "After I saw it was close to the eaves, I didn't really need an accurate figure. My neighbor, who I begged to come with me, didn't make it. I saw one of those painted messages in front of his house." Jo shivered and rubbed her hands along her arms.

"Our place in Metairie got six feet," Roxanne added. "They still won't let us in, but a policeman who lives on our street called everyone and gave them the bad news. James is still upset over losing the baseball cards he's collected since he was five. Of all the stuff in the house, that's what's got him down."

"I know a little bit about the way he feels," Jo said. "Some woman in a gas station on my way back here told me I should be happy because I was safe and my family was all right. She said the rest is just stuff."

"She's right about the family part, but hell if it isn't our stuff and we liked it, huh? Losing it all isn't exactly a picnic," Roxanne said with a laugh.

"After so many died, I hate to complain about things, but some of the furniture I had belonged to my grandmother. Pottery Barn can't replace those memories." Jo exhaled at length. "But enough morbid thoughts."

"True." Roxanne patted her on the knee and turned to Tully and Libby. "Jo and I were in touch the whole time we were on the run, as it were, and we also spoke to Pasco a few times."

"After that we donned our WWTD bracelets," Jo said.

"WWTD?" Libby asked.

"What would Tully do," Roxanne supplied, getting a snort out of Tully. "After we got the information Pasco passed on to us, we made a few appointments."

"Not without a little difficulty, mind you," Jo said. "We worked on the case file and have a court date Wednesday in Baton Rouge with a Judge Archibald Raymond. With Pasco's help we were able to serve Neil Davis at Children's and their attorney, Victor Williams."

"I hope you both realize that right now we can't prove that Evangeline died because Kara was taking an illegal substance. We all know she was, but unless we have a witness willing to come forward to testify to that, all we have is speculation," Tully said as she flipped through what they had filed.

"That's why we're going to court Wednesday—not on the Hebert case, but to argue that Dr. Nicolas should be barred from practicing until all this is sorted out. We have enough evidence to back us up on that one." Jo got up and flipped to the final page of the brief so Tully could see the meat of the document she'd compiled. "The meeting with Neil and Victor tomorrow morning is merely a courtesy on our part, but I think Victor is going to see that our getting that injunction Wednesday is the first step in winning our case."

"A little speculation never hurt anyone, huh?" Tully asked with a laugh.

"If you were a gambling woman, you'd be putting your money on us not even needing to go to court tomorrow. Victor's going to talk the board into settling this as quickly as possible."

"Let's roll the dice, then," Tully said. She stood up and put the brief under her arm. "And let's get back to work."

❖

"You need to call Neil and tell him to contact someone on Victor's staff and get me out of here," Kara said through the glass. "Once you get through, you should try and get some sleep, Jessica—you're not looking too good."

"I haven't slept in days, so I'm sorry I'm not up to par, and dragging Neil into this isn't the wisest thing to do right now. We need to get an appearance in court and see if we can't post bail so we can leave for Texas."

Kara laughed, but her eyes remained cold. "I've never been in jail, but on TV part of the deal is you don't leave the state, baby. These hicks will most likely outfit me with one of those ankle devices, just to stay on Tully's good side."

"I'm trying my best to help you, and I think it's time you start listening to me."

"Wait." Kara put her fingers up to the side of her head and closed her eyes as if trying to read Jessica's mind. "You gave up everything for me, and I'm supposed to just roll over and play your bitch now, right?"

"I did give up plenty to be with you, and if it isn't enough, then you need to tell me. This is about both of us and what we have to lose." Jessica tried taking long, deep breaths to keep her temper under control. "You didn't believe me about Tully and what she's like when she gets her teeth into something. It's bad enough when she has to work for the truth, but you've been more than accommodating when it comes to just handing yourself over on a platter."

"I thought you said not to give her that much credit."

Jessica laughed, starting softly and gathering steam that ended in tears. "When it came to me, not her job. It was the job that made her forget all about me a long time ago, and it didn't matter enough to me to fight to get her back."

"So what are you trying to tell me?"

"That it's not just you that's going to lose out big on this one. I have a lot on the block too, and Tully is going to exploit every weakness we've exposed, and she's going to start stripping us of everything important. You have your career to worry about, and I have my kids. Tully might have been a lousy spouse, but she's a brilliant attorney, especially if she's pissed at something and someone. Up to now we've done an excellent job at ratcheting up her anger, so it's time to stop poking the bear with a sharp stick and go into survival mode if we're going to get through this."

"You can't walk away from me," Kara said with her hand on the glass. She appeared close to panicked.

"I'm trying to fix this, not leave. If that's what I wanted, I wouldn't be here."

"Do what you have to, but get me out of here and I'll do whatever you ask."

Jessica nodded, then got up to talk to the guard. She knew that the only way to get Kara out was to talk to the sheriff—which wouldn't be easy; he'd known Tully since kindergarten. To her surprise, she was immediately taken to Carl's office.

"Thanks for seeing me so quickly, Sheriff," Jessica said, grimacing when she saw the moose head.

"Anytime." He waved to the chair across from his so she'd take a seat. "What can I do for you?"

"I need you to help get Dr. Nicolas a court appearance for a bail hearing."

"Between you and me, if she volunteers to take a drug test I can have her in front of Judge Larkin within the hour."

"And if she doesn't?"

"I don't know if you've noticed, ma'am, but we had a storm blow through here not that long ago. Things are moving like molasses these days."

She glared at Carl, literally biting her tongue, as his smile grew wider. "I believe that's what's called extortion."

"Make accusations like that and our meeting is over. Good luck in getting that court date, and please let me know if there's anything I can do for you."

When Jessica stood up abruptly, her chair scraped along the tile floor, filling the quiet room with a screech. "I thought you were innocent until proven guilty."

"And I thought you and the yahoo you came into town with took an oath to first do no harm. Life's a bitch, ain't it?"

"You'll be hearing from our attorney."

"Looking forward to that. But before you go off hunting for one, make sure you'll have a room at that place you're staying. It's going to be a long search."

"I'll leave the hunting up to you, since it seems to be a barbaric hobby of yours." Jessica gestured at the moose head.

"Freddie here proves a point of mine, so that's why I keep him hanging around." Carl stood up and patted the trophy on the snout.

"That you have the ability to kill a defenseless, stupid animal?"

"That I have the ability to bring down what I'm hunting for. A doctor who likes to use recreational drugs might just be good to keep Freddie company, but I wouldn't want to stink up the place."

"Fuck you, Carl."

"You have a nice day now, Jessica, and happy hunting."

Chapter Thirty

Tully felt Libby grip her hand as they drove through New Orleans on their way to Children's Hospital. The streets were still mostly empty, with only a few lost souls walking around as if dazed amidst the police and National Guard troops still occupying the city. With so much debris everywhere, it was hard to figure out where to begin.

"Honey, do you think it's smart to go home once we're able to?" Libby asked.

"I'm not going to force you to do something you don't want, but I don't want to abandon the city. The kids love it here too, and you have a year of school left, whenever they open it up again. Do you really want to walk away from that?" They were driving past Tulane, which appeared to be locked down tight.

"At least I have a job." Libby turned away from the window as she teased Tully.

"That you do, darlin', and while it's not going to be easy, I think it'll be good for us to start fresh here together. If we're going to build a life, this seems like a good time to start. From the looks of this place, we're at least a little ahead of everyone else, since our damage is minor. For now, though, we'll stay with Mom and Dad and live on the boat if things get tight."

Jo looked out the window as they drove along, appearing lost in thought. "Do you think Victor's going to recognize you without the power suit?"

Libby ran her nails along Tully's jeans and smiled at the question. When they had evacuated, Tully hadn't packed any work clothes, so casual was the style of the day. "Maybe when they see your ass in these pants, they'll give you whatever you want. I know I would."

"Can I quote you on that when I see Roxanne again?" Jo asked Libby.

"No more comments from the cheap seats," Tully said. "We're here."

The same police officer Tully had spoken to when she'd gone in on the day of the evacuation was again on duty when she stepped into the lobby. With no patients and only a few staff people trying to clean up the storm damage, the hospital was quiet and calm.

"If you're Tully Badeaux, that short guy said he was waiting for you in the executive boardroom. Said you'd know where he was talking about."

"Thanks, Officer, and it's nice to see you're all right."

Neil's appearance stopped her from saying anything for a long while. The man actually appeared older than the last time she'd seen him, and a bone-deep exhaustion clung to him like lint. Next to him Victor wore chinos and was freshly showered, smiling as if he were waiting for a tee time.

"We appreciate you stopping by today, Tully. It saved us from having to call you in for another talk. After all the excitement we've all lived through, it's time to start fresh, without this old business hanging over our heads." Victor stood up and offered her his hand.

"Considering what you all are facing," Tully responded, "I appreciate you making the time."

After shaking hands they sat down and exchanged pleasantries on how they had made out in the storm. Throughout the entire meeting, Neil just stared at her, letting Victor do the talking.

"Like I was saying, Tully, we want to put this to rest and concentrate on getting the hospital back up and running," Victor said as he retrieved a file from the folder in front of him. "We're prepared to make another offer based on what you presented to us before the storm. Since Dr. Nicolas is no longer here, we can't enforce the apology the Heberts wanted, but we'll try our best to get in touch with her and have her comply."

It was too easy. Victor never gave in that easily to anything, especially admitting some culpability on the part of one of their doctors. Tully thought about what she'd told Jo and Roxanne the day before.

They couldn't prove Kara's sobriety the day of the surgery, which was a fact. But sometimes fate gave you the chance to gamble, not because you got a glimpse of the other guy's cards, but because you could see the beginning of the moisture on his brow. Victor was holding shit for a hand, but he thought he was doing a good job of bluffing.

"I figured with all the excitement around here you haven't had a chance to put this case on the fast track you threatened me with at our last meeting, so we went ahead and arranged that. I believe you were served with those papers yesterday."

"If you accept the offer that won't be necessary," Neil said, speaking for the first time.

"I'll even give you a break and waive a jury trial and let the judge decide the outcome." Tully kept talking over him. "We're ready to go tomorrow."

"The papers your people filed were for injunctions against Nicolas, and she's no longer here, so what does that have to do with the hospital?" Neil asked.

"If you need to find Dr. Nicolas, who's still in your employ, by the way, since I haven't seen any evidence to indicate otherwise, she's sitting in central lockup in Montegut, Louisiana. She was stopped for driving under the influence of some undetermined substance." Tully took the videotape out of her briefcase and laid it on the table. "This is the tape of that traffic stop and consequent arrest. Before the storm she was documented buying illegal drugs from a known dealer in New Orleans east." She laid down the pictures Pasco's team had taken, thumping them on the table in one big wad. "And we have a few more photos and video of her taking those drugs on the campus of this very hospital before the storm."

"What does this have to do with the Hebert case?" Victor asked.

"On second thought, we'll wait and have that jury trial," Tully said as she fanned the photos out. "What does this have to do with the Hebert case? It shows a pattern of behavior, a pattern that was like pointing a loaded gun at an innocent little girl and firing without thought or conscience. Because that's what a doctor operating under the influence is, a loaded gun. I'll paint the jury a map that might need to get from point A to point B via points LMNOPQ, but I'll get them there." It was as big a bluff as the one Victor had tried, but Tully had a much better poker face.

"You still have to prove that she was high the day of that surgery." Neil slammed his hand down on the table. "And I really don't see that happening."

"Like I said, I need to prove a pattern of behavior, first off." She raised her index finger. "Then I put the dealer on the stand to see just how long Dr. Nicolas has been a loyal customer," another finger went up, "and I finish with a witness from the hospital."

"Who'd you talk to?" Neil demanded.

"And ruin the surprise for you? Where's your sense of adventure, shorty?"

"You bitch," Neil said with a sneer. He stopped when Victor put his hand on his forearm and squeezed hard.

"What do you want?" Victor asked.

"Three and a half million for pain and suffering, and Dr. Nicolas doesn't step foot in an operating room in this hospital again, not even to clean the floors, until we decide on a length of time she can prove sobriety. That means you help me enforce that restriction, even if she decides to seek work somewhere else, no matter the state."

The room was silent, as if everyone was waiting to see where the dice would land. "Done," Victor said finally. "You'll have the papers in the morning."

"I'll have the papers now, thank you. The aftermath of the storm will make it difficult to get all the signatures you need, but it's not impossible. We'll wait, but if you want the deal and for Josephine here to call off tomorrow's court appearance, then you'll get it done."

"Fine, give me an hour and I'll have it ready for your signature."

"That gives me plenty of time to call the Heberts so they can sign as well." Tully saw Josephine already on the land line, but from the way she was hitting the disconnect button, there was still no dial tone. The deal was really more than they wanted, way more, but she thought the turn of events wouldn't exactly upset the Heberts.

Tully didn't know if Victor or Neil knew of Kara's past, but she had been willing to gamble and guess they did. Having knowledge of such reprehensible behavior made them as responsible for what had happened to Evangeline as Kara. Tully wanted to believe that they didn't, but they weren't willing to let Tully weave a tale of such neglect in front of a jury.

"Kara might have problems, but she would've made a fine surgeon," Neil said. The angrier he'd gotten, the deeper the crease in his brow had become. "She'll never live up to that potential now because of you."

"It doesn't sound like you believe she can keep clean. If Kara Nicolas had aspired to be a rock star, then I still wouldn't have understood her addiction, but murdering a few notes in a song is different from what she did. In this line of work so many things can go wrong, without any outside factors like drugs coming into play."

"I know all that, so don't preach to me, Tully."

"I'm not preaching. I merely mentioned it because you have no idea how many clients I turn away when I think a surgeon did his best and something just went wrong because of the patient's health or unexpected bleeding." She accepted the papers Victor's assistant handed her and placed them on the table in front of her. "You never mention all those cases where I explain to a grieving family that no matter how much pain they're in, the doctor and the hospital aren't to blame. It's just fate."

"That's because for all the ones you turn down, some other vulture's ready to take your place. You lawyers will ruin health care."

"When it comes to people like Kara, that's not such a bad thing, is it? I'm sure if one of your kids had been on that table, your thoughts on the subject would be different."

Ignoring Neil, Tully started reading, not wanting to waste her time trying to convince him of something he would never admit—at least not publicly until, as he said, a vulture like her came along and convinced him it was in his best interest to give a little instead of lose everything he held dear. Three and a half million sounded like a fortune to most, but she was willing to bet four times that amount that the Heberts would trade it for just one more week with their daughter.

❖

"How do you plead?"

Kara blinked a few times, trying to curb the craving for a fix. She was standing in front of an elderly judge.

"Shouldn't I have a lawyer?"

"You can have a clown on a tricycle if you want, ma'am, but there's a line of people waiting to see me. If you'd like bail, then go ahead and enter a plea." He looked up at her over his glasses.

"Not guilty," Kara said.

"No record, from what I can see," his attention went back to the papers, "so I'm going to release you on your own recognizance. The district attorney's office will send you your court date information. Make sure you give accurate information on where we can find you, or we'll write a warrant to put you back in here so quick it'll make your tail spin."

"I can go?"

"As soon as you sign a few things." The judge signed first, then slid the document toward her. She didn't read a line before signing, and he shook his head.

It took another twenty minutes, but Kara traded her orange scrubs for her blue ones and walked outside the building, blinking in the brightness of midmorning. After a few failed phone calls to Jessica, she figured cell-phone service was still a victim of the storm. Unfortunately, when Jessica had droned on about where she was staying, Kara had tuned her out. Even if she wanted to start walking, she had no idea which way to go.

The oak tree across the street cast a large patch of shade close to Bayou Terrebonne, so, after being locked up for all those hours, she headed in that direction, planning to sit and wait for Jessica to come for her afternoon visit. The car stopping behind Kara made her turn around and squint to try and make out the driver, but with the glare of the sun on the front windshield, all she could make out was the outline of someone's head.

"Need a ride?"

Kara kept her hand up to her brow. "Is there a place to stay around here? I'm actually trying to find a friend of mine."

"There's a place about four miles from here. We can start there if you want. Hop in."

The voice sounded familiar, but Kara ignored the warning bell, wanting to get back to the small bag she'd hidden in the trunk of Jessica's car.

"Thanks, I appreciate not having to sit out there for hours."

The car made a U-turn and headed south, and when they passed the large house with the bed and breakfast sign and Jessica's car parked in front, Kara decided to turn and study the driver's face. The fog finally cleared. For what seemed like an eternity she didn't recognize it; then an arrow of fear pierced her brain, and she reached for a nonexistent door handle. She was thinking she might able to escape when the car stopped, but the fist connecting with the side of her face sent her world into darkness.

❖

"I can't believe you got that done so quickly," Libby said as they walked to the car. "And I can't believe you found a witness and didn't tell us about it."

"Oh, there was no witness." Tully smiled at her. "I guess there were plenty the day of the surgery, since it's something that doesn't happen in a vacuum, but none of them were willing to talk."

"Should I be worried that you bluff so well?" Libby gave her a pointed look.

"You don't have to worry about that. I don't think I could bluff you at all, since you have ways of wheedling things out of me that Neil can only dream about."

"I'm actually more shocked that he didn't take you up on your offer to go to trial, even with the witness."

"Neil knows the golden rule of civil law."

"Another rule?" Libby asked, slipping her hand into Tully's.

"Well, it's my rule anyway." Tully leaned over and kissed her on the side of the head. "This case would've been hard to win even with a real witness and all the evidence we gathered on Kara's obvious habit, if Kara had been the kind of doctor a jury wants to believe."

"I don't follow."

"Good doctors are cocky but human. Confidence is a desirable personality trait for them because they have to believe in themselves to do what's necessary to get the job done. They should give you a sense that, despite what's wrong with you, they have the talent and the know-how to fix the problem. But they also have to make you think that they care a little about you as a person. It doesn't have to be a warm fuzzy feeling, but you have to walk away believing that they connected with you on some level. Kara hadn't gotten to that place yet. A jury would've convicted her on principle, and he realized that."

"So what happens to Kara now?"

"I'm sure with what she just cost the hospital, she'll have a hard time finding another job for a long time, even if she does stay clean. If she decides to go somewhere else, our agreement won't be binding, but since it isn't a closed settlement, I'll be happy to write a nice long letter to whoever decides to employ her. We can't bring her up on any charges unless I do find a witness to testify she was high, but even then we don't have any blood work or tests to back that up. Elijah and Simone will get what they wanted, just not in the way they thought they would."

CHAPTER THIRTY-ONE

A car drove up before they got to Tully's SUV, and a young blonde waved to Jo from the driver's seat.

"I'll find my way back to your folks', guys," Jo said, "but I called a friend who I might be staying with until I decide what I'm doing with my house."

"Have fun," Libby told her.

After they left, Tully pressed Libby to her and rested her chin on the top of Libby's head. "I have an idea, Mrs. Badeaux."

"I'm getting some of my own, Mrs. Badeaux." Libby bit her gently on her chest just above her heart. "We have a house with a pine tree in the pool, but the new bed looked really good the last time we were there. Care to go have an official christening?"

"We haven't been together for years, but you can already read my mind?"

"I could spend the afternoon trying to read your mind, or I could spend it trying to memorize every inch of you. I'm sure there are some spots that I haven't gotten to yet."

Tully laughed and kissed the top of her head while letting her hand drop down to Libby's backside. "The parts you *have* gotten to know well are incredibly happy, though."

The drive to the house knocked some of the playfulness out of Libby as they went through some areas that obviously had gotten about five feet of water. On one block the houses had stayed like theirs, high and dry; then in the next she saw small piles of Sheetrock already sitting out front waiting for the trash man. While the extent of the damage was disheartening, the little signs of life gave her hope that the misery would eventually end.

"Can I tell you something?" Libby stopped Tully from getting out of the car.

"You can say anything you want, baby, you know that."

"I want us to come back here, no matter how hard it is at first. You were right about that. We belong here, and I want to build our family in this house." They had parked in front, and the place appeared as serene as it would on any other summer day. "I love you, and the one thing I admire about you is that you never back away from a fight."

"Let's go get started on that. Besides, I want to show you something." Tully opened her car door and went around to open Libby's. Libby hadn't been on her feet very long when Tully picked her up and carried her up the stairs to the porch. "I've gotten such a reputation of being a workaholic that I don't want you to ever think I'm not romantic, so I thought today would be the perfect day to start proving that to you in spectacular form."

"Planning on sweeping me off my feet, huh?"

"I'm planning on so much more than that." Tully stopped at the door, and when Libby bent to turn the knob, Tully took a step back. "I think the elves will get it, baby."

"Elves?" The door opened and Bailey and Ralph stood there smiling, as if they knew a secret that was bursting to come out. "Elves," Libby said again.

"Elves who'll be leaving with their grandmother, but helpful nonetheless," Tully said, giving her kids a wink.

"Have fun, guys, and we'll be fine, I'm sure," Bailey said. She grabbed Ralph by the back of his collar and dragged him out. "Since you're holding the girl, I guess you don't have time to recap what happened today, huh?"

"Tomorrow, Bailey Bean, I promise." Tully kissed both of the kids and nodded in her mom's direction when she drove up.

"They all know we're going in there to have sex, don't they?" As Libby made the comment she felt the heat rise from her chest all the way to her ears.

"In the future we might not make such blatant declarations, but today I think we deserve to have a good time no matter who knows about it."

"It's still kind of embarrassing."

Tully carried Libby through the open door and pushed it closed with her foot. The house was still warm, but a slight breeze came in from the windows the kids had opened since the electricity was still not up and running. Libby didn't say anything until Tully stopped at the entrance to the master suite. The candles, the bowl of strawberries next to the bed, and the soft music from the battery-operated radio made her heart overflow.

"They'll most probably tease us mercilessly from now until the end of time, but today they wanted to give us a wedding present," Tully said. She sat at the edge of the bed, which was covered with fresh new linens, and kissed Libby's cheek. "It's their way of showing us how much they love us, and welcoming you into my life."

"I know sometimes you feel like you could've done a better job when it comes to Bailey and Ralph, but they're great kids." Libby put her hand on Tully's cheek and kissed her on the lips. "That shows you did a great job."

"I didn't think I'd succeeded in making them proud of me until just now. You made that possible for me." Tully leaned over and laid her down. "I love you, and I want to show you how much."

As Tully leaned over her, Libby started on the buttons of the blue shirt Tully had picked to wear with her jeans. The overwhelming urge to feel Tully's skin pressed up to every naked inch of her took Libby by surprise, but Tully appeared more surprised when, after the second button, Libby just ripped the shirt open, sending a shower of buttons to the wood floor.

"Remind me to order some rugs for this room," she told Tully. Tully's deep laugh as she took off her pants made Libby's nipples harden to the point of pain as they fought the confinement of her bra. Tully sat her up and helped the situation by unhooking the undergarment with one hand.

Any notion of decorating fled Libby's mind as the rest of their clothes landed on the floor. A groan laced with want escaped her as Tully's lips latched around her left nipple and sucked it past her teeth and into her warm mouth.

"What else would you like for this room?" Tully asked after she released Libby's nipple with a soft pop.

"I'd love a few things, but they have nothing to do with decorating."

Tully had yet to touch her anywhere below her breasts, but as

Libby straddled Tully's legs she could feel her clitoris pulsing in a way that begged to be touched.

"You are so beautiful," Tully said, her teasing put aside as she stopped and simply gazed at Libby's face. "I could tell you the exact moment I first saw you."

"There's a chance I could sound really sappy, but I can tell you that story too." Libby ran her fingers along Tully's jaw, then just under the skin around the bottom of her eyes. "I don't know how many cups of coffee I served in a morning, but it was enough to make the people I handed those cups to become almost invisible after a while. But when you talked to me over that counter, I fell into your eyes."

"I felt the same way. You had your hair in a ponytail and looked a little frazzled with the pace, but your smile just set off your face."

Libby ran her fingers back down until she linked them behind Tully's neck. "All those days and all those cups of coffee, you were the one thing I always waited for. It's childish, I know, but you always made me feel that someone thought about me, which made me feel special."

"You *are* special, love, and what makes me the luckiest woman alive is that you're mine." Libby's nipples had softened a bit, but at Tully's declaration they became rock hard again.

"Prove it to me."

As the words left Libby's mouth, Tully squeezed her hand between them and in one short thrust had two fingers buried deep inside her. When the palm of her hand brushed against Libby's clitoris, it instantly sparked the beginning of her orgasm.

With her knees on the bed and her hands behind Tully's neck, Libby thrust her hips forward and groaned. She tried to pay attention to Tully's words, but she could concentrate only on Tully's fingers sliding in and out and how good Tully's skin felt pressed against her. The last thing she wanted was for the sensations to end, but she couldn't help speeding up her hips and claiming the touch that was hers. She pulled Tully's hair as she reached the pinnacle, coming down on Tully's hand and enjoying the way her clitoris pulsed against Tully as the spasms died down.

"This feels so good that I may demand that the honeymoon not end," Libby said, feeling as limp as overcooked pasta.

"That sounds like a hardship." Tully stopped laughing only when Libby pinched her nipple and tugged.

"Don't make me get rough with you, Badeaux."

"You might want to remember where I have my hand before you go making threats, beautiful." For emphasis Tully pushed her fingers in far enough to make Libby gasp.

"If that's your form of punishment, I might take up threatening you as a hobby." Libby smiled innocently at her, then put her index finger on Tully's forehead and pushed her to lie flat on the bed. "Swing your legs onto the bed for me, baby."

Tully did as she was told. "Comfortable up there?"

"If you bent your knees up for me and put your feet flat on the bed," Libby leaned back as soon as Tully did it, "I'd be more comfortable."

The new position made Tully's fingers go in as far as they could. "I love feeling you inside me," Libby said, pushing her hips back enough so just the tips stayed inside. "I love it because I know it turns you on as much as it does me."

With that Libby leaned back enough so her fingers landed between Tully's legs. "So…so wet," she said. She was having trouble staying focused as Tully brought her thumb forward, so when Tully moved her fingers back in, Libby felt a delicious stimulation.

Before the sensual haze set in, Libby started stroking Tully slowly but firmly. Her fingers moved easily through Tully's wetness, and as soft as the path was, it was difficult to miss her hard clitoris.

The thought of bringing Tully the same pleasure she'd just received made the walls of Libby's sex clutch at Tully's fingers. Despite her inexperience she tried to hang on so she could watch Tully let go for her.

She whispered, "I love you," and the words brought Tully to the same peak she was rapidly climbing again. She claimed it readily with one last grunt as Libby joined her. After that they lay together just sharing soft touches and kisses until they fell asleep, making love again when they woke up.

"You know the only problem I didn't plan for," Tully said as she tried to get her breathing back to normal after her fourth orgasm of the afternoon.

"What?" Libby asked from where she'd landed on Tully's chest.

"The shower here doesn't work."

"If the kids and your mother being here wasn't enough to make me die of embarrassment, running into them before we get back to the boat might just do it."

"I'll run cover for you, honey." Tully rested her hand in the middle of Libby's back and laughed. Though it was getting warmer in the house, she had no desire to move, but the later it became, the more realistic she had to be.

The city authorities had instituted a curfew, but some unsavory characters were still running around, so Tully wanted to get them out of harm's way before the sun went down. If they didn't leave soon, they'd be stuck for the night.

"Do you think it'll be a while before we're able to come back?" Libby asked.

"I'd love to say it won't be, but this is the Big Easy, and the only thing moving fast around here is the current of the river." She sat up after Libby rolled off and searched for her underwear. "Why, ready to move in?"

"It's just been such a long time since I had a place I really considered home that the timing of this storm really sucks."

"We'll make a home on the boat for now, and I promise we'll be in here as soon as we can."

Libby put her pants on and went to help Tully with her shirt, laughing when they fastened the three remaining buttons. "I hate to whine."

"Libby, you were stuck in foster care at sixteen and left to fend for yourself at eighteen. You're entitled to a little whining."

They walked around locking the place back up, and Tully felt the temperature rise the second the windows were closed. The silence outside was still disconcerting, making it seem as if someone had bled the soul out of the city.

"Let's get going so we can stop by the Hebert place after we get cleaned up," Tully said.

"Are you glad to get this one behind you?"

"I'm thrilled not only to finish it, but also with the outcome. It's done, and while it couldn't bring Evangeline back, it's over."

Despite the warmth of the room Tully watched Libby run her hands up her still-naked arms and shiver. "I hope you're right."

CHAPTER THIRTY-TWO

When was this?" Jessica asked the deputy who'd signed her in that morning for her visit with Kara.

"Like I said the last three times, the judge released her this afternoon. I don't know where she went after that."

"Why didn't anyone call me?"

"Because Dr. Nicolas isn't a minor and you aren't her legal guardian, from what we could tell." Sheriff Carl stepped up and waved his deputy off. "She walked out of here under her own steam, so what's the problem?"

"She didn't have a ride and had no way of getting in touch with me." Jessica hit her fist against her leg. "You knew she didn't have anyone else to turn to."

"She couldn't have gone far. Just take a ride and find her, but tell her not to forget her court date before she decides to try anything cute."

The place where Jessica was staying wasn't far, but she hadn't seen Kara on the way to the jail. She tried again before doubling back and heading in the opposite direction, then stopped at every open store, café, and hurricane shelter she came across. No one had seen Kara. Everyone was either helping those who had evacuated out of New Orleans or talking about the storm that had changed the landscape in more ways than just flooding.

By seven that night Jessica was frantic and still hadn't found the first clue that would lead her to Kara. That desperation led her to the last place she wanted to be. Alma and Gaston's driveway was loaded with cars, but none of them belonged to Tully. She was debating the wisdom of her choice of turning to Tully again when she heard voices coming from behind her.

She recognized Tully's laugh first, sounding so carefree that Jessica squeezed the steering wheel until her fingers hurt. She ignored the pain and squeezed harder when she saw her walking up the drive holding hands with Libby. After sharing her life with Tully for such a long time Jessica felt strange at the sight of her being so demonstrative with someone else.

Tully's and Libby's hair was damp, and they were chuckling as they walked up the drive. All that ended when Jessica opened her car door and stepped out.

"What's wrong?" Tully asked, sounding concerned, but she didn't let go of Libby.

"I need to talk to you and I need your help." Jessica blew out a long breath, trying to control her emotions.

"Let me go in and tell everyone we're back," Libby said. She brought her other hand up and sandwiched Tully's between hers. "It's okay, sweetheart."

"If this has to do with Dr. Nicolas—" Tully started.

"Trust me, Tully, if I could deal with this alone I would." Jessica started crying, and before Tully could move away she stepped forward and just fell into Tully's chest. "I just don't…" She stopped to release some shuddering sobs.

"Come on." Tully turned her around and led her to the porch. Libby walked away from them, going through the open front door toward the back of the house. "Sit down and let me go get you something to drink, and then you can tell me what's wrong."

Libby met her in the hallway just off the foyer of the house with a large glass of ice water.

"I'm sorry about this, baby," Tully said.

"For what? Caring about the mother of your children?" Libby pressed the glass into her hand. "I have no doubts about where I stand in your life, my love, and I also know the path you had to take to get you to this point."

"Thanks, and could you keep Bailey and Ralph in the house until I see what this is about?"

"Just try to talk her into staying this time, for their sake."

Tully nodded before going out and handing the glass to Jessica.

Her crying had slowed and she just appeared fatigued. "Try to drink some water and tell me what's wrong," Tully said softly.

"They let Kara out today." Jessica didn't take her eyes off the ice in her glass as she spoke.

"I'd think that should be making you happy."

"I can't find her and I think something's happened to her, but Carl won't do anything about it."

The wood under Tully's rocker creaked when she sat down and set it in motion. Had this been the afternoon she'd found Jessica in bed with this woman, she would have welcomed the news. "What makes you say that? She could just have caught a ride out of town."

"I know how you feel about this whole situation, but she wouldn't have done that. Kara wouldn't have left without me."

"Okay, then why automatically assume something's wrong?"

"Tully, no offense to your hometown, but there's one way in, and the only way out is to turn around and head in the opposite direction. If you're looking for someone, it's hard to miss them, even if they're walking on the opposite side of the bayou." She lifted her head and looked Tully in the eye. "I've been driving up and down the road all afternoon. She's not here, and since she wouldn't have left without me, then something's wrong."

"What would you like me to do about that?"

Jessica put the glass down and put her hands over Tully's. "Talk to Carl and have him look. It's getting dark, and if she's hurt I want to find her before it's too late. He knows you and would do it for you if you ask."

"I'll talk to him, but I want you to stay put here with the kids after I do. You're tired. There's no sense in something happening to you too." She stood up and waved Jessica into the house. "Actually, I'm going to have to drive over to the sheriff's office since the phone isn't working yet."

Bailey and Ralph came out and faced Jessica. "Grandma set up the room upstairs for you to get some sleep after you take a shower," Bailey said.

After hearing Bailey's flat tone, Tully put her hand at the back of Bailey's neck and kissed her on the forehead. Bailey's lack of emotion signaled that she had figured out Jessica's sudden return had nothing to do with her and Ralph.

"Tully, I think I should come with you," Jessica said, ignoring Bailey's offer and grabbing Tully's bicep.

"Mom said she'd do it, so let her," Ralph told Jessica as he jerked her hand off Tully and pointed her into the house.

Tully could tell that Jessica's continued indifference had really upset Bailey and Ralph. "Try to get some sleep, and I'll wake you if there's any news," she said as they stood at the foot of the steps inside.

"Thank you, Tully. I know this is the last thing you want to be doing, but I really appreciate it."

Tully nodded and held her hand out to Libby. "Want to come with me?" she asked when they were outside.

"Sure." They crossed the street to the Land Rover. "What do you think could've happened to her?"

"What was it Chase called her? A crankhead? Well, someone with a habit who's been in jail for a couple of days would probably make for the nearest dealer to get a fix. We may be in the middle of nowhere, according to Jessica, but that doesn't mean there aren't drugs around here. Someone in jail could have told her who to call, and she made for an address after she got out."

"It's really depressing to think someone can be so dependent on something that she can't live without it." Libby picked up Tully's hand and kissed her knuckles.

"You mean you're not addicted to me and can live without me?"

"No, I'm a certified Tully junkie, but you're not exactly bad for my health, lover."

They arrived at the sheriff's office as Carl was walking out the front door, and he stopped at the driver's side window and smiled. "I might have to start hanging out with you, Tully, if this is the kind of company you keep."

"You told me I couldn't flirt with your wife, so the same goes for you." Tully introduced the two before telling him why they were there. "I'm sure she's sleeping off her high somewhere, but in case I'm wrong, could you send out a directive to the deputies on patrol to keep an eye out for her? If they find anything, send them over to Mom's and let us know. I left Jessica over there taking a nap."

"Sure thing. Can't be too careful since the woman couldn't shut up about having everyone's badge for what she thought was unfair treatment. All I need is for her to fall into the bayou and float on out to the Gulf."

"Thanks, Carl. If you need me I'm going over to Elijah and Simone's place to talk over a few things." They both waved as Carl headed back inside.

"If she got out this morning and something happened to her, she could be in trouble now that it's dark. Walking out here at night is a dangerous proposition even for the locals, and if she's not sober it could be suicide," Tully said as she turned back to the main road.

❖

When they drove up, Elijah was sitting outside mending a net, which he dropped into his lap when Tully got out of the car. She knew Jo had been able to get in touch with them that afternoon, by some miracle, so he already was aware of the settlement. Still, he didn't look like a man who had just won his case.

"Came by to see if you or Simone had any questions," Tully said as they reached the porch stairs.

"She's inside watching television." He tilted his head that way as his line of sight came to rest on Libby.

"Why don't I join her?" Libby took the obvious hint.

"Something on your mind, Elijah?" Tully sat close to him and picked up a casting net that was next to be fixed. In their talks she had learned that Elijah mended equipment as a sideline to his fishing. She wasn't as practiced as he was, but she had the skill to do a good job, and she guessed he would open up if she wasn't staring him down.

"Are you still my attorney?"

"Unless you want other counsel, I am."

"So nothing we talk about, you can tell anybody, right?"

Tully worked the needle through the edge of the hole and started to make new webbing. "That's correct."

"I was brought up to think your life was like the seasons." Elijah gripped the wooden block that held the line he used to repair nets and kept his eyes on Tully's hands as she tied and wove. "You sprout, you grow, you bear fruit, and then you enjoy watching the seeds you sow grow and continue the process."

"That's a good way to think about life."

"I'm not going to have that last part now. My baby, she's gone, and Simone and me won't have any more."

"I was brought up to believe that God works in mysterious ways, my friend, so don't count yourself out on a family just yet. None of us know what the future holds in store." Tully double-knotted the last stitch and cut the line before standing up and folding the net to hand back to him. "Why do you think you need an attorney for that story?"

"Because we might not know what the future is, but sometimes our pasts come back to haunt us when we least expect it. If that happens to me, I want to know you'll help me out. I don't want Simone left alone. She's suffered enough."

"Is there something you want to tell me? Like you said, the conversation would be just between the two of us."

Tully stepped off the porch and waited for him at the bottom of the stairs, and they walked to Elijah's boat, moored across the street like her father's. It was the most private place to have this conversation since Tully didn't have the use of her office.

"I don't need to talk with you now, Tully, but the day might come when I do."

"Did you understand Jo today when she explained that Dr. Nicolas is going to be let go from Children's Hospital?" She felt like she had cast her line and was looking for a bite. "It's not the jail sentence you were hoping for, but you took away the one thing she loved."

"You're right." Elijah stepped closer and put his hand on her shoulder. "Kara Nicolas got what she deserved, and her sentence was no less punishing than what my little girl got." He squeezed her shoulder, but his face showed no expression. Then he just let her go and started walking down the road, staying close to the water.

Tully watched him leave and knew that no matter how much she pushed him, he wasn't going to say anything else on this subject, and most probably wouldn't for the rest of his life. Her gut was warning her, though, that there was plenty more to this story and that Jessica's worries weren't unfounded. "Her sentence was no less punishing," she repeated softly. "What in the hell is that supposed to mean?"

A patrol car was driving slowly toward her, and the deputy rolled his window down and stopped. "Evening, Tully."

"Any luck with Dr. Nicolas?"

"We drove up about twenty miles and came back on both sides of the bayou, but no one's seen her. Even stopped and talked to most of the old-timers who like to sit outside and watch the world go by. They promised they'd be watching for her, but they hadn't seen her either."

"Thanks for stopping. I'll take a drive myself before I head on back home." Tully said the words, but she was willing to bet a month's salary that she wouldn't find anything either.

At midnight, after an extensive drive through some of the less populated areas of Montegut, she and Libby found Jessica waiting for them in the living room wearing a new T-shirt and jeans. When Tully just shook her head, Jessica didn't ask anything.

"Get some sleep and we'll start looking in the morning. I talked to Carl's night commander, and he said they'll keep up the patrols tonight. If she's still in the area they'll find her."

"I'll go back to the bed and breakfast."

Alma stepped in from the kitchen and took Jessica by the hand. "Nonsense, there's no reason for you to be alone, so go upstairs. The kids fixed up one of the beds for you. Tully, the kids are waiting for you across the street. Your father's over there keeping an eye on them until you two got back."

When they stepped on board the boat, Gaston was sitting in a lawn chair peering out at the water. He kissed them both and headed off to bed.

They carefully stepped around the air mattress they'd put out for Chase on the floor, with Bailey and Ralph sleeping in the bunks.

"Is something wrong?" Libby asked. She'd tried the same question a couple of times while they were riding around in the car, but Tully had just shaken her head and turned down another street. "And please don't tell me it's nothing."

"I just have a bad feeling about this, and I have a clue as to why, but I don't want to believe I might be right."

"Right about what, baby?" Libby asked.

"We can't have this conversation now." Tully pointed to the kids sleeping around them. "Because when we do, it's going to be as attorneys talking about our client, not as partners."

"You don't have to tell me at all if you don't want to. I just thought you'd feel better if you talked about whatever's bothering you." Libby snuggled closer to her; the air conditioner was set low enough to hang meat.

"When we're out looking again tomorrow, we'll discuss it as much as you want." They shared a long kiss before Libby drifted off to sleep.

❖

Another deputy stopped by in the morning to tell them they still hadn't had any luck in finding Kara. Tully wasn't surprised—the real shock would've been if they'd found any evidence of Kara at all.

Jessica joined them and Tully gave her the job of trying to get in touch with Kara's family in Texas while they went out to look again. The phones were still sporadic, but the assignment would keep Jessica busy while they continued their search.

"I don't think we'll find Kara Nicolas no matter how hard we try," Tully told Libby as soon as the car door closed. They were going to drive to some of the more out-of-the-way locations that hadn't been covered yet because Carl lacked the manpower.

"What makes you so sure?"

"My talk with Elijah yesterday. He didn't come out and say it, but I think he had something to do with her disappearance." She told Libby verbatim the words Elijah had used when he talked about punishment and his daughter.

"What are you going to do?"

"There isn't anything I can do. He was smart enough to make sure I'm still his attorney. I can't tell Carl about this because of privilege. My hands are tied until Elijah decides to say something or Carl puts together a case."

"Did you try to talk to him about it?"

Tully took a road with marsh on both sides, and because of the storm, the water was lapping over the edge, which made her take it slow. She was sure, though, that if Elijah had done something to Kara, she was currently somewhere well offshore feeding the crabs and the fish. If that was the case, Kara would never be found, and for as much misery as she'd brought into Tully's life, Kara wasn't some rabid dog to be taken out back and disposed of. If that was what he'd done, Tully understood his motivation, but it wouldn't be easy living with the fact that she hadn't tried to do something about it. Kara's parents deserved better.

"This is the part of this career path that's going to take some getting used to." Libby placed Tully's hand in her lap and rubbed her fingers as she scanned the area. "You must get tired of carrying the weight of other people's secrets."

"I try to always do right by my clients, but I also steer them to do the right thing. Problem is, darlin', you can drag them to the pool, but you can't always make 'em swim."

"Does it bother you?"

Tully nodded. "I don't go out of my way to help people break the law and get away with it."

"That's not what I meant. I know you better than to believe that about you."

Seeing a tree that the storm had more than likely put across the road, Tully turned the SUV around. "It bothers me that if Elijah is involved, he would gamble with his future like that, because Simone loses here too. But in his soul he blames Kara for the death of his child. If it was Bailey or Ralph that I'd lost, who knows what my grief would push me to."

"I guess I spoke too soon when I said this is over. If something happened to her, this is just the beginning. And you know Jessica will find some way to blame you."

"Jessica's going to have to accept that karma came back to bite Kara in the ass, and I certainly didn't have anything to do with her choices."

Tully turned down another road with a few homes built up at least fifteen feet in the air, keeping them out of harm's way when it flooded. Everyone they passed waved, but stayed on their porches watching them.

By the end of two days, Tully and Libby had covered the same territory four more times, with still no luck.

When they returned every afternoon they found the kids sitting with Jessica, who would start a fresh bout of crying when Tully shook her head. It was as if the ancient land with its cypress knees and moss hanging from the tree branches had opened up and swallowed any sign that Kara Nicolas had ever existed.

CHAPTER THIRTY-THREE

As the days ticked off, Tully realized they faced a new problem. Another storm, Hurricane Rita, was churning its way through the Gulf, bearing down on what everyone first thought would be the Texas coastline. As if Katrina hadn't been enough, every day the forecasters placed Rita closer to Louisiana, and everyone in Montegut was preparing, knowing the kind of storm surge that could result from being on the eastern side of a storm of that size.

With Rita right offshore and predicted to come on land late that night or early the morning, Tully parked next to Elijah's boat, figuring one more day of driving to the same places she'd covered would yield the same results. He was on board, folding his nets and storing them inside the cabin.

"This thing is going to churn things up around here, don't you think?" Tully asked him, staying on land, out of his way.

He only nodded and kept up what he was doing.

"And it can permanently get rid of things that are lost."

"What can I do for you, Tully?"

"At least tell me if I'm spinning my wheels here."

He took his cap off and scratched the top of his head, making her think he was just going to clam up. "First, tell me why you're looking so hard."

"Not because I owe my ex anything and not because I have illusions of caring for Kara."

"Then why?"

She turned her head and gazed down the road. From where she was standing she could make out the steeple of St. Bridget's Catholic Church. Behind it was the cemetery that had been used from the time the land had been settled. Evangeline had been laid to rest in one of the new sections.

"Why?" Tully repeated. "Because no matter her sins, her parents deserve the last comfort you had. They should be able to bury her and know her life is finished. It doesn't matter how they get that knowledge, but it's only humane to give it to them and spare them the agony that will haunt them if we don't."

"Wish I could help you and them, but I can't."

"If you're sure you can't, then I'll have to accept that. I'm not here to push you into giving me something you're not capable of, but if you change your mind you know you can count on me to help you."

It had been worth a try. Now she had a reasonable idea of the truth and the comfort that she had tried her best. "Good luck with the storm, and if you and Simone need anything, let me know."

"You think less of me?" Elijah asked as he jumped from the boat to the shore to follow her toward her vehicle.

"I understand you, Elijah, and I respect you. What happened to you is my worst nightmare, so no, I don't think less of you. The burden of truth, whatever that might be in this case, might get heavy over time, though." She opened the door to her car, but didn't move to get inside. "I've found that sometimes that kind of strain leaks over into other aspects of your life. With everything you and Simone have been through, you don't deserve any more added to your plate."

"Thanks, and I'll remember that. You all evacuating for this thing?"

"My father keeps telling me how that house has been there for over a hundred years and he isn't leaving, and the kids and Libby already went through the trauma of having to leave what they knew, so we're staying for now." She gazed up at the overcast sky and felt the moisture in the air. Rita was shaping up to be a rainmaker, from all the reports. "I'll keep my eye on the Weather Channel just in case. How about you and Simone?"

"I'm packing the boat just in case. If things get bad I'm going to float her up the bayou as far as I can and try and ride it out."

They shook hands, and Tully headed on back to the house to help with the hurricane preparations. She had sent Roxanne and her family, as well as Jo, back up north with the office files, but Chase and her mother, along with Jessica, had stayed.

The first big gusts came in at ten that night, and Tully sat with her family flipping between the local stations and the Weather Channel. At its current rate Rita would really get going past midnight, and since it was coming in right at the Louisiana/Texas border her decision to stay was starting to give Tully a headache. When the grandfather clock in the foyer chimed twelve thirty, she was about to tell everyone to pack their bags to get on the road for a couple of days when there was a knock on the front door.

Waving her father off, Tully opened the door to Elijah and closed it behind her just as quickly when she saw the way he was twisting his hat in his hand.

"I'm taking Simone and my boat out of here." He pointed across the street, which wasn't visible because of the driving rain. "I docked by your daddy's so I could come and see you before I headed out."

"Need some help?"

"No, I wanted to see if you tried looking down by Jim Bob Delacroix's place over by the pass." The place he mentioned was ten miles farther south than where they were standing, a huge chunk of private land owned by a New Orleans oilman whose hobbies were fishing and making money. "I thought about what you said, and whatever you find, I might need help carrying the weight of the truth when you get back and this is over."

She shook his hand. "That's something you can count on."

Neither Libby nor the kids were happy with her decision to go out alone, but she didn't want them to get hurt if the storm got any worse. Tully almost caved in when Libby grabbed the front of her T-shirt.

"You better come back to me. I'll be lost if something happens to you. I went through the pain of losing my parents and finally saw the end of being alone when I found you, so you better not let me down, Tully."

"I won't," was all Tully said before she kissed Libby to show her how much she meant it. "I love you, and I'm planning on a long life with you, so I'll be right back."

Her own words echoed in Tully's head as she turned onto the main road and drove almost to the end where the pavement ended abruptly in the water, her vehicle swaying from the wind the whole time. The private drive stretched for three miles, ending at one of the nicest houses on the bayou. Jim Bob used the place a couple of times a year as a fishing camp to entertain some of his bigger clients, and other than a caretaker who came out once a week, the place sat empty and secluded.

She took her time walking around searching for clues at the end of her flashlight. If the front of the house was nice, the back was spectacular. After a lot of excavating, Jim Bob had created a series of ponds in his backyard that were fed by the pass that ran alongside the eastern part of his property.

After extensive dredging, what had started as a small feeder off Bayou Terrebonne years before had turned into a quick route to the Gulf. He allowed his neighbors to use it, but its main purpose was to get his large fishing cruiser out to blue water.

The boat was gone, probably brought in because of the storm, so Tully walked slowly along the back banks of the ponds watching where she put her feet because of the local reptilian population. Not finding anything from Elijah's cryptic clue, she was about to turn back when she spotted a flash of blue out in the distance on a small island. She put her flashlight right on it and saw Kara huddled against the trunk of an ancient oak.

Tully ran back to the mud boat she'd seen earlier and pushed it into the water. The pole in it was long enough for her to guide the boat out to the land that was rapidly disappearing in the rising water. "Kara!" Tully lost a shoe in the thick mud when she landed. If the wind and rain hadn't roused Kara, Tully figured she was dead.

"Kara!" she screamed again, finally getting some response when she got closer. The large bruise on the side of Kara's head made Tully grimace, but she was relieved that Kara was still alive. "Come on, we have to get out of here. The levee must be topped for the water to be coming up this fast. We don't have much time."

Kara shook her head and wrapped her arms even tighter around her legs.

"You can't stay here and ride out a hurricane holding on to a tree." Tully lifted Kara's head to make sure she understood what she was saying.

"I can't swim, and I'm not getting on a boat in this weather." With that statement Kara jerked out of Tully's grasp and turned her head to the tree trunk, as if it would hide where she was.

"I can't leave you here, so I apologize ahead of time," Tully said. She hated to hit her in the same place as the bruise, but if Kara wouldn't go willingly she would have to be carried out.

With a grunt Tully slugged Kara, hefted her up, and carried her back to the boat. Before she could push off, the electricity went out at the house, cutting off the floodlights in the yard and plunging the area into total darkness. The rain was now flying horizontally because of the gusts of wind, and Tully prayed she was going in a straight line toward the shore. If she missed too far to the left they would go into the pass and possibly out to the Gulf once the current changed with the wind, if they were lucky enough to stay afloat that long.

She stuck the pole into the water and propelled them closer to the shore, but on the next stroke she wasn't prepared for the sudden drop-off, and the wood slid through her fingers. The depth could only mean she'd aimed too far out and they were in the pass. With no way to steer she had no idea where they'd end up.

"Libby, forgive me if this doesn't work out," she shouted into the wind as she removed her other shoe. The rocking made it difficult to walk to the front of the boat where the tie-off rope was. When her fingers closed around it, Tully quickly found the end and fastened it around her waist.

Another miscalculation now and they would both be lost, but she could figure no other way out. She took a deep breath and jumped off the front of the boat into surprisingly warm water with a very strong current. The storm surge from Rita was driving it, but Tully started swimming in what she hoped was an easterly direction. With the weight of the boat she was dragging and the force of the water, her limbs quickly felt like lead, but she knew to give up now would lead to certain death, so she ignored the fatigue and pushed harder.

After what felt like hours, no matter how much Tully wanted to keep going, she could push her arms over only once more; then she surrendered to the current. She rolled over to her back, hoping to keep her head above water and thinking about Libby, Bailey, and Ralph. For the first time in her life she felt like a total failure for abandoning the people she loved most for something they might not understand. As her tired body started to sink, she lamented all the things that she'd left unsaid. She was sure that her words, along with the remainder of her days, would be swept away along with the debris swirling around her.

❖

"Libby, you really need to move away from the window, honey," Alma said. At Libby's request Gaston had unboarded one of the windows facing the road so they could keep an eye out for Tully. "If something comes flying through there, you could get hurt."

A glance at her watch showed Libby it was after one in the morning, close to an hour since Tully had gone out into the storm. It had seemed surreal to watch the taillights of Tully's car disappear and know she was left behind with the Badeauxes and Jessica.

"Did she tell you where she was going?" Jessica asked.

"Mama, Libby answered that already," Bailey said in an exasperated tone.

"She didn't really say. She just said she'd be back in a little while," Libby answered.

Alma put an arm around Libby's waist and brought her other hand up to make her let go of the curtain.

"If she said she'd be back, she will. Tully's good at keeping her word," she said softly.

"Yes, she always was the white knight every girl dreams of," Jessica added. "Until some other cause came along, and then forget it."

"She's coming back, right, Libby?" Ralph came up on her other side and stared at her as if begging her for reassurance. His question gave Libby the opportunity to ignore Jessica.

"We have a house to get ready, and she told me she wanted your help getting that tree out of the pool, buddy, so of course she is. You think she'd miss the opportunity to put you and Bailey to work?"

Libby turned away from Alma so she could put her arms around him, gazing over his shoulder at Bailey sitting with Chase. The house shook with a ferocious gust of wind, and Libby pressed him closer, putting her body between the window and Ralph. What had started as a bad rainstorm was turning into hurricane-force winds.

"Come on, Ralph, let's me and you go check the house," Gaston said.

"Do you think we should've evacuated?" Chase asked when Ralph and Gaston left to go upstairs. "It's getting bad out there."

"Jeez, Chase," Bailey said, getting up and going into the kitchen.

"What?" Chase asked, seeming perplexed by Bailey's reaction.

"Her mom is out there, so it's not a good time to remind her about how bad it's getting," Libby said before going after Bailey, Jessica behind her.

Bailey was sitting at the kitchen table holding herself and rocking as if she was in pain. "You okay?" Libby asked gently.

"She promised," Bailey said, not stopping her rocking.

"Promised what, sweetheart?"

"That she wouldn't leave us and that we'd be okay—she promised. If something happens to her, what happens to us?"

"You have me." Libby knelt down in front of Bailey's chair and rested her hands on her lap. "And since when do you count her out so easily?"

Jessica crossed her arms over her chest. "Because she knows Tully would rather play the hero than stick around for the mundane things in life for too long. You can't expect her to be happy just playing house. Don't be that naïve."

"I can't force you to think like me, or to have my faith, but you know that's not true, Bailey Bean." Libby took a chance and used the nickname, rewarded when Bailey fell into her arms and cried.

Libby held Bailey until Alma came into the room and guided her back to the living room. When Jessica began to follow, Libby stopped her with a forceful, "Wait."

"As soon as the weather clears I'm taking my children out of here and home," Jessica told her.

"They have a home to go to after this, and they aren't going anywhere until Tully gets back. And if you talk about her to Bailey or Ralph like you just did again, I'll put you out of this house myself. I don't care what the weather is."

"Yeah, right." Jessica ran into Gaston when she turned around to leave.

"I'd listen to her, Jessica, because I agree with her," he said. "If I were you I'd sit down and shut up before you find yourself out the front door."

Not expecting an answer, Libby asked Jessica, "What did life do to you to make you so angry?"

"It cheated me when it came to making choices. All the ones I've made up to now except for Kara were to please someone else," she spat out.

"How sad for you that you think that," Libby said, trying to find some reason to feel sympathetic toward Jessica. "But that doesn't give you the right to make your family pay for your mistakes or bad choices. Tully is my choice, and I won't stand for one more snipe at her expense."

Jessica didn't answer her and just walked out, leaving Gaston and Libby alone, and it was Libby's turn to cry.

"I don't want to add to your worry, Libby, but the water out back's starting to come up," Gaston said. "That's got to mean the levee breached somewhere along the line. Even if we wanted to leave we can't, at least not without some ferrying back and forth to the *Alma Mae*."

"Do you think that's why Tully's not back?"

"Could be, darlin', so you and I have to have a talk."

"I'm not leaving without her," Libby said, meaning every word.

"While Tully's not here you're in charge of those kids, and if we have to move them to the boat I need your help."

"Do you think it's going to get that bad?"

He unlatched the shutter to one of the kitchen windows and pointed outside. "The tide was high when the wind started, and these southern gusts are pushing even more water in. The last time that happened we ended up with eight feet over flood stage here. We're up twelve feet, but if this is anything like what just hit New Orleans, I don't want to be stuck in this house if we can help it."

"I'm not going to let anything happen to her family, but I won't desert her either."

Gaston secured the window again just as the power went out. "Just remember you're her family too." His smile was as bright as the beam of his flashlight as he said it.

Libby stayed behind to light some candles, remembering how her mother would do the same thing before saying a prayer in church. "Please, God, if it has to be one of us, pick me," she said as she lowered the match to the wick. "Bailey's right, Tully. You did give your word, and I'm holding you to it."

CHAPTER THIRTY-FOUR

Tully's lungs screamed for air and she struggled weakly to the surface. The true panic set in when no matter how hard she tried, she couldn't make headway against the current. After spending her life on the water, she never figured it would end this way.

It was hard to accept that it would, but when she couldn't get her head above the surface she had no choice. Her lungs felt like they were about to burst so she tried again, but the total blackness she was submerged in gave her no clue as to how far she had to go to save herself. As she swam in what she assumed was an upward direction, the churning water slammed her into a thick wooden surface she at first thought was a tree. In reality it was the answer to her prayers—she'd run into Jim Bob's dock.

Tully wrapped her legs around it just as the rope tied to her waist became taut, and in her weakened condition it almost ripped her from the lifeline, but she refused to let go. With the will of someone who embraced life, she shimmied up the pole until just her face was above the water. The gulps of air that filled her lungs were like a gift, and she greedily sucked them in between coughs.

"Now if you could only figure out how to haul yourself onto the dock," she thought as she clung to the piling. The rope from the boat was biting into her waist, so whatever she did, it'd have to be quick before the pain gave her no choice but to let go.

A huge bolt of lightning split the night, followed by an instant boom, making goose bumps break out on her arms and legs from its nearness. Though being fried in the water scared Tully, the only way to get out of the situation filled her with dread. The illumination of the lightning helped her see the ladder about fifteen feet downstream from her, curving down from the dock and used to board smaller boats in low tide. It was the last thing between safety and the unknown.

The only way she could reach it was to release the piling and pray she could grab the ladder at the right moment. Guessing wrong would push her farther up the channel and she would drown, she was sure. Her other option was to cut Kara loose and hope the boat didn't capsize, bringing Kara the same fate. That was the best option, because keeping herself tethered to the boat would only drag her away from the pier. With her mind made up, Tully took a deep breath and let go.

Working on pure adrenaline, she pushed her body out of the water and threw both her hands above her head. She wanted to cry when she felt the solid iron of the ladder under her fingers. Knowing the force of the boat was coming, she quickly looped her arm through the lowest rung. She willed herself to move and looped her other arm through the next rung, high enough now to put her feet on the lower one and pull up. Not for the first time she was extremely grateful for all the exercise Libby had encouraged her to do. If this had happened a year earlier she'd have been fish food by now.

Once out of the water she looped the rope over the top of the ladder to take the strain off her waist. Standing on the pier, she reeled Kara in, and when Kara was close enough Tully could see she had come to and was gripping the side of the boat with white knuckles.

"Hang on," Tully yelled. "Kara, you have to let go and get out."

For once Kara didn't argue. She grabbed the hand Tully was holding out to her and didn't let go even after she was on her feet. They were safe for the moment, so it was time for Tully to tackle their next problem—the water was lapping at the boards under their feet.

"We have to get out of there before the water gets any higher," Tully yelled over the wind.

"How?" Kara asked, her voice sounding raspy from a couple of days' nonuse after she'd finally quit screaming for help.

"By finding something that floats and has a motor attached to it." With a squeeze to Kara's fingers Tully dragged her to the large boathouse at the end of the dock. She put her shoulder into the door to force it open, wishing she hadn't lost her flashlight.

The inside of the building was dark, and she could barely see two boats hanging overhead on straps that kept them out of the water. They both had motors, but the winch that lowered them was electric and she didn't have time to look for the manual override. Inside, most of the noise disappeared since the caretaker had thought to lower the door that led to the channel.

Tully felt around for something either sharp enough to cut through the straps or capable of unhooking them from the winch itself. Her fingers closed around a wrench, meaning she was in for a climb. "Get up on the worktable in case the water's coming in faster than I think."

"Where are you going?" Kara grabbed Tully's bicep so hard Tully was sure she would have a bruise.

"I'm going to make sure Jim Bob Delacroix sues me for destruction of property." Tully made it to the first boat and turned on the spotlight on board. She worked to get the bolts out of the front of the boat, figuring she only had to release one side and the craft would slide out. Hopefully it would stay afloat once it hit the water at such an odd angle. The first bolt came out, then the second bolt came loose, and she banged it out the rest of the way by using the wrench as a hammer.

The bow of the boat went below the waterline up to the first set of seats when it hit, but the vessel popped back up like a cork. When she was sure it was going to stay afloat, Tully retrieved the gas can from the other boat and climbed down.

"How are you going to get us out of here?" Kara asked.

"The door should have a crank. If not, I'm crashing through it." Tully got on board. "Hell, it works in all those Bond movies I've seen through the years."

"Are you sure you know what you're doing?"

Tully connected the gas can to the motor, keeping her fingers crossed that the thing would crank. "Do you mean am I going to kill you in the hurricane or in a fiery crash in the boat?"

"I can see why Jessica didn't like you much—you're a smart-ass."

"Jessica didn't like me because she decided to start cheating on me and I took offense to it." Tully walked back to the bow and looked over the edge to make sure Kara had a clear path to the boat. "Let's get going."

"I thought you said she did you a favor."

The manual crank to the rolling door was where she thought it would be, and she opened it just enough for the boat to clear. She didn't need to trash everything in the place just to escape. "You both did," she said. "If anything, you showed me that I was just cruising through life instead of enjoying the hell out of it like I used to. A long existence doing nothing but hanging around is only fun if you're a priceless piece of art—for people it's a cop-out."

The higher Tully lifted the door, the more the noise increased, and Kara just sat clutching the back of the seat. "Why did you come back for me, then? If you have everything you want now, why chance it?"

They would have to duck to get out, but Tully secured the line to the door and moved back to work on the motor. It took ten yanks to get it started, but thankfully it sputtered to life. "Because I want my kids to always think of me as someone who does the right thing, no matter who it's for. I might not always be successful, but at least I try."

Tully squatted on the floor of the boat and signaled for Kara to put her head down. The wind was still blowing stiffly, filling the channel with whitecaps. "Hang on, because we're going to have to go through some choppy water before I can get us to safer ground."

"I don't think I would've come back for you," Kara screamed at her.

"Aren't you glad I'm not you, then?" Tully yelled back before she gunned the engine.

In the channel the spotlight was a godsend, but it also let her see just how extensive the flooding was and just how much trouble they could've been in if she hadn't reached that ladder to get out. The dock wasn't visible anymore, and the island Kara had been stranded on had all but disappeared. Figuring the water was deep enough to accommodate the boat's motor, Tully headed toward her parents' house, planning to continue down the drive she'd come up if there was water all the way to the road. The last thing she wanted to do was wait out the storm with Kara while her family was miles away and worried.

Tully noticed more debris and fallen trees than she would've expected, but the water was still a few feet from flooding the first floor of the elevated houses. She was relieved that Libby was safe and surrounded by family and not going through this alone.

When she'd given in to her feelings for Libby, Tully had worried about the demons of Libby's past and what had happened to her parents. Not that she didn't love Libby deeply, but a small part of her had feared

Libby was picking the safe choice, not one that would bring her the most happiness.

"I'm an idiot," Tully said to herself. Libby could no more hide her feelings than she could be outwardly mean to someone just for kicks. It just wasn't in her.

"Did you say something?" Kara asked.

"Talking to myself, don't worry about it. We're getting close, so try and hold out a little longer."

"Good. I'm tired of being wet."

As Tully steered the boat toward the front steps of the porch, she noticed the house was dark, but it had never looked better. The anxious faces pressed to the window of the living room made her smile again. As much as she loved her whole family, it was the three people closest to the door that made her give thanks that she'd had the will to fight her way back. Seeing the relief in Libby, Bailey, and Ralph's faces made every agonizing moment worth it.

Thankfully, no one stopped Libby as she threw the front door open and ran into Tully's arms as soon as she made it on the porch. Tully was soaked through, her T-shirt clinging to her and her chinos hanging low because of the weight of the water, but she was alive, and that was all that mattered as Libby greeted her with a long kiss.

Kara sat in the boat, then finally stood up when Jessica called her from the door of the house.

After they dried off, Tully spent the remainder of the storm in her old room sleeping with Libby, the kids close by on air mattresses.

❖

At daybreak the water was still there, but the wind had died down to a stiff thirty-mile-an-hour breeze. Tully knew that as long as it blew in from the south and the levee was damaged, the flooding wouldn't go anywhere. As she checked to see if she'd damaged Jim Bob's boat in any way, she watched Ralph and Bailey be cordial to Kara. Earlier that morning they had told Jessica who they wanted to live with and why. They would agree to a visitation schedule, but they wanted to stay with Tully and Libby.

"I guess you won all the way around, huh?" Jessica asked Tully when they were alone on the porch.

"I didn't realize I was in a contest."

With the water still high she was planning to return the boat to the boat shed before anyone missed it, then have Gaston give her a ride back in his small boat.

"The kids don't want anything to do with me, and your young bride can't stand me either."

"The kids will come around if you give them the time and attention they want from you, and Libby was probably just taking up for me."

Kara walked out and put her arm around Jessica's waist, still appearing dazed from her experience. The bruise on the side of her face had gotten darker from the extra blow Tully had delivered, but she had no apparent long-term damage.

Jessica continued her tirade. "There's one place you're going to lose, Tully, and this time there's nothing you can do about it."

"What's that?"

"I'm going to take pleasure in bringing down your precious clients who started this whole mess on a whim. Elijah did that to Kara, and now he's going to pay for it with the longest sentence I can talk a judge into. He left her out there to die."

"A wise man told me just recently that your life was like the seasons. You blossom, you sow and reap a family, and then you spend the autumn and winter of your life enjoying all that you've planted." Tully sat on one of the rockers and welcomed Libby to sit on the arm of the chair.

"Well, Elijah is going to spend his seasons in a small cell, if I have anything to do with it," Jessica said.

"That same wise man told me something else," Tully said with a relaxed smile.

"What, a poem about a tree?"

"No, the truth about a small girl who died at the hands of a woman her parents entrusted her to, and because she was just a little bit high when she stepped into the operating room, it turned out disastrously. I've already settled with the hospital for the mistake so there's no going back for more, but criminally there's still plenty of legal maneuvering room."

Jessica pushed away from Kara and put her finger in Tully's face. "It's her word against some kidnapping sadist."

"It's her word, all right, or should I say words? She confessed, Jessica, and Elijah got it on tape. I'm not a criminal attorney, but I might dabble a little to tell my own story about a man driven to do what he did because of grief. Grief and suffering that *she* inflicted, and he and Simone were right all along." Tully nodded toward Kara. "Maybe you should consider this a wash and let it go. Think of it as a second season, as it were, and try to forget the mistakes of the first one, because that's exactly what I'm planning to do."

"He has to pay for what he did to her," Jessica said again. "Whatever she said to him was because she was trying to get out of a bad situation."

"She's right, Jessica, let it go." Kara moved Jessica's hand away from Tully's face.

"I can't accept that," Jessica said.

"You don't have to. It's up to me to decide, and I say let it go." Kara turned Jessica around to face her. "Things happen and people act like they aren't expected to—that goes for all of us. I made a mistake and those people paid, and Elijah made a mistake that Tully paid for by coming to get me," Kara said. "It's over."

"Finally, something we can all agree on," Tully said as the rest of her family came out to join them. "Let's go get this boat back, and I'll tell you the true meaning of being up to your ass in alligators," she said to Libby.

They all laughed when the kids ran down to the boat, acting like they didn't want to be left out of any more adventures.

EPILOGUE

Easter Sunday 2006

In the name of the Father, the Son, and the Holy Spirit, amen. Our mass is ended, go forth in peace and enjoy your Easter Sunday," said Bishop Goodman. The ten o'clock service at the St. Louis Cathedral was so full that people were standing in the back, unable to find an empty pew.

Libby and Tully and their family sat with the whole Badeaux clan, including Alma, Gaston, and Tully's two brothers and their families. Even though they weren't regular churchgoers except for Alma, they had given in to Alma's request of a day off from house repairs to give thanks for the blessings that had come from so much misery less than a year before. At Alma's insistence, Simone and Elijah had joined them.

"How long now?" Simone asked Libby as they walked out together. Their case hadn't been the only thing that had brought them together, and they had spent a lot of weekends in the city so Elijah could help Tully get the house ready and do some carpentry work.

"Three more months, and I'm thanking God it's going to be before it gets real hot again."

"Is Tully ready for this new baby?" Simone asked. They were standing on the slate tile in front of the cathedral with little children running around them in their pastel clothes.

Libby watched Tully as she walked Bailey and Ralph to the corner where Jessica was waiting to pick them up for brunch. She would return them later to the house to spend time with their friends and cousins.

"Since she has a little more experience than I do, I think she's actually more ready than I am." Libby laughed at how quickly Tully made it back to her side.

"How are you feeling, Simone?" Tully asked, placing her hand over Libby's swollen midsection.

Libby smiled at the way Tully's chest puffed out when the baby gave two quick healthy kicks in response to her touch.

"I'm a month ahead of Libby, but I feel great. Being able to give Elijah a family has been the best thing that came out of all this."

Simone put her hand on her back in a gesture that Libby recognized as an attempt to balance her load, and Elijah was at her side in an instant.

"After being told for so long there'd be no more children because of my first pregnancy, finding out we're having twin boys has been the miracle I've prayed for," Simone said. "I still miss my little angel, but this has been a blessing."

"I feel the same way," Libby said. "After all that happened to us last year it feels good to create something new that will only bring happiness into our lives."

"That's until they turn sixteen, then all bets are off," Tully joked. "We'll meet you back at the house to eat the food Mama's been cooking since Friday."

Once Simone and Elijah walked off, Tully and Libby stood facing each other, knowing these were their last minutes alone until the door of their bedroom closed that night. With Chase and Dana still with them, they didn't have much privacy. And during that precious time alone, Libby had shown Tully just how much she'd missed by staying in a relationship that wasn't working anymore.

"Want me to go and get the car?" Tully asked. At Libby's request she had put on her seersucker suit and a crisp white shirt, which fit in with what many of the other parishioners were wearing as they welcomed spring Southern style.

"Honey, you do know I'm not going to collapse if I walk a few blocks, right?"

"I just want to make sure you don't strain yourself."

"Women have been having children for a long time, so please don't worry so much."

Tully took her hand and started walking to Jackson Square. "It's my job to worry about you."

"Uh-huh, good-looking." Libby slid her hand around Tully's

elbow. "That suit still looks fantastic on you, by the way. It was always one of my favorites when you wore it into the coffee shop. I thought you looked hot in it."

"Thank you, even though this is a smaller version of the one you first fell in love with." Tully laughed. "It's nice to know that pregnancy hasn't killed your libido."

"You're complaining?" Libby laughed even harder.

"Like hell. After the last couple of months, those ten other kids you want sound like a great idea."

Libby pinched her side. "Just a couple ought to do it when you add them to the two Badeauxes we have living in the house already. Speaking of the kids, did they get off okay?"

"Jessica promised to have them back by one, and when they left with her, for once they actually looked like they weren't being led to the gallows."

"How's she doing?" Libby still sounded less than enthused when she talked about Jessica, but the relationship was getting easier. They'd never be best friends, but Libby was willing to make the best of it for Ralph, Bailey, and Tully.

"Jessica's still a bit lost, but I think she's coming around. Kara's still in rehab, and from what I understand they're not seeing each other anymore." Tully stopped at one of the park benches when Libby slowed down and helped her sit. "Jessica started working in the emergency room, and the change seems to be good. I never realized just how much she resented her father, but really for no good reason."

"What do you mean?" Libby rubbed her abdomen in an obvious effort to get the baby to calm down, smiling when Tully took over for her.

"When it came to mapping out her life, he didn't really put any pressure on her. She put it on herself, using a sort of twisted logic to make him and her mother happy. You miss out on a lot when you try to live up to made-up expectations." Tully moved closer to her and kissed her forehead. "With the new changes in her life she's trying to find something she thinks she missed out on after medical school."

"Just as long as she doesn't try to find something she had and lost after medical school," Libby said with another pinch to Tully's side. "That prize has sailed, Counselor."

Tully put her hand back on Libby's middle and kissed her lips this time. "A year ago I was lost. My children were beyond my reach, and the reality of that made me feel like no matter how much I tried to make a family, I was alone."

"Not anymore, honey." Libby put her hand over Tully's. "You'll never be alone again."

"I know that because, like I told Kara, you're my second chance. You found me, and in your eyes and in your arms is where I want to be lost for the rest of my days. I love you."

"You know what?"

"What?" Tully asked.

"When you tell me things like that, if I wasn't already madly in love with you and having your baby, I'd do it all over again."

"You bring out the romantic in me." Tully stood up, bowed at the waist, and held her hand out. "You ready to go?"

"If it's with you, then the answer is yes."

Tully helped Libby to her feet, got as close to her as she could, and kissed her like a woman in love.

"You know what?" she asked when they drew apart.

"What?"

"I'm really glad I love coffee too."

They started toward the car, holding hands in the one part of the city that the storm had left relatively untouched. Outside the French Quarter, the city needed extensive rebuilding, and native New Orleanians knew the Big Easy would never be the same.

But Tully embraced that realization. Walking next to her was the foundation on which she was rebuilding her future, and just like Libby's crystal blue eyes, it looked enticingly bright.

About the Author

Originally from Cuba, Ali Vali now lives right outside New Orleans with her partner. As a writer she couldn't ask for a better, more beautiful place, full of real-life characters and exciting events to fuel the imagination. When she isn't writing, working in the yard, cheering for the LSU Tigers, or riding her bicycle, Ali makes a living in the nonprofit sector.

Ali's is the author of *The Devil Inside*, *Carly's Sound*, and *The Devil Unleashed*, all published by Bold Strokes Books. *Deal with the Devil* is scheduled for release in 2008.

Books Available From Bold Strokes Books

Such a Pretty Face by Gabrielle Goldsby. A sexy, sometimes humorous, sometimes biting contemporary romance that gently exposes the damage to heart and soul when we fail to look beneath the surface for what truly matters. (978-1-933110-84-4)

Second Season by Ali Vali. A romance set in New Orleans amidst betrayal, Hurricane Katrina, and the new beginnings hardship and heartbreak sometimes make possible. (978-1-933110-83-7)

Hearts Aflame by Ronica Black. A poignant, erotic romance between a hard-driving businesswoman and a solitary vet. Packed with adventure and set in the harsh beauty of the Arizona countryside. (978-1-933110-82-0)

Red Light by JD Glass. Tori forges her path as an EMT in the New York City 911 system while discovering what matters most to herself and the woman she loves. (978-1-933110-81-3)

Honor Under Siege by Radclyffe. Secret Service agent Cameron Roberts struggles to protect her lover while searching for a traitor who just may be another woman with a claim on her heart. (978-1-933110-80-6)

Dark Valentine by Jennifer Fulton. Danger and desire fuel a high-stakes cat-and-mouse game when an attorney and an endangered witness team up to thwart a killer. (978-1-933110-79-0)

Sequestered Hearts by Erin Dutton. A popular artist suddenly goes into seclusion, a reluctant reporter wants to know why, and a heart locked away yearns to be set free. (978-1-933110-78-3)

Erotic Interludes 5: Road Games, ed. by Radclyffe and Stacia Seaman. Adventure, "sport," and sex on the road—hot stories of travel adventures and games of seduction. (978-1-933110-77-6)

The Spanish Pearl by Catherine Friend. On a trip to Spain, Kate Vincent is accidentally transported back in time—an epic saga spiced with humor, lust, and danger. (978-1-933110-76-9)

Lady Knight by L-J Baker. Loyalty and honor clash with love and ambition in a medieval world of magic when female knight Riannon meets Lady Eleanor. (978-1-933110-75-2)

Dark Dreamer by Jennifer Fulton. Best-selling horror author Rowe Devlin falls under the spell of psychic Phoebe Temple. A Dark Vista romance. (978-1-933110-74-5)

Come and Get Me by Julie Cannon. Elliott Foster isn't used to pursuing women, but alluring attorney Lauren Collier makes her change her mind. (978-1-933110-73-8)

Blind Curves by Diane and Jacob Anderson-Minshall. Private eye Yoshi Yakamota comes to the aid of her ex-lover Velvet Erickson in the first Blind Eye mystery. (978-1-933110-72-1)

Dynasty of Rogues by Jane Fletcher. It's hate at first sight for Ranger Riki Sadiq and her new patrol corporal, Tanya Coppelli—except for their undeniable attraction. (978-1-933110-71-4)

Running With the Wind by Nell Stark. Sailing instructor Corrie Marsten has signed off on love until she meets Quinn Davies—one woman she can't ignore. (978-1-933110-70-7)

More Than Paradise by Jennifer Fulton. Two women battle danger, risk all, and find in each other an unexpected ally and an unforgettable love. (978-1-933110-69-1)

Flight Risk by Kim Baldwin. For Blayne Keller, being in the wrong place at the wrong time just might turn out to be the best thing that ever happened to her. (978-1-933110-68-4)

Rebel's Quest: Supreme Constellations Book Two by Gun Brooke. On a world torn by war, two women discover a love that defies all boundaries. (978-1-933110-67-7)

Punk and Zen by JD Glass. Angst, sex, love, rock. Trace, Candace, Francesca...Samantha. Losing control—and finding the truth within. BSB Victory Editions. (1-933110-66-X)

The Devil Unleashed by Ali Vali. As the heat of violence rises, so does the passion. A Casey Clan crime saga. (1-933110-61-9)

When Dreams Tremble by Radclyffe. Two women whose lives turned out far differently than they'd once imagined discover that sometimes the shape of the future can only be found in the past. (1-933110-64-3)

Stellium in Scorpio by Andrews & Austin. The passionate reunion of two powerful women on the glitzy Las Vegas Strip, where everything is an illusion and love is a gamble. (1-933110-65-1)

Burning Dreams by Susan Smith. The chronicle of the challenges faced by a young drag king and an older woman who share a love "outside the bounds." (1-933110-62-7)

Fresh Tracks by Georgia Beers. Seven women, seven days. A lot can happen when old friends, lovers, and a new girl in town get together in the mountains. (1-933110-63-5)

The Empress and the Acolyte by Jane Fletcher. Jemeryl and Tevi fight to protect the very fabric of their world...time. Lyremouth Chronicles Book Three. (1-933110-60-0)

First Instinct by JLee Meyer. When high-stakes security fraud leads to murder, one woman flees for her life while another risks her heart to protect her. (1-933110-59-7)

Erotic Interludes 4: Extreme Passions, ed. by Radclyffe and Stacia Seaman. Thirty of today's hottest erotica writers set the pages aflame with love, lust, and steamy liaisons. (1-933110-58-9)

Unexpected Ties by Gina L. Dartt. With death before dessert, Kate Shannon and Nikki Harris are swept up in another tale of danger and romance. (1-933110-56-2)

Broken Wings by L-J Baker. When Rye Woods, a fairy, meets the beautiful dryad Flora Withe, her libido, as squashed and hidden as her wings, reawakens along with her heart. (1-933110-55-4)

Combust the Sun by Andrews & Austin. A Richfield and Rivers mystery set in L.A. Murder among the stars. (1-933110-52-X)

Tristaine Rises by Cate Culpepper. Brenna, Jesstin, and the Amazons of Tristaine face their greatest challenge for survival. (1-933110-50-3)

Passion's Bright Fury by Radclyffe. When a trauma surgeon and a filmmaker become reluctant allies on the battleground between life and death, passion strikes without warning. (1-933110-54-6)

Sleep of Reason by Rose Beecham. Nothing is as it seems when Detective Jude Devine finds herself caught up in a small-town soap opera. And her rocky relationship with forensic pathologist Dr. Mercy Westmoreland just got a lot harder. (1-933110-53-8)

Grave Silence by Rose Beecham. Detective Jude Devine's investigation of a series of ritual murders is complicated by her torrid affair with the golden girl of Southwestern forensic pathology, Dr. Mercy Westmoreland. (1-933110-25-2)

Too Close to Touch by Georgia Beers. Kylie O'Brien believes in true love and is willing to wait for it. It doesn't matter one damn bit that Gretchen, her new and off-limits boss, has a voice as rich and smooth as melted chocolate. It absolutely doesn't… (1-933110-47-3)

Carly's Sound by Ali Vali. Poppy Valente and Julia Johnson form a bond of friendship that lays the foundation for something more, until Poppy's past comes back to haunt her—literally. A poignant romance about love and renewal. (1-933110-45-7)

Of Drag Kings and the Wheel of Fate by Susan Smith. A blind date in a drag club leads to an unlikely romance. (1-933110-51-1)

100th Generation by Justine Saracen. Ancient curses, modern-day villains, and a most intriguing woman who keeps appearing when least expected lead archeologist Valerie Foret on the adventure of her life. (1-933110-48-1)

The Traitor and the Chalice by Jane Fletcher. Tevi and Jemeryl risk all in the race to uncover a traitor. The Lyremouth Chronicles Book Two. (1-933110-43-0)

Whitewater Rendezvous by Kim Baldwin. Two women on a wilderness kayak adventure—Chaz Herrick, a laid-back outdoorswoman, and Megan Maxwell, a workaholic news executive—discover that true love may be nothing at all like they imagined. (1-933110-38-4)

Erotic Interludes 3: Lessons in Love, ed. by Radclyffe and Stacia Seaman. Sign on for a class in love...the best lesbian erotica writers take us to "school." (1-9331100-39-2)

Punk Like Me by JD Glass. Twenty-one-year-old Nina writes lyrics and plays guitar in the rock band Adam's Rib, and she doesn't always play by the rules. And oh yeah—she has a way with the girls. (1-933110-40-6)

Forever Found by JLee Meyer. Can time, tragedy, and shattered trust destroy a love that seemed destined? When chance reunites two childhood friends separated by tragedy, the past resurfaces to determine the shape of their future. (1-933110-37-6)

Sword of the Guardian by Merry Shannon. Princess Shasta's bold new bodyguard has a secret that could change both of their lives. *He* is actually a *she*. A passionate romance filled with courtly intrigue, chivalry, and devotion. (1-933110-36-8)

Sweet Creek by Lee Lynch. A celebration of the enduring nature of love, friendship, and community in the quirky, heart-warming lesbian community of Waterfall Falls. (1-933110-29-5)

Wild Abandon by Ronica Black. From their first tumultuous meeting, Dr. Chandler Brogan and Officer Sarah Monroe are drawn together by their common obsessions—sex, speed, and danger. (1-933110-35-X)

The Devil Inside by Ali Vali. Derby Cain Casey, head of a New Orleans crime organization, runs the family business with guts and grit, and no one crosses her. No one, that is, until Emma Verde claims her heart and turns her world upside down. (1-933110-30-9)

Chance by Grace Lennox. At twenty-six, Chance Delaney decides her life isn't working, so she swaps it for a different one. What follows is the sexy, funny, touching story of two women who, in finding themselves, also find one another. (1-933110-31-7)

Erotic Interludes 2: Stolen Moments, ed. by Stacia Seaman and Radclyffe. Love on the run, in the office, in the shadows...Fast, furious, and almost too hot to handle. (1-933110-16-3)

Turn Back Time by Radclyffe. Pearce Rifkin and Wynter Thompson have nothing in common but a shared passion for surgery. They clash at every opportunity, especially when matters of the heart are suddenly at stake. (1-933110-34-1)

Promising Hearts by Radclyffe. Dr. Vance Phelps lost everything in the War Between the States and arrives in New Hope, Montana, with no hope of happiness and no desire for anything except forgetting—until she meets Mae, a frontier madam. (1-933110-44-9)

Innocent Hearts by Radclyffe. In a wild and unforgiving land, two women learn about love, passion, and the wonders of the heart. (1-933110-21-X)

Protector of the Realm: Supreme Constellations Book One by Gun Brooke. A space adventure filled with suspense and a daring intergalactic romance featuring Commodore Rae Jacelon and a stunning, but decidedly lethal Kellen O'Dal. (1-933110-26-0)

Course of Action by Gun Brooke. Actress Carolyn Black desperately wants the starring role in an upcoming film produced by Annelie Peterson. Just how far will she go for the dream part of a lifetime? (1-933110-22-8)

Coffee Sonata by Gun Brooke. Four women whose lives unexpectedly intersect in a small town by the sea have one thing in common—they all have secrets. (1-933110-41-4)

The Temple at Landfall by Jane Fletcher. An imprinter, one of Celaeno's most revered servants of the Goddess, is also a prisoner to the faith—until a Ranger frees her by claiming her heart. (1-933110-27-9)

Rangers at Roadsend by Jane Fletcher. Sergeant Chip Coppelli has learned to spot trouble coming, and that is exactly what she sees in her new recruit, Katryn Nagata. The Celaeno series. (1-933110-28-7)

The Walls of Westernfort by Jane Fletcher. All Temple Guard Natasha Ionadis wants is to serve the Goddess—until she falls in love with one of the rebels she is sworn to destroy. The Celaeno series. (1-933110-24-4)

The Exile and the Sorcerer by Jane Fletcher. First in the Lyremouth Chronicles. Tevi and a shy young sorcerer face monsters, magic, and the challenge of loving. (1-933110-32-5)

Force of Nature by Kim Baldwin. From tornados to forest fires, the forces of nature conspire to bring Gable McCoy and Erin Richards close to danger, and closer to each other. (1-933110-23-6)

In Too Deep by Ronica Black. Undercover homicide cop Erin McKenzie tracks a femme fatale who just might be a real killer…with love and danger hot on her heels. (1-933110-17-1)

Hunter's Pursuit by Kim Baldwin. A raging blizzard, a mountain hideaway, and a killer-for-hire set a scene for disaster—or desire—when Katarzyna Demetrious rescues a beautiful stranger. (1-933110-09-0)

Erotic Interludes: Change of Pace by Radclyffe. Twenty-five hot-wired encounters guaranteed to spark more than just your imagination. Erotica as you've always dreamed of it. (1-933110-07-4)

Justice Served by Radclyffe. Lieutenant Rebecca Frye and her lover, Dr. Catherine Rawlings, embark on a deadly game of hide-and-seek with an underworld kingpin who traffics in human souls. (1-933110-15-5)

Justice in the Shadows by Radclyffe. In a shadow world of secrets and lies, Detective Sergeant Rebecca Frye and her lover, Dr. Catherine Rawlings, join forces in the elusive search for justice. (1-933110-03-1)

A Matter of Trust by Radclyffe. JT Sloan is a cybersleuth who doesn't like attachments. Michael Lassiter is leaving her husband, and she needs Sloan's expertise to safeguard her company. It should just be business—but it turns into much more. (1-933110-33-3)

Fated Love by Radclyffe. Amidst the chaos and drama of a busy emergency room, two women must contend not only with the fragile nature of life, but also with the irresistible forces of fate. (1-933110-05-8)

Storms of Change by Radclyffe. In the continuing saga of the Provincetown Tales, duty and love are at odds as Reese and Tory face their greatest challenge. (1-933110-57-0)

Distant Shores, Silent Thunder by Radclyffe. Dr. Tory King—along with the women who love her—is forced to examine the boundaries of love, friendship, and the ties that transcend time. (1-933110-08-2)

Beyond the Breakwater by Radclyffe. One Provincetown summer, three women learn the true meaning of love, friendship, and family. (1-933110-06-6)

Safe Harbor by Radclyffe. A mysterious newcomer, a reclusive doctor, and a troubled gay teenager learn about love, friendship, and trust during one tumultuous summer in Provincetown. (1-933110-13-9)

shadowland by Radclyffe. In a world on the far edge of desire, two women are drawn together by power, passion, and dark pleasures. An erotic romance. (1-933110-11-2)

Love's Masquerade by Radclyffe. Plunged into the indistinguishable realms of fiction, fantasy, and hidden desires, Auden Frost is forced to question all she believes about the nature of love. (1-933110-14-7)

Honor Reclaimed by Radclyffe. In the aftermath of 9/11, Secret Service Agent Cameron Roberts and Blair Powell close ranks with a trusted few to find the would-be assassins who nearly claimed Blair's life. (1-933110-18-X)

Honor Guards by Radclyffe. In a wild flight for their lives, the president's daughter and those who are sworn to protect her wage a desperate struggle for survival. (1-933110-01-5)

Love & Honor by Radclyffe. The president's daughter and her lover are faced with difficult choices as they battle a tangled web of Washington intrigue for…love and honor. (1-933110-10-4)

Honor Bound by Radclyffe. Secret Service Agent Cameron Roberts and Blair Powell face political intrigue, a clandestine threat to Blair's safety, and the seemingly irreconcilable personal differences that force them ever farther apart. (1-933110-20-1)

Above All, Honor by Radclyffe. Secret Service Agent Cameron Roberts fights her desire for the one woman she can't have—Blair Powell, the daughter of the president of the United States. (1-933110-04-X)

BOLD
STROKES
BOOKS